Something was definitely moving through the trees, and quickly. The stride sounded long and heavy, but the spacers couldn't see anything through the dense bushes that grew along the sides of the trail.

An anthropoid stepped out of the bushes then, watching them through milky blue eyes. "Holy shit," Nickson whispered. He'd read about the creatures but had never actually seen one before. They were native to Heinlein.

"Stay calm," the captain said. "No sudden movements." It was a muscular creature, a biped two meters tall, rippling with muscles and possessed of gray, leathery skin. Its head, shoulders, back, forearms, and legs were covered in coarse, bluish-gray fur. Its face was mostly hairless. It didn't have a nose; these creatures breathed through gill-like organs on their necks. But it did have a large, almost circular mouth, full of gleaming white teeth. It hunched forward, striking an aggressive posture toward them, and let out a guttural growl.

The captain's laser was already in her hands. "Nix, do you have a weapon?"

"What? No! You said to bring outdoor clothes, not a gun."

"Next time, bring a gun, too," she said.

BAEN BOOKS by MIKE KUPARI

Dead Six (with Larry Correia)
Swords of Exodus (with Larry Correia)
Alliance of Shadows (with Larry Correia)

Her Brother's Keeper
Sins of Her Father

To purchase any of these titles in e-book form,
please go to www.baen.com.

SINS OF
HER FATHER

MIKE KUPARI

SINS OF HER FATHER

A Baen Books Original

Baen Publishing Enterprises
P.O. Box 1403
Riverdale, NY 10471
www.baen.com

ISBN: 978-1-4814-8381-0

Cover art by Dave Seeley

First printing, March 2018
First mass market printing, February 2019

Library of Congress Catalog Number: 2017053734

Distributed by Simon & Schuster
1230 Avenue of the Americas
New York, NY 10020

Pages by Joy Freeman (www.pagesbyjoy.com)
Printed in the United States of America

For Cathe.

SINS OF
HER FATHER

CHAPTER 1

The Privateer Ship *Madeline Drake*
Deep Space
Rashid-231 System

Nickson Armitage awoke suddenly to an obnoxious buzzing sound in his compartment. He sat up quickly, bumping his head on the padded ceiling of his berth. He was soaked in sweat, and the air was insufferably dry; the environmental regulation systems were still being repaired.

"Yeah?" he said, into the intercom, checking his chrono. He'd been asleep for about ninety minutes. More time than he'd hoped for.

It was Reg, the flight medic. "Nix, you need to come down to sick bay. The skipper is asking for you."

"Huh? He's up? Is he doing better?"

Reg was silent for a moment. "No. You . . . you should come down here as soon as you can."

"I . . . yeah, okay. On my way." He tapped the controls and the hatch to his berth slid open, allowing slightly cooler air to flow in. The ship was still under acceleration, maybe 0.75 gravity, which was a good sign. It meant the engines were holding up and they were still on course. There were twelve berths on the crew deck, but no one else was around. Red emergency lighting provided illumination, and the air tasted stale. Nickson wiped the sweat from his face as he made for the hatch.

Sick bay was just below the crew deck, between it and the cargo hold. Sliding down the ladder, Nickson's feet hit the deck with a thump. He turned around in the narrow ladder compartment and banged on the hatch to sick bay before opening it. The auto-open functions were disabled to save power, so he had to unseal the heavy hatch and push it open manually. Inside, the ship's modest medical facilities were over-crowded. All four medical bunks were full, and two more injured crew were lying in gurneys, secured to the deck, with IV tubes stuck in their arms.

Reg stepped across the cramped bay to greet Nickson as he came through the hatch. He looked tired, like he hadn't slept in days. He probably hadn't; Dr. Mugabe, the flight surgeon, had been seriously injured during the battle and had succumbed to his wounds hours later. Reg wasn't as well trained as the doctor, but he was an experienced rescue medic and had been doing his best to treat casualties. Between his efforts and the autodoc, no one else had died since Dr. Mugabe passed. Of the *Maddy*'s original complement of thirteen, only five were uninjured, not even enough to conduct proper damage control. They really couldn't afford to lose anyone else.

Captain Ogleman's pained expression brightened when he saw Nickson. Half his head was bandaged, and he'd lost an eye, but he was awake for the first time in days, and alert. "Nix," he croaked, barely able to speak. "It's good to see you."

"It's good to see you awake, Skipper," Nickson said. Captain O was in bad shape. He was sealed, from the armpits down, in an emergency body cast in a last-ditch attempt to keep him alive. "How are you feeling?"

"I'm dying," he said flatly.

"Bullshit. You'll pull through."

"No, I won't, Nix," he said sadly. "The autodoc told me. The cast has not been able to stop the internal hemorrhaging." He'd had a five-centimeter-wide chunk of hot metal tear through his chest. "I'm surprised I made it this long."

Nickson forced himself to smile. "You always were a stubborn bastard."

"Too stubborn. I should have listened to you."

"It doesn't matter now, Skipper. You should just try to rest. Save your energy."

The captain laughed, coarsely. "Save it for what? I'm dying, man. The only reason I'm coherent enough to talk is because of the painkillers this . . . this burial shroud is injecting me with. Listen to me now. How's the ship?"

"Not good, Skipper. Weapons are offline still. The cargo bay is a hard vacuum." An incoming missile had blown the doors off the cargo bay, depressurizing it. "Only five of us are still on our feet. We lost a radiator, so we have to be careful about how much heat we generate, and that's part of the reason it's so damned hot in here. We're not atmospheric right now. But we've got navigation, we've got propulsion, we've got life support, and the transit motivator is still functional. We should be able to make it back to Nantucket Station and get patched up enough to get us home."

Captain Ogleman exhaled heavily, as if relieved. "Good. Good. My stupidity hasn't doomed us all, then."

"Skipper..."

"Save it. I was stupid. I got the doctor killed, and myself too, it would seem. I just want to let you know that I'm sorry."

"The captain never apologizes for command decisions," Nickson said.

"I'm not the captain anymore. You are." He sat up a little more in his bed. "Reg? Come here, please."

The beleaguered medic stepped over, putting on a fresh pair of sterile gloves. "What do you need, Skipper?"

"I need a witness. Tell the computer to record this, too. My name is Clarence Ogleman, owner and captain of the *Madeline Drake*. I hereby transfer all command authority to my executive officer, Nickson Armitage, and charge him with the duty of getting the ship home to port on Heinlein."

Nickson felt numb inside. He'd assumed command while the skipper was incapacitated, but this formality drove home the point that he was dying. "I accept command, and will discharge my duty to the best of my ability."

"Good," the skipper said, weakly. "Good. End recording." He turned back to Nickson. "Get the lads home, will you?"

He nodded solemnly. "I will, Skipper. I swear it."

Captain O clenched his eyes shut, obviously in pain. "Thank you," he said, breathlessly, a moment later. "Now get going. The crew needs their captain. I'm tired. I need to rest."

"It's been an honor working with you."

"You too, son. I know the ship is in good hands."

Nickson shook hands with his shipmate, turned, and left the sick bay without another word. He resolved that if they made it back to Nantucket Station, he was going to take a day and drink himself unconscious.

CHAPTER 2

Heinlein
Faraway System
One Standard Year Later

Sitting up in bed, Nickson was briefly unable to remember where he was. He'd had that same nightmare again, reliving Captain Ogleman's last moments. He rubbed his face vigorously with his hands, and looked around his bedroom. He might as well get up; he wasn't going to be getting back to sleep tonight.

SNORK! ZZZZzzzzz . . .

He looked down at the woman next to him. She was asleep, snoring away peacefully. *Oh . . . right.* He remembered going out and chatting her up, but the rest of it was . . . fuzzy. *Katy.* Her name was Katy. Maybe. Kylie? Carly? Feh. It would come to him. The sun was beginning to lighten the horizon, but it was still early. Too early to be up after the night he'd had, but Nickson hardly ever slept for more than a few hours at a time. His doctor said it was to be expected after his ordeal in space, but he wasn't sure that it was really that.

6

No, he was restless. Not in the sense that he had difficulty sleeping. He'd been dirtside for a year, mostly drinking his savings away, wondering what in the hell he was going to do with himself. As he'd promised the late Captain Ogleman, he'd managed to get the *Madeline Drake* home to Heinlein. With the captain's death, legal ownership of the *Maddy D.* had passed to his estate. The ship was promptly sold off to ensure the crew still got paid, and that all debts were settled. It was a grim necessity since they'd failed to complete their last contract. Nickson's share was enough to pay his rent and keep him well supplied with booze, but he was still unemployed.

He needed to get back to work. He needed to get back into space. Dirtside life had a lot going for it: every creature comfort imaginable, women, real sunshine, all the air you could breathe, and natural gravity. It was the environment humankind was meant to live in. Yet, for all that, it was . . . dull. Space was an intrinsically hostile environment and, despite the routine of interstellar travel, remained quite dangerous. It was home to the spacer, though, and Nickson Armitage had been a spacer all his life. He'd been born on a ship. He had been more than a standard year old before he was ever brought down to the surface of a planet.

Barefoot, dressed only in his shorts, Nickson found himself lured to the kitchen by the smell of brewing coffee. The appliances were programmed to start making it as soon as he got out of bed. He tapped a control panel to get its attention. "Bacon, six strips, crispy." The appliances acknowledged and got to work making his breakfast. It'd be a few minutes before it would be ready. Sitting down at the table, he picked up his tablet and tapped the screen.

He disinterestedly browsed through local, colonial, and interstellar news, skimming the headlines but not reading any of the articles. Colonial market reports. The city of Coventry, Heinlein's colonial capital and Nickson's home, was going to begin an expansion of the spaceport. Sports stories. Comical videos of people's pets. The weather forecast. Apparently the Concordiat Defense Force was sending troops to far-flung Zanzibar in an attempt to stabilize the recently annexed colony. Then an icon flashed on the screen: new job listings that might interest him. *Hmm.*

Pouring himself a cup of coffee, Nickson sat back down and opened the listings. He'd been watching the job boards for ships looking for officers to add to their crew. There were usually a fair number of spacer jobs to be found this way, but officer positions were much less common. The turnover rate for ship's officers was much lower than for regular crew, and most captains preferred to keep their same core staff as they got to know and trust them. He had it set up so that he'd be immediately notified of any officer billet that opened up, on any kind of ship, just to keep his options open.

A free trader named the *Marco Polo* was looking for an experienced astrogator. Astrogation was not his area of expertise, but he knew enough to do the job and could fake the rest for an interview. He tagged that one for later. La Garda Interstellar, the largest freight company on Heinlein, had numerous officer positions open. That would be a last resort. It was steady work, but the pay was mediocre. Serving on a bulk freighter was about as dull as being in space could be.

A local energy conglomerate needed engineers for its transport and refinery ships. This type of work involved harvesting helium-3, hydrogen, and deuterium from the Faraway system's gas giants, refining them into useable reaction mass and fusion fuel, and transporting them across the system. Working in the energy sector was also good, steady work, though possibly even more dull than serving on an interstellar freighter. The ad stated the employee would stay planetside for a few months out of the year, and would never leave the system. It was the kind of work a spacer looked for if he had a family and wanted to settle down, which was, more or less, the opposite of Nickson Armitage. In any case, he wasn't an engineer by trade, and all the other listed positions paid substantially less.

The last ad caught Nickson's eye. A privateer called *Andromeda* was looking for a new first officer. He pulled up the publicly available registration information for the ship. *Not bad*, he thought. She was bigger than the *Madeline Drake* had been, and better armed, too. She was a *Polaris* class, from Winchell-Chung Astronautical Industries. The type had been recently superseded in low-rate production by the *Polaris-II*, but was still very formidable. Something like that, Nickson thought, would make an ideal privateer. Her class had the right combination of reaction-mass tankage, armament, cargo capacity, and crew berthing. She had a pretty impressive record, too. She'd been operating out of Heinlein for twenty-five local years, which equated to about twenty standard years. Staying in the business that long and still being both profitable and in one piece told Nickson that this ship's skipper knew what he was doing.

The pay was listed as negotiable, but that was standard practice for that sort of position. Nickson was, by his own estimation, a pretty good negotiator besides. He sent an inquiry along with his resume. The *Maddy D.* had had a pretty good service record, before her fateful final contract, and he had references to verify his experience. He'd worked his way up from pilot to XO under Captain Ogleman, and had done everything from cargo runs to pirate hunting. A ship like the *Andromeda* was exactly what he was looking for.

"Nickson?" It was a woman's voice. He looked up to see his guest standing in the doorway to his bedroom, naked except for the patterned stockings he'd left on while undressing her, which she'd fallen asleep in. She was tall, curvy, and...*buxom.* Blonde curls spilled over her shoulders and down her back.

"Hey...you!" he said. *Harley? Was it Harley?* "I didn't wake you, did I?"

She smiled with those full lips of hers. "No, hon. It's so early. What are you doing up?"

"Just checking the news and such. You want some coffee? Breakfast?"

"We could have breakfast...or you could get back in here and say good morning the proper way."

Nickson raised his eyebrows. "Well. It is rude to leave a guest wanting for company." He stood up, his coffee forgotten, doffing his shorts as he followed *what's-her-name* back to bed.

CHAPTER 3

Heinlein
Krycek Estate
Northern Hemisphere

"Good morning, sir!" the steward bot said, in a cheery, synthesized voice. It rolled to a stop in the grass. "There is an aircraft approaching the estate."

Zander Krycek didn't look up. It was a beautiful summer day, and he was spending the morning down in the dirt, pruning his roses. "Are you sure?" Air cars, VTOLs, and other aircraft passed close to the property from time to time. Sometimes the machines confused rude pilots with potential visitors.

The steward bot bobbled a little, gyroscopically stabilized on one large wheel. "According to telemetry, the vehicle's trajectory will take it directly over the house. It is decelerating and descending."

This was enough to give Zander pause. "I see," he said, standing up. At 197 centimeters tall, he towered over the robot. "Let's go see who they are, shall we? Head out to the front yard and wait for them. If they land, ask them what they want and tell them to wait.

I'll be out momentarily." He started to walk away, but paused. "Jerkins, if you detect weapons, send an emergency signal at once." This would cause the house to go into full lockdown mode.

"Of course, sir," the robot said, just as cheerily, before rolling away.

Zander didn't get many visitors. He lived out his exile on Heinlein quietly, not socializing very much. Given his controversial reputation, there were many who wanted nothing to do with him. He'd written several books, given a few interviews, and occasionally indulged in the services of a high-end courtesan agency, but rarely did anyone bother to come to his home. It was unusual.

He had enemies, back home on Ithaca. They'd left him alone for all these years, but in the back of his mind, he wondered if today was the day they'd come for him. Such a thing had always been a possibility, albeit an unlikely one. Traveling across interstellar space to kill someone was almost always more trouble than it was worth.

Nonetheless, he activated his home's defense system and retrieved a personal weapon. He checked to ensure his pistol was loaded; of course, it was. He studied the weapon for a moment. The beautifully engraved emblem on the grip always caught his eye. It was the presidential seal of the Colony of Ithaca, from back when there *was* a president.

When *Zander* was president.

Armed and smiling humorlessly, Zander made his way through his home. Pausing in the foyer, he brought up the security feed on a small display. Jerkins was waiting in the yard, its boxy blue body standing out against the dark green of the rich Terran grass. The unmistakable whine of engines could be heard now, if only barely, through the well-insulated walls of Zander's home.

Cameras locked onto the aircraft and zoomed in as it circled around the estate, descending toward the front yard. It was an ungainly looking craft, with a blunt nose housing a cluster of sensors and antennae, held aloft by a pair of circular, ducted rotors in place of wings. Wind buffeted the lawn and Jerkins as the helicopter adjusted the pitch on its rotors, lowered its landing gear, and settled onto the lawn.

Zander frowned. It took a lot of work and maintenance to keep this particular species of bluegrass growing on this part of Heinlein. He was tempted to go out there and tell the interlopers to get the hell off his lawn, but he waited. As the aircraft's engines spun down, Jerkins approached, rolling across the grass to the side of its fuselage. The steward bot came to a stop as doors to the helicopter's passenger compartment slid open. A set of steps unfolded, and a tall man stepped out onto the grass.

The security cameras automatically zoomed in, linked with a feed from Jerkins's optics. Facial recognition software scanned its database and attempted to identify the visitor, but Zander didn't need the machines to tell him who he was. Even after all these years, there was no mistaking Erasmus Starborn. Shaking his head, Zander opened the door and stepped outside.

It had been fifteen years, or more, since he'd seen this man. Then-Lieutenant Starborn had been with Zander from the beginning, serving him faithfully through the overthrow of the king and the colonial civil war that followed. He had been a trusted intelligence officer and advisor after Zander assumed the presidency. He looked older, despite the life-extending miracles of space-age medicine. His hair, which he'd always kept cropped very short, was longer now, and he had a beard.

"Mr. President," the visitor said, extending a hand.

"Ras," Zander replied, his mind full of questions. He took the offered hand and shook it firmly. "My God man, it's been how many years?"

"Almost twenty standard years, sir." He studied Zander's home for a moment. "It seems like you're doing all right for yourself."

Zander chuckled. "I had assets put away when I left. It was enough to set me up here." His tone lowered slightly. "You've come all the way from Ithaca, I assume?"

"I have."

"I'm certain you didn't travel so far to admire my home. What do you want, Ras?"

"Sir, the situation back home has been steadily worsening since your departure."

"I told you it would."

"None of that was up to me. In any case, I was sent here to find you. I have a message for you."

"From who?"

Ras took a deep breath. "From your daughter, sir."

Zander's heart fell into his stomach. His knees grew weak. Sensing the changes in his vital signs, Jerkins rolled over and grabbed Zander's arm, ensuring he wouldn't fall. "Adisa?" he asked. "She sent me a message?" She'd been a child when he'd been ousted from office. Friends of her late mother had sent her into hiding as Zander was sent into exile. He'd long since come to accept that he would never know her, and now she sends a message?

Zander looked up at the slowly darkening sky as he regained his composure. Clouds had been rolling in all afternoon, and a cool wind was blowing in from the mountains to the north. He stood up straight, his steward bot backing out of his personal space. "Yes, well, I expect it'll rain soon. Please, come in. We have much to discuss."

The study was a large, cozy room, lit by large bay windows on the south side. The floor, several bookcases, and the desk were all made of native Heinleinian oak and hickory hybrid. A holographic globe, showing a 3D image of the planet and its satellites hummed quietly against the wall. As the two men sat down, Jerkins rolled in and asked if anyone wanted refreshments.

"Scotch, neat." Zander didn't imbibe often, but he needed a drink just now. "Care for a drink, Ras? It's local, thirty years old."

"Just tea, please, if you have it."

"I have Assam and Sencha," Jerkins replied.

"I have not heard of these."

"Assam is black," Zander explained, "and Sencha is green. They call them Ebony and Emerald back home."

"Ah, I see. Sencha, then, please."

"Scotch and Sencha," Jerkins confirmed. "Just a moment." The robot pivoted around and rolled out of the room.

"That's a fine machine you've got there," Ras noted. "I've never seen a robot with such good speech recognition and cognition."

"It's all right, as long as you don't expect too much. Still, cheaper than hiring a human staff."

"I would like to think that you were well served by human staff, at least for a while." Ras had been one of Zander's aides as a young lieutenant, when Zander was himself a colonel in the Royal Guard. He saw great leadership potential in the young man, and took him under his wing. He'd promoted him to major and kept him in a trusted position after becoming president.

"You certainly had more initiative than Jerkins," Zander mused, as the steward bot rolled back into the room. "Though, I couldn't help but notice your absence at the end." His tone had changed. The room felt a little colder.

"I did what I could, sir," Ras said, looking down into his tea. "For what it's worth, I helped convince them to let you go into exile. They wanted to hang you, and I told them that would have started another civil war."

Zander sipped his scotch. "You were probably right about that. How's your boy, by the way? Jeb, right?"

"Grown, with kids of his own. I'm a full colonel in the Guard now. Counterintelligence."

"Oh? Do they know you're here?"

Ras smiled. "Not exactly."

"I always did know you'd go far. Let's get down to it, then. Please show me this message from my daughter."

"Of course," Ras said, reaching into his jacket pocket. He retrieved a small holographic projector and placed it on the desk. "You should know that I have not seen the message. It's encrypted and can only be unlocked with your biometric data. Just place a thumb on the pad on the projector, and it should play automatically."

Hesitating for just a moment, Zander downed the rest of his drink and put his thumb on the pad. The holographic projection above the device flashed a red icon, then a green one. "Access granted," a synthesized voice announced. The icon disappeared and was replaced with a three-dimensional projection of a young woman with black hair, brown eyes, and skin the color of mocha.

"Adisa," Zander whispered. She looked so much like her mother, there was no mistaking her. His little girl was all grown up.

"Hello, Father," the woman said as the message began. "I know this must come as a shock to you. It's not easy for me, either." She looked down, briefly, a sadness in her eyes. "First, let me prove to you that it is really me, by telling you some things only I would know. First, my name is actually a boy's name, but despite mother's protests, you thought it was pretty and insisted upon it. And second . . . when I was small, you would tell me a story every night. You wouldn't let my nanny do it, and you wouldn't let me just watch a show. You would tell me about the Adventures of Princess Adisa, and her journeys from one magical planet to the next. You made it up as you went along, but I loved it. You only stopped after mother died."

Zander struggled to not tear up. It had been so long he'd almost forgotten.

"For much of my life, I was told that you were a madman. The Butcher of Sargusport, the man who destroyed an entire city. The war criminal who had to be deposed."

The old man looked away from the projection for a moment, even though Adisa couldn't see him. He had indeed ordered the destruction of Sargusport, via a nuclear artillery round, but the decision hadn't been one he'd made lightly. It had haunted him ever since.

"I tried to find objective analysis of you, of what you did. It wasn't easy. Much of the truth has been erased, replaced with propaganda. Since your exile, you've been blamed for many things that are not your fault: the current strife, the economy, the poverty, all of it. You've been a convenient scapegoat for the Council government. For what it's worth, I'm sorry I never got to know you, father. I don't believe that you're the monster you've been made out to be. I still remember my father, smiling as he told me stories, even making sound effects."

Zander fought back tears once again.

Adisa took a deep breath. It was apparent she had recorded this message in one take, and didn't seem to be reading off a script. "That is not the purpose of this message, though. I wouldn't have sent Colonel Starborn so far just to say hello. I don't know how closely you've been following the situation here on Ithaca, so included with this message are detailed files, and Colonel Starborn should be able to answer any questions you might have. The short version is, the situation is grim. After your departure, the Council was never able to maintain control over the entire colony. The southern region is, for all practical purposes, fully autonomous, and doesn't recognize the authority of the Interim Government. In fact, they have prospered more, and many of our citizens resent them for it."

That made sense. The southern region had a smaller population and vast mineral wealth. It was more rural, and the inhabitants tended to be less trustful of the central government. This went back many, many years.

"The economy is struggling, and there are some troubling signs that we may be facing a total economic collapse. We've been experiencing runaway inflation and the dinar is all but worthless, despite the price controls the Council has implemented. There are shortages everywhere. People are going without medicine, and some are even going without food. There is talk of using this emergency to implement a command economy fully controlled by the Council, of having the government seize farms and manufacturing facilities to ensure quotas are met."

Zander frowned. Many of the people involved in the revolution were idealistic, passionate, and economically illiterate. Such a move would start a civil war.

"The Council is growing desperate and afraid. They fear there might be yet another revolution, one that sees them overthrown, backed by the Southern Autonomous Zone. Their side has the population advantage, but that doesn't mean victory. They always find someone to blame for the failure of their plans. Usually it's you, father, but sometimes it's also *greedy corporatists* or *Southern militants* or even the native population.

"They're desperate, Father, and they're afraid. They have sent envoys to the Orlov Combine."

Dear God, Zander thought to himself. *The fools have all gone mad.*

"No one else will back the Council now, and the Combine promises technological investment that will solve the shortages of critical resources. They claim to be the most efficient planners in all of inhabited space. A colonial referendum is being drawn up, and Colonel Starborn's sources have told him that the results of that vote have been decided ahead of time. Already our networks are being bombarded with pro-Combine propaganda, promising a new age of cooperation and prosperity. You and I both know the truth, Father. If that treaty is signed, then Ithaca will be nothing but a client state, and all who oppose their rule will be killed.

"The situation is dire, but all is not lost. There are many of us opposing them, and even though we are extremely outnumbered, we are pursuing advantages of our own. As I record this, I'm attempting to set up a meeting with the native Elders, to ask for their support. They don't respect the Council, though, and they don't respect me. The only human they truly respect is you, Father. You're the one who brought them to the negotiating table and got them to agree to the peace treaty."

He was quite proud of that fact. He'd written a book about it. The king, when he was young, had blundered into a war with the alien inhabitants of the world, turning over centuries of peaceful coexistence. It had fallen to Zander to strike at them hard enough to bring them to the negotiating table. It worked: They signed the peace treaty, the first such interspecies agreement in living memory.

"I'm asking you to come home, Father. I know there are many who will oppose you, but if anyone has a chance of uniting the opposition against the Council it's you. You have many supporters even today. Without your help, I fear war is inevitable, and I don't believe it's a war that we can win.

"I await your reply. I know you'll do the right thing."

The message ended, and the image of Adisa disappeared.

Ras spoke up after a moment. "I know it's a lot to take in, sir."

Zander ignored him. "Jerkins, another scotch. Bring the bottle."

"At once, sir," the robot said, and rolled off.

"This is a hell of a thing to drop at a man's feet, Ras."

"Desperate times call for desperate measures. You and I both know what will happen to the colony if the Combine comes in. If you need some time to think about it, please take it, but time is of the essence."

"I'll go," Zander said, as Jerkins handed him another glass of scotch.

Ras blinked a few times. "Just like that, sir? It will be dangerous."

Zander smiled. "Ras, you don't go from being an officer in the Colonial Guard to dethroning a king to being appointed president of the colony if you're prone to hesitating. In any case, retirement is dreadfully dull. I've written books, I've traveled, I've given talks, and now I live with a robot and prune my roses. Returning home might be dangerous, but this will kill me."

"It's good to have you back, sir," Ras said, smiling.

"I'll need a few days to get my affairs in order. Do you have a ship?"

"No. We bribed our way onto a high-speed courier, under assumed identities. I tried to keep everything as low profile as possible. We will need to find another way home."

"I see. How many people did you bring?"

"There are three of us. I told the others to let me initiate contact with you alone."

Zander nodded. "We'll need a ship, then. How

much money do you have at your disposal? We're going to need a lot."

"It shouldn't cost that much to charter a ship, should it?"

"I don't intend to book a berth on some tramp freighter, Ras. We may need fire support. I want to hire a privateer." He sipped his scotch again. "One last thing...does she know?"

Ras was quiet for a moment. "No. We never told her. There are rumors, but the Council has made an effort to quash them. It's the stuff of conspiracy kooks now."

"Good. Good. It may be time that she learned the truth." He never imagined he'd get to see Adisa again. He found himself wondering what she was like. What kind of woman had she become?

CHAPTER 4

Ithaca
Ionia-5589 System
Southern Hemisphere

Shoulders aching from the weight of her pack, Adisa Masozi paused to catch her breath and take a sip of water. Guiding her were a pair of experienced Rangers from the Southern Autonomous Zone Civil Defense Force. They were in a small clearing at the floor of an overgrown forest, one full of life-forms that resembled trees. Their stalks consisted of several thick vines, or roots, wrapped around one another like a braid, and rigid. They varied in color from dark green, brown, gray, and black. Twisting upward for dozens of meters, they were capped with great, colorful, feathery blossoms that soaked up ultraviolet radiation from Ionia-5589. The lowest canopy was almost thirty meters overhead. The uppermost canopy was more than forty. The canopy was so dense that little sunlight got through to ground level. Between the darkness, the humidity, and the mist that hung in the little clearing, the air felt claustrophobic and oppressive.

"You doin' all right, love?" one of the Rangers, Roc, asked, slinging a rifle over his shoulder. He was a slender man with Asiatic features. His camouflage fatigues, a mottled pattern of greens, browns, and blues to match the alien forest around them, were visibly damp with sweat.

"I'm fine," Adisa said, her dark skin glistening from her own sweat and the murderous ambient humidity. "We should be close now, yes?" They were hundreds of kilometers from the nearest human settlement, and probably twenty klicks from the clearing where they'd been dropped off by aircraft. Moving on foot under the dense foliage kept them hidden from any reconnaissance drones that might be lurking overhead.

The Ranger wiped the condensation off the screen of his wrist-mounted display with his sleeve, tapped the device a couple of times, and looked up. "Yes. A few more klicks and we'll be at the rendezvous point. I think."

"You think?"

"SATNAV doesn't work down here. The trees, they create natural electromagnetic fields. The denser the jungle, the worse it gets. Plays hell with the equipment. They should have briefed you on all this before you came out here."

"How...how do you even know where we are, then?"

"Inertial navigation," Roc said, tapping his wrist-top display, "and a hard-copy map. And, you know, I've been here before. I know where we're going. Do you need to rest a bit?"

Adisa finished a long pull from her drinking tube. "No, let's keep going. I want to get there before night-fall." Some of the nastier predatory creatures liked to hunt during Ithaca's long night.

"As you wish," Roc said. "Let's move." He led the

way, negotiating a path through the foliage. His partner, a short, stout man with broad shoulders and tanned skin, took up the rear. The two Rangers kept Adisa in between them for safety. She was a native Ithacan, but the flora, fauna, and terrain of the Southern Autonomous Zone were foreign to her. The terraformed zone she had grown up in, thousands of kilometers to the northwest, was cooler, flatter, and much dryer.

Those final "few klicks" took hours for the trio to traverse. The terrain grew more rugged, and they spent quite a bit of time navigating down into a ravine. It was lined on either side with huge pseudo-trees, and had a small stream running down its base. The sides were almost vertical, and were riddled with natural caves.

"This is it," Roc said, dropping his pack.

Adisa looked around anxiously. It was dark at the bottom, so dark that it was difficult to see unaided. "What now?" she asked, scanning the cave openings for movement. "Do we have to signal them?"

Roc shook his head. "No, they know we're here. They'll approach when they're ready. They know me, but they don't know you. Just set your pack down and rest for a bit. I'll keep watch so you don't get surprised."

Adisa didn't need any more encouragement than that to take a load off. She unfastened the waist belt of her backpack and removed it, setting it down on the smooth, cool stone of the ravine floor. She sat down next to it, took another drink of water, and retrieved her handheld. She quickly typed in an encoded message to her compatriots that she was in position and awaiting contact with the aliens. The device didn't have enough signal, at the moment, to push the message out, but it would keep trying until it did.

"Adisa," Roc said, his voice little more than a whisper. "They're here."

"Where?" she asked, looking around. She'd lived on Ithaca her entire life and had never seen one of the natives before. Roc pointed up, drawing her eyes to the edges of the ravine above them. Several gaunt figures loomed overhead, shrouded in shadow. They seemed to be armed with bows and spears, but it was difficult to tell. Despite the superiority of the humans' weapons, they were outnumbered and at the bottom of the ravine. If the aliens had hostile intent, Adisa and her Ranger companions were as good as dead.

"No sudden movements," Roc warned. "Just follow my lead, and keep quiet until I tell you to speak. They're nervous around strangers." Adisa nodded her understanding, and the Ranger stepped forward, leaving his rifle resting on his pack. "Hello, friends!" he shouted to the beings at the top of the ravine. "It's me, Roc! We come in peace, yeah?"

"They understand Commerce English?" Adisa asked, her voice a whisper.

Roc raised a hand to silence her. "Hush, let me do the talking." He turned his attention back to the aliens. "I'm here to speak with Follower of the Storm."

The beings at the top of the ravine shifted slightly, but there was no immediate response. After a few moments, though, Adisa noticed three aliens moving down into the ravine, following the same path the humans had taken. "Roc, look!" she said excitedly.

Roc nodded quietly and waited for the beings to approach. As they drew nearer, Adisa got a good look at them for the first time, and she was in awe. They were saurian in overall structure, tall and barrel-chested.

Small heads sat atop their elongated necks, and vestigial tail stumps protruded, upswept, from behind them. The aliens reminded Adisa of nothing so much as sawn-off brontosaurs. Each of the creatures stood over two meters tall. Their leathery skin, light gray in color, was smeared with paint to make them blend into the jungle better. They looked down at the humans through black eyes as they drew near.

The trio of aliens were dressed in clothing made from animal hides. Their wide feet were wrapped in thick leathers. The apparent leader of the three had more ornate apparel, his hides embroidered with patterns and symbols. The two flanking him...her? It? They seemed to be body guards. Both carried human-made assault rifles, though the weapons' grips, stocks, and sights had been substantially modified to be compatible with their nonhuman anatomy. One wore a pack made of animal hides and plant material, while the other had a hiking pack of obvious human origin.

The leader stepped forward and approached Roc. Their faces seemed lifeless, but Adisa wondered if that was only because she didn't know their body language. Standing close to Roc, the being extended a zygodactyl hand with four digits. Roc grasped its hand with his and, much to Adisa's surprise, the two shared a very human handshake.

"It's good to see you, friend," Roc said, speaking a little bit more slowly than he normally did. The alien responded in a deep voice, barking out a string of words, clicks, and other noises that Adisa couldn't possibly decipher. Roc turned to Adisa. "This is Follower of the Storm, love." Turning back to the alien, he said, "Stormy, this is A-dis-a." He said her name slowly, enunciating every syllable. The alien responded with more clicks and grunts. "No, she's not my mate. What? Oh, no, it's just a figure of speech. I don't actually love her. I just met her the other day. She's here because she seeks an audience with the Elders of your people."

Follower of the Storm moved toward Adisa. His movements were graceful and quiet, despite his looming presence, and he looked down at her with his dark eyes. "Why...did...you...come?" he asked, pausing between words as if trying to remember what to say.

Adisa's mouth fell open, and she was overcome with excitement. "You speak our language? My God, this is incredible! I never would have dreamed that I'd be having a conversation with you like this! It's like something from the old stories!"

Follower of the Storm looked at her quizzically. Roc, chuckling, told Adisa to slow down and speak very clearly. "Human speech can be just as confusing for them as their language is to you. Use short words and be concise."

"I apologize," Adisa said slowly. "This is very exciting for me."

Follower of the Storm dipped his head slightly. "Under-stand. Good for me to practice your speech, A-disssss-ah. What...do you...?" He fell silent, and looked over at Roc.

"I think the word you're looking for is 'need,'" the Ranger said.

The alien dipped his head at Roc and turned back to Adisa. "Need. What do you need with Elders? Very strange for Elders to meet with...aliens."

"I understand," she replied. "This is very unusual for me as well. But there is a great threat to us all."

"Threat?" the alien asked, cocking his head slightly to one side much as a human would.

"Yes. Um . . . danger? A danger. A terrible danger is coming. We are all in danger, your people and mine."

"Under-stand dan-ger," Follower of the Storm said. "Tell me this dan-ger."

Adisa paused, trying to determine how to explain the complex political situation on Ithaca to a tribal alien. "The elders of the human tribe on this world are planning to make a . . . a pact, a bargain, with another human tribe. This other tribe will enslave us all. Your people and mine. If we resist, they will kill without mercy. Do you understand?"

Follower of the Storm's dark eyes blinked several times, as if he was processing what he'd been told. "Yes," he croaked. "I under-stand. Other human tribe from an-other world?"

"Uh, yes," Adisa replied, surprised by the question. "They're called the Combine."

"Com-bine," the alien repeated. "Why come here?"

"Conquest. They wish to take what they want."

"Why your tribe make pact with such . . ." He muttered some guttural word from his native language.

"Our elders are weak. They are afraid. The Combine tribe is much stronger. They seek to use their strength to stay in power."

"Under-stand. What you want from my people? Not concerned with human . . . problems."

"You need to be concerned," Adisa said firmly. "The Combine believes that all nonhuman beings are a threat. They will enslave your people and kill you all if you resist. You must believe me. We come seeking your help."

"What help?"

"A war is coming, Follower of the Storm. We wish to ask your Elders if they will be willing to fight with us."

The alien was quiet for several moments. He swayed slightly, as if deep in thought. "Will bring you to Elders of my tribe. They must decide, not Follower of the Storm."

"Thank you!" Adisa was beaming. "Thank you so much!"

"Rest now," Follower of the Storm said. "Must... discuss...with my warriors. We will leave in short time." He turned and strode off to confer with his people.

Adisa turned to Roc. "So far, so good, yeah?"

Roc shook his head slowly. "You know, I never thought they'd actually agree to take us to their Elders."

"Has it happened before?"

"It's rare. Your father was the last one who gained such an audience. They normally want nothing to do with human affairs. This is unusual. I'll need to send a report to HQ. Sit down for a spell, love. Drink water and change your socks. I don't know how far we have to walk yet. Rest while you can."

Log Entry 131
Mission 815-707-SSOC
Reconnaissance Ship 505

The predictions made by the AI/CORE have come to pass. Hostile factions intend to disrupt influence operations on Ionia-5589/Ithaca by returning the exiled president, Zander Krycek, to power. AI/CORE regards this plan's likelihood of success as MODERATE/HIGH, and advises immediate countermeasures. We are activating assets PLASTIC FLOWER and EXALTED PAWN.

CHAPTER 5

The Privateer Ship *Andromeda*
Heinlein
St. Augustine Spaceport

Dressed in cargo pants and hiking boots, Nickson Armitage made his way up the gangway connecting the landing tower to the *Andromeda*. He wouldn't normally have dressed so casually for a job interview, but the instructions he had gotten were quite specific about him needing to dress for outdoor work. The roof of the gangway had polarized transparent sections which automatically tinted when exposed to sunlight. Despite the tint, Nickson got a good look at the *Andromeda* as he approached, and she was a beauty. Her gunmetal gray hull was decorated with blue accents. Captain Blackwood, the ship's owner and commander, had told him that she'd recently gone through a major refit: new engines, updated systems, and a general refurbishment to keep the old girl flying. From the look of her, Nickson imagined she'd be good for another fifty years, at least.

The gangway was attached to the ship's cargo bay, and the bay doors were open. As Nickson approached, a short, stocky man in a sage-green flight suit appeared. He had curly hair, a neatly trimmed goatee, and a transparent eyepiece over his right eye.

"Greetings!" the diminutive spacer said, beaming. "You must be Gentleman Armitage."

"I am," Nickson answered, extending a hand. "Permission to come aboard?"

"I'm Kimball, the *Andromeda*'s cargomaster," the spacer said, accepting the handshake. "Permission granted, of course. Please, follow me. You're right on time! That is fortunate, as the captain favors punctuality. You'll be meeting with her up on the astrogation deck. Did you have any trouble getting here?"

"Not at all. I caught the tube from Coventry yesterday, and got myself a room in the Duty-Free Zone for the night."

The cargomaster raised an eyebrow. "I hope Portside didn't treat you too badly."

Nickson grinned. The Duty-Free Zone around the St. Augustine Spaceport, Portside, was the sort of place that had sprung up around every major port since the age of sail. Business could be conducted, and goods could be sold tax free, so the place was a bustling commerce hub. Every type of enterprise imaginable, all designed to separate spacers from their accumulated pay, packed the crowded Zone: bars, brothels, virtual reality arcades, massage parlors, and recreational drug dens. It was a place where thieves, pickpockets, and scammers of every stripe would clean you out if you didn't keep your wits about you, and the police patrolled in pairs. "Ah, I stayed out of the bad side of town. They've really cleaned up the north end in the last couple years."

"Very good. Let us begin the tour, shall we? This is the cargo deck, as I'm sure you're aware. We are currently replenishing our stores, and much of the open space will be filled before we depart." They came to a ladder, which led through a hatch to the deck above. "After you, Gentleman."

"Odd that a ship this big doesn't have a lift," Nickson mused, climbing the ladder.

"She was designed as a military patrol ship," Kimball said, following him. "*Polaris*-class ships have been made in dozens of configurations, and the contract specified that there would be no lift. It saves mass and cost."

"Makes sense."

Kimball joined Nickson on the upper deck a moment later. "This is the crew deck. We have thirty berths here, though our normal complement is sixteen to twenty."

"I'm sure the extra berthing comes in useful," Nickson said, looking around. This deck took up nearly the entire diameter of the primary hull. In the center was what looked like a common area, with tables and benches fastened to the deck. This area was ringed by two rows of one-man berths, fifteen in each row. The top row was slightly offset from the bottom and was accessible by a metal catwalk.

"The showers and heads are on this deck, as well as a galley area for preparing rations. If you enjoy manual meal preparation, you are welcome to do so."

Nickson smiled. He'd never cooked anything by hand in his life. "Where to next?"

"We continue upward, Gentleman, until we get to the astrogation deck. Please, follow me."

A short while later, Nickson found himself standing

outside the hatch to the astrogation compartment. Kimball tapped the console next to the hatch.

"Cargomaster Kimball reporting, Captain," he said. "I have Gentleman Armitage with me."

"Very good," a woman's voice replied. Nickson recognized it as belonging to Captain Blackwood; the Scotch-Avalonian accent was unmistakable. "Send him in."

"Right away." Kimball turned toward Nickson. "She awaits you. Good luck to you."

Nodding at the cargomaster, Nickson tapped the hatch control. The door slid opened, and he stepped inside. In the center of the compartment was a large holotank, on which was displayed a three-dimensional schematic of the *Andromeda*. Captain Blackwood stood on the far side of the tank, her face lit up amber from the hologram, studying the image.

"She's a fine ship," Nickson said, as the hatch closed behind him, "with an outstanding service record."

"She is," the captain agreed, smiling. She was tall, almost as tall as Nickson, with fair skin and a strong jawline. Her dark hair hung over her right shoulder in tight braid. "Flattering my ship is a good start to your interview. Captain Catherine Blackwood," she said, stepping around the holotank and shaking Nickson's hand. "Welcome aboard."

"Thank you, Captain. It wasn't flattery, though, just a professional observation. You know as well as I do the state most privateer ships tend to be in."

"I do. That's why I'm rather particular about who my exec is. There's no secret to keeping a ship in fighting shape. It's a matter of maintenance, discipline, and morale. I expect my officers to be dedicated to all three, to take care of the ship and my people both. Complacency has killed more spacers in history than any other hazard."

Nickson wasn't sure about that statistic, but he understood where she was coming from. In deep space, there was only a razor-thin margin between life and death, and spacers often didn't live to see old age if they neglected the little things. "We had the same philosophy on the *Maddy D.* Captain Ogleman was personable and laid back, but displaying a lackadaisical attitude toward maintenance or your duties was the fastest way to get booted off the ship."

"I see. Tell me about your duties as XO."

The responsibilities of a ship's executive officer had millennia of tradition behind them, but they did vary from ship to ship. "Given our small crew, I wore a few different hats. My primary job was overseeing the maintenance of the ship and the welfare of the crew. The crew was small and we'd worked together for years, so the second part was easy. Maintenance was my primary focus most of the time. The *Maddy D.* was a great ship, but she was old, and she needed a lot of upkeep. We were planning on a major refit when we got back from our last contract."

"One of the primary reasons I'm considering you for the position is that you have experience on a licensed privateer. My other applicants all have a merchant fleet background. This job can be dangerous, as you're aware, and merchant officers generally lack combat experience. While I try to avoid combat, sometimes it is unavoidable. I can't expect my exec to garner much respect from the crew if my junior officers have more combat experience than he does."

"Oh, I agree, Captain," Nickson said, with a grin. "I think you'll find I'm a perfect fit for the position."

"We'll see. Your last contract didn't go so well. The publicly available records on the *Madeline Drake* show that she limped home, so badly damaged that she couldn't land. Captain Ogleman was reportedly killed, and the ship was auctioned off in orbit."

Nickson looked down for a moment, his smile gone. "That about sums it up. It was a bad tour."

"Can you tell me what happened? I'm not trying to imply that you were responsible. I am just curious as to what lessons could be learned from your experience."

Nickson took his jacket off, folding it neatly over his arm. "I loved the *Maddy D*. I was hired on as a pilot, and over the course of eight standard years I worked my way up to XO."

"Eight years? That's impressive."

"She had a small crew, as I said. Things were less formal than on, say, a military ship. Captain Ogleman and the previous XO, Aziz, took me under their wing as soon as I came aboard. I guess they saw leadership potential in me. I was thrilled. My previous ship, the *Eledore*? If you didn't play politics, you had no shot at promotion. The skipper liked to play favorites.

"Anyway, our last contract was with the colonial government of New Babylon. They couldn't afford much of a military of their own, so it was easier to just pay privateers to do it." Many smaller or less prosperous colonies either relied on mercenaries completely, or used them to supplement their own armed forces. Maintaining an astromilitary was a technically challenging and enormously expensive endeavor. Colonies with small populations and modest economies often couldn't manage it on their own, but soon found that a lack of a military left them vulnerable to pirates, raiders, and hostile governments. Outside of Concordiat space, especially on the frontier, privateering was big business as a result. "We were steadily employed by them for a couple of local years."

"That sounds like the kind of work many privateers would be thrilled with."

"We were, at first. The pay was good, and New Babylon is a nice planet as far as planets go. Good air, clean water, and soil that took to Terran crops without much difficulty. The colonial government spent most of their budget on terraforming, and had been doing so for years and years. The terraformed zone was huge, covered in forests and grasslands. The rest of the planet was a little bleak still, but there was plenty of room to grow."

"That doesn't exactly sound like a recipe for conflict."

"I'm willing to bet that if they'd been left alone, New Babylon wouldn't have much use for privateers, or even a military."

"I take it that they weren't left alone?"

Nickson paused before speaking again. "Have you ever encountered a lost fleet, Captain?"

"I haven't," she answered, after a moment. "They're rare." Lost fleets, rogue fleets, homeless fleets, whatever you wanted to call it, were usually groups of ships that, for one reason or another, didn't have a home port. Their crews and passengers lived perpetually in space, constantly on the move. Such notions were often romanticized in pop culture: the truest of spacers, wanderers, explorers, mysterious societies harboring lost technology or arcane knowledge. "I haven't read up on New Babylon, but do recall hearing something about a small colony being attacked by a raider fleet."

"The troubles began before we were hired," Nickson explained. "Attacks on ships coming and going to New Babylon, ships disappearing, things like that. The government of New Babylon got nervous and started sending their patrol ships out to do reconnaissance. I guess one of them reported a massive fleet, dozens and dozens of ships, in deep space, in an uninhabited system. Nobody knew who they were, but they knew they were outnumbered. They took the threat seriously enough to be proactive and beef up their pretty meager defenses with privateers."

"Fascinating. This lost fleet, where did it come from?"

"You know, we never found out. It's possible that the New Babylonians have learned something since I left, but we had no idea. They didn't answer any communications. Their ships were old, some of them *centuries* old, of many different makes and models. They had everything from large people-haulers with rotating sections, to atmospheric-capable ships, freighters, military ships, everything. Intelligence estimated their number at a hundred and five, total."

The captain's eyes went wide. "A hundred and five!"

Nickson nodded. "The New Babylon Space Patrol had all of three ships in its inventory, and they were search-and-rescue cutters, not warships. They were badly outnumbered and started hiring every privateer they could afford. There was something like thirty of us at the height of it all, based on New Babylon. The Colonial government went all out, spending every credit they could spare on defense. They'd send us out on regular one- or two-thousand-hour patrols, searching the nearby systems in pairs or threes for any sign of the lost fleet. There were a few scattered engagements in the beginning, and they grew more and more frequent as time went on. After a year of this, we finally encountered what seemed to be a main war fleet. Not the whole thing, but the bulk of the combat-capable ships. We found them two translations away from the Babylonian system, and they were headed right for it. We engaged them one translation away from New Babylon."

"I see. Is that where your ship was damaged?"

"No. The battle was over by the time we got there, and the lost fleet ships scattered. That system had four transit points, and different ships made for all four of them. Captain Ogleman opted to have us pursue what seemed to be the lost fleet's flagship, a midsized cruiser. It headed for the fourth transit point alone, and we followed. We chased them for weeks, through two systems, before we caught up to them in Rashid-231."

"I take it the engagement didn't go well?"

Nickson was quiet for a moment. He didn't like talking about this. "That's putting it mildly. I pleaded with the skipper to give it up. We were by ourselves. The cruiser was damaged, and had to have been two hundred years old, but it was a lot bigger than us. He just wouldn't listen. If we killed it, or captured it, we'd get a huge bonus from the client. The damned thing was his white whale."

"I see."

"We never even closed to laser range. They kept

fleeing, lobbing missiles at us. It's like they just wouldn't run out. They hit us, more than once. By the time we broke off and turned around, only five of us were uninjured. The ship's doctor was dead and Captain Ogleman was on life support. He died before we translated out of the system, and I was left in command." Nickson paused again, looking at the hologram of the *Andromeda*. "I know this is a fantastic-sounding story, Captain, so here." He handed her a data drive. "This is a record of the *Madeline Drake*'s logs. You can review it all yourself, if you care to. Consider it part of my resume. We made back to port and got repaired enough to make the flight back to Heinlein. We had been badly damaged enough that the client was contractually obligated to let us go."

The captain studied the plastic drive in the palm of her hand for a moment, then looked back up at Nickson. "So, what you're telling me is, you thought your captain was making a poor decision, and you tried to talk him out of it?"

"You're damned right I did, Captain. I didn't think the cruiser was as badly damaged as the reports said it was. That ship had killed two of the ships in our fleet and had badly damaged half a dozen more. Captain Ogleman was less pessimistic and thought we could take them. He reasoned that if they kept running from us instead of engaging, then that meant we were a real threat."

"That's a reasonable assessment. I can't think of any other reason for a cruiser to run from a single patrol ship."

"My gut told me something was wrong, though. She was flying too straight to be that badly damaged.

I tried, and failed, to convince the skipper that we should just let it go and regroup."

"What did you do when he didn't take your advice?"

"What could I do? I did everything I could to get the crew ready for a fight. I programmed the best representation of the cruiser into the computer that I could and ran drills on my people. We went over contingencies again and again. It just wasn't enough."

"And after this experience, you want to go back to privateering?"

"I do. Dirtside life is ... well, you know how it is. I got the itch, Captain. No sense in denying my nature. I love it out there, and I'm bored down here. I'm a spacer. I need *space*."

"I see," she said, looking at the drive in her hand again. She was quiet for a moment. "Well, I need to be honest, you're a strong candidate. I'm also pleased to see that you followed my instructions regarding your attire. Let's go for a hike, shall we?"

"A ... hike, Captain?"

"Yes. I know of a trail that leads to an overlook, to the south of the spaceport. It gives quite the view! Consider this part of your interview, Mr. Armitage. A physical assessment, if you will."

It was unorthodox, but if that's how she wanted to do it, Nickson wasn't going to argue. "Lead the way."

"This is it," the captain said. "Quite the spectacular view, isn't it?"

"Yeah," Nickson said, breathing heavily. "Spectacular." They were several kilometers from where they'd left their vehicle, and every damned meter of it was uphill. Taking a long drink from her canteen, the captain sat down on a small boulder. Catching his breath, Nickson sat next to her and took in the view. Surrounded by hybrid evergreen trees, they sat a few meters short of a sheer cliff face. Far below and several kilometers away was the St. Augustine Spaceport. It was a massive facility, spanning hundreds of hectares cut out of the dense forest. It had seven launch pads, arranged in a circle around the central terminal. Four of the pads were occupied, tall ships locked into landing towers, casting long shadows in the afternoon sun. One of those ships was the *Andromeda.*

"Thank you for coming up here with me," the captain said. It was quiet, save the singing of birds and the buzzing of insects.

"Hey, no problem," Nickson said, grinning. "I hope this proves that I really want the job."

"You'd be surprised at how many spacers let their health go to hell, Mr. Armitage."

"It wouldn't surprise me at all, Captain. I've seen spacers so fat you wonder how they can even get around if they're not in freefall."

Captain Blackwood laughed at that. She reached down into her pack, which she'd set at her feet, and retrieved her handheld. She tapped the screen a few times, then offered the device to Nickson.

"What's this?" he asked, taking it.

"Your contract. The job is yours if you want it. Take a moment and read it over."

Nickson quickly scanned the contract. Most of it was standard privateer fare, nothing he hadn't seen before. After scrolling to the bottom, he signed it with a thumbprint, then handed the device back to the captain.

"Welcome to the crew, Mr. Armitage," she said.

"Please, Skipper, just Nix."

The captain smiled. "Nix it is." They shook on it. "Now that that's taken care of, we have a contract offer. It's a short-notice affair, but it's too promising of an opportunity to pass up. How soon can you be ready to leave?"

"I need a couple days to get back to Coventry and move out of my apartment."

"That's right, you live in Coventry, don't you?" She looked thoughtful for a moment. "Do you feel up to starting a little sooner?"

"How much sooner?"

"Immediately."

Nickson didn't miss a beat. "Absolutely. What do you need?"

She tapped her handheld a few times. An image of a tall man with hard lines in his face and gray hair appeared in the holotank. "This is Zander Krycek. He's our client. He has requested passage to Ithaca."

Nickson had never heard of Ithaca. "I'll read up on it. What do you want me to do?"

"I'm going to meet with him to hammer out the details of the contract. He's currently staying in Coventry, and since you're headed there anyway, I want you to join me. Consider it the start of your on-the-job training."

She wants to have this meeting in person? It was strange, especially considering that the St. Augustine Spaceport was a continent away from Heinlein's colonial capital, but if that's how she wanted to do it . . . "Skipper, if you prefer negotiating contracts face to face, then I'm all for it. Do you want to fly back to the city, or take the tube?"

"You know, let's take the tube. The costs for chartering a flight from the spaceport are outrageous anymore."

"Are we in a tight financial situation, Skipper?"

She frowned. "You could say that. I'll let you look over the ship's logs when we get back. We sustained significant damage on our last mission, and . . . well, keeping a ship spaceworthy is expensive."

"If you're not flying, you're losing money."

"Indeed. This contract could be a boon for us, if the money is as good as it seems." She looked him in the eyes. "Listen, Nix, there's something else I need to tell you about. The reason I hired you is because my previous exec was killed on our last mission."

"I'm sorry to hear that, ma'am. Believe me, I know how hard it is to lose a crew member. May I ask how he died?"

She was quiet for a moment. "You know, I've never actually discussed this with someone who wasn't there. Our last mission took us to Zanzibar. Have you heard of it?"

"Yeah. That's that failed colony the Concordiat is going to annex, isn't it?"

"The same. As fantastic as it sounds, we had a hand in the chain of events that led to that. I was hired by my own family, back on Avalon, to go there and rescue my brother Cecil."

"Your brother? What the hell was he doing on Zanzibar?"

"That was my question. He was there on a treasure hunt, hoping to save the family business by obtaining antecessor artifacts. Before you ask, yes, we found them, but it's a very long story. It's all in the logs. In any case, on the way there, we had to pass through Orlov's Star."

"Oh, shit."

"Indeed. There was an incident, and we left the system with the Combine quite unhappy with us. The mission to Zanzibar was successful; I got my brother back, and we only lost one member of the crew. Well, technically, he was one of the mercenaries we hired, but..."

"If he's working for you, if he lives on the ship with you, he's part of the crew."

"That's how I saw it. His name was Randall Markgraff, and he died on the ground on Zanzibar. I was hoping that would be our only loss, but as we were leaving the planet, we were engaged by a Combine light cruiser. They'd come looking for us."

"You took on a cruiser?"

"We did. We prevailed, too, but not without cost. Wolfram, my XO, died in the battle, as did my assistant engineer, Charity. We were hit badly, you see, and they were conducting damage control. Wolfram had been with me since I took command of the *Andromeda*."

"I'm sorry, Skipper."

"These things happen, I suppose. It's a risky business."

"That doesn't make it any easier."

"No, it doesn't. I've been in no rush to replace him, even though it needed to be done. Somehow it felt wrong. But, there's nothing for it. I can't stay dirtside forever on account of a lost friend. Wolfram would have wanted me to get back into space." She looked up at the spaceport once again. "It's well past time I did. Shall we get back? It'll be dark in a few hours, and it's not good to be out here after dark."

"Yeah...wait, what? Why is it not good to be out after dark?"

"You... aren't much of an outdoorsman, are you, Nix?"

Truth be told, Nickson rarely left the city. He liked being surrounded by people. It was a welcome contrast to the dark emptiness of space. "I prefer the urban lifestyle is all."

"I see. Well, some of the local wildlife likes to come out at night, and some of them can be quite aggressive."

"You mean like bears?" Nickson had read about bears. They were imported from Earth and lived in the forests of the terraformed zone.

"There are worse things than bears out here. Let's get—" She fell silent and looked up. There was a bright light in the afternoon sky, accompanied by a deep rumble. The light, a brilliant orange, glowed through the layer of clouds several thousand meters above the spaceport. The glow intensified as the rumble grew louder, echoing across the hills, as if an angry god was descending from on high to smite the world. Then, all at once, the clouds parted, pierced by a column of smoke and thermonuclear fire. The rumble turned into a roar as the descending ship broke through the cloud layer, on final approach to one of the open landing pads.

The ship slowed as its altitude decreased, balanced on a column of thrust. The captain raised a pair of binoculars to her eyes and watched it as it descended, making minor course corrections to ensure it would land on the pad.

"That's the *Eowyn*," she said. "She's a privateer, same as us. That's the competition." She was as tall as the *Andromeda*, but slenderer. The sleek lines of her hull and spaceframe were only interrupted by four stubby fins and two radiators jutting out from the lower part of the fuselage. Instead of the four-engine cluster that powered the *Andromeda*, the *Eowyn* relied on a single, massive fusion rocket, around which the rest of the ship was built.

"It's a bold design," the captain said, watching the *Eowyn* as she settled onto the landing pad. "One of those new single-engine types coming out of the Inner Colonies."

"She looks new," Nickson said. "I bet she's only a couple of years old." Having a single engine reduced complexity and, more importantly, mass. It required less piping, less shielding, fewer support structures, and freed up more of the internal volume of the ship for other purposes. Plumes of smoke and fire shot upward, away from the pad at forty-five-degree angles, as blast diverters dispersed the *Eowyn*'s thrust. Such a design was not without its drawbacks, however. There was no redundancy in her propulsion. If the engine failed, there was no limping home at reduced thrust. At best, it'd be a huge inconvenience; at worst, it would be catastrophic.

The *Eowyn* cut its engine, plunging the spaceport into an almost eerie quiet. The rumble of the ship's landing echoed through the hills for a few moments and was gone. "The business is getting more and more cutthroat. The longer we rest on our laurels, the more time newcomers have to establish reputations and win contracts." Inhabited space was vast, but it wasn't so vast that a privateer could afford to sit around and let herself be crowded out of her own market.

The captain put her binoculars away. "I love these

long hikes into the wilderness. Wolfram used to go with me all the time. Once, I even managed to get the entire crew, save Mordechai Chang, to go on a hike together."

"Chang? He's the purser, right? Why didn't he go?"

The captain smiled. "You'll understand when you meet him. We camped out here for a week, living out of tents and cooking meals over an open fire. Spacers like us spend half our lives in a sealed can. It's good to get outside once in a while."

Nickson nodded. "That sounds like—hang on. Did you hear that?"

"Hear what?"

"I think there's something in the woods," he said, quietly. "I heard twigs breaking, like something moving through the trees."

More twigs snapped. "I heard that," the captain said. She placed her hand on the grip of a laser pistol that she carried in a holster across her chest. The foliage rustled again. Something was definitely moving through the trees, and quickly. The stride sounded long and heavy, but the spacers couldn't see anything through the dense bushes that grew along the sides of the trail.

An anthropoid stepped out of the bushes then, watching them through milky blue eyes. "Holy shit," Nickson whispered. He'd read about the creatures but had never actually seen one before. They were native to Heinlein.

"Stay calm," the captain said. "No sudden movements." It was a muscular creature, a biped two meters tall, rippling with muscles and possessed of gray, leathery skin. Its head, shoulders, back, forearms, and legs were covered in coarse, bluish-gray fur. Its face was mostly hairless. It didn't have a nose; these creatures breathed through gill-like organs on their necks. But it did have a large, almost circular mouth, full of gleaming white teeth. It hunched forward, striking an aggressive posture toward them, and let out a guttural growl.

The captain's laser was already in her hands. "Nix, do you have a weapon?"

"What? No! You said to bring outdoor clothes, not a gun."

"Next time, bring a gun, too," she said, aiming at the creature. The anthropoids fell somewhere on the evolutionary scale between apes and early protohumans. They were strong, fast, and aggressive. They had to be, to survive on Heinlein, which was home to all manner of dangerous, carnivorous species. It growled again, but didn't approach. "Just keep your distance," the captain said, even though the anthropoids didn't use or understand language. "We can both walk away from this." It was rare for them to venture this deep into the terraformed zone. While Heinlein's native ecosystem was somewhat compatible with the imported Terran one, its native species wouldn't eat Earth-native plants. This generally kept the whole food chain out of human-inhabited areas.

"Uh, Captain? There's more of them." A second anthropoid stepped onto the trail from the other side. This one carried a meter-long wooden club in its hand, made of a thick tree branch. Bolstered by the arrival of its troop mate, the first creature lunged forward, sprinting toward the captain at frightening speed. She barely had time to squeeze the trigger. The laser pulsed rapidly, emitting a loud crackling sound, the beam shimmering slightly as it ionized the air through which it traveled. The creature screeched as a messy wound opened on its chest. Pink and white fluids splashed, and the air stunk of ozone and burnt hair.

As its troop mate died, the second anthropoid charged, holding its club high over its head. "Look out!" Nickson shouted, lunging toward Captain Blackwood. He shoved her out of the way just as the beast swung the club, which *wooshed* to the ground with an earthy *thud*. The captain twisted around, shoved Nickson out of the way in turn, and fired her laser. Its pulses tore into the creature. The creature dropped its club and collapsed to the ground, bleeding into the dirt.

Heart pounding, Nickson watched as the captain ejected the power cell from her weapon and replaced it with a fresh one. A laser pistol powerful enough to be effective on large and dangerous animals quickly went through batteries, and generated a lot of waste heat on top of it. It had done its job, though: they were both still alive.

They didn't linger at the scene. The spacers stepped past the bodies of the dead anthropoids and headed back down the trail. They were, technically speaking, a protected species. "It's strange that they're so close to the spaceport," the captain said. "We need to report this to the wildlife service."

"Yeah, well, let's get out of here alive first."

"Keep your eyes open. They tend to travel in groups, from troops of four or six to packs of dozens, if they've formed a large hunting or war party. Laser pistol or no, if we run into a large group they'll rip us to pieces. Let's pick up the pace."

"You don't have to tell me twice," Nickson said, speeding up to a jog. Together, the spacers moved down the trail as quickly as they could without falling. The path was long, rocky, uneven, and in places quite steep. For more than a kilometer they ran. A throaty roar echoed through the trees, driving home why they really didn't want to risk falling.

"This is a hell of a first day!" Nickson said, struggling to keep up. He worked out occasionally, but running was never a thing he enjoyed doing. There were multiple roars and cries coming from the forest now, from both sides of the trail. They didn't know for certain how many of them there were, but it sounded like a lot.

"I think it's a war party!" Captain Blackwood said.

"A war party? What the hell is a war party?"

"Exactly what it sounds like, Nix!"

"Holy shit, we're going to die."

"We're not dead yet. Keep moving! Cam!"

"What? Who's Cam?"

"It's my virtual assistant. Cam, I need you to start my car and bring it to me!" Her pace slowed just a little. They were both tired.

"Starting the car now," Cam replied, its synthesized baritone voice loud enough for Nickson to hear. "However, you are not near a road. I cannot bring the car to you."

"It's an emergency and I don't give a damn about bloody traffic regulations! Start the car, put it in off-road mode, and get it as close to me as you can without disabling it! I don't care if it gets damaged as long as it drives!"

"I understand. Are you sure you want to do this?

Your insurance may not cover damage to the vehicle if—"

The captain didn't let Cam finish its standard disclaimer. "Yes, I'm sure, damn you! Now! Do it now!"

"Very well. I will get the car as close to you as I can. Please stand by. If there's an emergency, I can contact the authorities for you."

"Contact the wildlife service," she said, picking up the pace again. "Just get the car up here." The trailhead was still more than a kilometer away, and judging from the angry, bestial growls coming from the trees, they wouldn't make it.

ROAAAR!

An anthropoid crashed through the bushes then, stepping onto the trail behind them. It held a large stone in its hands, above its head, and hurled it at the spacers. Nickson dodged to the left as the skipper dodged to the right. The stone impacted the dirt where they'd been standing with a loud *thud*. Taking a knee, the captain brought her heavy laser pistol to bear and shot the beast in the chest, the rapid-pulsing laser stitching a gory wound across the creature's torso. Screeching in pain and gushing pink and white fluids, it turned and retreated into the trees.

"Nix, let's go! I think they're trying to encircle us!" They turned and took off back down the trail. Coming to a switchback, the captain led Nickson off the trail, and together they cut through the thick underbrush and slid down a steep embankment. Covered in mud, they landed back on the trail, on a lower level of the switchback, and kept going.

Nickson was beginning to wonder if she hadn't warded the marauding anthropoids off. Their roars and cries had stopped. There was something very primal and utterly terrifying about being hunted. It was all he could do to remain calm and keep pushing on, toward the captain's vehicle.

"There it is!" she said. A hundred meters or so down the trail, on the far side of a thick, fallen tree, was her car. The hydrogen engine was quietly running, waiting for them. The vehicle had good ground clearance and decent off-road capability, something that came in handy in the terraformed zones of Heinlein. In many areas, the roads weren't paved. In some areas, they could scarcely be called "roads" in the first place. "Come on!" They sped up to a flat-out run, a desperate final dash to the vehicle. Behind them, they heard something crash through the brush, followed by heavy footsteps. They were being chased. Nickson had never run so hard in his life.

They didn't get far. The captain cried out in pain as a thrown tree branch caught her in the backs of her legs, causing her to stumble and fall. She landed facedown in the dirt, grinding the palms of her hands into the rocky trail, and lost her laser.

"Captain!" Nickson said, sliding to a stop. He turned and ran to her just as she was pushing herself up. A hulking anthropoid, this one larger and darker in color than the others, loomed over them. It had another tree branch in its massive, three-digit hand. "Get away from her!" He punched the creature in the face as hard as he could. Pain shot through his hand as it connected with its bony jaw. The anthropoid backhanded Nickson, sending him flying. The wind was knocked out of him as he hit the ground.

Turning back to Captain Blackwood, it raised its

crude weapon as she scrambled to get away. She tried to protect her face with her arms as it swung.

CRACK!

She cried out in agony as the bones in her forearm snapped. The beast roared, long and guttural, its spittle hitting her face as she crawled desperately backward, trying to get away.

Struggling to sit up, Nickson's hand touched something solid. It was the captain's laser! As the anthropoid hefted its club again, this time for the killing blow, he picked up the weapon, pointed it, and held the trigger down. In a flash, it was over. The heavy laser's rapidly pulsing beam ripped the anthropoid open. It didn't even shriek in pain like the others had; it just fell over backward, bleeding, dead before it hit the ground. The air stunk of the putrid odor of the creature's internals, burnt flesh, and singed hair.

Both spacers sat there for a moment, breathing heavily, not saying anything. They listened carefully for the telltale sounds of more of the creatures moving through the brush, but only the sound of the wind sighing through the hybrid evergreens and the quiet hum of the car's hydrogen engine could be heard.

"Captain!" Nickson said, getting to his feet. He ran to her and helped her up. She cradled her injured arm against her body. "Are you okay?"

"I'm fine, Nix, thanks to you. Help me to the car, would you?" The door automatically opened as they approached. Nickson aided her as she took off her pack, trying not to further injure her broken arm, and tossed it in the back. He eased her into the passenger's seat before climbing into the driver's seat himself. "Get us out of here, if you please."

Nickson cautiously drove down the trail, trying not to damage the vehicle on the uneven terrain. Cam, her virtual assistant, spoke up again, its voice resonating over the car's sound system. "You appear to be injured, Catherine. Do you wish me to call for a medical response?"

"No. It's not critical, just a broken arm. Send a message to the wildlife service. Tell them we made it out, but killed several of the anthropoids in self-defense."

"Message sent."

"Good. Call Harlan."

"Calling Harlan," Cam repeated.

"Harlan is my flight surgeon," she explained. He answered the call after a few seconds, his image appearing on a small, transparent display on the dashboard.

"Captain, good to see you. What can I do for you?"

As Nickson drove, the captain carefully raised her broken arm so that the doctor could see it. It was already bruising up. "Would you mind if I stopped by? I'm afraid it's broken."

"I'm afraid it is, too," he said, leaning in closer to the screen. "Are you all right?"

"I'll live. I've about had my fill of dirtside life for the time being, though. Be a dear and have a drink ready when I get there, would you?"

"I'll have some brandy waiting for you, Captain. We'll get that arm put back together."

"Very good. Oh, Harlan? This is Nickson Armitage, our new executive officer."

"It's a pleasure," Nickson said, keeping his eyes on the road.

"Good to meet you, sir," the doctor said.

"Nickson here saved my life today. I think hiring

him was a good choice. I'll have him drive me to your place. See you soon." The call ended, and the captain looked over at Nickson. "I meant that, Nix. Thank you."

"I meant it, too: hell of a first day."

CHAPTER 6

Portside Tube Station
Duty-Free Zone, Twenty Kilometers South
of St. Augustine Spaceport
The Next Day

"You know, I've never actually taken the Tube before," Captain Blackwood said. The train was finishing its acceleration and would soon settle in to its cruising speed. "I've always preferred to fly." The Tube, as it was colloquially known, was a network of high speed-trains that crisscrossed the surface of Heinlein, connecting the major population hubs. The trains traveled in an elevated, sealed pipe, which was kept as close to a vacuum as could be reliably maintained. Suspended in a magnetic field, the trains zipped back and forth at a thousand kilometers per hour.

"I would have been happy to fly this time, Skipper," Nickson replied, sitting next to her. Her arm was in a thin cast.

"As I said, it's gotten too expensive. We need to maintain a budget. Our financial situation is not ideal."

"I've been going over the financial records, and I

see what you mean. Getting the ship repaired in the Llewellyn Freehold really set you back."

Captain Blackwood scoffed at the mention of the Freehold. "The entire bloody planet is nothing but political cover for pirates. If you're just passing through, and haven't paid the right bribes to the right people, everything costs a fortune. And since they have some trade relations with the Orlov Combine, having us there posed a risk to them, and they charged us a daily *security fee* while we were planeted."

"You had to pay them not to turn you over."

"Exactly. The ship was due for the refit anyway, and after being so heavily damaged there was no sense in putting it off. When all was said and done, our profit margin was small, and a lot of that has been eaten up by berthing fees."

Parking a ship at a spaceport was a significant expense. The *Andromeda* had been sitting for nearly two standard years, much of that waiting for the upgrades to be completed.

"Aside from me dragging my heels on getting the crew roster filled back out, the market has been slow. Mordechai has been analyzing the situation, and he thinks privateering is undergoing a market correction, as he calls it."

"What does that mean?"

"Piracy is largely an economic problem, and the factors that make piracy profitable are changing, at least in this part of inhabited space. The Outer Colonies can't really be considered the frontier anymore. There are fewer and fewer ports willing to harbor a ship that is at all suspicious, and fewer avenues for the selling of stolen property. The Concordiat having annexed Zanzibar means increased military activity out that way, too, and increased paranoia on the part of the Combine. They're one of the biggest traffickers in illicit goods, but few pirates want to risk getting caught between them and the Concordiat fleet."

"You know, Captain Ogleman was concerned about this before our last contract. He was convinced that Heinlein just wasn't going to be a viable base of operations for privateer work in coming years." Nickson looked down, for just a moment. "I think that may have been part of his reasoning for pursuing that cruiser."

"Financial desperation has gotten many privateers in trouble over the years. Either way, Captain Ogleman may have been right."

"What then? Are you considering a move?" Nickson didn't have any family, and wasn't particularly attached to his adopted home of Heinlein. Even still, one did not simply up and relocate to another planet. Making such a move was a massive logistical problem, and bore no small amount of risk.

"I don't know. It may be necessary, in order to stay in business. In any case, there's no sense in stressing over it now."

"Hey, Skipper? There's something else I wanted to ask you. Like I said, I went over the logs from your last time out. What happened with the *Agamemnon*?"

She was quiet for a moment. "Ah, yes. That."

"I mean, finding a Second Federation vessel, completely intact, after it had been drifting out there for what, eight hundred years? It's incredible."

"It was too big for us to salvage, mind you. The damned thing was seven hundred meters long. We investigated, but found nothing useful. Did you review the logs and the video from that?"

"I did," Nickson said, vividly recalling the helmet-cam footage of the ship's bridge. Frozen gore was stuck to the walls and floor. Mangled bodies were strapped into chairs. "What in God's name happened?"

"We still don't know. I worked out a deal with my brother. I sold him the salvage rights for a pittance, accepting a percentage of the salvage profits instead of a big up-front fee. A fleet from my family's business went out to Baker-3E871 and began the recovery process. They disassembled it, piece by piece, and brought it back to Avalon. We've yet to make any money off the salvage."

"What? That ship is priceless!"

"Oh, it is, but there were...complications. I don't know of this first hand, mind you, only what my brother told me in his correspondence. Several workers were killed in the salvage effort. The whole process was plagued with problems. When they finally got it back home, the government got involved. They declared it a matter of colonial security, and the whole thing has been shrouded in secrecy since. That ship had an AI, you see, a genuine, pre-Diaspora AI. Last I heard, they were attempting to reactivate it, to find out what happened to the crew, but I don't know if they had any success."

"Is your brother still involved?"

"He is, along with his partners from Zanzibar. My father saw to that. I don't know what they'll learn, if they ever get that AI operational, but I don't expect it will be pleasant."

Nickson thought again about the grisly discovery

on the ancient derelict. He had no idea what could have done something like that. He'd heard stories, of course, old spacers' tales of ghost ships, vanished crews, and other horrors to be found in the darkness of outer space. Until his own encounter with a mysterious lost fleet, he'd never put much stock in those tales, but now? He wasn't superstitious, but he wasn't ready to dismiss such things out of hand, either. "Anyway, I've been reading up on our client, Skipper," he said, changing the subject. "He's got what you'd call a *checkered* history."

"Oh? Beyond being the ousted and exiled leader of a colony?"

"Yeah, beyond that. It took a while to find some of this stuff. I had to run a detailed search, and I had to try and weed out any less than truthful propaganda from either side, which there was plenty of. He himself has written several books, but I haven't had time to read them."

"Summarize it for me. I haven't had time to go over everything I should have. This is all happening on short notice."

"Zander Krycek was deposed in a coup about twenty standard years ago. He was still popular with a sizeable portion of the colonial population at the time of his ouster, and in order to avoid sparking a second civil war they allowed him to go into exile. Since then, the colony has been in a long downward slide, socially and economically, and the ruling Interim Government is struggling to maintain order."

"I suppose that's why they want him back," the captain said.

"Maybe, but some people won't be happy about it.

He is still known, in the official Ithacan histories, as the Butcher of Sargusport. It seems that after months of trying to crack a royalist stronghold, the remote city of Sargusport, he destroyed it with a tactical nuclear weapon."

"Royalist?"

"That's what it says. I guess they were supporters of the king, whom our client had overthrown. That's odd. You don't see a lot of actual kings these days."

"Mm. Go on."

"Anyway, twenty thousand colonists died, and not just the militants. Noncombatants, children, the elderly, and the sick and wounded all died with the city."

Nickson watched as his captain mulled that over. They were privateers and, yes, mercenaries, but that didn't mean they were without conscience or morality. "What happened after that?"

"I hate to say it, but it worked. Destroying Sargusport, I mean. After that, the last remaining royalist holdouts came to the negotiating table, and a cease-fire was declared. It ended eight local years of war."

"And they ousted him after that?"

"Yeah. The Interim Government, which is run by something called the Revolutionary Council, blamed President Krycek for the civilian deaths, but took credit for negotiating the armistice. They said he was a dangerous, reckless war criminal, and that too much power had been consolidated in his office. They voted to remove him from office, and dispensed with the office of the presidency altogether. Scapegoating him helped unify the colony somewhat, and the cease-fire held after his departure."

"Yet it seems he still has allies there."

"It makes sense. Apparently, he was quite popular before the coup. He even managed to negotiate a peace treaty with the native sentient species, a first in modern history. Why? Having second thoughts about this?"

"No. We need this contract, Nix. If I keep my crew planetside for much longer, I won't *have* a crew. Besides that, there's something larger at stake here. Mr. Krycek explained to me that this Interim Government, ruling council, whatever they call themselves, are planning on extending diplomatic relations with the Combine."

"What? Why? Why would anyone do that?"

"When you get some time, you should read up on the Combine's propaganda machine. To hear them tell it, Orlov is a wonderful, communitarian society free from corruption, inequality, poverty, and the petty squabbles of democratic politics. Instead of fighting amongst themselves, they say, everyone has a place, everyone contributes, and they're working to make that Godforsaken rock they live on a paradise."

Nickson was incredulous. "And people actually believe that?"

"Some people do. You'll find pro-Combine agitators on almost every world. Some of this is organic, born of ignorance and wishful thinking, some of it is a deliberate influence effort on the Combine's part. You'd be surprised at how well it works. Their methods are incredibly sophisticated."

"I think securing that trade agreement with the Llewellyn Freehold, what, twenty years ago? I think that emboldened them."

"I'm inclined to agree. They were willing to send a cruiser after me, all the way to Zanzibar, unusual for a supposedly isolationist hermit-state. They also had designs on Zanzibar itself, I suspect. I don't think they would have been content with selling weapons to the local warlord."

"I've gone over some of your logs from Zanzibar, Skipper. A previously unknown antecessor civilization, with intact artifacts left behind? If there was even a chance the Combine could secure alien technology, they wouldn't hesitate to try to annex that planet."

"Indeed. I suppose that's why the Concordiat claimed it first."

Nickson grinned. "Surely you don't doubt their noble intentions, Skipper? They insist it's just about humanitarian relief and peacekeeping."

Captain Blackwood laughed. The train was speeding along at close to a thousand kilometers per hour now, across rolling, forested hills. The tube, constructed with many transparent sections, was elevated. It stood about twenty meters above the ground, and every so often a tree flashed past the window. "You know," she said, still looking out the viewport, "this is actually rather pleasant."

"Well, this is a first-class cabin, too, Skipper. If we were in the cheap seats, we wouldn't have this little compartment to ourselves."

"Even still. I come from Avalon, and technically I'm still Lady Blackwood of Aberdeen. My father sits on the ruling council, and he always insisted that mass transit is for peasants." She chuckled. "It wouldn't do for a man of his position to ride with the commoners."

Nickson's tablet started vibrating in his hand. He was receiving a message. Tapping the screen, the image of Mordechai Chang appeared.

"Cap'n, Mr. Armitage," the purser said. "I apologize for bothering you, but you ought to see this." His image disappeared as the screen went black for a moment. "This is a live netcast coming from our client. The media picked up on it."

The screen now showed the face of Zander Krycek. He was sitting in what looked like a plush hotel room, and was in the middle of an address when the audio cut in: "...worse than that, the Council has been making overtures to the Orlov Combine. There are even reports that suggest they're looking to consolidate their own power by signing a mutual defense agreement with the Combine.

"This cannot be allowed to happen. I accepted my exile because I thought it was for the best for my people and my homeworld. The colony had already been torn apart by revolution and civil war. I was a divisive figure, and I had hoped that with my departure, some semblance of normalcy would return to Ithaca. Clearly, that has not come to pass. I cannot, and will not, allow my homeworld to become a client state of the Combine. That is why I intend to return home; I'm going back to Ithaca.

"Unlike the cowards on the Council, who make deals in secret, I announce my intentions openly, and I am not afraid. Let them be put on notice: Everyone will know of their treachery, should they go through with this. To them I say this: It is not too late to change course. It is not too late to put your homeworld before your own petty self-interest. It is not too late to stop this madness. Work with me. Together, we can rebuild our government and our homeworld. We can set aside our past differences and work toward giving our people a brighter future, one where they are not cogs in some great, indifferent machine.

"If you're unwilling to do this, if you're unwilling to defend your home from foreign intervention, then you have no place on Ithaca. You have been warned."

The netcast ended. Nickson looked up from his tablet at his captain; her face had gone a little paler.

"That colossal idiot," she said, quietly.

Nickson just sighed. *What have you gotten yourself into this time?*

CHAPTER 7

Coventry
One day later

"Fancy enough for you, skipper?" Nickson asked, as they made their way down a hallway on the fifty-first floor of the King's Tower Hotel. The carpet beneath their feet was plush, and the lighting was cozy without being too dim. It was one of the most expensive hotels in the city of Coventry, and their client had booked himself an executive suite on the top floor.

The King's Tower was one frequented by the rich and famous of Heinlein, as well as foreign diplomats. It was heavily constructed, its walls designed to be impervious to gunfire and to contain explosive blasts. The doors were reinforced, the windows were made of armored transparency, and the grounds were patrolled by armed security day and night.

"This is a good sign, Nix. This tells me he has money to spare. That's good, because after his stunt yesterday, our fees are going up."

"You really expecting trouble?"

"It's hard to say. It's certainly more likely now, thanks to his speech."

Nickson's stomach twisted a little, though he didn't mention it to his captain. He really didn't want to get into combat if it could be avoided. Memories of the desperate slugfest with the lost fleet cruiser flashed through his mind: screaming klaxons, the ship shuddering as nearby bursting missiles peppered the hull with fragmentation, seeing his shipmates burned and wounded, watching his captain die.

"Nix?" It was the captain. She looked concerned. "Are you alright? We're here. This is the room."

"Yeah! Yeah, I'm fine, Skipper, just going over some things in my head. Shall we let him know—" Before he could complete that sentence, the door quietly slid open.

"Welcome!" The two spacers were greeted by a robot with a cheery, synthesized voice. It had a cylindrical body balanced atop a single large wheel. A pair of tentacle-like mechanical arms hung from its sides, and its angular head was a cluster of sensors, cameras, and antennae. "Captain Blackwood, Mr. Armitage, please follow me. Master Zander is expecting you." The robot's body rotated one hundred eighty degrees, its single wheel remaining stationary, and it rolled away, humming a pleasant tune.

Nickson and the Captain looked at each other for a moment. He shrugged, and they followed the machine into the ostentatious hotel suite. An airy, vaulted ceiling was complimented by marble floors, while the main living area was carpeted. Large windows on the northeast corner provided a spectacular view of the city. Coventry was built around a semicircular bay, six kilometers across at its widest, and the city was lit up as Heinlein settled into its long, warm night.

Zander Krycek was waiting in the living room, lounging in a big leather chair. Ancient classical music played over the sound system as the old man studied a tablet screen. Three other people, two men and a woman, were in the room with him. He rose as the spacers approached.

"Captain Blackwood and Mr. Armitage, sir," the robot said.

"Very good. That'll be all, Jerkins." The robot beeped an agreeable tone and rolled away. "Captain," he said, extending a hand to her, "it's good to meet you face to face."

"And you as well," she said, as the two exchanged an Earth-style handshake. "This is Nickson Armitage, my executive officer."

"Nice to meet you," Nickson said, shaking the man's hand.

Zander Krycek indicated a tall, thin man with short-cropped hair and an ebony complexion, as was the majority on Ithaca. "This is Colonel Erasmus Starborn, of the Ithacan Colonial Guard." He gestured to the woman, who was shorter, had a lighter complexion, curly black hair, and a pair of smart glasses on her face. "This is Kya, an attaché from the Southern Autonomous Zone, and . . ." he paused, looking around. "Ras, where did Sebastian get off to?"

"He told me he was going to check on the lobby," Colonel Starborn said. "I'll contact him."

"Please do. In any case," Zander said, "Sebastian is with Ithacan Foreign Affairs."

"And this didn't raise suspicion when you left?" the captain asked.

The colonel looked at Zander.

"Go ahead, Ras, you can tell them. They're going to be working with us, they need to know."

"We didn't tell them where we were going," the colonel replied. "This was supposedly a diplomatic outreach to several independent colony worlds. We weren't actually on the transport ship we were supposed to be on. We transferred to a courier ship, after paying a hefty bribe, and traveled here in cold sleep."

"Yes, well... Mr. Krycek, do you mind if we sit?" the captain asked. "We have a lot to go over."

"Yes. Everyone, please, have a seat, and let's get down to it," Zander said. "I'll have Jerkins bring us some refreshments."

"Jerkins?" Nickson asked.

"My steward robot."

"Yes, but Jerkins?"

Captain Blackwood spoke up. "Mr. Krycek, we caught your netcast yesterday."

"Oh? What did you think?"

"What were you thinking?" the captain asked, pointedly. "We had the element of surprise. We could have gotten you to Ithaca with little to no risk of resistance. Instead, you announce your intentions to the entire galaxy."

Zander raised an eyebrow. "Are you saying you're not interested in the contract anymore, Captain? I'm sure I can find another privateer."

"I'm saying that you've substantially increased our risk, and we will need to factor that into our fee schedule. Help me understand, sir, why you chose to do it this way."

"It does seem a little, er, counterintuitive," Nickson suggested.

"Indeed, it does. In fact, it's probably the last thing my enemies on Ithaca would have expected."

"It also serves to rally support back home," the woman named Kya said. "President Krycek is still considered by many to be the rightful leader of the colony. He's a hero, the man who overthrew a tyrant, made peace with the natives, and ended a bloody civil war. He was unfortunately scapegoated by political opportunists, but the announcement of his return will embolden our allies and send our opponents scrambling."

"Yes, that's a lovely bit for a press release, but it still significantly increases our risk."

"Hang on a second," Nickson said. "Tell me about this king."

"What?" Kya said.

"It's not common. There are some colonies that have hereditary monarchies, but in most cases, they're honorary titles and the royalty lacks real political power. You almost never hear about a king wielding absolute authority."

"Such was the case on Ithaca," Kya answered. "King Khari the Fifth was the last of his dynasty. His family had ruled Ithaca since the colony was founded over four hundred and fifty standard years ago."

"The Khari family, wealthy traders from the Inner Colonies, launched the expedition to Ithaca about the time of the signing of the Interstellar Concord," Zander explained. "Much of inhabited space was still recovering from the dark years. The Kharis weren't content with the wealth and power they had. They wanted an entire world to themselves."

Kya continued, "Ithaca, at the time, was inhabited

by a few thousand explorers from Olympic Interstellar Expeditions. The Kharis landed with dozens of ships and tens of thousands of colonists, and laid claim to the whole world. Eventually, OIX was driven off, and Valdemar Khari declared himself King Khari the First. His family members were set up as a nobility."

"By the time I was an officer in the Colonial Guard," Zander said, "things were getting bad. Khari the Fifth was a deeply troubled man. His ill-advised economic policies drove a once prosperous colony into the ground. Off-world trade dwindled, a lot of people lost their jobs, and unrest ensued. In his paranoia, he saw enemies everywhere. Those suspected of treason or sedition simply disappeared. In doing so, he created many new enemies. Something had to be done, so we removed him."

Captain Blackwood raised an eyebrow. "Removed?"

"Yes. Unfortunately, this started a civil war. The king had an heir, but she abdicated the throne, leaving a power vacuum. The rest of the nobles squabbled over who was next in the line of succession, and their royalist supporters tried to crack down on everyone who had opposed them. It wasn't long before we were in open conflict."

"So, you deposed the king, then declared yourself president?"

Zander's eyes narrowed. "I declared myself nothing, Captain. I was selected by my peers. It was the closest thing to democracy Ithaca has ever seen."

"I see. In any case, you were declared an enemy of the state and were sent into exile. Upon your return, they will try to kill you, correct?"

"I'm sure they'll try."

"Right. Mr. Krycek, the *Andromeda* is a fine ship,

and she has more fight in her than a ship her size ought to. I have complete confidence in both my ship and my crew. However, we are just one ship. Now that they know we're coming, what kind of reception are we going to receive? Am I going to be dragged into a colonial civil war?"

"Ithaca doesn't have a functioning astromilitary anymore, Captain, if that's what you're worried about. Our space patrol wasn't large to begin with, and I'm told it's been grounded indefinitely in recent years."

"That's good to know, but there are still other concerns."

"They could hire corsairs to come after us," Nickson suggested. "They could try to shoot us down when we land."

"I understand all that, I assure you both. It's a risk I'm willing to take. If it's a risk you're willing to take as well, there's a substantial payout waiting for you. I think you'll find my offer quite attractive."

Nickson looked down at his handheld as Mr. Krycek sent the contract offer. The offered payment was substantial, covering the fees, plus some large bonuses. It amounted to tens of millions of credits.

If the captain was impressed, she didn't let it show. "I see. I'm sending you the revised fee schedule. I'm afraid the increased risk of loss of life and damage to my ship, as well as the risk of political entanglements, requires some adjustment of the original terms."

The client frowned when he saw the new counteroffer. "Captain, I don't think..." he trailed off. "Ras, what is it?" Colonel Starborn had turned to the window. His body language told Nickson that something was wrong.

He spun around suddenly, running toward the others. "Get down!" he shouted, shoving Zander to the floor with both hands. A deafening roar filled the suite as a stream of armor-piercing bullets first pockmarked, then spider-webbed, then ripped through the protective windows, luminescent tracer rounds tearing into the far wall in a cloud of dust and debris.

Nickson, reflexively, dove to the floor, dragging his captain down with him. "What the hell is going on?" he shouted, trying to hear over the roar of machine-gun fire.

Colonel Starborn already had his sidearm drawn. "There's an armed drone outside! Stay down!" Driving the point home, the machine made another pass, pouring fire into the luxurious suite from a different angle. Chunks of flooring and wall material flew through the air as the drone sprayed bullets into the suite. Everyone was on the floor, huddling underneath the window, trying to utilize what little cover was available.

"Skipper, are you alright?" Nickson asked.

The captain had produced a compact laser pistol from under her shirt. "I'm fine. Are you armed?"

"What? No! I didn't think we'd get into a firefight while meeting the client!"

"Bloody hell, Nix! Fine. I'm going to try to and get a shot at it. Get ready to run." The firing had ceased, at least for the moment. The drone could be heard, barely, over the wind whipping through the shattered windows, and the alarms sounding throughout the hotel.

"Skipper, no!"

"Stay where you are!" Colonel Starborn shouted. "It's waiting for us to come out!"

Zander Krycek had an angry, yet calm expression on

his face. "Enough of this." He tapped the screen of a tiny device he wore on his wrist. A moment later, his steward bot appeared from the other room, moving more quickly than it had before. A boxy attachment with what looked like a pan-tilt-zoom camera lens had slid up from its back and locked into position on its shoulder. The air shimmered as the robot fired its laser turret, pulsing it at thirty shots per second.

Jerkins ceased firing and came to a stop. "Threat neutralized," it said, its voice more baritone than before. "Standing by."

"Move, move, move!" Colonel Starborn shouted. "Out the door, go!" He grabbed Zander Krycek, pulled him to his feet, and shoved the old man forward, toward the door. He sent Kya after him next, then motioned toward Nickson and Captain Blackwood. "Come on, let's go!"

The captain was already on her feet. Nickson scrambled behind her, hoping like hell the would-be assassins didn't have a second drone out there. Colonel Starborn waited until everyone else was out of the room before exiting. Jerkins followed, rolling quietly behind the group with its laser weapon armed.

The ornate, carpeted hallway of the hotel was quiet, save the warning klaxon sounding over the PA system. In an attack like this, the doors of the hotel automatically locked, and residents were warned to stay in their rooms. Nickson and the group were the only people in the corridor.

"We need to get to the lift!" Kya said. She was shaking, and it looked like her bladder may have let go, but she was still on her feet.

"No," Colonel Starborn cautioned. "The lifts are

locked out in an emergency like this. The stairs are our only way down." Moving to the end of the hall, the lanky officer shoved the door open, gun drawn, making sure it was clear, before signaling the others to follow him.

The doorway led to a landing, with dozens of floors below. There was a man in a nice suit waiting for them, his face pale and sweat trickling down his forehead.

"Sebastian!" Colonel Starborn said. "Where the hell were you?"

"I was down in the lobby," he said, huffing and puffing. "When the alarm sounded, I ran up the stairs. All fifty-one floors. Is everyone alright?"

"No casualties." He turned toward the group. "Okay everyone, we need to keep moving and get out of here. Stay alert. That drone might not be all there is to our attackers."

"Hold up a moment," Zander said, leaning on the railing, breathing heavily.

"Are you injured, sir?" the colonel asked, holstering his sidearm and stepping toward the former president.

Zander smiled. "No, Colonel, I'm just old. I need to catch my breath before we tackle so many flights of stairs. Check Kya."

"I'm... I'm okay," Kya said, shakily. She appeared to be uninjured, but she didn't sound fine. "Mr. President, we—" *BLAM!*

It took Nickson what seemed like a long time, over the ringing in his ears, to realized that that loud noise had been a gunshot. Time seemed to slow down as he watched, helplessly, as Colonel Starborn collapsed to the cold ceramicrete landing, a bullet hole in the back of his head.

Behind him was Sebastian. He held a compact pistol out in both hands. The air stunk of burnt propellant. Eyes wide, face blank, he turned the gun toward Zander Krycek.

Jerkins moved, more quickly than Nickson would have thought possible. "Threat detected," it reported, an instant before opening fire with its pulse laser. A crackling, electric roar and several gunshots briefly filled the stairwell, followed by eerie quiet.

"Is everyone all right?" Captain Blackwood said, laser pistol pointed at Sebastian. She lowered it a moment later. The assassin was dead, his chest ripped open and his face gone. High-intensity directed-energy weapons tended to flash-evaporate the water in living tissue, resulting in a steam explosion not unlike when lightning strikes a tree. At thirty pulses a second, the results were often gruesome. The air stunk of burnt hair, blood, propellant, and the telltale ozone smell of a laser weapon.

"Jesus Christ," Nickson said. He clenched his hands into fists to get them to stop shaking. Sebastian had been a mole, it was apparent. He conveniently missed the drone assault and then attempted to kill the client himself. "I'm alright, Skipper. How about—oh, shit!" Zander Krycek was down, leaning against the wall. He had a hand on his shoulder, and blood was pouring down his left arm. "Mr. Krycek!"

"I'm fine!" the old man insisted, through gritted teeth.

"Mr. President!" Kya cried, running to him.

"Stand back, Kya!" Nickson insisted. "Mr. Krycek, let me see that wound."

"I think it went all the way through."

"I think so too," Nickson said, finding the exit wound on the back of Zander's shoulder. "Keep pressure on it. Does anyone have a first-aid kit?"

"Excuse me, sir," Jerkins said, its voice returned to its normal pleasant tone. "I have medical supplies." Its tentacle-arms reached behind it, retrieving a red first-aid kit from its back. The robot handed the kit to Nickson. "I can read Master Zander's vital signs. His heart rate is elevated, but his blood pressure is dropping. Remove two self-sealing wound patches from the kit. Wipe the blood away from the wound, remove the adhesive cover, and place the patch over the wound. Press firmly, ensuring the patch achieves a positive seal. The patches will apply a coagulant and a pain killer."

"Uh, thanks," Nickson said, opening the kit. He was trained in first aid and didn't need the robot to tell him what to do.

"If Master Zander goes into cardiac arrest, I am equipped with a defibrillator. I have already contacted the authorities and have requested an ambulance."

Zander grunted in pain as Nickson applied the necessary pressure. "What about Ras? Is he dead?"

"He is," Captain Blackwood said, kneeling by the colonel's body.

Zander nodded, his face grim. "What about Kya?"

"I'm still here, sir," she said, tears in her eyes. "Please don't die."

"I'm not going to die, young lady."

"You're all patched up," Nickson said. "We need to get moving."

"Jerkins, help me up," the exiled president said. The robot did as it was told, moving to him and gently helping him to his feet.

"Can you walk?" Nickson asked. "You've lost blood. We can stay here."

"No. They were prepared. The lobby is where most of the hotel security will be. We're safest there. Jerkins will help me down the stairs."

"Can he get down the stairs, on that one wheel?"

"I am capable of navigating stairs," Jerkins answered. It was odd, but his synthesized voice seemed less cheery just then, as if it were offended.

"What about Colonel Starborn!" Kya cried. "We can't just leave him here!"

"We have to, my dear," Zander answered. "There's nothing we can do for him. We will claim his body later." He looked to Captain Blackwood and Nickson. "Captain, Mr. Armitage, thank you both for your help. I wish to further amend the contract."

"Sir, now really isn't the time—"

"Hear me out," he insisted. "Captain, I need you to get me off this planet as soon as possible. Kya and my robot, too, as well as Colonel Starborn's body. I'm going to need a protective detail. I have liquidated all my assets and holdings. I'll pay you whatever price you want. Get me home."

Nickson leaned in and spoke into the captain's ear. "How are we going to get him a protective detail before we leave? There's no time to screen and vet one."

"There isn't," Captain Blackwood answered, "but we may be able to pick one up along the way."

"You have someone in mind?"

"I do."

CHAPTER 8

New Austin
Lone Star System
Cimarron Territory
Southern Hemisphere

"I really wish you'd have called for backup, boss," Deputy Marshal Wade Bishop said, scanning the cluster of old, prefabricated buildings through his rifle scope. "There are a lot of guys down there."

Colonial Marshal Marcus Winchester agreed, as he studied the situation through smart binoculars. "We're out of line-of-sight communications range." He looked down at his radio. "I've got no signal on sat-comm."

"Jammers?" Wade asked.

"Most likely," Marcus answered. "It'd take a tac team hours to get out here even if we could call for backup, and I don't trust the locals." Cimarron Territory was at the very edge of New Austin's terraformed zone, where it was difficult to distinguish the terraforming from the rocky, windswept wastes that lay beyond. It was a region of rugged mountains capped by ancient glaciers, where very little of the imported Terran ecosystem was in evidence. The sun had already disappeared behind the mountains to the east, the light slowly fading in the long twilight.

The marshal and his partner were crouched behind a boulder, one partially covered in bright red, native pseudo-lichen. Below them, in an alcove hidden on all sides by cliffs and towering rock formations, was what had once been a survey camp. It was over a hundred years old, dating back to the Second Interstellar War, and had been used by some of the first explorers to land on New Austin. It had supposedly been abandoned for many years, but a months-long investigation had led them to this remote place.

"What do you want to do?" Wade asked, ducking back down.

Marcus frowned. He'd gotten a warrant to raid this encampment and arrest the squatters. Technically the facility was still the property of the Colonial Government, though no one would have bothered if the people taking up residence there weren't also suspected of manufacturing and distributing Red Eye. The territorial sheriff had been especially uncooperative with the marshals, and Marcus hadn't been keeping them informed of his plans.

A dangerous synthetic drug, Red Eye was being used by more and more of New Austin's criminal element. In the right mixture, called Beast Red Eye, the drug would increase strength, stamina, speed, and aggression. Another mixture, known on the street as Chill Red Eye, induced a euphoric high while decreasing inhibitions. Both versions were a thick, red fluid commonly administered by droplets to the eye, hence the name. Both versions were also incredibly addictive and had severe side effects. Chill was usually taken by abusers of Beast to help them calm down. Taking too much of either would result in brain injuries or death. Red Eye was so dangerous that it was one of the few drugs banned by the Colonial Government, which otherwise took a laissez-faire approach to such regulation.

"They haven't spotted us," Wade continued. "There's two of us and at least six of them down there, and most of them are armed. The smart thing would be to get out of their jammer radius, call for a tac team, and guide them in."

"Even if we get ahold of HQ, have you checked the weather?" Marcus asked, not putting down his binoculars. "There's a huge dust storm north of here. They won't release an aircraft until it's cleared up."

Shit, Wade cursed to himself. New Austin's rugged outback usually provided sunny, clear weather, but every so often the winds would pick up, creating dust storms hundreds of kilometers across, which sometimes lasted for days. "Well, we can still head back to Canyon City and get the sheriff to help us, maybe come back tomorrow. Maybe now that we have proof that something is going on out here he'll be more helpful."

"I don't trust that son of a bitch as far as I can throw him, Wade. I think he just might be . . . Hold on." He lowered his binoculars and looked at his partner. "Take a look."

"Huh?" Wade shuffled around, peeking out from behind the boulder and shouldering his rifle again. "What do you—son of whore."

"Yup," Marcus acknowledged. The Colonial Marshals

watched as, far below them, one of the squatters walked a woman to a small outbuilding. He was a large man with long hair, who had a weapon slung over his shoulder. He shoved the woman in front of him and made her walk. Her hands were bound together and another line was tied around her waist. The long-haired man held the end of it, as if it were a leash. "She look like she's being held against her will, Wade?"

"She sure as hell does, Marshal," Wade answered, watching as the man pushed her into the outbuilding and waited by the door. "Looks like they're taking her out for a piss break. Christ only knows what they've done to her. Did you ID her?"

"The binos say there's an eighty percent chance she's Misty Esteban. She's a known grifter and con artist. She did time in prison for fraud, was out early for good behavior, but she dropped off the map a few months ago. Guess we know where she ended up." Criminal or not, Colonial Marshals couldn't abide a person being held in captivity by a gang of thugs. Once they realized what was happening, Marcus and Wade were obligated to intervene.

"We can't risk her being used as a human shield. The guy guarding the door, can you hit him from here?"

Wade reached under his coat and retrieved a metallic cylinder. Attaching the sound suppressor to the muzzle of his rifle, he braced the weapon on a rock and looked through his scope. "Say the word, Marshal."

"We won't have good comms until we shut that jammer off. I'm gonna creep down there, as close as I can get. You watch him. If he spots me, or tries to sound the alarm, or if the girl comes back and he goes to leave with her, you drop him. Make it a clean shot. Don't put her in danger."

"You got it. I just hope to hell this is what it looks like, and not some crazy sexual fetish or something. I wish Devree was here."

"Hell, I do too, Wade," Marcus said, making his way back from the boulder as quietly as he could. "She's a much better shot than you."

"Yeah, yeah, just get your butt down there before it's too late. I gotcha covered."

In the failing light, Marcus made his way down the rocky slope at a crouch, staying in the shadows of stony outcroppings and avoiding loose rocks. The wind blowing through the hills helped drown out any noise that he might have made, and the long-haired man guarding what he was guessing was the latrine seemed to be none the wiser.

As he approached, the stench of the outbuilding filled Marcus' nose. *That's the shitter, no doubt about it.* The long-abandoned camp's plumbing clearly no longer functioned. He was close now, as close as he could get without being seen. Crouched behind a boulder, carbine in his hands, he waited for the woman to come out of the latrine. A few lights turned on, in the main part of the encampment, as darkness overtook the alcove, but the latrine building remained in the shadows.

A moment later, the woman exited the latrine, her hands still bound together in front of her. She looked like she hadn't been treated well. Her clothes was dirty and her hair was tangled. Marcus didn't want to think about the things these drug peddlers had been doing to her. It was hard to tell in the poor light, but he agreed with his binoculars' assessment: she was Misty Esteban.

Her handler, the big, long-haired man, stepped forward with another length of rope in his hands. He was about to reattach his leash to her when his head burst open with a wet *splat*. A sonic crack echoed through the hills, but Marcus barely heard the report from Wade's rifle. He didn't waste any time. He was on his feet and moving before the long-haired man's body hit the ground. He startled the woman, who was staring at the corpse in shock, blood splattered on her face. Before she could scream, Marcus clamped a gloved hand over her mouth.

"Shh," he said. "Look at me. I'm a Colonial Marshal. We're getting you out of here, but I need you to be quiet. Can you be quiet?" Eyes wide, Misty slowly nodded. "Good," Marcus said, removing his hand. "Come this way." He led her behind the latrine building, where they were concealed in shadow and out of sight of the rest of the compound. "Are you Misty Esteban?"

"Y . . . yes," she stammered, her voice hoarse. "Are you looking for me?"

"Your probation officer would probably like to hear from you, but I'm after these guys, not you. Hold still." He drew a combat knife from his vest and quickly cut the bindings around her wrists. "Are you injured? Can you walk?"

She nodded, shivering as a cold wind blew through the camp. Marcus took off his long, brown duster coat and put it around her. "Climb up there," he said. "My partner is waiting for you. Is there anyone else? Anyone they're holding?"

"There's another girl, Rochelle. Her name is Rochelle." Misty said. "I don't know where she is most of the time. They kept me in a locked room, but not her. I don't think . . . I don't think she's one of them. She's nice. She tried to protect me. I think she's there against her will."

"Damn it to hell," Marcus muttered. He'd been hoping he could just sneak away with Misty. "Get going up this hill, and stay out of sight." He looked up at where Wade was hiding, and waved for him to come down.

"What are you going to do?"

Marcus straightened his wide-brimmed hat and raised his carbine. "I'm gonna go get that other girl."

"What am I supposed to do if you get killed?"

"If you get over this hill and keep going due east, you'll come to a dirt road. Follow the road north and you'll come to our vehicle. It's got a transponder in it, so just stay there. Sooner or later somebody will come looking for us."

"That's it?" the woman asked, incredulously. "That's your plan? You're going to have me go wait while you kick in the door and shoot the place up?"

Marcus grinned. "Lady, I didn't plan on you being here at all. I'm improvising. Which building is Rochelle being held in? How many of these guys are there?"

Misty pointed to the largest of the blocky structures, and the only one with two floors. "There, the main building. They kept me locked in a room in the basement. I don't know how many of these skags there are. Seven, eight?" She looked over at the dead man. "Oh. One less, now, I guess."

"Great. Get going, okay? About the worst thing that can happen to you is that my partner and I get killed and they recapture you."

Misty agreed, wiping the blood from her face. "Right. I'm going."

"Oh, and I want that coat back when we get there," Marcus added, as she began the climb up the rocky slope. She reached Wade, who was on his way down. He helped her up a particularly steep ledge and pointed her in the direction she needed to go before continuing on his way down. A few moments later, he joined Marcus behind the latrine building, crouched in the shadows.

"Holy hell," he said, crinkling his nose. "That's a powerful stench. What's the plan?"

"That was Misty Esteban. She said there's another captive, a gal named Rochelle, in there, too. Main building, probably, but she said she wasn't locked up."

"What the hell is she doing with these guys, anyway?"

"I didn't ask. We'll question her later. Right now we gotta get in there and get that other girl out. Misty said there might be six or seven more guys, not including the one you killed. Nice shot, by the way."

"How you wanna do this? I could scramble back up the hill, fire some shots to lure them out."

"Not with just two guys," Marcus said. "We need to cover each other's backs, especially when we go in that building."

"This is a bad op, Marshal. We're outnumbered and we're going to try to clear this camp by ourselves?" Wade grinned. "The legend of the Mad Marshal, Marcus Winchester, continues to grow."

Marcus looked over at his partner. "The . . . what? What legend?"

"I'll tell you later. We gotta do this now before they come out and see the body. And Christ, I need to get away from this shitter before I puke."

"It doesn't get better with time, that's a fact," Marcus agreed. "And I'm cold. Let's go."

"Hold up, Marshal," Wade said.

"What are you doing?"

The deputy retrieved from a pouch on the side of his vest a bulky monocular with an eyepiece at one end and cluster of lenses at the other.

"What is that?"

Wade took a knee, lifted the device to his eye, and scanned the compound from the shadows of the coming night. "It's my snooper scope, and it sees everything. It has night vision, it has infrared, it even sees through walls."

Marcus crouched next to his partner. "How does it see through walls? X-rays?"

"No. Radar, something about the Doppler effect on a moving target. I don't know. Here, just look. Use the buttons on the side to zoom in and out."

The marshal took the device from Wade and looked through it. Gyroscopically stabilized, the scope presented a remarkably clear, enhanced image of the compound, better than Marcus's own smart goggles. A ghostly image, a silhouette, of a person walking appeared briefly, then disappeared as it stopped.

"It's basically a motion detector. It doesn't work so well if they stop moving, but you can track people with it. Kind of gives you a limited 3D picture of the inside of the building."

Marcus noted several signatures of moving people. None of them seemed to be in a hurry, which meant that they likely didn't suspect anything. One appeared to be heading down a flight of stairs, somewhere in the building, then vanished. "I can't see the basement."

"I'm not surprised. Too much dirt in the way. The effective range is pretty limited, too. It wouldn't have worked from up there on the hillside."

"I see at least five guys moving around, not counting the guy who went downstairs." He lowered the optic and looked at Wade. "We ought to give them the chance to surrender."

"It'll put the hostage at risk."

"We don't know that there is a hostage. All we have is the word of a known criminal who might be trying to keep us busy so she can get away. Besides, we already shot that one hooplehead unawares. We go in guns blazing and it might look bad. I don't want another investigation from Internal Affairs."

Wade sighed heavily. "Fine. You wanna do the callout or should I?"

"I'll do it," Marcus said. "Get to cover and provide overwatch."

Clutching his rifle, Wade nodded, and moved off into the shadows, taking up a position behind a pile of boulders. Marcus stood up, adjusted his hat, and strode toward the middle of the compound, stepping into the light. There was no sign of movement in the compound, save vortices of dust being kicked up by the cold wind.

"Gotcha covered, boss," Wade said, into Marcus's earpiece.

Marcus tapped his earbud, activating a voice amplifier. "Colonial Marshals!" he announced, his voice booming over a loudspeaker on his vest. "You are all under arrest! Lay down your arms and come out with your hands up!"

CHAPTER 9

Ithaca
Ionia-5589 System
Southern Hemisphere

It had been days since Adisa Masozi had been able to
have a proper bath. She found herself making do with
a scrub in a river, watched over by Follower of the
Storm and his warriors. The SAZ-CDF Rangers had
laughed at her uptight northern modesty, but she'd
told the men to stay away when she was bathing. Even
if they were nothing but professional, having them
around while she was so vulnerable made her uneasy.

Not so with Follower of the Storm and his companions. The aliens had about the same level of sexual
interest in humans as humans had for beetles, and their
lack of interest was strangely comforting. In the days
she'd spent with him, Adisa had learned much from
Stormy, as the Rangers affectionately called him. He
was, in fact, male, or a close equivalent. His people
almost always chose one mate and pair-bonded for
life, and couples separating was all but unheard of.
It seemed to Adisa that the aliens had, perhaps, a

more limited emotional range than humans, experiencing neither the soaring heights of passion nor the crushing depths of depression. She'd had many long conversations with Stormy, learning everything she could from him, and he gave the impression that his people simply got along more easily than humans did.

The lack of emotional depth did not mean the aliens weren't intelligent, however. Quite the contrary, Follower of the Storm seemed remarkably perceptive, and could grasp most of the concepts of human interaction, even if the reasoning behind it was alien to him. He found the concept of envy most puzzling, though.

"I don't mean it like that," she explained, drying herself on the rocky bank of a cool, calm river. "If someone wrongs you, or takes from you, or hurts you, then being angry at them is expected. But sometimes humans resent . . . uh, dislike, even hate other humans who have more than they do."

"But these hu-mans did not take the things they have from others?" Stormy asked, again.

"No. They are angry that another has more than they do. More possessions, more wealth, more power, or a higher station in life, even if those humans did nothing wrong. Sometimes humans get so angry at those that have more that they want to hurt them, take away what they have, even kill them."

"That is . . ." Stormy paused, as if trying to remember the word he needed. "Not good thinking. Ir-ration-al."

"It is," Adisa agreed, "and yet, it has been one of the great motivators of my species. Often, humans convince themselves that those that have more did, in fact, get what they have by stealing from others, but it is often not really the case. Pride and envy are two things nearly every human religion warns against. Where you find one, you'll often find the other, and they can be very destructive. Does any of this make sense?"

"Makes sense," Follower of the Storm echoed. "Humans grow angry at those that have what they do not, even though...wise ones...warn against this. Humans are not rational. Humans land here, many solar cycles ago. Entire world available, countless worlds available, and they come here to our...ancestral... homelands. We fought humans, but humans attacked first. This is known. I was there."

"You were there?" Adisa asked, surprised. It had been well over a hundred standard years since the Colony of Ithaca was founded. Stormy's people must live for a very long time. "At the time, we were at war with a species more powerful than ourselves, and they were trying to exterminate us."

"We know of the..." He reverted to his harsh, native language, briefly, before speaking Commerce English again. "This one...I...do not know the human name for them. But we know of them."

"We called them Maggots," Adisa said.

"Mag-gots. What is mag-got?"

"It's, ah..." She paused, tapping the screen of her handheld. A few seconds later and she had brought up video of a terrestrial maggot, depicting its life cycle, growing into a typical housefly. "This."

Follower of the Storm didn't nod his head or anything, but Adisa was learning to pick up on his body language. The way he moved conveyed understanding. "I under-stand now," he said, returning her handheld to her. "I see the phys-i-cal res-em-blance. Humans give names to things that re-sem-ble other things."

"Yes!" Adisa said, beaming, as she put her clothes back on. "Ahh. I feel so much better now."

The olfactory organ above Stormy's eyes flared slightly. "Your ... scent ... is better now."

She laughed, and turned her attention back to her alien companion as she picked up her pack. "Tell me, how do you know of the Maggots? You said that your people know of them."

"This one said too much," he said, after a long pause. "Not my place. Elders must decide this."

"I apologize, Follower of the Storm. I did not mean to offend you."

"O-fend?"

"Uh ..." Adisa paused, struggling to come up with good synonyms. "Insult. Upset. Anger. I did not mean to cause, um, bad feelings."

Stormy swayed again, in his people's equivalent of a nod. "Not angry. No ... bad feelings. There is much about us that we do not discuss with ... aliens. It has been decided. It is not for Follower of the Storm to ... over-rule."

"I understand, and I respect your customs. Will we meet with your Elders soon?"

"Yes," Stormy answered, looking back over his shoulder. "Your ... companions ... approach."

"You all done washing up, love?" It was Roc, accompanied by his teammate.

"I am," she said, picking up her pack.

"We got some food warmed up. You should eat. You need the calories. We'll be moving again soon."

"How much farther?" Adisa asked.

Roc turned to the alien. "What do you say, Stormy?"

"One more solar cycle of walking. Less, possible. Not far now."

Adisa sorely wished that she could have taken an aircraft to meet with the alien Elders. What would have been a short flight for a VTOL had translated into many days of walking through dense foliage and rugged terrain. They had only been able to move during daylight hours, since it was unsafe to trek at night. "Do you think your Elders will agree to help us?"

"Can not say. Big questions not for Follower of the Storm to decide."

She hoped that she'd be able to bring the aliens on board. What she was doing, attempting to form an alliance with an alien species, was unprecedented in the modern era. If she pulled it off, she might go down in history as a pioneer in interspecies relations. If she failed?

She didn't want to think about that.

CHAPTER 10

New Austin
Lone Star System
Cimarron Territory
Southern Hemisphere

His carbine held at the low-ready, Marcus Winchester surveyed the scene in front of him and smiled. In the open center of the complex, faces down in the cold dirt, lay the remnant of the gang of drug manufacturers. Their hands and feet were bound with flex-cuffs. They had constantly complained of their treatment until the marshal put a bullet in the dirt a few centimeters from one of the survivors' heads. They'd been quiet after that.

Marcus was pleased. Two marshals had done all this. Outnumbered, outgunned, but not outmatched by the band of thugs, he felt like he had lived up to the reputation the Marshals Service had earned over the last century. Life on a frontier world like New Austin was hard, even with all the comforts and conveniences modern technology allowed for. You had freedom like nowhere else, but there were always those who would prey on the weak and the innocent. It was the job of the Marshals Service to bring the law to every corner of the colony, no matter how remote, and they'd done just that.

Wade stood nearby, rifle tucked under his arm, talking to someone on his headset. "Copy that. Out."

"What'd they say?" Marcus asked.

"The storm isn't clearing up, but they've got a high-speed transport aircraft inbound. Should be here in an hour, at most."

"That fast?"

"It's supersonic. They're going to go over the dust storm and land right here. I guess our new friend over there is kind of a big deal."

"She certainly seems to think so," the marshal said, looking over at Rochelle. She paced back and forth, angrily tearing some poor bastard a new asshole on her handheld. When her conversation was finished, she strode over to the marshals, anger still in her eyes. She was a pretty thing, Marcus thought, tall and fit. Her hair was tightly pulled back, and she had subtle lines around her mouth and eyes from, he assumed, being angry all the time.

She was also, apparently, an agent of the Office of Strategic Intelligence. She'd flashed implanted, hidden credentials as soon as the marshals burst in to rescue her.

"There's a high-speed transport on its way," Wade began.

"I know that!" she snapped, dropping the device into her pocket and sealing up her coat. "This is . . . this is unbelievable!"

"Will you calm down?" Wade said, angrily. "We probably saved your life. You're welcome."

"Saved my life? Saved my...are you serious? Surely, you're playing a joke on me, you unbelievable scratching colonial yokel! Do you have any idea how long I've been working this investigation? Any idea at all? You idiots just kicked in the door, guns blazing, kill the marks I've been working for months, and what? You want a thank you? You expected to carry me out like some damsel in distress from an ancient fable?"

"I'm a married man, ma'am," Marcus said.

"Of course you are," the OSI agent hissed. "You probably have a gaggle of illiterate, dirt-covered brats, too."

Anger pulsed through Marcus's body, causing an eye to twitch and his grip on his weapon to involuntarily tighten. "Listen, lady, I've had about enough of this."

"*Agent,*" she corrected. "You will address me as *Agent.* If you think you've had enough now, you just wait until my report makes its way up the chain. This investigation has been ongoing for years, across multiple planets and who-knows-how-many light-years of space, and you two come along and ruin it all!"

"What in the hell is the OSI doing on New Austin, running around with drug manufacturers?" Wade asked. "How is that in any way the jurisdiction of the Interstellar Concordiat?"

"I just said it was a multiplanetary, interstellar operation," the agent retorted. "I shouldn't be surprised that you can't see the big picture here. It wasn't just about manufacturing drugs for the dregs of a backwater colony to fry their brains with. These people were part of an interstellar operation that extends outside the Concordiat and is therefore a matter of interstellar security. At least it was, until you two killed the man who was their contact with off-world assets. You know what? Never mind. This operation is classified and I don't have to explain myself to the likes of you."

"There's where you're wrong, *Agent*," Marcus replied, controlling his anger but unable to hide the contempt in his voice. "Under Article 31 of the Interstellar Concord, all Concordiat officers or authorities are required to inform the colonial government of any official business they intend to conduct on that colony world, regardless of whether or not it's secret. You people failed to do that. Had you bothered to inform us of your operation, this whole mess could have been avoided, and your precious asset would still be alive."

"Don't you quote the damned Concord to me—"

Marcus was having none of it. "Second, the whole reason we intervened tonight was because when we were scouting the place, we saw a woman named Misty Esteban, and had reason to believe she was being held against her will. As soon as that happened, as a peace officer, I became legally obligated to intervene, and between that dust storm and these hoopleheads' commo jammers, waiting for backup wasn't an option."

"None of this is relevant."

"Let me finish. Misty Esteban told us that there was another captive in the facility, a woman she called Rochelle, and that she believed she was being held against her will as well. She said that you were, and I quote, *nice* to her, and tried to protect her. Is that true?"

"Of course I tried! I did everything I could without compromising my cover! I wasn't being held against my will, I just told her that so she'd trust me."

"Right. So what you're telling me is, you did your best, but if you couldn't stop them from raping her or doing God knows what else without blowing your cover, oh well, too bad. Is that an accurate assessment of the situation, ma'am?"

The agent's eyes narrowed. She leaned in, pointing a finger in Marcus's face. "Now you listen to me, *Marshal*. I don't know who you think you are, or where you think you're going with this, but you can stop this line of questioning right now. This operation was classified level Omega, and some jumped-up farmer with a plastic badge has no business questioning my methods. You have no idea how long it took, how many lives were risked, to get me where I was. I did what I had to do, and I wasn't about to let some two-credit con-artist compromise my operation!"

"I see. You can be assured, ma'am, that all of this will be in my report."

The agent laughed in Marcus's face. He wondered how in the hell she maintained deep cover for so long when she was such a pompous, angry skag. "Go ahead, Marshal, write up your report. If you want to keep your job, you'll sign a nondisclosure agreement and never speak a word of this again." She jammed her finger into Marcus's shoulder. "So, you can take your little report and go fuck yourself with it."

Marcus took a deep breath. He was a veteran of the Concordiat Defense Force's Espatier Corps, and spent a good chunk of his military career in special operations. He'd worked with OSI spooks before and, like most spec-ops veterans, didn't think very highly of them. Many of them, in his experience, were good people: professional, mission oriented, willing to cooperate to get things done. But a lot of them were just like her: arrogant, grossly overconfident in their own capabilities, and utterly convinced that the secretive nature of their work meant the rules didn't apply to them. As a chief warrant officer in the Espatiers, there wasn't much he could do about it. He had his orders, and had to put up with these self-important asses. But as a Colonial Marshal, he had authority here, even if the condescending OSI agent didn't think so.

"Agent," he said, looking down at her from under his wide-brimmed hat, "I'm placing you under arrest."

She looked back at him, mouth agape, as if she didn't understand what he was saying. "I'm not impressed with your petty threats, Marshal."

"I don't make threats, ma'am. Wade?"

"On it, Marshal," Wade said. He pulled a pair of restraints from his vest and grabbed the OSI agent's hands. Before he could lock them around her wrists she spun around, incredibly fast, and brought a knee up into Wade's groin. He was wearing a protective cup, but even still, it looked like it hurt. She followed up with a palm strike to his chin. He stumbled backward and fell onto his butt in a puff of dust. His big 12mm revolver was out in a flash, extended in his left hand, pointed at the OSI agent's face. Marcus raised a hand, and his partner lowered the gun.

A couple of the restrained drug makers, who had been silent throughout the exchange, were laughing. The OSI agent clearly had training, and probably bionic implants, but that wouldn't stop Marcus from giving Wade hell about having gotten beaten up by a woman half his size. Even though that would amuse him endlessly, he'd had about enough of her.

She turned to him, a sneer on her pretty face. "If you're quite finished—AAAAIIIIEEEE!" She shrieked in pain as the less-lethal compliance round from the under-barrel launcher on Marcus's carbine hit her in the stomach and latched on. Doubled over from the impact, she fell to the dirt, convulsing, as the device shocked her over and over again. The electrical pulses were specifically contrived to disrupt the human nervous system, rendering the target immobile, and they usually did a number on bionics, too.

"Wade, if you're done screwing around, will you please restrain her?"

Cussing, Wade stood up and then knelt by the now-incapacitated OSI agent.

Marcus disabled the compliance round so that he could restrain her without being shocked himself. "Agent," he said, kneeling next to her, "you are under arrest, as I said."

"Fuck you," she hissed. "You'll pay for this."

"You're under arrest for threatening a peace officer, violating Article 31 of the Interstellar Concord, knowingly endangering a kidnapping victim while operating in an official capacity, and, of course, resisting arrest."

If dirty looks could kill, Marcus would have been struck dead by the icy glare the OSI agent gave him. The New Austin government always resented it when the Concordiat interfered in the colony's domestic affairs. He didn't imagine that they'd put her in jail or anything, but until her handlers came to fetch her, she could lay there in the dirt with the rest of the criminals. "I am obligated to advise you that you are being recorded, and this interaction can be admitted as evidence against you in a court of law. I suggest you remain silent."

"I'm going to destroy you," she said, coldly.

"We'll see."

Log Entry 132
Mission 815-707-SSOC
Reconnaissance Ship 505

The first countermeasure effort has failed. Asset PLASTIC FLOWER is dead. Authorities on Faraway/Heinlein are on elevated alert. Asset EXALTED PAWN has been ordered to return to standby status and conduct no further operations. Colonial authorities blame the government of Ionia-5589/Ithaca. OPSEC has not been compromised. AI/CORE recommends continuing passive surveillance and taking no further direct action at this time.

SIGINT has revealed that Zander Krycek was with an individual named Catherine Blackwood at the time of PLASTIC FLOWER's death. AI/CORE is CONFIDENT/HIGH/HIGH that this is the same individual who is wanted in conjunction with the destruction of Commercial Space Station 015 and Cruiser 247. AI/CORE scans of the Heinlein planetary network reveal that she is the operator of the Polaris-class patrol ship Andromeda, which was involved in the incident in the home system and is suspected in the incident at Danzig-5012/Zanzibar. CAPTURE/KILL order is still in effect for this individual. We will continue reconnaissance until AI/CORE recommends a direct course of action.

CHAPTER 11

The Privateer Ship *Andromeda*
Heinlein
St. Augustine Spaceport

Standing in the long shadow of the *Andromeda,* Nickson Armitage watched as missile after missile was loaded into the ship's dual rotary launchers. Each launcher held five of the fat, nine-meter-long missiles, which served as the *Andromeda*'s primary armament. The weapons, powered by high-density solid-state motors, could accelerate at more than a hundred gravities. Thrust-vectoring nozzles provided them with maneuvering capability. Each was equipped with an armor-piercing, high-explosive warhead, consisting of a tungsten penetrator cone at the nose and a powerful main charge intended to detonate inside the enemy ship.

They were also incredibly expensive. Rearming the ship for the upcoming mission was costing millions of credits. Fortunately, the *Andromeda* had other ways of defending itself: two laser turrets and a 60mm railgun. A laser turret sat on either side of the ship's primary hull, giving it a full three hundred sixty degrees of coverage. While lasers were limited in effective range, and generated a lot of waste heat, they didn't require ammunition and could be fired for as long as the ship had power. They were also invaluable as point-defense weapons, targeting incoming warheads before they could hit the ship.

The railgun was probably the ship's most versatile weapon. Firing half-meter-long slugs of tungsten or depleted uranium, the railgun could destroy an enemy ship in a single shot if it hit it under the right circumstances. It was effective against both space and surface targets; the slugs were dense enough to make it through even a thick atmosphere without burning up, and produced tremendous kinetic energy upon impact. The major downside to the railgun was its limited range of traversal. The length of the magnetic accelerator meant the weapon had to be built into the ship's hull instead of bolted on as a turret. The gun could track only ten degrees in any direction from its storage position. Aiming the railgun often meant rotating the ship, which brought its own set of problems.

The ordnance hauler—a huge wheeled vehicle designed to transport munitions to ships at the spaceport; raise them up to the launchers, tubes, or bays; and feed them into the ships' magazines—had finished loading one launcher and was retracting its telescopic arm. Nickson was confident in the capabilities of his new ship. She had a better thrust-to-mass ratio, more delta-v, and packed a lot more firepower than the *Madeline Drake* had. He had little doubt she could take on anything in her size class, or even larger, and prevail.

The attack at the King's Tower Hotel had been

the subject of round-the-clock news coverage and an intense investigation. He and the captain had been interrogated by the police, as had the client and his people. The fact that Zander Krycek's robot had killed a man had muddied the waters at first, to the extent that they had all spent a night in the Coventry Police detention center. A playback of Jerkins's on-board recorders, combined with everyone's testimony, had gotten them released. No charges were expected to be filed.

The police still hadn't figured out who had carried out the attack, so far as he knew. Whoever they were, they had covered their tracks well. The drone had purged its own memory before it could be recovered, and from what Nickson had heard, no useful forensic evidence had been gained from it. It was apparent that Sebastian, the attaché from the Ithacan foreign office, had been a mole. With Colonel Starborn dead, there was no way of knowing how he had infiltrated the conspiracy to return Zander Krycek to power, but it was clear that they were compromised. It was possible that there would be further assassination attempts.

Worse, Captain Blackwood and Nickson had been taken into custody with their client. Arrests were a matter of public record, as was the fact that the captain was the owner of the *Andromeda*. Anyone willing to look into the matter might be able to figure out what was going on. They had to launch soon; information could only travel across interstellar space as quickly as a ship could carry it. If the *Andromeda* got underway soon, they'd have a head start and would have a much higher chance of getting to the Ionia-5589 system unopposed. If they delayed? There was a courier ship in the system currently, and it would embark soon. Courier ships all talked to each other whenever their routes crossed paths. They also paid noncouriers to carry and deliver information uploads to places that they didn't normally go, even if it took longer.

In other words, even with the absolute speed limitation, information could propagate across inhabited space remarkably fast. The longer they delayed, the more likely it was that their client's enemies would know exactly what ship he was taking. They already knew where he was going. Even if they didn't know the exact route the *Andromeda* would take, the geometry of space-time and the necessity of replenishing stores and reaction mass left them with a limited number of paths that they could realistically follow.

Time was of the essence, and every day they stayed on Heinlein, the more danger they were possibly in. This hadn't stopped Zander Krycek from capitalizing on the attack on the King's Tower Hotel. The very next day, he held a public press conference. His arm in a sling, he condemned the attack and those who would endanger innocent people to carry it out. He renewed his call for Ithacan patriots and foreign volunteers to join his cause, and announced that he was willing to meet with investors. Word was, several wealthy venture capitalists were interested in backing his effort. It was a gamble; if the revolution failed, they would lose everything they invested. But, if it was successful, they might get first and exclusive access to the largely untapped resources of Ithaca.

The Heinlein colonial government was outraged that such an assassination attempt had taken place on their soil. It was the sort of thing that could spark a diplomatic crisis. But, given their noninterventionalist policy, and the fact that Heinlein didn't have diplomatic relations with Ithaca, nothing would likely come of it. It did, however, serve to make the government sympathetic to, and possibly willing to support in some way, Zander Krycek's cause. Perhaps not overtly; his infamy as a war criminal made him toxic to many, but there were discreet ways of lending support.

Still, Nickson had an uneasy feeling that he just couldn't shake. He'd nearly been killed his second day on the job, and they hadn't even lifted off yet. The brush with death in Coventry had rattled him even worse than he'd originally thought. He hadn't slept well since, and sometimes couldn't get the image of the bodies of Colonel Starborn and Sebastian out of his head. He was pleased that he'd held it together while in the heat of the moment, enough that he'd been able to get the captain to cover and apply first aid to Zander. But, seeing the death and smelling the stench of burnt flesh and smoke had brought some very bad memories flooding back. He'd felt helpless, just as he had when the lost fleet cruiser was ripping the *Maddy D.* apart, and he found himself wondering if going back to privateering was such a good idea after all.

He looked down at the tablet in his hands, as the ordnance hauler slowly crawled to the other side of the ship. The crew was still short an assistant engineer. They had been taking on supplies as well. Kimball was overseeing that, as rations, raw material for rapid fabricators, spare parts, and Zander Krycek's robot were all loaded into the cargo bay. There was one other small package as well: the cremated remains of

Colonel Erasmus Starborn. He was being taken home so that he could be laid to rest in Ithacan soil, and so that his family could have the dignity of a proper funeral for him.

They had a long journey ahead of them, and the *Andromeda* hadn't had a proper shakedown cruise since her refit. Per the captain, the route they were planning on took them through the Lone Star system, at the ragged edge of Concordiat space. According to the logs, she had hired a team of mercenaries from the planet New Austin before, and she reasoned that even if those same people weren't available, finding others would be easier. Plus, New Austin was far enough out of the way that the odds of Ithacan assassins lying in wait for Zander Krycek were practically nil.

At least, that's what he hoped. In any case, the captain had ordered him to get trained up on the use of a laser pistol, and start carrying one with him while off the ship, whenever local laws permitted it. He'd never thought about carrying a weapon before, save a good knife. Captain Ogleman had mandated that all arms on board the *Madeline Drake* were to be secured, accessible only by himself and the master-at-arms. He reasoned that, in the lonely depths of space, with the hours of tedium and moments of fear, guns in the hands of a crew were more likely to result in an act of rage, or even a suicide, than they were in a legitimate case of self-defense. After all, the crew had all been vetted, and there was no reason to think anyone would attempt to harm anyone else.

Captain Blackwood saw things differently. Apparently, people had tried to kill her often enough that she never left the ship unarmed, if it could be helped.

After the incident at the King's Tower Hotel, one could hardly blame her. Had the robot not been there, it would have been down to her to stop the gunman before he killed them all.

Nickson wasn't sure how he felt about this. He was a *spacer*, damn it, not a soldier. Despite what you saw in the media, privateering rarely involved exciting laser battles, and often involved long hours of preventative maintenance and training. But, the skipper had given him his orders, and she obviously knew her business. He would get with the security officer, Mazer Broadbent, once they were underway, and begin training on the use of the laser pistol.

He had an unsettling feeling that such training would prove necessary before this contract was over.

CHAPTER 12

Ithaca
Ionia-5589 System
Southern Hemisphere

By torchlight, Adisa Masozi was led deep underground. Follower of the Storm was ahead of her, and the two SAZ-CDF Rangers trailed behind. They had been met at the tunnel entrance by a guide, one of Follower of the Storm's people. In a silence broken only by their breathing and the shuffle of their feet, the group followed the guide down a long, narrow, sloping tunnel. It wasn't natural; it had been dug through the dense, Ithacan soil and reinforced with beams made from the local pseudo-trees. Its very existence defied the commonly held belief that the native Ithacans built no works or cities, and Adisa suspected she was the first human to have ever been brought here.

As exciting as it was, she was concerned. The fact that she was being shown this place was either a very good sign or a very bad one. Perhaps she had earned their trust, or perhaps they weren't going to let her leave. The cool, damp, still air, weighing heavily on her like a bad mood, didn't help her anxiety any. Adisa wasn't claustrophobic, exactly, but she had no love of being underground.

Deeper into the tunnel, however, the air changed. As they came around a bend, Adisa felt a breeze on her face. The air grew warmer and smelled fresher. The passage grew wider and more open, until it terminated at a narrow opening covered with a curtain made from the skin of some jungle beast. The guide disappeared behind the curtain, taking his torch with him, leaving the passageway engulfed in oppressive darkness. The only light came from under the curtain.

"This way," Follower of the Storm said, pulling the curtain back. He extended a hand to Adisa, to lead her through the opening. Her own hand was dwarfed by his wide, leathery, two-thumbed appendage, but he was very gentle with her. Adisa stepped through the opening, into the unknown.

"My God," she said, her voice little more than a whisper. A vast, dome-shaped cavern stretched out before her, probably a kilometer across. Entire sections of the walls and roof, hectares across, were covered with bioluminescent pseudo-algae, illuminating much of the cave with a dull, orange glow. Natural columns of stone, the size of buildings, extended from the floor to the ceiling, supporting the roof. Some of them had been hollowed out and were dotted with lit windows. Structures, some made of stone, some made of plant materials, crowded seemingly every flat spot. Far below her, a great, subterranean river cut through the geofront, its flowing black waters splitting the hidden city in two.

"This is home," Follower of the Storm croaked,

matter-of-factly. "You are first hu-mans to ever come here."

"We thought you to be nomads," Adisa managed, still awestruck. Thin wisps of smoke, probably from cook fires, filtered up from many of the structures, gathering in a haze at the roof of the cavern. Up there, a breeze caught it, and carried it down another tunnel. There had been rumors, mostly from wild-eyed crackpots, that the native Ithacans had secret underground cities. The planet was covered in networks of underground caverns and waterways, and it was believed that some of the underground rivers ran for thousands of kilometers.

"No-mads," Stormy repeated, as if to consider the word, as the guide led them along a path hewn from stone. "On the surface, we wander. Always mov-ing. Too dangerous to stay in one place. But here is safe."

"Are there other cities like this?" Adisa asked, recording everything on her handheld.

"Yes," Stormy answered, but he didn't elaborate.

"Where are you taking us?" Roc asked. He seemed less sure of himself now. This was unfamiliar territory even for a pair of experienced Rangers.

Stormy looked back. "To meet-ing of Elders. Do not be afraid. This one has..." He paused, as if trying to figure out how to phrase what he was trying to say. "This one has spoken for you. You are safe. Do not wander."

"You don't need to worry about that, mate," Roc replied, looking around. "Like as not we'd never find our way out of this labyrinth."

A labyrinth it was. Adisa and her companions were led out of the main chamber, down a series of winding passageways. Along the way, they saw very few of the native Ithacan people, and those that they did encounter hurried away without making eye contact. It was unsettling, and the Rangers held their slung weapons close. In every chamber and passageway, a slight breeze could be felt. It was almost as if the underground city was breathing. This air circulation was surely vital to maintaining an adequate oxygen supply so far beneath the surface.

At the end of this winding journey, they came to an ornate stone door, covered with intricate carvings. The guide said something to Follower of the Storm, who then turned to the humans. "A-diss-a, only you go. Others stay. Warriors not . . . allowed . . . in presence of Elders."

"I mean your Elders no harm, mate," Roc said. "I'm not leaving her."

"You mussst. Only she goes on."

"It'll be okay," Adisa said. She hadn't come this far only for her chance to be lost over a petty disagreement. "I will go, alone."

The guide pulled open the stone door, which seemed to move easily despite its weight. On the other side, Adisa found a large, airy chamber, lit red and gold by a small fire pit in the middle. The room was ringed with imposing statues of the native Ithacan people, and other . . . *things* . . . beings, creatures, that Adisa didn't recognize. Some of them resembled the Ithacans, others were utterly alien. Were they animals? Demons? Gods? There was no way to know. The fire flickered in the slight breeze, causing the shadows of the statues to dance eerily. She startled as the door clunked shut behind her. Turning back around, she noticed three cloaked figures sitting in front of the fire now. Either they hadn't been there before or she hadn't noticed them, but either way Adisa gasped. The figures ignored her.

Spinning up her courage, Adisa approached the fire pit, keeping a watchful eye on the three cloaked figures. Their build and shape told her that they were native Ithacans, but they were smaller than Follower of the Storm and the others of his people that she'd seen. Their necks and appendages were much slenderer, and their heads were pointier. She estimated that, standing up, they'd be no taller than her. None of them seemed to pay her any mind as she sat, cross-legged, in front of the fire herself. All three of them gazed intensely into the fire, the dancing flames reflecting in their black eyes.

"Hello," Adisa said, surprised by how loud her own voice sounded. "Hello," she repeated, in more hushed tones. "I am Adisa. I have traveled far to meet with you. Thank you for seeing me."

There was no response. The three aliens continued to gaze into the fire. *Do they even understand me?*

"Why have you traveled so far, young one?" the beings asked, in unison, shocking Adisa. Three singsongy voices, higher in pitch than Follower of the Storm, in melodious synchronization. None of the aliens moved. Their mouths didn't move. She wasn't sure if they'd actually said that, or if she had imagined it.

She hesitated for just a moment. "I . . . I have been sent to ask for your help."

"The troubles of your kind are not our concern. We only wish to exist in peace."

"That is all I want, too, but our problems will soon be your problems. What is coming will affect all who live on this world, regardless of what they wish."

All three of them looked up at her, simultaneously, the fire still flickering in their glassy, dead eyes. Adisa's heart jumped up into her throat. "Speak, young one," the three voices said. Now she was *certain* that their mouths weren't moving. "Tell us of what is coming."

"My people have suffered many years of strife," she began. "It began after the last war, when Zander Krycek was removed from power."

"We know of this change. Zander Krycek forged a pact with our people. There was peace, and there was trade. With him gone, your rulers drove our people from your lands, forbidding us to even pass through them. This broke the pact. We do not trust your kind."

"I don't blame you, but there are larger things at stake here than our past differences. My . . . rulers, as you call them, they are weak now. They are weak and afraid, and that makes them dangerous. Not just to my people, but to yours as well."

"We do not fear you, young one," the voices sang.

"It is not us who you need to fear," Adisa replied, meeting their unsettling gaze. She reached into her bag and retrieved a small, holographic projector. She set the device on the cool stone floor and tapped the controls, causing it to display its first image: a human being with heavy cybernetic augmentation. His right eye, both of his arms, and both of his legs were replaced with bionic implants. On the left side of his head was another implant, his *electronic comrade*. "It's them. My rulers, in their weakness, have called out for help. Their call was answered."

The three looked up at the projection in silence. "Who are they?"

"They're called the Orlov Combine. They are a

militant, oppressive, dangerous civilization. Nowhere amongst the thousands of human colonies are people so enslaved. Each human born on their miserable world is monitored and controlled and directed and commanded for his entire life. The majority of the population is bred to be...submissive. Obedient. Not especially intelligent. The rest have more will, but are no more free."

"This is why we stay out of your affairs, young one. Humans are..." The voices hesitated for just a moment. "Complicated. Perplexing. You have primitive emotions, base impulses that drive you to conquer and kill and steal. You prey on each other as much as you prey on others. Your cruelty, your greed, and your violence is boundless. We know much of your history, of the terrible wars across the stars, of worlds burned from the sky and billions of souls crushed between metal and wheels. We know of the machine-god and his disciples, and of the darkness that followed their war. We remember your encounter with the..."

Adisa didn't understand the word the aliens used next. Did they mean the Maggots? "How...how do you know of this? Did other humans tell you about us?"

The three didn't answer her question. Instead they asked questions of their own. "Why do you seek our help? Why should we involve ourselves in your struggles? We trusted you before and we were betrayed."

"Because *they*," Adisa answered, pointing up at the hologram, "are coming *here*. Their numbers are vast. Their weapons are terrible. When they get here, they will ravage this planet, stripping it of every useful resource. They won't care how much of it they destroy in the process. They will either enslave or exterminate your people, every last one of you, without mercy.

They were attacked by the Maggots in the last big war, and they hate all nonhuman life."

The song of the three voices was much sadder now, even fearful. "We were once strong, but no longer. There are many of us, but we live as primitives, hiding in the dark, fearful of the sky. What would you have us do against such...evil?"

"It's not too late," Adisa said, leaning in slightly. "They're not here yet. My rulers are fearful because they are weak. They are weak, and they are vulnerable. Many oppose them. If we strike, if we remove them, we can stop this from happening." She looked up at the hologram. "We can stop them from coming."

"You wish us to fight in your war," the three sang. "You ask us to not only trust you, but to fight for you, to die for you."

"Not for us. For your home. For this world. For... for *all of us.* Together, your people and mine, fighting as one. We will give you weapons. We will fight at your side. We will...we..." Adisa trailed off, forgetting what she was going to say. She felt a pressure behind her eyes not unlike a sinus headache. Then there was faint buzzing in her ears that gave way to a shrill whine. It grew louder and louder, almost deafening, then ended abruptly as it began.

"You believe what you say," the aliens said, musically. "You are afraid."

"What did you..." Adisa shook her head. It didn't matter. "Yes, I am telling you the truth. There's more. Zander Krycek is my father. He was the one who forged the pact with your people. He was the one who chose peaceful coexistence after years of war. I am his blood, and I, too, want peaceful coexistence with your people. We are willing to fight for you, if you will fight for us. That is why I ask for your help, now, in defending this world. Your home. *Our* home. Please. For all of our sakes, will you help us?"

The three elders didn't answer. Adisa's hologram flickered and went out. The aliens returned their gaze to the fire, seemingly ignoring their human visitor.

"Well?" Adisa asked. Behind her, the great stone door quietly slid open. "That's it? You're just sending me away without an answer?"

"Zander Krycek is coming back?" they asked, as one.

"What? Yes. At least, I hope so. I have sent an envoy to bring him home."

"You are his blood. You share his fire. This is good."

"Will you help us, then?"

There was a long silence. "Go now, young one," the voices finally answered, once again in perfect synchronization, so clear that they must've been in her head. "We will summon you if we wish to speak again."

Adisa stood up and looked down at the three aliens, defiantly. "Whatever you're going to do, I suggest you do it quickly. There isn't a lot of time left." She left the chamber without another word.

Log Entry 133
Mission 815-707-SSOC
Reconnaissance Ship 505

We have been tracking the Polaris-*class cruiser* Andromeda *since its departure from Faraway/ Heinlein/St. Augustine Spaceport. Original analysis predicted with a confidence level of MODERATE/ HIGH that the ship would refuel in orbit and*

*initiate a trajectory for Transit Point Alpha. This
would be the most direct course to Ionia-5589/
Ithaca. However, the* Andromeda *has... surprised... AI/CORE in this instance. After refuel-
ing, the ship began a long out-system trajectory,
toward Transit Point Delta. Several possible
routes to Ionia-5598/Ithaca are possible through
this transit point, but none of them are direct,
and there are a limited number of supply points
along the way.*

*AI/CORE is CONFIDENT/MODERATE/
MODERATE that the* Andromeda *is en route to
Lone Star/New Austin. This system is in Concordiat space. AI/CORE advises caution, but the
mission has not changed.*

We are now shadowing the Andromeda, *and
are far enough behind them that our presence
should not be alarming. We have filed a flight
plan with Faraway/Heinlein space traffic control, stating that we will follow the trade route
through Concordiat space, to Lone Star/New
Austin, terminating at STLR Rockwell's Sun/
Llewellyn-A. Traffic control queried as to why
we had remained in the system for as long as
we had without planeting or docking. They were
informed that a business deal fell through, and
that we are returning home. This explanation
was accepted without further query.*

*AI/CORE advises against directly engaging
the* Andromeda *between Faraway and Lone Star
systems. This is a common trade route, and the
navigation beacons have data recorders that
upload to courier ships. Any direct action could*

compromise OPSEC and render RS-505 unable to conduct further missions. We will wait until an opportunity to complete the mission without compromising ourselves presents itself. AI/CORE has informed us that we have assets available on Lone Star/New Austin, and recommends using them. We concur.

CHAPTER 13

New Austin
Lone Star System

"State your name, for the record."

"Marcus Winchester."

"What position do you currently hold?"

"I'm the Colonial Marshal for the Red River Sector of Laredo Territory."

"Do you have any family on New Austin?"

"I immigrated here from Hayden with my wife, Eleanor, and my daughter, Annabelle. We have since had a son, David."

"I see. What are their vocations?"

"Huh? Eleanor is a miner and a geologist. Anabelle is enrolled at the Spaceflight Academy. David is a toddler."

"Understood. How many deputies do you have on your staff?"

"One."

"Excuse me? According to this, Marshal, your office is budgeted for four deputies."

"That may be the case, ma'am, but I haven't received any new deputies in several years."

"Have you asked?"

"The main office is aware of my personnel situation, ma'am."

Another voice spoke up. "Is it true that you took a leave of absence last year, to travel off-world?"

"I don't see what that has to do with—"

The impatient-sounding woman interrupted him. "Answer the question, please."

Marcus sighed. "Yes, I took a leave of absence. I was hired as a security consultant by a licensed privateer."

"The *Andromeda*."

"That is correct."

"And what did you do while in the service of this . . . privateer? You disclosed that you were well paid."

"I did nothing that was in violation of the Marshals Service code of ethics, Colonial Law, the Interstellar Concord, or the Laws of Outer Space. I would go so far as to say that I wouldn't even be ashamed to tell my mother what I did, if she were still with us. I couldn't tell her, mind you, because I signed a nondisclosure agreement that is still legally binding. I signed an affidavit saying as much when I was reinstated into the Marshals Service, backed up by neuroscopic analysis verifying that I was telling the truth."

"Marshal, this inquest—"

It was Marcus who interrupted this time. "With all due respect, ma'am, this inquest can't, legally, obligate me to violate that nondisclosure agreement any more than it could require me to testify against myself." Only a grand jury, convened in a nonpublic hearing, could require that of him.

She didn't like that. "We'll come back to this later.

Now, what were you doing in Cimarron Territory? That's a long way from Laredo Territory, isn't it?"

"A Colonial Marshal has jurisdiction planet-wide, ma'am."

"I'm aware of that." She was getting testy. "What I'm asking is, what were you doing so far out of your specific, assigned area of responsibility?"

"I was conducting a criminal investigation. My office spent most of the last year trying to track down and apprehend the people behind a Red Eye manufacturing and distribution network. In this, we were successful."

An unpleasant looking man with a beard asked the next question. "Why not simply hand this over to the Cimarron Territory office?"

"Cimarron Territory currently has no Marshals office, sir. Like I said, we're undermanned. This isn't just a problem for my office."

"I see. Tell me, then, why did you not inform the local sheriff of what you were doing?"

"Mainly because Sheriff Coltrane was completely uncooperative. I talked to him about it, at the beginning, and was rebuffed. You gotta understand, the locals out there don't much care for the Colonial government. He was elected on a platform of territorial rights, and apparently, those rights include refusing to cooperate with the marshals. That's only speculation on my part, mind you. He wouldn't even talk to me, directly, so I'm only guessing at his reasoning."

"According to your report, Marshal, backup was unavailable because of a dust storm."

"That is correct."

"Why didn't you back off and wait for backup to become available?"

"That was my intention, until we saw one of the suspects leading a woman to their outdoor latrine. She was tied up, and, in my estimation, being held against her will. Upon making that assessment I was legally obligated to intervene."

"Even using lethal force?"

"If necessary."

"Was it necessary for your partner, Deputy...uh, Bishop, to shoot the suspect in the head, without giving him a chance to surrender?"

"I didn't want to risk her being taken as a hostage."

"Commendable, Marshal, but after that, five of the suspects were killed in the ensuing gun battle. Three of the surviving four were injured."

"That's correct."

"That's it? No justification? You killed people, Marshal."

"I did. It was their choice. I told them to lay down arms and come out. They responded by shooting at me."

"Why didn't you just retreat?" the testy woman asked. "You'd already freed the person being held against her will this, um ..." she looked down at a screen. "Misty Esteban."

"The Marshals Service is not in the business of being driven off by gangs of criminals, ma'am."

"I'm not sure I agree with that method of policing."

"Regardless, that was my duty. I carried it out. They could have surrendered at any time, and as soon as they did, they were arrested without further use of force. The wounded were given medical treatment."

The bearded man spoke up again. "According to your report, Ms. Esteban told you of another woman being held against her will, and that this factored into your decision to escalate the use of force."

"It did. If there was a chance someone was being held against her will in there, I couldn't very well just walk away and wait."

"You could have, you simply chose not to."

"Have you ever seen what happens to victims of kidnapping and human trafficking? I have. You look in the eyes of someone who's being held prisoner, getting raped *every single day*, and you tell her that it's okay to *walk away* and *wait*. I made a decision and I stand by it. The Marshal Code of Conduct agrees with me."

"There's no need to raise your voice, Marshal. We're simply trying to establish what happened. Tell us what happened next, with the OSI agent."

"She was, apparently, the other so-called captive that Misty Esteban told me about. I say so-called because, according to what she told me, she wasn't being held against her will. She was deep undercover."

"And then you arrested her."

"I did."

"Why would you do that, Marshal?"

"As stated in the arrest report, she violated Article 31 of the Interstellar Concord, threatened a peace officer, assaulted my deputy, and resisted arrest. She also allowed a citizen to be victimized and held against her will while acting in an official capacity. That is a serious crime, and her status as an OSI agent doesn't excuse her for committing it."

"You don't think the law makes allowances for extenuating circumstances, like being deep undercover?"

"I'm not a lawyer, sir, but I have read the text of

that particular statute. There's nothing in it about an exception for OSI agents."

"The OSI agent involved provided us with a significantly different report than the one you submitted, Marshal. She stated, being very blunt, that you were reckless, too eager to use force, overstepped your authority, and as a result, you ruined a long-running investigation and killed several people."

"My interaction with the agent was recorded, ma'am. You can judge for yourselves."

"That recording was surrendered to the Office of Strategic Intelligence, Marshal. Recording her face and voice was in violation of, let me see..." She tapped her screen a few times. "Section 214b, Paragraph 4, of the latest addendum to the Interstellar Defense, Security, and Espionage Act. We were required to surrender the recording."

Marcus' hands clenched into fists under the table. "I see. And the Colonial Government chose not to challenge this?"

"The situation was reviewed, and it was determined that there was no standing to challenge the order."

"Well, that is just great," Marcus said, bitterly. "In that case, I've said all I care to say. You have my report and testimony. If you have any other questions, I want a lawyer present."

"This inquest is not a criminal investigation, Marshal. You don't need an attorney."

"See, I disagree. Seems to me my career is on the line, and y'all just let the OSI take off with evidence I submitted that would back up my case. I'm not saying anything else without consulting with my lawyer."

"Very well, Marshal. Your lack of cooperation with

this inquest will be noted, though we are obligated to tell you that you're within your legal rights. You are hereby suspended from duty for a period of not less than fifty days, after which time you will be notified of our final decision. You are dismissed."

Marcus was seething. Teeth grinding, fists clenched, he held it together long enough to stand up and leave the room.

Wade was waiting for him outside. The Marshals Service headquarters was a plain, fifteen-story building, its Spartan design typical of government buildings. The street in front of the courtyard was jammed with traffic.

"How'd it go, boss?"

Marcus put on his sunglasses and frowned. "I'm suspended for fifty days."

"Same. That OSI bint had our body camera recordings confiscated. It's our word against hers."

"They're spineless, terrified of the big bad OSI. It's pathetic." Marcus already had a low opinion of the current Colonial Government, and its unwillingness to stand behind law enforcement. This incident only served to confirm his attitude. "Like as not we'll be out of a job."

"You think so? Hell, there'll be no one left in Red River Sector."

"The sheriff will have to handle everything, I guess. It won't be our problem anymore."

"Well, shit. Your family gonna be okay, Marshal?"

"We'll survive, but keeping Annie in the Spaceflight Academy might be a problem."

"Really? With as much money as you brought home from Zanzibar?"

"A lot of that went into investments for Ellie's

mining business. Also, I don't know if you know this, but that school is really God damn expensive."

"Aww, poor kid. I hope you figure something out."

"She's home on break now. I'll have to talk to her and Ellie about it when I get home. What about you? What are you going to do with yourself?"

"Me and Devree still got some savings left, even after buying the house. You know, after this shit, I'm kinda glad she didn't sign up for the Marshals."

"You about ready to head home?"

Wade nodded. "I'll split the fee for an aircar with you."

"Deal." A ground car would have been much cheaper, but it was at least a ten-hour drive to Red River from the colonial capital. "Let's get some chow, first, though. I'm starving."

CHAPTER 14

The Privateer Ship *Andromeda*
Deep Space
Faraway System

"Ah, Gentleman Armitage! You're here for weapons training, yes?"

"I am," Nickson said to the cargomaster as he came off the ladder. "Hello, Kimball."

"Gentleman Broadbent is waiting for you," Kimball said, indicating an open area in the middle of the cargo deck. "He has the trainer all set up for you."

"Uh, great. Where are you off to?"

"To my rack. I've been on duty for fourteen hours now. I could use some rest."

The *Andromeda* was undermanned. The ship had sat in port for nearly two standard years. There had been no extra funds available, without a contract, to hire new crewmembers. The rapid departure from Ithaca meant that there had been no time to fill the personnel shortages. Cargomaster Kimball had no assistant. Neither did Indira Nair, the chief engineer, whose assistant had been killed at Zanzibar. All three junior officers, Luis Azevedo, Nattaya Tantirangsi, and Colin Abernathy, had been retained, but of the three only Colin was a rated pilot. The others had rudimentary flight operations training, but only enough to be watch standers.

"I'm sorry there wasn't time to hire you some help," Nickson said.

"Not to worry, sir. Jerkins has been quite helpful, and never complains."

Across the cargo deck, Zander Krycek's robot rolled out from behind a stack of crates. It came to a stop over a pair of tie-downs, and extended its mechanical tentacles to the floor. Grasping the tie-downs, the robot locked itself into position and powered down. They were approaching the transit point, and Jerkins had the good sense to power down before translation.

"I will manually disengage its battery connector before we translate," Kimball said, as if reading Nickson's mind, "and remove the power cell from its laser weapon."

"Good thinking."

"Yes, well, we've transported an AI on this ship before. I've seen for myself what happens when they go through translation. I'll not have Jerkins armed and on the loose when it may be affected by transit shock. Have a good training session, sir. I'll be on the personnel deck if I'm needed."

Nickson had read the logs from when the *Andromeda* had transported an AI named Ember from Folsom-4101-B to New Peking. The machine intelligence's reaction to translation ranged from simply locking up to becoming verbally abusive, screaming obscenities at passing crew members. Jerkins wasn't nearly so sophisticated as an actual AI, of course, but it did have a powerful pulse laser. Better safe than sorry. "Have a good night, Kimball. I won't make a mess."

The ship was still accelerating at a steady 0.85 gravity, and would continue to do so for another ninety minutes or so. This allowed Nickson to walk across the deck, though the fifteen percent reduction in apparent weight meant that one had to be cautious. It was easy to take bigger steps than anticipated.

"Hello, sir." In the center of the cargo deck was an open space, surrounded by stacks of crates placed in such a manner as to ensure radial mass symmetry. Mazer Broadbent was waiting for Nickson, and he struck an imposing figure: tall, muscular, with a cybernetic ocular implant taking up a good-sized portion of the right side of his head. Around his waist was a gun belt; on his right hip, in a low-slung holster, was a laser pistol.

"Mr. Broadbent, thank you for meeting me here," Nickson said. "I appreciate your help in this matter." It was a little embarrassing that the executive officer needed to be taught something like this, and he worried that it made the crew think less of him.

"Not at all, sir. I've run several members of the crew through this training regimen. You're not the only spacer to not be very experienced in the use of small arms. I'd say you're in the majority, as a matter of fact."

"You know, it's really never come up before."

Broadbent smiled. "It seldom does, but it's better to have the training and not need it than the other way around. Are you ready to begin?"

"I am. Let's do this."

On a cart behind the security officer was another

laser pistol and several power cells. Broadbent picked up the weapon and turned, offering it to Nickson butt-first. The XO took the weapon in his right hand.

"First thing," Broadbent said, in a polite but firm tone, "please take your finger off the firing stud."

"Oh? I'm sorry. What...where do I put my finger?"

"Just index it along the side of the weapon, or on the outside of the trigger guard. As a rule, you want to keep your finger off the trigger until you're aiming at your target and are ready to shoot. Negligent discharges can be avoided this way."

"I see," Nickson said, adjusting his grip as instructed. The laser pistol in his hand had a solid feel to it, constructed of high-strength alloys and composites. The grip and frame were boxy, but the barrel was rounded, and colored blue. "Why is it blue?"

"That's a training weapon. It operates virtually the same as our issue service weapons, but takes a lower-density power cell and projects a visible green laser when you fire. It's harmless, so long as you don't habitually point it into your eyes. The main practical difference is that it creates no sound when you fire."

Nickson had experienced, first hand, how much noise lasers can make. He remembered the awful, electric crackling as Jerkins's rapidly pulsing laser ripped Sebastian open from face to stomach. He turned toward the target that Broadbent had set up.

"Watch your muzzle, sir. You almost pointed the lens at me as you turned. Another rule of safe weapons handling is to not point the weapon at anything you don't intend to kill."

"Oh. Sorry. So, how do I hold it? Do I point it up, like this?"

"That'll do for now. We'll get into drawing from a holster and the various ready positions later. Now, facing the target, I want you to extend the weapon in both your hands, pointing at the target. Don't blade your body off to the side, or only use one hand. Like this." Drawing his own weapon, the security officer showed Nickson where to put his left hand, and how to grip the gun. Nickson followed suit, pointing the pistol at the target some five meters away. "Holding it both hands helps mitigate recoil in projectile weapons. In lasers, it helps steady your aim."

"Got it. What now?"

"Look through the sight. Do you see the green dot? That's your aiming point. The sight has power as long as the weapon does, and is regulated to the point of the laser's impact. The sight doesn't have to be perfectly aligned. No matter which angle you're looking at it from, wherever the dot is, your laser will follow."

"Okay. That seems easy enough. Uh, where is the safety?"

"This weapon doesn't have a manual safety. The primary safety is you, being mindful about where the weapon is pointing and keeping your finger off the firing stud. Now, I want you to go ahead and squeeze the trigger. If you apply about two-point-seven-five kilos of pressure, you'll feel a clean break, or a click. That's when the weapon will fire."

Nickson squeezed the trigger. *BEEP!*

"Very good. That tone was just to let you know you fired. If you look at the target, you can see where your point of impact was."

The target displayed a glowing dot, three centimeters

to the right of the orange circle Nickson had been aiming at. "I missed."

"You did, but only by a little. On a man-sized target you'd still be in the kill zone. I think you jerked the weapon a little to the right when you fired. I want you to do it again, but focus on pulling the trigger straight back."

Nickson continued to train, following the security officer's instructions as closely as he could. He was shown how to eject and replace the power cell, which was stored in the weapon's grip. Mazer Broadbent explained the basic functioning of the laser, and how firing it too rapidly drained the power supply faster. The training gun didn't generate heat, but a real one would, he said.

"I think that does it for today, sir. Let me know when you want to do this again."

"There's more?"

The security man smiled. "There's a lot more."

"Okay. It won't be until after we translate. I'll get with you when I get some more free time. And hey, thanks for doing this."

A warning klaxon sounded; ten minutes until freefall. A moment later, Nickson's communicator chirped at him. He tapped his headset. "This is the XO."

"Sir? This is Azevedo. Could you come up to the flight deck, please?"

"On my way. Is it an emergency?"

"No, sir, just something I think you might want to see."

"I'll be right there." He looked up at the security officer. "Thank you for your time today. I guess I'm needed upstairs." He turned and made for the ladder.

Nickson strode onto the command deck, where Luis Azevedo and Nattaya Tantirangsi were waiting for him. Colin Abernathy was up on the flight deck.

"Sir, you should strap in," Azevedo said. "We'll be cutting thrust in less than a minute."

Nickson sat in the command chair and fastened the restraint just as the freefall klaxon sounded again. A moment later, the dull rumble of the *Andromeda*'s engines ceased, and Nickson's stomach lurched as he was thrust into microgravity.

"Good timing, sir," Nuchy said. That was her nickname, *Nuchy*. Nickson was glad for it; her real name was a mouthful.

"Azevedo, what seems to be the problem?"

"There's another ship, sir."

"Okay. And?" A quick check of his displays told Nickson that there were presently twenty-one ships under thrust in the Faraway system, and more in space dock.

Nuchy spoke up next. "It's just a little strange, sir. After we stopped to take on remass, and began the burn to Transit Point Delta, then it started on a similar course."

"I see. Did it do this immediately?"

"No, sir. It waited for over twelve hours. There's no way it can catch up to us now."

"So . . . what's the problem?"

Azevedo seemed nervous, as if he regretted calling Nickson back up to the command deck. "Sir, it's not doing anything suspicious or threatening. It's just weird. I've got a weird feeling about it."

"Okay. Send it to my displays. Let me take a look at it." Nickson wasn't sure what the kids were on about, but it was better to humor them. He didn't want them to be afraid to bring things like this to his attention, even if it turned out to be nothing. It always paid to be vigilant.

The ship in question looked clunky, but otherwise unremarkable. Using a touch pad to rotate the image, Nickson examined the ship from every angle. It was big, seventy-eight meters from nose to tail. Its cylindrical body was topped with a blunt, aeroballistic nose. Three streamlined housings around the base of the primary hull contained its primary fusion rockets, and each was topped with a triangular airfoil. Large radiators jutted out from either side of the hull.

Based on its exhaust signature and general layout, the computer was seventy percent sure it was a *Galaxis*-class multirole cutter. That wasn't unusual. The *Galaxis* class was an ancient design, having been first produced in the Inner Colonies at the very end of the Interregnum. It was a simple, reliable design, widely copied, modified, and manufactured over the subsequent centuries. Their heyday had long since passed, but there were still thousands of them in inhabited space.

According to her transponder, the ship was the *Bonaventura,* a free trader registered out of the Llewellyn Freehold. To Nickson's mind, this meant that she was like as not involved in some illicit activity or another, given that a great many of the "merchants" who operated out of the Freehold were smugglers or pirates, but she didn't seem to pose a threat.

"Okay, guys, she's an old tub out of the Llewellyn Freehold. I don't see anything unusual, but something about this is obviously bothering you. Tell me what you're thinking."

"We checked her flight plan," Nuchy said. "She's going to New Austin, same as us, then onto the Freehold."

"It is a standard trade route. You seem to think we're being followed, even though she's in no position to catch up to us. What makes you think that?"

Luis Azevedo spoke up this time. "Well, sir, she waited for many hours after we departed to begin her burn toward Transit Point Delta. But, I checked the logs, and she *filed* her flight plan shortly after we left the fueling station."

Nickson thought about it for a moment, and pulled up the *Bonaventura*'s flight plan. "Hmm," he mused, rubbing his chin. "It's probably nothing. But *probably* isn't *definitely*. After what happened planetside, we can't be too careful. Good work, guys. I'll brief the skipper when she comes on duty."

"Thank you, sir!" the young officers said, looking pleased with themselves.

CHAPTER 15

Ithaca
Ionia-5589 System
Southern Hemisphere

Adisa Masozi was tired. Her chrono told her she'd been in the vast, underground city for almost twenty of Ithaca's 18-hour days. She had little to do while she waited for an answer from the alien elders, and had spent much of the time sleeping. Without being able to see the sky, her internal clock was off. She would sleep for twelve, sometimes fourteen hours at a time, and then she'd be up for nearly twice as long.

In her waking hours, she would explore and document the subterranean metropolis as much as Follower of the Storm would allow, which wasn't very much. She recorded video and took hundreds of photographs. Her devices were unable to link to the planetary network, so she couldn't upload anything, and only had an approximate location of the city, but there was so much to learn.

The Ithacans had lived here for centuries, as near as she could tell, and had kept it a secret for all that time. When her father had met with the Elders, years before, to forge the peace treaty, they had chosen the meeting place, and it had been on the surface. There were theories that the natives had secret holdfasts of some sort, but few would have imagined the scale of the underground city.

She made a habit of recording her thoughts into a journal, both to help pass the time and to keep her thoughts straight.

I'm getting frustrated, she wrote, tapping the virtual keyboard on her tablet. *I've been down here for twenty days now, and I've still heard nothing from the Elders. Even Follower of the Storm is being more distant than he had been. I suspect he's been told to stop sharing so much, but he won't tell me anything. I'm still not certain why I was brought here.*

That's not all I suspect. They deny it, but I believe I've seen electric lights down here. I've never been able to get close enough to confirm. It seems that every time I notice one, it is quickly put out, and I've not yet been able to get it on video. The Rangers have noticed them too, but we've made it a point to not discuss it in front of our hosts. If the Ithacans do, in fact, have a higher level of technology than they've let on, they obviously want to keep it hidden from us. There's no sense in jeopardizing our request for their help by being intrusive.

It would be an incredible discovery, even if it was something as simple as a water wheel being used to power a vacuum-filament light globe. Humans have been living on Ithaca for centuries and have never detected electrical power distribution. If this is the case, it might be indicative of not only deliberate camouflaging, but a sufficiently advanced understanding of electromagnetics to know that such a signature may need to be camouflaged. I may be reaching here. Perhaps I've been underground too long. Yet, I find myself wondering if the natives may be more advanced than we've ever suspected.

Adisa looked up from her screen, rubbing her eyes. The quarters they had been given were hewn from stone. A curtain covered the entrance, and another separated her from the two SAZ-CDF Rangers, to give her some privacy. The curtains rustled lazily in the constant, gentle breeze that blew throughout the city, carried from room to room by a series of carved vents and boreholes. Aside from the steady sighing of the circulating air, it was very quiet tonight. Today? It really didn't matter down here. Whatever time it was, she could tell that the Rangers were asleep. She could tell by dim light shining over and through the privacy curtain that their little fire had died down to embers.

Letting her eyes adjust to the darkness, Adisa felt a change in the air, as if the sleeping Rangers were no longer the only ones in the chamber with her. She heard the faintest shuffling of feet. A black shadow moved across a wall, cast only by the embers of the dying fire. Her heart was pounding so hard that she could almost hear it. She slowly reached for her pistol, as the approaching figure cast its looming shadow on her privacy curtain.

"Who's there?" she called out, her voice a raspy whisper.

"It is Follower of the Storm, A-disss-ah. Do not be . . . afraid." His halting, baritone voice was hushed.

Relief washed over the operative as Follower of

the Storm poked his head over the top of the curtain. "You scared me."

Stormy was quiet for a moment, awkwardly looking down at Adisa. "This one . . . did . . . not . . . mean to . . . scare you. This one was sent by the Elders. They wish to . . . see . . . you." His rumbling voice echoed softly in the chamber. "Please follow."

Adisa jumped to her feet. "Of course!" she said, excitedly. "Just let me wake Roc and tell him where I'm going."

Stormy bobbed his head from one side to the other. "No. They slumber. You come, alone."

"Okay. Just us, then, I suppose. Please, lead on."

Follower of the Storm guided Adisa through the subterranean metropolis. According to her chrono, it was nighttime on the surface, and indeed the city seemed to be asleep. Even underground, beings used to a day/night schedule prefer to keep one, she thought to herself, even though she had no idea how they kept time. She hadn't seen anything that she could identify as a chronograph.

After ten minutes of following Stormy through labyrinthine tunnels and into the structure that seemed to serve as the city's hall of government, Adisa once again found herself before the door that led to the chamber of the Elders. The path they had used to get there seemed different than it had before, even though they'd come out in the same place.

"This one will wait for you," her alien companion said. "A-dissss-ah must go alone." As he said this, the door to the Elders' chamber slid open. The room beyond was black, save for the red glow of the fire pit. "Do not be afraid."

"Thank you, Stormy," Adisa said, managing a smile for her companion. She turned and entered the chamber, keeping her eyes fixed on the fire as she crossed the room. The floor rumbled slightly as the door slid shut.

The three Elders sat on the floor, in front of the fire, as before. Adisa took her place opposite them, sitting cross-legged on a woven mat which had been placed on the floor since her previous visit. In front of her was a tray, made of the local pseudo-wood, and on it was a crude metal cup filled with a steaming liquid. It smelled almost like ginger.

"Is this for me?" she asked, not touching the cup.

"Yes," the Elders harmonized. "Drink, young one."

"What is it?"

"The elixir will clear your mind. It will allow us to show you things, and we have much to show you."

Adisa hesitated. "You . . . you're going to drug me? Why?"

"Do not be afraid, young one. We understand your anatomy. You will not be harmed. You must trust us. You ask us to trust you, to fight in your war at your side, do you not? Trust begets trust."

"Fair enough." She picked up the cup, which seemed to have been hammered out of a thin sheet of tin, and lifted it to her lips. The gingery scent of the beverage was almost intoxicating up close. Her muscles began to relax almost instantly, as if she were holding the universe's most perfect aromatherapy candle. Without further hesitation, she drank from the offered cup. The drink was thick, and spicy, and had flavors that she couldn't quite place. She downed it all and set the cup down, feeling warm inside, and maybe even a little drunk.

"Focus on the flame, young one," the Elders sang. "Clear your mind and lose yourself in the flame."

"Okay..." she said, quietly, gazing into the fire. Her alien hosts began to emit strange music, from the nasal cavities above their eyes. She tried to concentrate on nothing but the dancing of the flames, and found herself entranced. As the Elders harmonized, she was certain she was hearing their voices in her mind instead of with her ears. The flame faded away to darkness, and Adisa found herself gazing upon the Milky Way galaxy, as if from the Magellanic Clouds.

The image changed to an utterly unfamiliar, alien world, blue-green in color, swirling with yellow and brown clouds, and bathed in the light of a massive red star. At the top of a column of smoke and fire, a crude-looking chemical rocket appeared over the planetary horizon. "Long ago," the Elders began, "the children of this fetid, dying world crawled out of their primordial swamps and took to the stars. They did so not out of curiosity, but out of desperation. Powerful solar storms bombarded their planet with radiation, and soon it would be rendered lifeless. They chose not to surrender to their fate and go quietly into oblivion, but to spread across the stars and ensure the survival of their species."

The blue-green planet was gone now, replaced with fleets of oblong, organic-looking craft accelerating against a backdrop of millions of stars. Adisa recognized those ships from the historical records, or at least, the general layout of them. They were Maggot ships.

"You know them," the Elders sang, sadly. An image of an individual Maggot alien appeared, but it was different than Adisa remembered from her schooling.

It wasn't covered with technological devices, was less bloated, and was somehow more natural looking. Its smooth, ribbed body, like that of the terrestrial fly larvae from which they got their name, was propelled by a series of short legs. The creature morphed, then, with various technological apparatuses appearing on it. As it became more infused with technology, its body seemed to atrophy. It grew fat, its appendages withered, and it seemed more and more dependent on its machines.

"As their flesh succumbed to their machines, they grew colder. They created nothing of beauty or splendor. They forgot their songs and their old tales. They forgot the warm swamps from which they came. They saw themselves as masters of the galaxy, and so they were."

A massive fleet of Maggot ships, these ones more evolved than the last ones Adisa had been shown, moved toward a small, blue planet. As the ships entered orbit, they opened fire on the planet with their terrible weapons. Red-orange particle beams pierced the clouds and obliterated unfamiliar alien cities. Squat beings with round, blue bodies fled in terror as hell rained down on them from above. Oceans boiled, and the sky itself seemed to burn. The faintest scent of smoke teased Adisa's nose.

"The galaxy is full of life, as you know well. There are worlds uncounted that can bear the fruits of life. At the height of their power, though, they were as gods, and they would suffer no rivals. They claimed every star and every world as their own, foregoing only those which had been walked upon by the ancients. If any beings they encountered proved capable of taking to the stars, they were exterminated. For an eon, their empire spread across the galaxy, and there were none who could match them. A few had the means to resist, but all succumbed to their power."

The song of the Elders was mournful, now. "We were once as you are: young and proud. We left the bosom of our homeworld and discovered the Webway." Images of ships translating from one system to another appeared in Adisa's mind. "We walked on new worlds, and imagined ourselves to be the lords of all creation. How arrogant we were, how foolish."

The images swirled again, as if Adisa were looking at a reflection in a pool of water. She was now looking at one of the native Ithacans, except he wasn't on Ithaca. He was strapped into a seat in what was clearly the command center of a spaceship. He barked orders at others in his deep, guttural voice. It was a battle, and they were losing.

She watched, helplessly, as the Ithacans lost battle after battle. The Maggots were hunting them, mercilessly, relentlessly, slaughtering them everywhere they were found. They did not try to communicate with the Ithacans, nor did they make any demands, and they accepted no surrender. When orbital particle beam strikes didn't work, they would invade, take the fight to the ground. Adisa recognized their hideous war machines from archival footage, quadrupedal robotic war machines crawling out of their huge landers by the dozens. The Ithacans fought back, with incredible weapons of their own: monstrous, armored supersoldiers as tall as a building, powered by biological fission reactors and armed with energy weapons. Mass-drivers, hundreds of meters long, built into the ground, firing skyward. It was all for naught. While the Maggots had space superiority, surface weapons would eventually, inevitably be destroyed.

The images swirled again. When they came back into focus, Adisa was looking at a beautiful, blue-green planet, orbiting an orange star. Maggot ships closed in, pushing back the defenders. "We fought bravely for our homeworld, but it was hopeless. There were too few of us left."

Now the invaders were in orbit above the planet. The defending fleet was smashed, nothing more than expanding clouds of rapidly cooling debris. Particle beams lanced downward, rending the surface and vaporizing millions of beings. A massive asteroid was dropped, impacting the defenseless world with the force of a million fusion weapons. The atmosphere itself ignited, sending a wall of fire racing around the globe. Adisa's heart was filled with the sorrow of a long-dead people as their world was burned to glass.

"Those that survived, fled. We scattered in a hundred directions, but always were we hunted. As long as we could cross the gulf of space, as long as we had the technology to travel between the stars, they considered us a threat. We needed time, we needed a safe place to rebuild, repopulate, and to step back from the edge of extinction while there were still enough of us left to save our species."

Adisa recognized the world she was shown next, because it was her home, too. *Ithaca!* She watched, in awe, as alien ships made planetfall. The ships were disassembled, meticulously, and brought deep underground. It took years, many, many years, but the Elders' people hid every trace of their technology.

"We tried to fight, and we lost," the Elders said. "We tried to flee, but we were overtaken. We were left with one option: we hid. We buried our technology so deep that it could not be detected from space. We abandoned the stars and settled on this world. We lived as primitives, hunting and farming, as our forbears did ages ago. We built no cities under the open sky, created no works, and cast our eyes downward. We forgot much of our own history. Our achievements became legend, and those legends became fables.

"Those of us destined to be Elders were taught the truth. As our people multiplied, our true histories were passed from one generation to the next. For while those who had hunted us viewed themselves as gods, they were not gods, and they, too, were in decline."

An image appeared of a Maggot world. A strange city of angular structures and non-Euclidian geometries was laid out before Adisa, and it was dead. The city, abandoned, empty, was slowly overtaken by nature. Hideous vines slowly crawled up crumbling cyclopean structures, sprouting ghastly red flowers beneath an orange, alien sky.

"We are, all of us, mortal, young one. Nothing lasts forever. All civilizations fall. For all their might, for as vast as their empire once was, our conquerors were themselves dying. It was the slow death of ages; their civilization peaked, and declined. Their numbers were dwindling long before we ever encountered them. They became so dependent on their machines that they were as machines themselves. The drive, the will that pulled them out of their swamps and took them to the stars, had faded. In their malaise, they themselves faded as well. They had machines for every imaginable purpose, and in making them they lost their own purpose. Their empire, though incredibly vast, was but a shell, hollow and empty. It was only a matter of time before another race would challenge their dominance."

Everything Adisa had ever learned of the Second Interstellar War came flooding into her mind then. The confused, panicked first encounter, and the tense years that followed before the next one. The initial, losing battles. The outermost colonies succumbed first. Zanzibar fell. Orlov's Star was besieged. The Maggots pressed ever deeper into human space, plunging deep into the Concordiat like a dagger through the heart of mankind. Hayden burned, as did Nippon, and Hera, and Columbia. Countless millions died. Adisa's heart ached as the fear, the existential dread that comes from gazing into the abyss, filled her soul.

But then the tide turned. The Maggots' ships were powerful, and were so advanced that they required only one living being as an operator. Their weapons were terrible and deadly accurate, but their tactics never changed. They did everything as they had for ages, because it had always worked before. The Maggots, as ancient as they were, proved unable to adapt.

If there's one thing humans are particularly good at, it's adaptation. The war continued in Adisa's mind, everything she'd ever learned about the conflict, and some things she'd never known. The human race was unified as never before, and their wrath was terrible. In a matter of years, they went from slowly seceding territory to going on the offensive. Everywhere the Maggots were encountered, they were exterminated. Not a single individual being was allowed to escape.

Expeditionary forces pushed them out of Concordiat space, out past the frontier, and pursued them into their own space. Fleets of ships explored deeper into the unknown, while chasing the Maggots, than anyone had before.

Long the hunters, they became the hunted, and for the first time in thousands of years the Maggots knew real fear. The campaign of xenocide didn't end until humanity believed that their alien enemy was extinct.

"Your people did what ours could not," the Elders intoned, sadly. "Where we succumbed, you were victorious. You are, for now, the masters of all that is known."

Adisa's head was swimming now. The mosaic of images, the living story being played in her mind, faded away, leaving her gazing at only the flame. Coming out of the haze, she realized that she must have been sitting on that mat for hours. Her legs were cramped, and her back was sore. Her head hurt from the strange drink that they had given her. She rubbed her eyes and looked up at the three Elders, who still sat quietly across from her.

"My God," she croaked, her mouth incredibly dry. "You...you just told me more about your people than any human knows. This is simply amazing! This is..." She fell silent as her head throbbed.

"Gently, young one," the Elders cautioned. "The visions are much to endure, especially for a mind as undeveloped in psionics as yours. Breathe. The pain will pass."

"Why did you show me all this?"

"So that you would understand our terms."

"And what are your terms?"

All three of the Elders leaned in now, gazing at Adisa intensely, the red flames reflected in their large, black eyes. "We will fight for this world. We will not allow your Combine to take our home from us. We will not. We will not be driven to the brink of extinction again."

Adisa's heart leapt up into her throat. She almost couldn't speak. She had *done it!* "Thank you," she stammered, her response wholly inadequate. "What is it that you want in return?"

"You will tell Zander Krycek. We will fight for him, but when the battle is won, we have two conditions. One is that the humans leave our lands in peace. The terms of the old pact will be honored. You will make no attempt to return to this city uninvited, or to dig anywhere on our lands."

"I see. What else?"

"We wish to return to the stars."

"You . . . what?"

"We wish to return to the stars, and you will help us. For too long, we have been confined to this world. For too long, we have lived as savages, when once we walked as giants across the galaxy. You will help us relearn what we have forgotten. You will help us go back into space, to reclaim our birthright. In time, we will have our own ships, and the next great trial of our people will begin."

"What trial?"

"To find a new homeworld, and to find the rest of our race. Our ancestors were not the only ones to give up the way of machines and go into hiding. There are others, out there, somewhere, and we wish to find them. This you will tell to Zander Krycek.

This you will tell him, and if he agrees, then our people will join you in the fight. Do we have a pact, Adisa Masozi?"

My God, I hope so. "I can't speak for my father. I'm merely an emissary. But, if he is returning to Ithaca, I will relay your terms and advise him to accept them. I will do the same to my leadership should he not return. That is all I can promise you."

"Very well. Go now. Rest. You will need time to recover from the visions. You must sleep."

"I am very tired," Adisa said, standing up unsteadily. "No matter what is decided, thank you for trusting me enough to tell me your story."

The Elders sung one last warning for Adisa. "You should know, young one, that the path ahead is fraught with peril, dangers that even we cannot see. There will be suffering. There will be death. You must choose what it is you are willing to sacrifice, because sacrifice will be required before it is over. Now go."

Her head still spinning, Adisa made her way out of the chamber.

Log Entry 134
Mission 815-707-SSOC
Reconnaissance Ship 505

RS-505 has entered the Lone Star system. AI/ CORE is still offline, but we are continuing the mission on our own. It will take us 197 hours to make planetfall from the transit point we crossed through. The Andromeda *is well ahead of us, but we continue to track it as it approaches New Austin. Telemetry indicates it will make an orbital pass for aerobraking and then land at the planet's largest spaceport, outside its capital city.*

Before translation, AI/CORE informed us that there are assets available on New Austin, but declined to explain further. We will not have access to this information until AI/CORE comes back online. It is not known why the Andromeda *chose to take this route, as it adds a significant length of time to the journey to Ionia-5589/Ithaca. It is not useful to speculate. We will monitor the situation as it unfolds.*

We must remain cautious. We are in Concordiat space. We are not tracking any military ships in the system, but even a remote colony like New Austin has defenses and surveillance. We need to refuel. There is an automated station in high solar orbit, but utilizing it will require us to burn a substantial amount of reaction mass and take us farther from the planet. We have no choice but to land, despite the risk.

CHAPTER 16

**New Austin
Southern Hemisphere**

Marcus Winchester stopped short of his daughter's room. Her door was open, but she was having a video chat with someone. It sounded like her friend Liam.

"How are things going with Carlos?" the other voice asked. It was definitely Liam.

"Things have been . . . I don't know. He just doesn't get me." Come to think of it, she hadn't mentioned Carlos hardly at all in the month Marcus had been home, unemployed.

"Can I be honest?" Liam asked. "A lot of us don't. You're different, since you got back. What happened to you? You never talk about it."

"Liam, I told you, I *can't*. Look, we went to Zanzibar, okay? You ever heard of it?"

"I think so."

"Yeah, well, I was there, and things got ugly. People died. It's . . . I don't know how to talk about it with you. You wouldn't understand."

"Because I haven't done anything like that?" Liam

asked, pointedly. The kid sounded like his feelings were hurt.

"I didn't mean it like that. It's just..."

"Did you kill anybody?"

Marcus cringed. He'd been asked that question more times than he could count.

"What?"

"You said people died. Did you kill anybody?"

"I don't...no. Look, I have to go."

"Is everything okay? Did I say something wrong?"

"No, it's fine, I just need to go."

"But—"

"I'll talk to you later, Liam. Bye." Before he could say anything else, Annie ended the call and set her handheld down.

Marcus knocked on the frame of the doorway to Annie's room. "Hey, kiddo."

"Dad! How long were you there?"

"I wasn't trying to snoop, honey. Your door was open."

"Oh," she said.

He crossed the room and sat down next to her, on her bed. "I heard Liam say you're different."

"He just doesn't understand."

"He's right, you know. You are different. And no, he doesn't understand. He can't, because he hasn't seen what you've seen. He hasn't buried friends. He hasn't had to fight for his life."

Annie sighed. "It's hard sometimes."

Her father put an arm around her. "I know it is. And I am so, so sorry I put you through that."

"It's okay, Daddy," Annie said, with a sniffle. He could tell she was struggling to hold back tears. "I'll be okay."

"I know you will, Annabelle," he said quietly. "You take after your mother, and she's one of the strongest people I know. It just isn't fair to have your childhood taken away from you like that, and all because that little druggie shrew screwed with your horse."

"It's weird. I wouldn't be who I am now if she hadn't poisoned Sparkles. I guess I owe her a lot."

"That's a way to look at it."

"I don't hate her. Not after everything that happened. I never want to see her bitchy face again, but I don't hate her. She needed help."

Marcus was so proud of his daughter that he could bust. "That's mighty big of you, kiddo. Mature. And you're right, she was blitzed on Red Eye. I've seen that shit ruin a lot of lives. It makes people crazy, violent, and detached from reality. They say it feels like you're dreaming, and that you think nothing matters."

"I think I killed somebody, Daddy. When we were on Zanzibar, I mean."

"I know, honey. Kimball told me."

"I'm not sure, though. There were people everywhere, and your team was trying to get back to the ship. We were just shooting and shooting. I was shaking so bad I didn't think I hit anything, but this one guy . . . he was way off, couple hundred meters, but I pulled the trigger and he fell. He *fell*, Daddy." Tears rolled down her cheeks.

Marcus put a hand on her cheek and looked her in the eyes. "Listen to me, Annabelle Winchester. You didn't do anything wrong. You did what you had to do. If those men would have taken the ship, we'd have all been killed, or worse. I know it's hard, but you did the right thing."

Annie sniffled again. "That's just it. I *know*. I know I didn't do anything wrong. It's just...when he fell? I didn't feel bad. It happened so fast, I didn't feel anything. And then, when I thought about it later? I was glad. I was glad I killed him."

"Then why are you crying?"

"Because, it's not normal! Is there something wrong with me?"

He hugged Annie tightly. "No, baby, there's nothing wrong with you. That *is* normal. I just wish you would have talked about it sooner." Marcus had been hesitant to broach the subject with his daughter. He simply didn't know how to ask a teenage girl how she felt about possibly having killed a man.

"I wanted to. It's just...on the trip home, we were so busy, and I guess I kind of...I don't know, repressed it? I didn't want Mom to know, and I knew you'd tell her. I didn't want her to look at me like I'm a murderer."

"You're not a murderer. You were defending your ship, and it was *combat*. People die. And they're not always bad guys, either. That's why war is so awful, because good people die. No matter what side he fights on, every dead soldier has a mother or friends or a family that he doesn't get to go home to. You do it because it's your duty, or because you don't want to let your friends down. You did what had to be done. People who haven't been there, like Liam? They mean well but they don't get it. It's not something you can explain to someone."

"How do you do this? How do you kill people and come home and be normal?"

"Hell, I ain't normal. But I will tell you, the first

one is hard. After that? It sounds bad, but after a while you get used to it. You focus on the good in your life, on why you did what you did instead of the bad things you saw. Don't second guess yourself. But... baby, it changes you, and you'll never be the same." He didn't tell her about the dead girl from Mildenhall who still haunted his dreams. She didn't need to know about that. "It's the Mark of Cain," he continued. "The dark spot on a person's soul that comes from having taken a life. Don't try to pretend it's not there, but don't let it eat you up, either. That mark is a good thing. People who don't feel it, they kill without conscience. They lose their humanity. Aw, hell, I'm rambling on now. Does any of this make sense?"

Annie squeezed Marcus tightly. "I love you."

"I love you too, baby girl. You're the stars in my sky, and I'm so proud of you. You hear me?"

Annie nodded, but didn't say anything. Eyes closed, she hugged Marcus and cried. After a long moment, he felt his handheld vibrating in his pocket. Retrieving it, he tapped the screen and stared at it for a moment. "Well, I'll be damned." *Speak of the devil.* The *Andromeda* had returned to New Austin, and Captain Blackwood had a contract offer for Marcus and his team from Zanzibar. The message also stated that Annie would be welcome back as a crewmember if she wanted to go.

"What is it?" Annie asked.

"You'll never guess who wants to take us out to dinner."

"What? Who? Let me see?" Before Marcus could say anything, Annie grabbed his handheld and looked at the message. "Oh my gosh! They're coming back! We can go back into space!"

Shit. He knew she'd want to go the instant she saw the offer. He put his hands on her shoulders. "Cool your jets there, kiddo. We're not going anywhere until we discuss this with your mother. We're not just a family, we're a team, okay?"

"I'll go talk to her right now!"

"Hey, just hold on a second, will you? Let me go talk to your mom. You stay put."

Marcus found his wife in her office, sipping tea, frowning at a pair of computer displays. "Everything alright, baby?"

"I'm going to have to close the Jerome Mountain site." She sounded resigned. "The sphalerite vein isn't yielding germanium anymore, just zinc. It's not worth the effort to extract."

"I'm sorry," he said. He stood behind his wife and massaged her shoulders. "When it rains, it pours, hey?"

"Mm, that feels nice," she said, closing her eyes. "But yeah, seems like we can't catch a break. We may have to look at student loans to keep Annie in school, and we need to be saving for David's education, and I don't think I'm going to be able to stay in business much longer."

"Is it that bad?"

"The market is brutal right now, babe," his wife replied, eyes still closed. "Big companies are conducting large-scale extraction of minerals outside of the terra-formed zone now. Us little guys can't compete with that."

"I know what would make you feel better. How about we get dressed up and go to dinner in Red River?"

Ellie looked over her shoulder at Marcus. "Tonight? In Red River?" There wasn't anywhere else to go out to eat, and the town of Red River was over an hour away.

"We were invited. Also, there's something else I need to talk to you about."

Ellie sat up and swiveled around in her chair. "Marcus, what's going on?"

"Captain Blackwood is back on New Austin. She invited us to dinner, her treat."

She raised an eyebrow, arms folded across her chest. "And?"

"And . . . well, she . . ."

"She wants you to go off on some contract again, doesn't she? What Godforsaken rock does she want to drag you off to this time?"

Marcus took a knee in front of his wife, gently placing his hands on her legs, so he wasn't looming over her. "Ithaca. I don't know all the details yet, but I guess she's transporting a VIP that wants a bodyguard."

"She came all the way here to hire a bodyguard?"

"Like I said, babe, I don't know all the details. But yeah, I'd be gone again, up to a year maybe."

Ellie looked down at her lap. She unfolded her arms and placed her hands on top of Marcus's. "What am I supposed to do, all alone out here, with David, while you're off-world again? Do you have any idea what it was like for me last time? Do you? I spent every night wondering if you'd ever come home, if *my daughter* would ever come home, and I had nobody, Marcus."

Ellie had friends, of course, but Winchester Ranch was far enough out of town that she rarely got to see them in person. Annie seemed content to keep in touch with her friends virtually, but Ellie was raised in a big house with a big family. It was harder on her. The main reason they had settled so far out into the outback was so that she should be closer to her mining claims, and that didn't seem to be a viable path going forward.

"That's why I'm talking to you about this, babe. I don't have to go. I can tell Captain Blackwood that I can't help her this time."

"Maybe *you* won't, but you know as well as I do how headstrong that girl is. Even if you turn down the offer, she's liable to drop out of school and go. She takes after you, you know." At seventeen standard years, Annie was old enough to legally do just that if she wanted to, and there wasn't anything Marcus could do about it.

"I wish I could say you're wrong. Hell, I wasn't even going to tell her about the job offer until I talked to you, but she snatched my handheld and read it before I could stop her."

Ellie shook her head. "I worry about her lack of social skills."

Marcus worried too, sometimes. Annie had been raised on Winchester Ranch, and rarely saw the few friends she had. Until enrolling in the Spaceflight Academy, all her schooling had been done remotely. She was better about it now than she had been when she was younger, but she still had a bad habit of ignoring interpersonal niceties, like not reading someone else's messages in front of them.

"You know...maybe it would be better for David if he grew up around other people, aside from us."

"What do you mean? You want me to drive him to Red River every day for daycare or something?"

"No, I mean, maybe we should enroll him in a real school."

"What are you talking about? What school?"

Everyone on New Austin had access to home-learning curricula. There were interactive courses of study suitable for everyone from small children learning to read to adults seeking a university-level education. The courses were completely automated and were available for free. Actual physical schools, however, where students sat down together and learned in a group environment, those were rare, and they were often expensive. There weren't any in Laredo Territory, that Marcus knew of. Usually you only found such schools around the city.

"I'm sure there's a good school in Aterrizaje we could send him to."

"Aterrizaje? Are you saying we should move?"

"Maybe? I don't know. Look, we bought this place so you could mine. If you're not going to mine anymore, what do we gain from living way out here? Even if they want to reinstate me in the Marshals, I'm not sure I want to go back, not after this bullshit. We have twenty hectares of property that we don't do anything with. Annie doesn't have a horse anymore. I'd like David to be able to go play with friends sometimes, you know? Maybe we should move to the city."

"Marcus, you hate the city. That's why we emigrated out here, remember?"

It wasn't exactly like that. The entire world of New Austin had less people than the city they'd lived in on Hayden. Even the worst part of Aterrizaje, the largest city on New Austin, was nothing like the sprawling urban blight of Hayden. That world had its usable landmass severely limited due to lingering effects of orbital bombardment during the war, and its population was huge. Most people lived in towering arcologies, hundreds of stories high, and crime was rampant. The only reason Marcus lived there in the first place was because of the huge Concordiat Defense Force base he'd been assigned to. He'd left as soon as he'd separated from the service.

"Hon, no place on this planet is like Hayden. And I'm not saying we need to live downtown or anything. I'm saying maybe we look at getting a place on the outside of town. A place where it's not too crowded, but we're not out in the boonies, either."

"There are jobs available for geologists with mining backgrounds, with the big mining companies. Most of them are based out of the city, though."

"See? Maybe this is for the best."

"Are you sure? Out of the blue like this, and now you want to sell our home and move to the city?"

Marcus smiled. "Babe, how long did it take us to decide to come to New Austin? About a minute, right? We've always trusted our instincts, and they haven't let us down yet."

"You don't have to do all this because you want to go off with the *Andromeda* for a year, Marcus. I'm going to be lonely without you no matter where we live."

"I know, hon. This isn't me trying to bargain or anything. You just got me thinking. Maybe it's time for a change. Honestly, we should think about doing this whether I take the job or not. I'll have better job opportunities in the city, too, and we'll be closer to Annie."

"Marcus, you know as well as I do that girl will go, unless you can talk Captain Blackwood into rescinding the offer, and if you do that, she'll resent you. She's almost grown. She wants to get out there and have more adventures. And you know what? I think you're bored, too. You've spent the last month and a half just moping around the house, depressed. I don't blame you! You've put in years at the Marshals Service. You risked your life and worked damn hard, and as soon as the chips are down, what do they do? They throw you right under the wheels and wash their hands of you. They fucked you and Wade both. It's not right." She was bitter about the whole thing. Marcus was too, but he tried to not let it show. Rumor mill said that he and Wade weren't going to be reinstated.

"Baby, I don't want to go and leave you here with David, not if it's going to be that hard on you. I don't want you to resent me. I don't want this to come between us. If you want me to stay, I'll stay."

Ellie held Marcus's face between her hands. "Marcus Winchester, I know what kind of man you are, okay? I'm not going to stand in your way, and I'm not going to act like you leaving for work is abandoning me. The money you made last time paid off all of our debt and put Annie into the most expensive school on the planet. You made sure your family was taken care of. You do what you need to do, and I'll support you no matter what. I love you, you big idiot."

"I may be an idiot, but I'm your idiot. I love you too." Marcus leaned in and kissed his wife.

"Besides," Ellie said, "I'm sure Annie is hell-bent on going now. If she goes, I want you to go, too, and look after our little girl."

Marcus nodded solemnly. "I will, baby. I promise, I'll bring her home safe."

Ellie nodded too, a single tear rolling down her cheek. "Well. I guess I should start getting ready. Where is she taking us for dinner?"

"The Cactus Flower Steakhouse." It was the nicest restaurant in Red River, and probably in all of Laredo Territory.

Ellie perked up. She rarely got an opportunity to dress up. "How about that short, black dress? I haven't worn it in forever."

"That is a great idea," Marcus said, smiling. His wife looked damned good in that dress.

"Okay then. I know you like that one. You need to get cleaned up yourself. Shave off that scruffy beard. I don't want you meeting visitors looking like a caveman."

Marcus happened to think he looked rugged with his beard. He sighed. "Yes, dear."

The scent of steaks grilling filled Marcus's nose as he, his wife, and his daughter entered the foyer of the Cactus Flower restaurant.

"Over here, boss!" It was Wade, who looked halfway presentable for once; he was even wearing a tie. Devree Starlighter was with him.

"Good to see you," Marcus said, shaking his partner's hand. "You too, Devree." He shook her hand too.

"Honey, you look amazing!" Ellie said, stepping forward to hug Devree. She'd gotten to know the beautiful sniper after she'd shacked up with Wade, and they had become friends.

Devree smiled. "It's good to see you guys! How's the little man?"

"Why don't you ask him?" Marcus said with a grin. "How are you, Wade?"

Wade sighed. "You know..."

"David is kind of fussy on long rides," Ellie replied.

"And between you and me, mommy needs a night off. We left him with the Garcias, our neighbors." Devree's extensive bionic implants and prosthetics, a result of a violent attempt on her life years before, meant that she couldn't have children of her own. She'd never told Marcus that, but she did tell Ellie, and the Winchesters had no secrets between them. She had simply fallen in love with little David, and often volunteered to watch him while Ellie was away at one of her mining sites.

A hostess appeared and greeted the newcomers before turning her attention to Wade. "Mr. Bishop, is everyone here now?"

"These were our last holdouts."

"Okay, great! If you'll all follow me, I'll take you back to the private dining lounge."

"We wanted to wait up front for you," Devree said. "Captain Blackwood is already in the back."

The Cactus Flower had rustic, cozy décor. The floor and furniture were made of real wood. The tables were all decorated with lit candles, and the overhead lighting was dimmed, making for an intimate feel. The well-to-do of Laredo Territory enjoyed their meals, paying the newcomers no mind. Against a back wall, a trio of robotic musicians in wide-brimmed hats played twangy music on acoustic guitars.

After leading them across the main dining room, the hostess waved a hand in front of a sensor, and a door quietly slid open. Inside was a large table, lit by candles. Captain Blackwood and a man Marcus didn't recognize were sitting at one end. A single-wheeled robot was quietly parked against the wall, behind the man. The captain stood as the hostess announced the new arrivals, crossing the room to shake Marcus's hand firmly.

"Marcus!" the captain said, smiling broadly. "It's so good to see you again. And you as well, Wade."

"Captain," Marcus said with a nod. Wade and Devree shook hands with her next. Ellie politely greeted her, if not as warmly.

Captain Blackwood's eye lit up when she saw Annie. "Oh, Annabelle, how have you been?"

Annie didn't say anything at first. She stepped forward and, instead of a handshake, surprised the visiting spacer by giving her a big hug. "I'm glad you came back, Skipper," she said quietly.

The captain put a hand on the girl's shoulder. "I'm glad I did too, dear. Your father told me you've spent most of the last year enrolled in the local Spaceflight Academy, is that right?"

"I'm doing really good," Annie said, proudly. "I got a lot of credits for the time I spent on the *Andromeda*. I basically got to skip the first-year stuff."

"Very good. I knew you'd do well. Did your father tell you why I invited you all here? It's not just a social visit."

"He said something about you needing to hire people again."

"It's true. Everyone," she said, addressing the entire group, "I do have another business proposal for you all. This is Zander Krycek, from Ithaca. But first, let's order some food, shall we?"

Sometime later, after the steaks had been eaten, Captain Blackwood got down to business over dessert and drinks. Marcus listened intently as her client told the group about the attempt on his life on Heinlein.

"So, this why I chose to come back to New Austin," Captain Blackwood said. "My client needs people he can trust, and so do I. I know of no one else I'd rather have on board for such a task."

"Not that I'm trying to talk you out of it," Wade said, "but why didn't you hire some guys on Heinlein before you left?"

"Yeah," Devree agreed, looking at the screen of her handheld. "New Austin is kind of out of the way, if you're traveling from Heinlein to Ithaca. This has to be adding time and expense to your trip."

"It is," the captain admitted. "But, after the attempt on his life, Mr. Krycek wanted off Heinlein immediately. He paid us a handsome bonus for making that happen. There simply wasn't time to hire and vet the kind of people we need for this job, and there remained the possibility that an infiltrator could get on board. That risk was unacceptable to my client, so here we are. I understand that this is all very sudden. I don't like trying to pull things together like this at the last minute. We're short several crewmembers, my ship didn't get a proper shakedown cruise after some major upgrades, and now I show up here, out of the blue, asking you to work for me again. None of this is ideal, but the situation is what it is."

"I'm in, provided Devree can go too," Wade said, without hesitation.

"Just like that?" the captain asked. "You don't want to see the contract terms first?"

"I'll go over them, sure, but you paid us well last time, and didn't bullshit us about the nature of the work. And hell, I've been on suspension from the Marshals for a while now. The way they're railroading me, I got no problem telling them to get scratched right about now."

Captain Blackwood looked confused. "Rail-roading?"

"Figure of speech," Devree explained. "Wade's suspension is entirely political. A drug bust blew the cover of some OSI bitch, and now his career is probably over, and it's not right." She'd had a couple glasses of wine. The sniper was not one to hold her tongue under normal circumstances, much less when she'd been drinking.

"I'm not supposed to talk about the details, baby," Wade said.

Devree scoffed and sipped her wine again. "What are they going to do, fire you twice? Fuck 'em."

"I, ah, assure you, this meeting is confidential," the captain said.

Marcus said nothing, but Ellie had plenty to say. "In that case, I don't mind telling you that Marcus was caught up in that same crock of political horse shit. This man has served the Marshals for years, since we immigrated to New Austin. He's risked his life over and over again. Do you know how many nights I've laid awake, waiting for *that* call? Do you know how long I've thought about how I'd break the news to Annie that her father isn't coming home? We *all* sacrificed for the Marshals, in our own way, and this is how they repay us. They're too spineless to stand up to the OSI, so they're willing to toss Marcus and Wade aside just to make this all go away."

She took another long drink from her wine glass. "When do you think you'll be leaving? Marcus needs time to get his affairs in order."

"Honey, I haven't agreed to anything," Marcus protested.

"Eleanor," the Captain said, "I want to thank you for being so understanding. This can't be easy."

She shrugged. "I knew what kind of man he was when I married him, Catherine. I'm not going to stand in the way of him doing what he wants to do, make him choose between work and his family. That's not fair to him. Last time, you told me you'd look after my family, and you did. And with you, at least I know his employer isn't going to leave him flapping in the breeze."

"We never leave a crewman behind," the captain assured her.

"Good. Because my daughter wants to go again, too. Don't you Annie?"

"Your message to Dad said there was still a place for me."

Captain Blackwood smiled. "There is, dear. I'm afraid Kimball has had to make do without your assistance, and I can tell you he misses having you around."

"I won't let you down, Skipper."

Zander Krycek spoke up next. Marcus could tell he was used to giving speeches. His demeanor was too calm, his words too smooth. "I'm afraid I don't know all of you. I too have a daughter, and I haven't seen her in many years. I know this isn't easy for you. I want you all to know, though, this isn't just some job. For me, it's not, anyway. The future of my home-world, millions of lives, hang in the balance. Even if I'm paying you all a lot of money, I'm grateful that you're willing to help. I'm short on allies these days."

"Mr. Krycek, we'll get you there safely," Marcus said. He reached across the table and the two men shook hands.

"We have much to do, and we're pressed for time," the captain said. "Marcus, I need you to try to recruit a few more people for your team. We'll be leaving as soon as possible."

"I don't know how many operators I'll be able to scrape together on such short notice, but I'll try."

"What about your former teammates? I would hire any of them again without hesitation."

"Ken Tanaka went home to Nippon. Last I heard from him, he was engaged to be married, so he's out."

"I still talk to Hondo from time to time," Wade interjected. "I'll message him, but I wouldn't count on him going. He's got seven kids now. You wanna look up Halifax?"

"I s'pose it wouldn't hurt. I haven't kept in touch, but I'll see if I can get a hold of him." The stout, red-bearded mercenary was cut from a different cloth than the military and law enforcement people Marcus had worked with last time, but he was reliable and trustworthy. "I've got a few friends I can ask, too, Captain. Send me a sample contract and I'll rustle the bushes for you."

"Uh, Skipper?" Annie asked. "I have this friend who might be interested, too. He's in my class at the Spaceflight Academy, but he's crazy smart. He'll learn quick. You said you were short people."

"I am. What is his area of study?"

"Engineering is his major. His minor is astrogation."

"Really?" Captain Blackwood rubbed her chin. "You don't say."

Marcus knew immediately whom Annie was talking about, and it made him chuckle. Poor Liam didn't know what he was in for.

❖   ❖   ❖

Liam looked surprised to see Annie. "Oh, hey! I was going to screen you. Everything okay? I'm sorry if I got too pushy last time we talked. I hope—"

Annie cut him off. "Shut up and listen for a minute. I'm leaving again."

"What? You're dropping out of school?"

"No! Well, yeah, I guess, but I'm going back into space!"

"Is this a joke?"

"No, it's not a joke. The *Andromeda* came back to New Austin, they're going on another mission, and they want to hire me again!"

"That's . . . wow. Congratulations, Annie." It wasn't unheard of for Academy students to get picked up as technicians-in-training, or for internships, by captains looking for talent. Many preferred to recruit their crewmembers young and train them on the job. Such candidates would often expect a smaller salary than an experienced, fully trained one. "When do you leave?"

"Soon. Couple of weeks, tops. There's more."

"What do you mean?"

"I mean I want you to come with me, Liam."

"What? That's . . . Annie, that's crazy! I'm only in my second year!"

"So? You'll learn on the job, same as I did. You learn all of the important stuff in the first two years anyway."

"That's . . . not at all true, Annie."

"It is if you're just going to be a crewman apprentice, dummy. Obviously, you're not going to be the astrogator or head systems tech. They'll train you, just like they trained me. You learn more from actually doing than from the sims."

"Are you sure about this?" Liam had always been the most straitlaced, rule-following kid in Annie's circle of friends. She had no doubt that his hesitation stemmed mostly from the fact that this amounted to *cutting class* and not finishing school.

"Liam, look. I know it's not the curriculum the Academy laid out." Students typically didn't actually get to go on a real training flight until the third year. "Just this once, can you not worry about what the plan is supposed to be, and do something spontaneous? You might not get a chance like this again. And you know, you get Academy credit for time served aboard a real ship."

Liam's eyes moved back and forth. Annie could tell he was doing the math in his head. "I . . . I need time to think about it."

"I understand. Think quickly, though. We ain't got a lot of time before we leave."

Log Entry 135
Mission 815-707-SSOC
Reconnaissance Ship 505

RS-505 has been planeted on Lone Star/New Austin for six local days. AI/CORE recommended landing at a remote, automated spaceport to avoid drawing attention to ourselves. The facility is on the very edge of the terraformed zone. There are no other ships present, and we have refilled our reaction mass stores. Colonial traffic control has been informed that we have landed for repairs, and will be on the surface until we are safe to leave again. This explanation was accepted without further query.

AI/CORE established a hard connection with the colonial network after we landed, and made contact with asset GLORIOUS BOTTLE. We have not been informed of any of the details, per SOP, but AI/CORE has confirmed that Zander Krycek is on Lone Star/New Austin. GLORIOUS BOTTLE has been ordered to terminate him at any cost.

We will be departing soon. If GLORIOUS BOTTLE fails, more direct measures may be necessary.

CHAPTER 17

New Austin
Aterrizaje
Equatorial Region
Several days later...

"The Rusty Rocket," Marcus said, looking up at the sign over the establishment's entrance. The sign played an animation of a dilapidated-looking ship struggling into space, belching black smoke behind it. "This must be the place."

"Classy," Wade commented, looking around. The Rusty Rocket was not in the nice part of New Austin's largest city, and seemed to cater primarily to jetcycle clubs. Cycling culture went back to the founding of the colony, another cultural import from Ancient Earth. A dozen of the two-wheeled, high-speed road machines were lined up outside. Most had enclosed cockpits, but a few left the riders exposed to the elements. They were powered by afterburning hydrogen turboshaft engines. Each had large air intakes on the front, and an exhaust nozzle at the rear. For extremely high speeds, up to four hundred kilometers per hour, the driver would engage the afterburner. Steering was aided by small airfoils, although doing a lot of steering at that kind of speed wasn't advisable.

"Didn't you used to have a bike, Marcus?"

"I did, back on Hayden. It made getting through traffic easier. It wasn't a jetcycle, though. These bikes make mine look like a scooter. Hell, some of them can probably top four hundred on a straight stretch, maybe faster."

"Jesus. That sounds terrifying."

Marcus looked at his partner. "You know, for a guy who used to disarm bombs for a living, you sure are a wet blanket sometimes."

Wade shrugged. "I took enough risks as part of my job that I didn't see the need to take them in my spare time, too. You know how many of these guys get killed every year? Upwards of three hundred KPH, you hit a rock on the road, or a coyote, or an armadillo, and you're going to go flying."

"You're not wrong. The only reason they aren't involved in a lot of accidents is they do most of their riding out in the outback."

New Austin's terraformed zone was vast, with very low population density outside of the towns and cities. Infrastructure, including a network of highways, was built at the founding of the colony, during the Second Interstellar War. As part of the Concordiat Contingency Colonization Initiative, the population of the frontier world was expected to expand rapidly as refugees from beleaguered worlds were resettled there.

The war ended before any displaced populations were settled on New Austin. The few cities were spread out, with the road network stretching from the coast of the Southern Ocean to the edges of the terraformed zone, and beyond. There were many remote areas where motoring enthusiasts could see what their machines could do, without worrying about running into a lot of traffic.

"Well, let's go see if Halifax is here," Marcus said, heading for the door. The interior of the club was dark. Music thumped heavily over the sound system, and screens mounted all over showed different sporting events. There was no one sitting at the bar, but groups of riders clustered around several tables. A pair of server robots rolled back and forth, taking food and drink orders to patrons.

"What the hell are they doing?" Wade asked, indicating two men at a table, hitting their arms with injector guns.

"A lot of these guys use reflex boosters to give them an edge at very high speeds. You'll see them shooting up before a ride. Hell, some have 'em rigged so they're steadily injected *as* they ride. You juice too much, and you come down real hard. You get the shakes, you get sick, sometimes you rage out."

"That doesn't seem like a good idea."

"Will you relax?" Marcus said, his voice hushed. "We're not marshals anymore. Everyone in here is already looking at us sideways. Stop acting like a cop."

According to the publicly available records, Benjamin Halifax was the owner of the Rusty Rocket. Marcus had tried several methods of getting ahold of his former teammate, to no avail. Going to his place unannounced was the last resort.

"What can I get you, gentle-men?" The robot bartender was a humanoid torso, with two arms and a cluster of lenses on its head. It moved up and down the bar on a gantry arm coming down from the ceiling. "Frontier Brew is half off during happy hour."

Marcus wasn't interested in a glass of horse piss like Frontier Brew. "I need to speak with the owner. Is he here?"

"I'm sorry. I don't understand the question. Would you like to see a menu?"

"No, I don't want to see a menu. I want to speak to the owner, Benjamin Halifax!"

The robot stared at Marcus, motionlessly, for a few moments. "I under-stand. Please wait." Following its track, it zipped off to the right and disappeared through a doorway.

"I hate robots," Wade said.

"Number one, that's prejudiced," Marcus said. "Number two, you're full of shit. All because you got rid of your love bot when Devree moved in, doesn't mean you get to act like a robo-phobe."

Wade's face flushed, just a little. "I told you I won that stupid thing in a raffle. I never used it. I pawned it as soon as we got back from Zanzibar."

"You shouldn't tease your friend for being a closeted robosexual," a woman said, appearing from the doorway behind the bar. The bartender followed her closely, sliding on its gantry track, as she walked over to Marcus and Wade. "Now who the hell are you two, and what do you want? You boys law?"

"No, we ain't law. My name is Marcus Winchester, and I'm looking for Benjamin Halifax."

"Supposedly he's the owner of this place," Wade added.

"I know him," the woman said. She was tall and

intense, with long black hair and a muscular build. Her arms, chest, and neck, all the skin exposed by her tank top, were covered in intricate and colorful tattoos. She leaned onto the bar, showing off her ample cleavage, but also the butt of the pistol on her hip. "What do you want with him?"

"We're not here to cause trouble," Wade answered.

"Look, this is private. Would you tell him Marcus Winchester is here, please?"

"Who says he's here? Maybe I don't know where he is."

"Seriously? It's going to be like that? We just want to talk to him."

"Lorelei, stop giving those boys a hard time," a rough, accented voice said. Benjamin Halifax appeared from the room behind the bar, with a mischievous gleam in his eye. His red beard was trimmed and braided, but the strip of hair on top of his otherwise-shaved head had grown taller. "Marcus Winchester, you son of a bitch." Grinning, he roughly shook Marcus's hand, then Wade's. "How the hell are you, boys? What brings you to my humble establishment?"

Neither Marcus nor Wade had heard from Halifax since they landed back on New Austin a year before. He hadn't changed much, and still seemed to have that entrepreneurial spirit. That was a good sign. "We came down here to discuss a little business venture with you."

"Let me guess, you're here to recruit me for another off-world adventure," he said, laughing. Lorelei glared at him.

Marcus and Wade looked at each other, then back at Halifax. "Actually..."

"Well ain't that a hell of a thing," Halifax said, a toothy grin splitting his face. "Come on back to my office and tell me what's going on."

Halifax smoked a cigar while he listened to what his visitors had to say. Lorelei stood in the corner of the office, arms folded, listening quietly. An automatic flechette gun was propped up behind her, and the walls were decorated with memorabilia from Halifax's adventures. On one shelf, against the far wall, were jars of dirt with labels on them. Some of them were unfamiliar, but others Marcus recognized, like New Austin, Opal, Zanzibar, Llewellyn-A.

"I take some from every world I've set foot on," he said, offering Lorelei, Marcus, and Wade a stogie. Marcus enjoyed a cigar on rare occasions (just never at home, since Ellie hated the smell), and took one, but Wade declined.

"You sure, lad?" Halifax asked. "It'll put hair on your chest."

"I'm good, thanks."

"Your loss," Marcus said, lighting his cigar. "Damn, that's good."

"I get these imported from Nuevo Santiago. They're pricey, but they're not turned out by the millions. They're hand rolled on the thighs of sultry women, if you believe the marketing material."

Wade cocked an eyebrow. "So, they taste like tobacco and sweat? Gross."

"You'll have to excuse him," Marcus said. "He just can't appreciate the finer things in life. That's why he prefers robots to real women."

"Ha!" Halifax blew a ring of smoke as he laughed.

Wade folded his arms across his chest. "You know..."

Marcus chuckled. "Anyway, that's the long and short of it. It's a last-minute, short-notice contract, but I don't think we'll be gone for as long as last time. I guess Captain Blackwood came here, specifically, to see if she could rehire all of us, but Ken is off-world and Hondo said no."

"His wife said no," Wade corrected.

"In either case he's not going."

Halifax puffed his cigar. "And Markgraff, God rest his soul, never made it home. What about the sniper lass, Devree?"

"She's going," Wade said.

"Please tell me you bedded that woman," Halifax said with a grin. "She was practically throwing herself at you."

"We moved in together a while back."

"Ha! Well done, lad, well done. You boys are Colonial Marshals, right? They inclined to let you take another long leave of absence?"

"Not . . . really an issue anymore," Wade said.

Marcus nodded. "It's a long story. Short version is, Wade and me both tendered our resignations. We're both just regular folk now. What about you? Seems you've been doing all right for yourself."

"Aye. Lady Blackwood paid us a handsome sum last go-round, didn't she? This place was a mess when I bought it, but I saw potential. Fixed her up, did a lot of the work myself. Now all the motorcycle clubs know me, and business is good."

"We're considering opening a second location," Lorelei said.

"We are," Halifax agreed. "It hasn't been without problems, mind you, but the future looks good."

"Your friend back there seemed mighty suspicious when we came in. You in some kind of trouble?"

The red-haired mercenary sighed, and mashed the butt of his cigar into an ashtray. "You know some of the jetcycle crowd ends up on the wrong side of the law. I never got involved in any of that, mind you. I run a legitimate business here. But some of my customers . . . well, let's just say they give the rest of my customers a bad name. Some of them run stolen property, things like that. But this one group? They call themselves the Devil's Due."

"I've heard of them," Marcus said, trying to remember.

"Wasn't there a report of a guy from some jetcycle club getting caught transporting Red Eye?" Wade asked.

"You're right, there was. I'm sure it was the Devil's Due guys, too. They wear the red gear, right? I remember now. They needed an aircraft to catch him."

"Aye. A couple of them brought some of that shit into my place. They were dropping it into their eyes, mixing it with reflex boosters. Two of them raged out and got into a brawl, so I told them to get out. They turned on me and ended up looking down the barrel of a gun, so they left."

"But they came back."

Halifax nodded. "The very next day. They came into *my* place, waving guns around like the sorry sons of whores they are. I shot one of them in the gut."

Lorelei reached behind her and patted the heavy, automatic flechette gun. "And I brought out Mavis here. Those skags decided they had somewhere else to be, and drug their friend right back out the door."

"I don't suppose you filed a police report?"

"Nah. Nobody died, you know?"

"Cops are bad for business," Lorelei said.

"You still having a problem with these guys?"

"The situation is . . . not ideal. I need to be careful when I go out. They smashed my ride up, so now I have to leave it locked in my garage. I don't get out much anymore. They won't likely try anything in the city, but out on the open road?"

"Way out in the outback, no witnesses, hell, it might be hours before anyone even finds you."

"Aye. So, I've become something of a homebody."

"Sounds like the perfect time for a vacation to me," Wade said.

Marcus agreed. "We'll be off-world for probably a year. Maybe things will blow over by then."

"Or maybe those assholes will land themselves in prison, where they belong," Wade interjected. "Between you and me, the Marshals are really going after Red Eye pushers right now. If you got ID on these guys, even security camera footage, I can send it to a friend on the down-low. Nobody suspects you of talking to the cops, and while you're gone, they end up in Purgatory Correctional Facility."

Halifax stroked his beard. "And you're sure your Marshal friends won't try to shut down my place?"

"Look, Wade and me both worked for the Marshals for years. Never once, in all that time, did we do a raid on a bar, and we weren't out on the highways hassling jetcyclers, either. Hell, our patrol vehicles couldn't catch 'em if we wanted to. Red Eye, though? That's different. That shit is poison. Any cooperation would be appreciated, and you didn't do anything wrong anyway."

"I'll be calling our lawyer anyway, thank you," Lorelei said, flatly.

"Fair enough. What do you say, Halifax? You in?"

He picked up a tablet and looked at the contract offer again. "It's tempting, Marcus, but I don't think so. I can't just leave my place for a year. Lorelei needs me here."

"Um, are you two, you know . . . ?"

"We fuck, yes," Lorelei answered, stepping forward. She put her hand on Halifax's shoulder. He looked up at her. "But don't kid yourself, Ben. I can run this place without you just fine."

"Truth be told, she handles most of the accounting," Halifax said, sheepishly.

"And I ain't scared of those Devil's Due shit-suckers, either. Mavis and me will handle them if they come back, and my brother is back in town. He's ex-Espatier Corps. I'll bring him on as security, and maybe some buddies of his. I'll be fine."

"Are you sure?" Marcus asked. "Look, I want Halifax on my team, but it's a hell of a thing, being gone for that long. I'm leaving my wife and my baby behind."

Lorelei's hard expression softened, just a little. "Ben, you go do what you gotta do. That day you gutshot that skag, I ain't never seen you that happy. I know you're bored. Go. Bring us back a bunch of money so we can expand, and so you can buy me a new house."

Halifax put his hand on top of Lorelei's. "Marcus, I don't mind tellin' you, I've bedded a lot of women in my day. Lost count. Hundreds, maybe."

Lorelei rolled her eyes.

"You may have mentioned that," Marcus said, with a lurid grin. Halifax had never been shy about boasting of his sexual conquests, often in detail.

"It's all true. I wasn't tellin' tales. But this woman? She's the best thing that's ever happened to me. She was what I was missing."

"It must be love," Wade mused, "for you to give up the threesomes."

Halifax grinned, devilishly, patting his girlfriend's hand. "I've given up nothing, lad. She brings a sexy little friend every now and again. Sometimes two."

Wade frowned. Halifax laughed, and picked up the tablet. He touched his thumb to the signature block at the bottom of the document. "I'm in. When do we leave?"

Oberth Hall was one of several large dormitories on the main campus of the Spaceflight Academy. The school was mostly deserted during its annual summer break, aside from a few maintenance personnel, a fleet of maintenance robots, and a few year-round holdouts like Liam.

"Hi, Annie," he said, anxiously, as he opened his door for her. The dorm rooms were Spartan: sixteen square meters of cold tile floor, eggshell-colored walls, and you had to share the bathroom with your neighbor. Each room came equipped with a bed, desk, dresser, and a chair. Students were free to decorate within certain guidelines, but Liam's room was barren. He'd been packing. All that remained of his belongings was stuffed into a pair of duffel bags.

"Is that all you're bringing?" Annie asked.

"Yes. I didn't have much else. I sold the stuff I wouldn't need. They . . . they said there was a fifty-kilogram weight limit for personal gear. I don't think I'm over, but I haven't weighed them."

Annie smiled and tried to be reassuring. She remembered how nervous . . . well, *terrified* is more like it . . . she was on her first day aboard the *Andromeda*. At least Liam had someone he knew to show him the ropes; Annie had had her father aboard, of course, but he had been as much a stranger on the ship as she was. Captain Blackwood told her that she'd be the senior-junior-crewman this time around, and that she'd be in charge of helping Liam get up to speed. "It'll be fine. I work for the cargomaster. It won't be a problem."

"Okay, good. I don't, you know, want them to think I'm a screw-up."

"You're not a screw-up!" Annie said, more forcefully than she'd intended. Her friend was quiet, and shy, and he had a tendency to run himself down. It made her angry, because he habitually underestimated himself. "Hellfire, Liam, you're at the top of our class. You'll do great. Isn't this what you've been working for this whole time?"

"It is! It is. I just, you know, thought I'd have more time to get ready. Two more whole years." His normally dusky complexion was looking a few shades paler.

Annie put a hand on her friend's shoulder. "Listen to me. I know you're nervous. I was too, my first day. First month, really, before I settled into the routine. It's okay to be nervous. You're leaving home. You're leaving New Austin! This is a huge thing, right?"

He nodded, haltingly. "I've dreamed of this since I was little. I'd sneak out past bedtime and climb up on the roof of the crèche so I could watch ships come and go from the spaceport. There's too much light pollution in the city to see the stars very well, but I could usually make out the Izanami Nebula. My whole life, all I've wanted to do was leave this planet. I never had much here. The Relief Society caretakers were all nice, but I never had a family. I imagined that being part of a crew is kind of like having a family. It was all I wanted for so long, and now that I have the chance, I'm ... I'm scared."

"I was too. I still kinda am. We got into a couple of battles on our trip to Zanzibar. We got into a fight with a Combine light cruiser, and the ship was almost overrun on the ground. We ... we were all firing out of the cargo bay."

Liam's eyes went wide. "Firing? You mean, shooting? Like shooting guns at people?"

Annie nodded slowly. "A laser, actually, but yeah. It was scary. We were locked into the landing tower and they wouldn't let us leave. My dad and his team had to go into the control room and release us manually. Then the cruiser was waiting for us in orbit. That's when the XO ... Mr. von Spandau, I mean, was killed. But we won. We beat a light cruiser with an old patrol ship." She felt a twinge of pride in her chest. She hadn't been able to tell very many people this story.

Liam, for his part, went a little paler. "Holy shit," he said, swearing for the first time that Annie could ever recall. "Why ... why didn't you tell us this?"

"I told you: I *couldn't*. I signed a nondisclosure agreement. The Combine will probably still attack the *Andromeda* on sight, and ... well, it's complicated. But you're part of the crew now, so I can tell you."

Liam stood up just a little straighter at that.

"You ready? I've got an autotaxi waiting for us. This is your last chance to change your mind, Liam. You step onto the ship and sign yourself in, you're in for the duration. I want you to be sure."

"What? Seriously? You spent the last few days talking me into going, and now you ask me if I'm *sure*?"

Annie shot her friend a lopsided smile. "I know this will be a good thing for you, and I knew your first reaction would be to stay no. I wanted to convince you that you could do it, but it's still your choice. Don't do this for me. Do it for *you*. But you know, you'll have some stories to tell when we come back."

He took a long look back at his dorm room, and through the window, at the campus grounds beyond. "Are you sure that we *will* come back?"

Annie shook her head, slowly. "I can't promise you that. But, you know, we probably will."

Liam took a deep breath, and grunted as he picked up his two heavy bags. "Let's get going."

Nickson Armitage sipped his coffee as he looked down at his tablet. The street-side café was cheery and bright, and not terribly busy. It was quiet enough to have a conversation without being so quiet that all the other patrons could also hear.

"Your academic record is impressive," Nickson said, without looking up at the young man sitting across from him. "You've gotten high marks in all of your classes, no disciplinary problems, and a letter of recommendation from the dean. How old are you, anyway? In standard years, I mean."

"Uh . . . ," he said, obviously trying to do the math in his head. The standard Earth year was still used as an almost universal unit of timekeeping, as every colonized world had its own orbital and rotational periods. New Austin's day was twenty-seven hours and fifteen minutes long, and it took 1.2 standard years for it to make its way around the Type G main-sequence yellow star the locals called Lone Star. "Twenty-two, I think? Somewhere in there."

Indira Nair was not impressed. Nickson had long since learned that she rarely was. "Have you ever been in space before?"

"Uh, no," the prospect said, fidgeting a little. His name was Enzo Zeks, and he was a student at New Austin's premier (and only) college of engineering. "I was born here. My great-grandparents immigrated here during the war."

"Interesting," Nickson said. The kid spoke with the slow drawl common to New Austin natives. "They were among the first wave of settlers then, right?"

"They were. I grew up hearing stories of what this place was like when they first got here, just a remote outpost far from anywhere. They helped build this colony. My great-grandmother was an engineer for the Contingency Colonial Authority. My great-grandfather was a farmer. They put down roots here, and...um... I wasn't trying to make a farm pun."

"I don't like puns," the hard-nosed engineer said, looking coldly at the young man. "You come from a family of groundhogs, you've never been to space, and now you want to be the assistant engineer on my ship? Why?"

Enzo fidgeted a little more. Nickson tried to sound less abrasive. "What Chief Engineer Nair means is, why do you think you'd make a good fit for the position? You've done well in school, but have you ever worked on a magneto-inertial fusion rocket before?"

"Yes. We have a couple working fusion engines in the offsite annex, out in the desert. It took three years on a waiting list, but I got a slot in that course."

"You waited three years to learn how to work on ship engines? You must want to do this pretty badly."

"I do, but I need an apprenticeship on an actual ship to get my AEG certification."

The certification that Enzo was talking about, from the Astronautical Engineering Guild, would be accepted across the entirety of Concordiat space, and on many independent colonies as well. With it, a qualified engineer could find work almost anywhere in inhabited space, and often would have his choice of ships.

Indira softened her tone, just a tiny bit. She was herself a member of the Guild. "That is a laudable goal. But most prospects take their apprenticeship cruise on a free trader or corporate merchantman. You are aware that the *Andromeda* is a privateer, and that we may be going into harm's way, correct?"

"Yes, ma'am," he replied, without a moment's hesitation. "The job listing made that clear."

Nickson liked that answer. He seemed confident about that part, at least. "Eager for a life of adventure as a swashbuckling corsair?"

"It will definitely be more interesting than a hitch on a corporate bulk freighter. I . . . look, can I be honest, sir?"

"Speak your mind."

"I grew up on a farm. I learned how to turn a wrench when I was a toddler, and cut my teeth as a kid working on farm equipment. My dad said that I'm gifted, and he really wanted me to pursue it. School costs a lot of money, and my family isn't rich. I got a scholarship that helps, but...I probably wouldn't have been able to go, if not for my dad's life insurance money."

"I see. How long since he passed?"

"Six local years. The way I see it, I owe it to him to do the best I can. Those bulk freighters? If somebody could make a computer that wasn't screwed up by transit shock, they'd probably be fully automated. Everything is routine. Each procedure for each contingency is written into company policy, and half the time, the assistant engineers just supervise maintenance robots or technicians."

Nickson knew how the kid felt. He hadn't wanted to work on a freighter, either, and for the same reason. "You think it would be dull."

"I guess," Enzo admitted. "I don't think I'd get the best opportunities to learn. Problem solving isn't really problem solving when all you do is whatever the manual says."

"Those manuals exist for a reason," Indira interjected. "You can't outsmart your reactor or your engine. You have to know them, their capabilities and limitations."

"I know, ma'am, but...I guess what I'm saying is, I want hands-on experience. I want to actually work on the engine myself, not sit back with a checklist and watch a robot do it. Even if that wasn't true... well, not a lot of ships come through here. There's a waiting list for apprenticeship opportunities, too."

The engineer tried very hard not to show it, but Nickson was good at reading people: She liked Enzo's answer. She was looking for an assistant who wasn't afraid to get his hands dirty, and wanted to learn the ship inside and out. She didn't let her façade crack for very long, though. "You seem bright enough, and enthusiastic, but we were looking for someone with more experience."

Enzo didn't let that faze him. "I understand, ma'am, but you're leaving in, what, five days?"

Nickson chuckled. He couldn't help it; the kid was right. There hadn't been much interest in the assistant engineer position. A privateer ship with a home port outside of Concordiat space, going on a mission with few disclosed details, and no specified return date, leaving on short notice, probably seemed questionable to more experienced engineers. "You got us there, kid. Indira?"

She frowned. "I'm not happy with this arrangement, but . . . I will need at least a semicompetent assistant."

"He seems semicompetent to me," Nickson said, gesturing to Enzo.

"Fine," she said, as if an annoying child was bothering her for a new toy. "I hope you're a fast learner, Mr. . . . Zeks, was it?"

"Thank you, ma'am!" Enzo said, excitedly. "You won't regret this."

"Maybe not, but you might," Nickson answered, grinning. "You get dropsick, kid?"

"I . . . I don't know, sir. I've never been in freefall before."

"Only one way to find out: The job is yours. I'll send you a packing list of what you ought to bring, along with reporting instructions. You need to be on board first thing tomorrow morning, no later than zero six hundred hours local. You'll officially sign onto the crew, meet the captain, get assigned a bunk, get your equipment issued, and we'll spend the rest of the day doing orientation. We've got another couple new crewman, so you won't be the only one. We lift off day after tomorrow."

Enzo was beaming now. "I'll be there! So, uh... where are we going?"

Personal protective detail work was not something Marcus had done a lot of over the years, though he had had training on it while in special operations. Instead of being loaded down with combat gear, he wore a suit jacket and slacks, with his 10mm pistol concealed. Wade was similarly dressed, and the two flanked Zander Krycek as he entered a corporate building in downtown Aterrizaje. They'd left his robot behind, even though it seemed like a good asset in a fight. The steward bot could navigate stairs, but not very quickly.

Devree Starlighter was trailing behind them, keeping their entrance and exit route under surveillance. Halifax was in the building's underground parking garage, staying with their rented, armored ground car.

Mr. Krycek had just emerged from a private conference room on the building's fortieth floor, and they were making their way back down to the parking garage. The New Austin headquarters of the Zoltan Corporation, an infamous deep-space resource extraction firm, seemed quite secure, but Marcus wasn't taking any chances. He had a throat microphone, and used it to quietly speak into his radio. "Halifax, check in."

"Quiet down here," Halifax said. "Nothing out of the ordinary."

"Good. Devree?"

"Your six is clear."

"Good. We're headed to the elevator. It'll be, uh, number six."

"Copy," Devree responded. "I'm headed down the stairs. I'll see you in the garage."

Mr. Krycek seemed to be in a good mood. His meeting had lasted almost two hours. "I think that was productive," he said, as the lift doors closed, and the three of them were the only ones in the elevator. "Zoltan put up a substantial investment in exchange for first-survey, first-dig rights in several places on Ithaca. We will need the money when the time comes." The ruthless interplanetary corporation had a reputation for not being afraid to get its hands dirty, and often found itself under investigation from Concordiat trade regulators.

"To be honest, sir, I'm surprised you found anyone willing to invest. Financing a coup has to be a risky endeavor."

"It is, but I assure you it's a time-honored tradition. In fact, I could've gotten substantially more money from Zoltan in exchange for exclusive mining rights worldwide, but I wasn't about to sell my entire homeworld to them. Their reputation, shall we say, precedes them."

"Any changes in the itinerary?" Marcus asked, as the lift came to a stop in the subterranean parking garage.

"No, we're right on schedule. I'm meeting a Mr. David Agnew for lunch at the Coeur des étoiles restaurant, and then we'll be returning to the ship."

Wade stepped out of the lift, scanning the parking garage before proceeding. Marcus and Zander Krycek followed. "We're in the garage," Marcus said, into his radio. Devree and Halifax acknowledged. He turned his attention back to his client. "Another investor, I take it?"

"Yes. He's an arms dealer."

"To be honest, I didn't know there were any real arms dealers on New Austin." As they approached the large, sleek limousine with one-way windows, the door to the VIP cabin quietly slid open.

"I suspect they try to keep a low profile," Mr. Krycek said. The door closed, and he was in the car.

"I'm in the garage," Devree said.

"I'll meet you at the car," Wade said, as Marcus climbed into the passenger's seat of the limo. They had two rental vehicles, the limo and a much more nondescript passenger van. "We'll be behind you."

The Coeur des étoiles restaurant was one of those places where the rich and powerful liked to eat. A single meal could cost hundreds of credits, and one could spot the movers and shakers of New Austin high society there on any given day. It was the kind of restaurant that, if not for his working on a protective detail, Marcus likely never would have set foot in. The food didn't look that good.

Annoyingly, this David Agnew wasn't there. They waited for almost an hour, standing watch while Zander Krycek sampled the overpriced appetizers, and other patrons (some with their own bodyguards) came and went. They were getting ready to leave when he received a message on his handheld.

"Ah, it's from Mr. Agnew," he said, tapping the screen.

"What's it say?"

"It's just a text message. He says he won't be able

to make it, and apologizes. Damn it all. What a waste of my time. Well, let's get out of here then, shall we?"

"We should, but..." Marcus trailed off as he cautiously scanned the restaurant, looking for anything out of the ordinary.

Wade was doing the same. "Something wrong?"

"I don't know. Just a bad feeling."

"Bad feeling?" Mr. Krycek asked, looking around. Marcus knew his history. There had been attempts on his life before. He was no fool. "The bill is paid. Let's go."

Marcus spoke into his microphone. "Head's up, we're moving him. We're going out the back."

"What?" Halifax asked. "What's wrong?"

"Contact was a no-show, just got a bad feeling. We're moving him now. Bring the car around to the service entrance."

"Aye. Moving."

Marcus walked close to his protectee, leading him toward the rear of the restaurant. Devree, who had been near the front entrance, quietly slipped out the front door. "The front looks clear," she said.

"Keep moving," Marcus ordered. "Get to your vehicle. All three of us will pile in the limo."

"Roger!"

"Excuse me, sir," a man in a nice dinner jacket said. He was the host. He went to put a hand on Mr. Krycek's shoulder.

Marcus was in between them in a flash. "Stop," he ordered. "Stand back. We're leaving."

"Sir, you cannot go this way! This way is for staff only!"

"I'm getting my client out of here. Now get out of my way." Marcus pushed the outraged host aside

and led his protectee down a corridor at the back of
the restaurant. Dodging utility robots, he followed the
hall until it ended at a pair of double doors. "Halifax,
we're at the back entrance. Are you in position?"

"Affirmative," the red-haired mercenary answered.
"It looks clear."

"Roger that. We're coming out." Slamming the door
open, Marcus assessed the scene as best he could
in the seconds he had. The big black limo was only
about ten meters away, with the door to the passenger
compartment open. Halifax had backed it down the
alley for a quick egress. The alley was narrow, hot, and
shady, with little direct sunlight pouring down from
above. There was no sign of movement or people.
He stepped out, first, hand under his jacket on the
butt of his gun. As he got close to the limo, he put a
hand on Zander Krycek's shoulder and went to push
him in. That's when Wade spoke up.

"Hey, what is—*contact rear!*"

Marcus whirled around, gun drawn. Wade had his
revolver drawn but, in a blur, something struck him
and sent him flying to the street. Marcus shoved his
pistol forward in his hands, aligning his sights on the
distorted blur. *Thermoptic camo!* He opened fire. Three
shots rang out, but the bullets struck the back wall of
the restaurant. The camouflaged figure moved so fast
the eye could barely track it, light footsteps tapping
the pavement as it ran. It circled around the car to
where Marcus lost sight of it. "He's coming around!"
He shoved Zander. "Get in the car!"

Wade was back on his feet, his big revolver up and
ready. *There!* Marcus caught the figure, shimmering in
the light, for a split second. He popped off two more

shots, but the figure disappeared upward in a blur. Wade fired, upward, at almost a sixty-degree angle. With an agonizing screech, the distorted blob landed on top of the armored limousine with a heavy *thump*. The damned thing was still moving! Before Wade could reacquire the target, it was scrambling toward the still-open door.

BLAM BLAM BLAM BLAM! Zander Krycek cringed in the seat as Marcus fired at the cloaked attacker on the roof of the limo. It shrieked again, its thermoptic camouflage flickering, and fell off the roof of the car, landing on the far side.

"What's going on?" Devree asked, over the radio, concern in her voice. "I'm coming around!"

"Go!" Marcus shouted, slapping the car's window. The vehicle's quiet hydrogen engine revved, its rear wheels squealing on the ceramicrete, as Halifax sped down the alley.

Marcus didn't have time to answer Devree. As the limo drove away, his gun was pointed to where the unseen attacker had to be. A shimmering, distorted blob flew upward into the air. "Look out!" Wade shouted, but it was too late. *WHAM!* The assailant hit Marcus so hard he saw stars. The next thing he knew, he was on his back, a heavy weight pinning him down. A gaunt figure with a ghastly grin was on top of him, cackling shrilly, long, stringy hair hanging from its head. It had flung its thermoptic cloak upward as a distraction. A long blade was jutting from its cybernetic hand, coming from under the palm, and the assassin tried to plunge it into Marcus's face.

All of his strength was barely enough to hold the cyborg at bay. Its eyes, a pair of gleaming red lenses, were cold and dead, but a psychotic smile split its face.

Its teeth, too, were metallic, and its mouth seemed wider than it should have been. Twisting his right hand free, Marcus stuck the muzzle of his pistol into the cyborg's side and rocked the trigger over and over again. The assassin flinched, but didn't relent, and an instant later ripped the gun out of Marcus's hand, nearly taking his finger with it. The blade was only centimeters from his face, now. The machine person kept laughing maniacally.

"Hey!"

Marcus and the assassin looked over at the same time, to see Wade, revolver leveled at them. *BOOM!* The cyborg's head snapped back as the explosive bullet hit it square in the right eye, blowing a chunk off its head.

SCREEEEEEEE! The assassin's death-rattle was almost deafening. It jumped to its feet, staggering backward, right hand ineffectually trying to cover the wound. Bright red blood poured down its face.

BOOM! Wade fired again. This round hit the cyborg dead in the chest. It screeched again and fell over backward.

"Marcus!" Wade ran to his partner, gun still pointed at the cyborg assassin. "You okay?"

Marcus coughed. His arms were shaking badly. He couldn't talk, so he just nodded. Wade grabbed him by the arm and helped him up.

"Jesus Christ. What *is it* with you and trying to fight cyborgs?"

The downed assailant was still twitching as the two mercenaries stood over it, guns in hand. It was so heavily augmented that it was barely human. Marcus couldn't tell if it had been a man or a woman. Its angular, androgynous face was covered in blood and other fluids.

Its long black hair was splayed out on the pavement, framing its face like a grim flower. The mouth had to be a quarter again wider than that of an average person, and its face was frozen in an agonizing, hideous smile.

"What the *fuck*?" Wade asked, not looking at Marcus.

Marcus, for his part, could only shake his head. He then spoke into his radio. "Halifax, this is Marcus, you copy?"

"I hear you, lad. Our package is safe and sound. Are you all right?"

"We're alive. Get him back to the ship. Will brief you later."

"Marcus?"

Both men wheeled around, guns pointing up the alley, at the sound of an approaching vehicle, but they immediately recognized the white passenger van. It was Devree. The vehicle screeched to a halt and she jumped out, carbine in her hands.

"What the hell happened?"

Marcus and Wade lowered their guns, and pointed at the body behind them. "This thing tried to kill us. Damn near succeeded."

"It was wearing a thermoptic camo cloak," Wade added. "It tossed it somewhere. Look for a lump of bent light."

Devree cautiously approached the fallen cyborg, which had finally stopped twitching. "What in the holy hell is that? I've never seen such heavy augmentation." That was quite a statement, coming from someone who was half machine herself.

"It was waiting for us back here, using active camo. It was this close to killing Krycek."

"Found it!" Wade said. Marcus and Devree looked

up at him. He was holding, in his hand, a shimmering blob of distorted light. "Should we take it?"

"No, leave it for the cops," Marcus said. "This is all evidence. Devree, get some pictures and videos real quick, before the police get here. We're in for a long day." Approaching sirens could be heard in the distance.

"Marcus?" Devree was standing over the cyborg's body, clutching her handheld. She started to back away as the assassin's armor-plated torso started to hiss and smoke.

Wade ran to her and grabbed her arm. "Devree get back!" He pulled her away just as the cyborg's chest started to glow, then split open, spewing sparks and white-hot flame upward. "Don't breathe in the smoke! It could be toxic!"

The three mercenaries stood back and watched, with Devree recording, as the fire spread to the cyborg's head and limbs. It was a fascinatingly morbid scene as the flames first erupted from the face and nose. Then the whole face collapsed into the fire. The alley stunk of burnt flesh and metal.

"Jesus Christ," Wade said, shielding his eyes from the flame. It was as bright as a plasma torch.

"All right, Devree, that's enough. Get out of here. I'll see you back at the ship."

"Good luck," she said to Marcus. "Be careful," she said to Wade, squeezing his hand. She got back into the van and drove away.

As the corpse continued to burn, a quadcopter drone, flashing red and blue lights, appeared from over the roof of the restaurant and descended into the alley. "This is the Aterrizaje Police," a synthesized voice announced over a loudspeaker. "You are under surveillance. Please remain where you are. Officers are responding." It descended until it was only a couple meters above the street, its cameras scanning the entire scene. It focused on the dead cyborg assassin for a few seconds, then turned to Marcus. "Do you need medical assistance, citizen?" it asked.

Marcus was hurt, but it wasn't bad. "Uh, no, I'm fine."

"Please give a statement."

"Not without my attorney present."

The drone beeped in acknowledgement, and continued patrolling the area.

Marcus turned back to Wade. "Notify Captain Blackwood. The cops might take us in for questioning. I'm calling my lawyer."

"If it's not one bloody thing it's another," Captain Blackwood said, stepping out of the taxi.

"An assassination attempt on Heinlein, okay, that's not too shocking," Nickson said, getting out after her. The automated vehicle quietly rolled away, leaving the two spacers standing in front of a police station in downtown Aterrizaje. "But here? There's no way anyone on Ithaca could have predicted that we'd swing through New Austin."

"I'm thinking that your suspicion about that so-called free trader was justified, Nix," the skipper said, as they entered the lobby of the police station. "You're correct; there is no way they could have arranged such an attack on our client ahead of time, not here."

Nickson checked his handheld. "I put in a query with traffic control about the *Bonaventura*. She put down at an automated spaceport way the hell out in the middle of nowhere, I mean at the ragged edge of the terraformed zone. It's normally used for cargo shipments to and from the mines. It was there for eight local days, then lifted off. They didn't file a flight plan."

"That's not unusual for Freeholder ships, but it is a little too coincidental, isn't it?"

"It is, Skipper. When we get underway, I'll run the crew through combat sims against a *Galaxis* class. Worst case scenario stuff, an example with every known upgrade."

"Excellent. Well, let's get this mess sorted out, shall we?" It had been hours since the shootout behind the restaurant downtown. The two hired mercenaries were being questioned by the police regarding the incident with the cyborg.

"Yeah, we...huh." Nickson trailed off. There was no one present in the lobby, but there was a hulking, bipedal assault robot parked against the back wall. Its ocular cluster tracked the two spacers as they approached, but it didn't move.

"May I help you?" the robot asked, in a synthesized baritone voice.

"Um...yes. My name is Nickson Armitage. This is Catherine Blackwood, captain of the *Andromeda*. I'm the ship's first officer. We're here about the, you know, shooting incident downtown today. It involved our client, Zander Krycek, and his bodyguards, Wade Bishop and Marcus Winchester."

The ocular cluster rotated, and a quiet series of beeps emanated from the machine. "Understood. Stand by." More beeps, then the robot was quiet.

After a few moments of silence, a pair of doors off to the side of the lobby unlocked and opened. A curly-haired, mustachioed man in street clothes, with a gun on his hip and a badge on his belt, came into the lobby.

"Captain Blackwood?"

"That's me," the skipper said.

"I'm Detective-Captain Miller of the Aterrizaje Police. Would you mind coming back with me? I'd like to ask you a few questions."

She folded her arms across her chest and didn't move. "I'm not sure I'm comfortable with that, Detective. I'm only a visitor to New Austin, not a citizen, and I don't have legal representation."

"Captain, you're not being detained. We just want to ask you a few questions about what happened. Your two contractors gave their statements, with their lawyer present. We're not pressing charges. It's not an interrogation. We're just trying to figure out where the assailant came from."

"Very well. I'll have my executive officer wait out here, if you don't mind."

"Thank you. Please, right this way. Oh, here they are." The doors opened again. Marcus Winchester and Wade Bishop stepped into the lobby, with a well-dressed woman that Nickson didn't recognize.

"Marcus, is everything all right?" Captain Blackwood asked. "Were you hurt?"

"I'm fine. We just had to clear up what happened with the police is all."

"I'm going to head back with Captain Miller and answer his questions. I want the three of you to head back to the ship. Nix, inform the spaceport authorities that we'll be departing a day earlier than planned, and get the ship ready for lift-off. Marcus, Wade, our client is to stay on the *Andromeda*."

"We're on it, Skipper," Nickson said, retrieving his handheld. "I'll call us a taxi and we'll head back."

"Captain Blackwood?" It was the woman who had come out with the mercenaries. "Serendipity Kim, attorney-at-law."

"Ah, Ms. Kim, I remember you. It's unfortunate that I get involved with the legal system every time I come to New Austin."

"I'd like to be present when you are questioned by Captain Miller."

The detective sighed. "Ms. Kim, Captain Blackwood is not under arrest. We're just gathering information."

"Even still, Captain, she has the right to legal representation."

Captain Blackwood smiled. "I suppose you ought to be there. I'm paying for your time, after all." She looked over at the exasperated detective. "Shall we?"

"See you at the ship, Skipper," Nickson said. He turned toward the door. "Let's get out of here, guys."

The sun had gone down over the eastern horizon as the trio exited the police station. The street outside was busy and noisy, which Nickson figured would confound the microphones of the security cameras on the building. "I'm glad you're all right," he said to the two mercenaries. "I think that ship that was following us, the *Bonaventura*, had something to do with this."

"You think?" Wade asked. "They were a free trader from the Llewellyn Freehold, I thought."

"Could just be a cover," Marcus said. "The question is, a cover for who?"

"Or whom?" Wade added.

"That we don't know," Nickson said. "Tell me you guys took some pictures that we can analyze." The

Aterrizaje Police weren't going to share their evidence or autopsy analysis with a bunch of privateers from off-world, and Nickson needed all the information he could get to ensure that the client got to Ithaca alive.

"Devree did before she left the scene. I didn't want to have anything like that on our handhelds, just in case. She got pictures and video before the body burned up. It had some kind of self-destruct mechanism."

Nickson nodded. "Perfect. Thank you. Oh, our ride's here. Let's talk more when we get back to the ship."

Log Entry 136
Mission 815-707-SSOC
Reconnaissance Ship 505

GLORIOUS BOTTLE has failed, and was killed. AI/CORE informs us asset's fail-safe initiated upon its death. If it functioned as designed, there should be nothing of intelligence value left. This is a setback, but the mission continues. AI/ CORE is CONFIDENT/HIGH/HIGH that it has accurately predicted the Andromeda's *route to Ionia-5589/Ithaca, given the limited number of resupply points in between there and Lone Star/ New Austin. We are on an out-system burn, en route to the transit point, with a significant lead on the target. AI/CORE has informed us that there is yet one more opportunity to complete the mission. Should that fail, direct action will be required.*

CHAPTER 18

The Privateer Ship *Andromeda*
Capitol Starport, Aterrizaje
New Austin

The astrogation deck was quiet, save for the constant hum of equipment and the cycling of the ship's air circulation system. The pictures and video that Devree Starlighter had taken of the cyborg assassin were being displayed in the holotank, translated into grisly three-dimensional imagery. Nickson listened quietly as Marcus Winchester analyzed the data they'd gathered about their assailant.

"Those cybernetics," Zander Krycek said, staring at the holotank. "And thermoptic camouflage, too? Was this...thing...even human?"

"As near as we can tell, mostly not. He wasn't wearing a body armor vest, but the rounds from my pistol had no effect. His torso seemed to be covered in lightweight composite armor plates. Both eyes were replaced with implants, as were the jaw and teeth. His arms and legs were both implants. They had to be, there was no way a human being could move like that. He jumped several meters up into the air, and flipped around like crazy. He had retractable blades in his hands."

"You saw this?" Zander asked.

Marcus nodded. "Up close. He tried to spear me with one, until Wade shot him off me."

"You said your pistol had no effect. How was it Wade's did?"

"My gun is a standard 10mm semiautomatic. The ammunition was regular poly-case antipersonnel rounds. They do a number on soft tissue but they don't penetrate armor very well. Wade's revolver is loaded with 12mm APHE."

Captain Blackwood looked at Marcus. "APHE?"

"Armor piercing, high explosive, ma'am. There's a tungsten-carbide penetrator tip backed up by a tiny explosive charge. The thing kicks like a mule, even with recoil compensation, but it's more effective on armored targets. Plus, he shot him in the face."

Zander shook his head. "I've never seen such extensive augmentation before."

Marcus looked grim. "I have. Sir, this is Combine tech."

Zander's eyes narrowed as he continued to study the image.

Nickson spoke up. "Marcus, are you sure?"

"As sure as I can be without doing an autopsy, sir. It's generally kept secret, but the Orlov Combine isn't as isolationist as the public is led to believe. They are invested heavily in asymmetrical warfare doctrine and external influence operations. Espionage, assassination, information warfare, political interference, weapons smuggling, you name it. It's widely believed that they have sleeper agents on every Concordiat world, and quite a few nonaligned ones as well.

"Mr. Krycek, some members of the crew are experienced net divers, and I had them do some digging on this David Agnew you were supposed to meet. It seems likely now that he doesn't exist. He was bait, intended to lure you out so that you could be killed. I believe your attacker was expecting us to come out the front. There was a news report about a vehicle bomb found parked a few kilometers away from the restaurant. I think it was intended for you. When you didn't show, the assailant came looking for us around back, and the bomb car just kept driving until it parked itself."

Zander Krycek rubbed his chin. "That might explain why he...it...went hands on with you. Why bring a gun if you have a bomb?"

"Well that, and there are gunfire sensors all over the city. Shooting firearms or energy weapons can trigger a response."

"The implications of this are unsettling," Zander said.

Captain Blackwood agreed. "It would seem that the Combine is after you. This makes me even more suspicious of that supposed free trader that followed us here from Heinlein."

"It's not my area of expertise, ma'am, but back when I was in the Espatiers, I read intelligence reports about Combine black-ops ships. They're disguised as traders, bulk freighters, private sloops, whatever they can pass off as. Usually they just do intelligence collection, but it was believed that they have other missions as well."

"We need to be ready for anything," Nickson said.

The captain frowned, her voice resolute. "If we

encounter that ship again, and I expect we will, I want the ship to go to battle stations immediately. I don't want to fire the first shot, but I will not let them threaten the *Andromeda*. Nix, I expect the same from you."

"Don't worry, Skipper. We'll be watching for it. If we're lucky, they haven't realized we're onto them. They've gotten a significant head start, though, and there are some stops we have to make between here and Ithaca. They could prep another attack. Mr. Krycek, I think it's best if you stay on the ship, even when we land or dock."

"I'll take that under advisement," he said with a sniff. "However, I'm paying you people a lot of money for bodyguards. They've already saved my life, so it's money well spent, but I may have to leave the ship on occasion. I'm trying to save my homeworld, Mr. Nickson, and I need all the allies and investment I can get. But, if what Mr. Winchester says is correct, then the situation is even worse than I feared."

Marcus seemed to agree. "It seems to me that the Combine would be doing everything they could to get their hands on Ithaca, and I don't think they're going to wait for the treaty to be signed to start preparing. You coming back is a threat, sir, especially since you announced your intention to do so. You may or may not succeed once you get to Ithaca, but you're guaranteed to fail if you never get there."

"It may get even more complicated than that," Nickson added. "Your would-be assassin burned up, but they're bound to be doing forensics on it, and they're going to suspect a Combine sleeper agent. A Combine operative attempting to kill someone on a Concordiat world could raise some alarms."

"Perhaps this could be used to garner some support from the Concordiat," Zander said, thoughtfully. "I don't think it'll make a difference. The war for Ithaca will be over by the time the Concordiat makes a decision." The sheer vastness of the interstellar polity meant that nothing happened very fast. Even if the government on Earth decided to declare war on the Combine, it would take months for just the announcement to get to the frontier. The distances involved often meant that interstellar politics was a ponderously slow affair at the best of times.

"Marcus," Captain Blackwood asked, "would it be reasonable to assume that the Combine is already making preparations on Ithaca? Not in response to Mr. Krycek's announced homecoming, of course, but wouldn't such preparations have already been in motion?" If a courier ship taking a direct route to Orlov's Star had left Heinlein on the day Zander Krycek made his announcement, it would get there in the same time frame in which the *Andromeda* expected to arrive in Ionia-5589.

"It's hard to say, ma'am. I'm no Combine analyst. That said, they've had plenty of time to prep. This has all been in the works for probably a year or more. I'd bet my hat they've been pulling strings to ensure that treaty gets signed one way or another."

"It's true," said Kya, the Ithacan political attaché. She'd been quiet up until now. "The Combine has been preparing. They've been sending aid for a year. An Ithacan year, I mean, almost two standard years. Their propaganda is all over the networks back home. *We come in peace*, they say. *We're here to help. Let's work together.* Things like that. The Council has been pushing it, too. Our intelligence people believe that more than a few of those humanitarian aid shipments were weapons, meant to supply the colonial government's forces. Their *advisors* haven't dared to show up in the Southern Autonomous Zone, but they've been all over up north. They talk about the treaty between Ithaca and the Combine as the thing that will save our colony."

"Even if Mr. Krycek's coup is successful," Marcus continued, "if the treaty has already been signed, the Combine might invade the system outright, claiming to be coming to the defense of an ally."

"They would have had the vote on the referendum by now," Kya said. "I'm sure the results will show overwhelming support for the treaty. The referendums staged by the Council only serve to give the illusion of democracy. The outcomes of the votes are all predetermined."

"Were there Combine ships in the Ionia system when you left, Kya?" Captain Blackwood asked.

"No. Their supply ships come and go regularly, but there were none when we departed. I have no idea if they'll be there when we arrive. They were all just bulk freighters, though, not even atmospheric."

"Really. How do they get their cargo to the surface? Does Ithaca have a shuttle fleet?"

"The colonial government does, but it's grounded most of the time. No, the Combine freighters just drop their cargo from orbit. The cargo containers have inflatable heat shields and limited maneuvering capability. Once they slow down enough, a big parachute deploys, and they just drift down to predesignated landing zones. A few have drifted off course and landed in our territory, so we got to examine them."

That struck Nickson as an efficient setup if all you needed to do was deliver cargo from orbit to the surface. It didn't provide a solution for getting goods from the surface to orbit, but in this case, such a solution wasn't necessary. *It would also be an efficient way of deploying troops dirtside in a hurry,* he thought to himself.

The captain frowned. "I see. As we've learned, though, they sometimes disguise their warships as something more innocuous. We may be in for a fight once we get in-system."

Nickson didn't like any of this. His first tour on board the *Andromeda* was getting more and more dangerous and complex by the hour. He could tell Captain Blackwood wasn't pleased with the way things were panning out, either. Their contract stipulated that they would get Zander Krycek to the Southern Autonomous Zone on Ithaca, alive, and in one piece. Possibly getting into a shooting war with the Orlov Combine was another matter altogether, especially since the captain had already had a run-in with Combine authorities. There was a very good possibility they were still looking for the *Andromeda*.

The money was good. They'd basically been paid the net worth of their client's entire liquidated estate, and it was a substantial pile of credits. Kya had promised that the Southern Autonomous Zone government would pay out even more when they arrived. But, what good is money if you're not alive to spend it?

Zander Krycek leaned on his cane. He looked tired. "Captain, the situation is even more fluid than I anticipated. We may need the *Andromeda* as fire support when we arrive in-system."

Nickson and the captain exchanged glances. There were clauses in the contract that covered the possibility of the *Andromeda* needing to fight its way to Ithaca. Those clauses did not obligate the ship to act as a combatant allied with the Southern Autonomous Zone.

"You're asking me to get my ship embroiled in your colonial civil war," the captain said, coolly. "That is outside the terms of our contract, Mr. Krycek, as I'm sure you're aware."

"I am," Zander said, leaning in. "But contracts can be renegotiated, can they not?"

"That very much depends on what you offer. What you're asking for substantially increases the risk to my crew, my ship, and myself. We go from merely transporting a controversial passenger to getting actively involved in your war. If we help you, and you lose, then what? Hopefully we can escape the system before we're captured and put to death. Besides that, my ship can't take on the Orlov Combine by herself. No amount of money will get me to sign a suicide pact, sir." The captain was a tough negotiator. Nickson was moved by the plight of the Ithacans, but she was right: The *Andromeda* was not obligated to die defending Ithaca from the Orlov Combine, however noble such a cause might be.

"I don't have any more money to give you now, Captain," Zander said, "and I can't promise you victory, as much as I would like to. I can, however, promise you rewards for your service if we are successful."

Captain Blackwood raised an eyebrow. "Go on."

"I talked this over with Kya already. We've been concerned about this for some time, even before our cyborg friend made his appearance. I am willing to offer you a safe port of harbor, free of charge, in perpetuity, at the Ithacan spaceport you choose. All berthing fees, maintenance, and other spaceport services will be covered. Additionally, I'm prepared to offer you a land grant and Ithacan citizenship if you want it."

One corner of the captain's mouth curled up in wry smile. "Generous, but you seem to be assuming I'm planning on spending a lot of time on Ithaca."

"You may want to. We will need to rebuild our own space fleet. We will need advisors to train and mentor our spacers, and ships willing to defend the system until our indigenous forces are capable of taking over. This could mean a long-term contract. But, even if you decline that, I have one final offer: a permanent royalty payment."

"Royalty payment?"

"You would be entitled to an annual percentage of the new colonial government's revenue," Kya said. "Not a big percentage, mind you, but still a substantial amount of money. It would be deposited into an account, accruing interest, until you come to withdraw it. Consider it a return on your investment, a reward for becoming a stakeholder in Ithaca's future."

They're scared, Nickson thought. *Or is it desperation? Or a negotiating tactic?*

The skipper wasn't impressed. "I mean no offense, but if I understand the situation correctly, I could fill my cargo hold with Ithacan dinars and it wouldn't be worth the remass I'd burn getting it home."

"That is a fair assessment," Zander said. "We wouldn't pay you in the local currency. You'd be paid in trade goods."

Information could only travel across space as fast as the ships carrying it. This complicated interstellar trade, as electronic representations of money were rendered useless. There was simply no practical way to transfer funds, electronically, from one system to another, and colonial financial systems varied widely on top of it. As such, hard currency, either Concordiat credits or valuable trade goods, were the preferred medium of exchange.

Nickson had to admit that this made for an attractive offer. It essentially amounted to free money, forever, and all they had to do was travel to Ithaca every so often to get it. That in of itself was no simple task, but it struck him as worthy of consideration.

The skipper seemed to agree. "I'll need time to consider this, and talk it over with my officers. Until then, we'll be preparing for departure. We're scheduled for lift-off at zero nine hundred hours tomorrow. I would advise you to stay on the ship until then."

Zander nodded. "I intend to, Captain, but there is one more thing I need to do before we leave."

"Oh?"

"Yes. I'd like to send a message to Concordiat authorities before we leave, preferably the Office of Strategic Intelligence."

Marcus frowned at the mention of the OSI. "What for?" he asked.

"Because," Zander said, grinning slightly, "we have information they might find interesting, and because I need all the allies I can get."

Marcus sighed. "I might be able to help you with that."

Marcus and Mr. Krycek were alone on the *Andromeda*'s command deck. They had an important call to make, and it had to be done in a secure manner.

Regular devices connected to the New Austin planetary network weren't secure, but the ship's communications suite was. That was important, because what they were about to do was of questionable legality.

"Are you sure about this, Mr. Winchester?"

"I think it'll work. They almost never change these frequencies, unless they get discovered. They'll probably change it after this. Heh." Coming from a background of special operations, Marcus had worked with the OSI a lot, on several different worlds. Every Concordiat colony had an OSI field office, whether it was publicly known or not. The one on New Austin, for example, was not publicly disclosed, but he knew it was there, and he knew their emergency contact frequency. He'd made it a point to look it up, when he was still in the Espatiers, before emigrating to New Austin. It paid to know such things.

"Okay, that should do it," he said, having punched the frequency into the console. "Let me do the talking, okay? Okay. Here we go." He tapped the screen and sent a priority hail. After exactly three seconds, someone answered.

"One eight seven four, please verify." There was no video, only audio.

Shit. "Uh..."

"One eight seven *four*, verify," the man said, sounding agitated.

"Look, I don't have an authentication code anymore. Mine was two six zero niner, but—"

The man on the other end of the communication cut Marcus off. "That code is invalid!"

"Hellfire, man, I know that! That's what I was saying!"

"What is your location? Identify yourself!"

"Listen, will you let me—"

"Sir, if you haven't identified yourself by the time we complete the trace, you will be looking at charges under the Interstellar Defense, Security, and Espionage Act."

That was bullshit, as far as Marcus knew, but this idiot wouldn't let him get a word in edgewise anyway. "My name is Marcus Winchester. I'm a former New Austin Colonial Marshal, and now I'm aboard the *Andromeda* in the Capitol Starport. I know you're an OSI field office, and I know you people know who I am. I had a run-in with one of your agents a while back."

There was a long pause. "What do you want?"

"I have information regarding the assassination attempt on Zander Krycek in Aterrizaje yesterday."

"I expect you do. You were there. We're aware of the situation."

"That's fine. Are you also aware that the assassin was a cyborg of Combine origin?"

Another pause. "How do you know that? The police haven't completed the autopsy yet."

Marcus grinned. "Because I have recordings and imagery of the assassin before he burned up. We analyzed it, and there's no doubt in my mind: It's Combine tech. I've seen it before."

"You shared this information with foreign citizens? That is a violation of—"

Marcus cut him off, this time. "Oh, horse shit, it is not. I was in special operations, all right? I worked with you people for years. Stop with the bluster, I ain't impressed. I'm a private citizen, I'm allowed to take videos of whatever I want, and you damned well know it."

There was no answer, only darkness and silence. Marcus looked back at Mr. Krycek and shrugged. A few moments later, the screen blinked alive, and Marcus found himself looking at the pretty, angry face of a certain OSI agent he had never wanted to see again.

"Well, well, well, if it isn't ex-Marshal Winchester," she said with a sneer. "I don't know what you're playing at, but the fact that you know this frequency is a crime."

"Holy hell, lady, you just don't quit, do you? I'm trying to hand you people information and it's threats and bluster."

"I don't make threats. I make promises. You of all people should know that."

"Yeah, well, it worked out for me. My new job pays several times what my old one did. Look, do you want the information on the Combine assassin or not?"

Her eyes narrowed. "Why are you doing this?"

"I don't suppose you'd believe it's because I'm a patriotic citizen of the Concordiat, a veteran, and I don't want Combine operatives loose on my homeworld?"

"Spare me the folksy, homespun bullshit, Mr. Winchester. If you have information that we don't, send it. We'll send it in for analysis. I suppose you want money?"

"I don't. I meant what I said." Marcus looked back and nodded at Mr. Krycek. "But, this gentleman would like a moment of your time."

The OSI agent frowned even harder. "Who is . . . oh. Zander Krycek, formerly of Ithaca, formerly of Heinlein, now on his way home. What is it that you want from us?"

"I would like you to forward a message to your superiors," the exiled president said. "As I'm sure you're aware, the current ruling council on Ithaca is on the verge of signing a mutual defense and trade treaty with the Orlov Combine. I think it's safe to assume that the result of this will be Ithaca becoming a vassal state of the Combine. The Combine will then have under their control a resource-rich system that's close enough to Concordiat space to be of strategic concern. I do not intend to allow this. I am returning home to restore the rightful government of the Colony of Ithaca, and I'm requesting Concordiat assistance."

"That sounds like an internal problem of a non-aligned colony to me," the agent said, tersely.

"We're giving you proof of Combine sleeper agents on a Concordiat world, and you're not worried about them annexing the system closest to your space? I must say, young lady, if you had been on my intelligence staff, I'd have fired you for that attitude. It's inexcusable in your line of work."

Marcus grinned. He didn't care if the OSI agent saw.

"I'm not going to apologize to the Butcher of Sargusport. That's right, Mr. Krycek, I know all about your history."

Zander Krycek was nonplussed. "Am I supposed to be impressed with that? For God sakes, I've written three books on the recent history of Ithaca. None of this is a secret. I assure you, we're not impressed with your station in the Office of Strategic Intelligence. However, I do think that your superiors will be interested in my offer. And, please, don't insult my intelligence by pretending that you're not going to forward relay it. I have no doubt this conversation is being analyzed in real time."

The OSI woman looked daggers at Marcus and Mr. Krycek both. "What is this offer?"

"The Combine has been engaging in so-called humanitarian aid efforts on Ithaca. Their ships come and go from the system, dropping off supplies and advisors. I would like the Concordiat Defense Force to send observers to the Ionia-5589 system to ensure that Combine forces don't interfere with our internal affairs. Ithaca is home to a primitive, indigenous species that may be subjected to exploitation or extermination if the Combine takes the planet."

She blinked a few times. "Are you serious? You think you can just call me up and get a squadron of warships sent to your home system? It doesn't work like that, Mr. Krycek."

"We'll see," he said, with a smile. "Just see that you pass the message on. I will say, however, that it would look bad for an entire star system to fall to Combine control simply because a certain few OSI officers didn't think it was worth worrying about. I'm having Mr. Winchester upload the data he recovered from my would-be assassin. Consider it a gift. Also consider the fact that I could have held a public press conference and announced this to everyone on this colony."

She didn't say anything.

"Yes, well, thank you for your time," Mr. Krycek said.

"You have yourself a fantastic day," Marcus said, sarcasm dripping in his voice. He terminated the connection before she could get the last word in.

"Thank you, Mr. Winchester. I could not have done this without you."

"You really think it'll work? I mean, you think the Fleet will send ships to Ithaca?"

"It's hard to say. I'd be surprised if they don't already

have spy ships visiting the system. If we're successful, we may be able to leverage the Concordiat against the Combine and preserve our independence. I hope so, because otherwise, if the Combine chooses to send a fleet of ships to take the system, there's nothing we can do to stop them."

Marcus nodded, but didn't say anything. His daughter was on board the ship, and now they were talking about possibly getting into a war with Combine. He was glad that Ellie didn't know what was going on.

CHAPTER 19

Ithaca
Ionia-5589 System
Southern Hemisphere

I have made history, Adisa wrote, collecting her thoughts in her journal, *but our troubles have only begun. I was led down another series of tunnels that led to the surface. We're in a clearing, and the electromagnetic interference from the jungle is low enough that I was finally able to upload my report to Command. The news I received back was not good: The referendum passed, by an overwhelming majority. A diplomatic envoy is already en route from the Orlov Combine to formally sign the treaty. The SAZ Congress has issued a proclamation declaring the vote illegitimate. The cease-fire that's held since my father was exiled will be violated. It's only a matter of time, now.*

Of course, the whole colony doesn't see it that way. The Council promises an end to poverty and inequality because of this alliance with the Combine. They claim that their advanced technology will allow everyone on Ithaca to be provided for. No one will be hungry, homeless, or wanting for basic needs. Combine freighters have been dropping supplies every few months, handing out food, medical supplies, and propaganda.

So many people are falling for it, and why wouldn't they? They've been indoctrinated that it's the colonial government's job to provide them with everything they need, and the Combine promises to do just that. They've been fed the lie that if the colony isn't united under the Council's rule, then we are destined to backslide into barbarism, if not outright extinction. They've been told the native peoples will attack and wipe them out if they are not kept at bay. They've been told that if the Combine doesn't become our benefactor, then the Concordiat will come in, forcibly take over the world, as they've done on Zanzibar, and put the welfare of the aliens ahead of that of the humans. Most of all, they've been told that the Southern Autonomous Zone and other groups resisting them are traitors, that they've been colluding with off-world forces to weaken the government and take over the entire planet.

All of that is the Council justifying the war to come. When it comes, they'll blame us, no matter who fires the first shot. Command believes the Colonial Guard has been receiving weapons and equipment from the Combine, a military partnership intended to bolster relations before the treaty was signed.

The Combine has been careful, up until now. Nothing they've done has been an overt act of hostility or interference. They weren't willing to risk the Concordiat intervening. As soon as the treaty is formally recognized, though, they will come, and they will come in force, and I very much doubt the Concordiat will be willing to risk war to stop them.

Adisa was so engrossed in her writing that she didn't

notice Follower of the Storm at first. She was sitting on a rock, under the shade of a juvenile pseudo-tree, on a hot, humid, but beautiful day. In front of her was a clearing in the thick jungle, where one could actually see the sky. Sunshine from Ionia-5589 poured down. Flying creatures soared above, occasionally swooping down to snatch rubbery seeds, the size of melons, off the towering pseudo-trees. A caravan of natives, riding hulking, eight-meter-long forest beasts, was entering the clearing from a jungle trail.

"What troubles you, A-dissss-ah?"

She was impressed with Stormy. He had gotten good enough at reading human body language that he could tell she was worried. "I'm just afraid for the future," she said, putting down her tablet and looking up into his dark eyes. "We may fail. We may fail, and we may all die."

"Yesss," Stormy agreed. "All die. Everything dies, A-disss-ah. My pee-pole. Your pee-pole. Plants. Beasts. Worlds. Stars. All fires are extinguished in time. Do not be ah-fraid."

"How can you not be? You know what's coming."

"Yesss. But you can not change that. You can not..." he paused, seemingly in thought, trying to find the words. "You can not stop the storm. The storm is coming. All that can be done is to...survive. Fight. If we die, then we die. It is the way of things."

Adisa was a little frustrated at Stormy's laid-back attitude about the coming war. She had to remind herself that, despite all of the barriers she'd overcome, he was still a nonhuman being, and he didn't operate on the same emotional level that she did. She envied him for that; he seemed much less stressed.

"There is good news," she said, trying to sound more upbeat. "I sent off a request for small arms, designed to the specifications of your people, and ammunition for them."

Stormy seemed confused. He looked at his thick forearm before looking back up at Adisa.

"Oh, I apologize. Guns. I asked for guns, built so that your people can use them." The natives' body configuration made it impossible for them to properly aim a rifle built for a human being. Their necks were too long, and their heads were shaped too differently. The weapons Adisa had requested would need significantly redesigned buttstocks, grips, and sights, so that Stormy's people could hold and aim them correctly. "It'll take a little time to get them, but the request was approved. The guns are coming." The weapons would need to be engineered, prototyped, tested, then put into serial production by automated mechanical assemblers. It was likely to take a few weeks.

"How many...guns?" Stormy asked.

"As many as you need. We have the capability to make them by the thousands. They have agreed to send all that they can. I will need to tell them how many warriors you have. The hardest part will be getting them to us, and distributing them to your people."

"We can...dis...dis...trib-ute," Stormy said, stumbling over a word he hadn't used much. He motioned toward the arriving column of pack beasts. "Our car-a-vans travel all over the planet. Hidden beneath the plants and trunks, in shadow. Hidden from the sky. Quiet. Slow, but...safe."

"Do you really think all tribes of your people will join the fight?" The native Ithacans outnumbered the human settlers by as much as two-point-five-to one, depending on which study you believed. She was grateful for this, as it was the only hope the Southern Autonomous Zone and its scattered allies had against the huge numerical superiority of the rest of the colony. There were almost twenty million people living on Ithaca, and the SAZ accounted for only about a quarter of the population.

It was mind-boggling. Adisa had read a lot of history. On Ancient Earth, billions of people shared the same planet. There was war, there was strife, and there was competition for resources, as one might expect. But Ithaca was an entire world with the population equivalent to a large city on one of the Inner Colonies. There was so much empty space, so much unspoiled, virgin wilderness, that it seemed silly to fight over it. There was plenty for all.

But the war was coming all the same. The Council would not abide a rival government on Ithaca, no matter how many kilometers separated them. Their "One Government, One People, One Colony" stance ensured that. Because of that, a pointless war was now inevitable.

Stormy seemed to ruminate on Adisa's question for a few moments. "Yesss. Elders are respected by all tribes. Elders..." he paused again. "This one...I... not sure how to say. Elders can talk, no matter how far apart. They all know what A-disss-ah said. It was decided. We all fight, or we all die."

"The Elders told me that human minds are undeveloped in psionics."

Stormy hesitated. "Si-on-ics? This one does not understand."

"They can talk with their minds. The Elders, I mean."

"Yesss. Only Elders have this . . . gift. Hu-mans do not. This one does not. The Elders saw into your mind. They know you tell the truth. That is why we fight."

"I hope you can appreciate how unprecedented this is. My God, Stormy, your people and mine have been living together for centuries and we had no idea!"

"We did not trussst your people. We trussst you, A-disss-ah. You speak for our people. We face death. There is no . . . reason . . . for secrets if we die keeping them. We are one. For now."

"You and I have advanced interspecies coopera- tion like no one ever has. I pray that we succeed. I would hate for all this to have been for nothing." Her father was the first human leader in the modern era to work out a formal peace and trade treaty with an alien species, at least on such a large scale. What Adisa had done was beyond even that. As far as she knew, no humans had ever fought *with* aliens in a war, instead of against them. If she survived the next year, she was seriously considering writing a book about it.

"Not for nothing, A-disss-ah. For . . ." he paused yet again. "For *freedom*. For survival. For the future. If we die, we die well. We die fighting. We do not go quietly into darkness. Not for nothing. For *everything*."

"How goes it?" Roc asked, approaching with a grin on his face. "Is she bothering you, Stormy?"

"What? No!" Adisa said, smiling. "We're conducting serious business here, I'll have you know."

"Biz-ness," Stormy agreed. He dipped his head. "I will relay this to . . . others, A-disss-ah." Without another word, he turned and walked off.

"Not much for saying good-bye, are they?" Adisa asked.

Roc sat down next to her, resting his weapon on his lap. "I think in their language, saying good-bye is only for when you don't expect to see someone again soon. Stormy told me it confused him how we say it every time we depart, even if we're coming right back. I tried to explain that it's rude to just walk away, but he thinks it's superfluous."

"I can't say he's wrong," Adisa said. "Any news?"

He shook his head. "Nothing new. Right now, it's only a matter of time before someone fires the first shot. Hey, can I ask you something? You're from up north, right? How did you end up in the jungle way down here?"

"My mother died when I was little. After my father left, I didn't really have anyone on Ithaca."

"I'm sorry to hear that, love. If you don't mind me asking, why didn't your father take you with him?"

"From what I've been told, he tried. My mother's extended family took me, hid me away. They didn't want me to go with him. They promised him they'd keep me safe."

"And he just accepted that and left without his own daughter?"

"I haven't spoken to my father since I was little. I don't know all the details. My mother was politically connected, you know. She had a seat on the original Revolutionary Council. People loyal to her weren't going to let my father take me off-world. Sometimes I wish they had."

"Where did he end up?"

"Heinlein."

"Never heard of it. Concordiat world?"

"No. It's nice, though. Very modern. Safe. No strife or political upheaval there."

Roc looked over at Adisa. His hair was blonde, and cropped short. She was certain his smile made him popular with the ladies back home. "Sounds like you're thinking about leaving yourself," he said.

"I'd be lying if I said it didn't cross my mind. Sometimes I wonder if my father didn't get the better deal. What about you?"

"Nah. This is my home. My father was a farmer, did I ever tell you that? His parents were farmers, too. I was the first one in generations who didn't want to be a farmer, because I love being out here."

"In the jungle?"

"You know it. It's beautiful, and...savage. Unspoiled and pure. There are secrets out there, too, things most people don't know about."

"Secrets? Like what?"

"I could tell you, but it's better if I show you. You up for a little walk?"

Adisa smiled. "Let me get my pack."

Two hours and several kilometers later, Adisa could hear the roar of water nearby. "What is that?"

"It's a waterfall, love. See?"

Stepping through the tangled vines, Adisa looked up, and her breath was taken away. A river cut through the primordial, alien jungle, dropping off a ten-meter-high cliff, into a deep pool in front of them. A rainbow hovered in the air as sunlight refracted through the mist. "It's beautiful," she said. "Is this the secret?"

"No, this is just a nice spot for swimming. Follow me." Roc led Adisa around the pool at the bottom of the waterfall, carefully navigating across the wet rocks. He brought her closer and closer to the waterfall. She was getting wet from the spray, and he kept on.

"Where are we going?"

"Behind the waterfall."

"*Behind* the waterfall?"

"You might get a little wet. Come on, it's worth it, I promise."

Adisa followed Roc as he approached the waterfall. As they got close, she realized the rock behind the water angled inward, and there was enough of a gap for a person to get through without getting completely soaked. The rocks were slippery. Roc went through first, found dry footing, and extended a hand to Adisa.

Taking his hand, she stepped through, and slipped. She fell forward, right into Roc. "Whoa there, careful. I got you. You okay?"

"I am," she said, looking up into his eyes. She felt her face flush, and pulled away. "So, um, what is it you wanted to show me?" She had to speak up to be heard over the roar of the falling water.

Roc retrieved a bright flashlight from his pocket. "This." He turned on the light and shined it on the rock behind the waterfall.

"Oh..." Adisa said, trailing off. She slowly stepped forward, running her fingers over the rock. On a smooth surface, lettering and pictograms had been carved, several centimeters deep. The lettering wasn't from any human language. "This is Ithacan script," she said. She turned back toward him. "We don't have many samples of this. How did you know it was here?"

"I've been swimming here before, is all. Explored a little bit, you know? Thought you'd like it."

"I love it!" she said, excitedly. "This is old, probably going back to ... well, going back a thousand years, at least." She turned back toward her companion.

"Can I tell you something? It's a secret. You can't tell anyone yet."

"Uh, sure, Adisa, I can keep a secret."

"The Ithacans aren't from Ithaca at all."

"Really? They told you this?"

"They did."

"Where did they come from, then?"

"They lost their homeworld long ago. They fought a war with the Maggots, and lost."

"Are you serious? They told you all this?"

"They didn't just tell me, they showed me. But, yeah, it's true. They scattered and hid, and now they don't know if they're the last of their kind or not. They've been here for more than a thousand years, and most of them have forgotten their true heritage."

Roc looked up at the carved glyphs and shook his head. "That's a hell of a thing, thinking you're a caveman when you come from the stars. All of them don't know, do they?"

"I don't think so. Stormy might, but I'm not going to ask him."

"Don't worry, I won't go prying."

"This will all come out sooner or later, but I was asked to keep it quiet for now. I just...look, I'm a xenoanthropologist. I know it seems boring, but I get excited about stuff like this. I had to tell somebody."

Roc smiled. "No worries, love. I know you're interested in things like this. That's why I brought you here."

"That was sweet of you. Thank you."

He nodded toward the clear pool on the other side of the waterfall. "You up for a swim?"

Adisa smiled. "You know what? I am."

CHAPTER 20

The Privateer Ship *Andromeda*
Deep Space
Shen Long–28 Binary System
1,200 Hours out from New Austin

"Wake up, crewman!"

Annabelle Winchester drifted in darkness, not certain where the voice had come from. She couldn't see nor hear anything else. In fact, except for the sensation of weightlessness, she felt nothing at all. She couldn't even move.

"Wake up, crewman!"

There it was again! It was louder this time, closer. Someone was telling her to wake up, but she wasn't asleep. Was she? Annie wasn't sure, and in her uncertainty she grew frightened. *What's going on? Why can't I move? Who is that? Oh God, oh God!*

SLAP! Annie's eyes snapped open as someone smacked her in the cheek, hard enough to sting. At first, her eyes wouldn't focus. Everything was blurry.

"What's going on?" she slurred, spittle dribbling out of her lips.

"You're experiencing transit shock," a woman said. The voice was stern, and accented. She was holding Annie by the collar of her flight suit. "Try to focus on me."

It took some effort, but with a moment of concentration her vision cleared. Indira Nair was the one holding her, her brow furled in what might have been concern or anger.

Annie's heart dropped into her stomach. "Ma'am!" she sputtered, feeling dizzy again. "I'm sorry. I'm sorry! I was cleaning the head and I don't know what happened and—"

The engineer cut her off. "That's enough, crewman. Are you alright?"

"I think so. I'm still a little dizzy. My stomach is . . . is . . ." Annie's eyes went wide as her stomach lurched. She cupped a hand over her mouth and used the other one to pull herself around to the toilet. Opening the lid activated the vacuum suction. She clung to handholds on the floor as she puked her guts out into the head she'd just cleaned.

The engineer just hovered there, holding onto a handhold, looking unimpressed.

Annie looked up at her, but before she could apologize again, the heaves started up and she threw up a second time. When it was over, she closed the lid and mashed the button to empty and sanitize the toilet.

"Are you finished, Miss Winchester?"

"Yes, ma'am," she said, her face ashen. "I'm sorry."

Engineer Nair didn't quite smile, but Annie could have sworn that her lip curled a little. "Transit shock is unpredictable like this."

"I've never blacked out because of it before."

"As I said, it's unpredictable. We left the physical

universe for a moment. It's hard on the human body. Now, I want you to report to medical. Can you make it up there on your own?"

"Yes, ma'am," she said, sheepishly.

"Good. On your way, then. Stop by the personnel deck and tell your counterpart to come down here."

"Liam?"

"Yes. Enzo is busy on the flight deck right now, and I want to show the boy how to run post-translation system checks. He seems bright enough to understand it."

"I'll send him down, ma'am," Annie said, pulling herself past the engineer, through the hatch. She looked back. "Thank you."

Indira Nair actually smiled, for the briefest of moments. "Move out, crewman. We have work to do."

Nickson Armitage relaxed in the command chair and waited for his head to stop spinning, taking an occasional sip from a bulb of nutrient-laced water. He'd known some people who seemed almost immune to transit shock, but he wasn't one of those people.

The assistant engineer, Enzo Zeks, was helping junior watch officer Nattaya Tantirangsi to reboot the primary flight computer. Enzo was somewhat familiar with such systems, and Nuchy had been cross-training as a systems technician. Together, they were doing the best they could, but the absence of a fully qualified systech was sorely felt. The crew was short-handed before they left Heinlein, and they were feeling it now.

"How we doing, Enzo?" Nickson asked, massaging his temples.

Nuchy was strapped into her workstation, and Enzo was floating next to her. "Flight computers are online, sir, but I wouldn't trust it just yet. Two out of three systems agree on the test problems. The third is just not cooperating. We're running at 67 percent."

"Good enough, Enzo." He liked the young assistant engineer. He was a bright kid, good with computers and electronics, and he helped make up for the lack of a systech. Nickson tapped his intercom control. "Colin, you with me up there?"

Colin Abernathy, up on the flight deck, sounded miserable when he responded. "We can proceed under manual control, sir, until the flight computer comes back. Optical tracking is online, and we've triangulated our position. We can begin the burn at your command."

"Very good. Start the burn. Ease us into it. That translation was a bad one."

"Roger that, sir."

Nickson liked the flight officer's enthusiasm. He respected a pilot who wasn't afraid to fly manually. "She's all yours." He turned his attention back to Enzo and Nuchy. "Enzo, grab a seat and continue diagnostics from there. Nuchy, when comms come back online, file our flight plan with Hannibal's Reach via a laser pulse transmission."

"Roger!"

The pilot's voice echoed throughout the ship as he made his announcement. "Attention, all personnel, stand by for burn, T-minus sixty seconds. I say again, stand by for burn, T-minus sixty seconds. One gee."

Mordechai Chang appeared on one of Nickson's screens, not looking any worse than usual. "Shall I contact the station and arrange us a berth, Mr. Nickson?"

"Please. We'll try to get in as much R and R as we can."

"Understood." His image was gone. As usual, he didn't say good-bye or anything.

Nickson closed his eyes, took another sip of his nutrient water, and waited for the acceleration to begin. After a minute, the ship began to rumble and vibrate as four powerful fusion rockets were ignited. A welcome sensation of weight came over him, increasing to Earth-normal as the *Andromeda* settled into its two-hour-long burn.

The system consisted of Shen Long–28A, a massive and ancient red giant, and Shen Long–28B, a blue-white main sequence star. The mismatched pair was orbited by several gas giants, one small, rocky, airless world, and a distant ice giant farthest out. It had no habitable planets, but had been permanently settled a century before the Second Interstellar war. The system's location and abundant resources made it a natural stop along existing, prewar trade routes. It was a bustling frontier crossroads.

Originally, Shen Long–28 was home to little more than an outpost of hardy pioneers, who began hollowing out an oblong asteroid some sixty kilometers long. The project sped up during the Second Interstellar War, when thousands of refugees, fleeing the Maggot onslaught, arrived in the system. Today, the asteroid, called Hannibal's Reach, was home to a quarter of a million people, and was a bustling transit hub along an otherwise lonely trade route.

There was a refinery complex from which they could purchase the reaction mass they needed without having to dock with the Reach, but Captain Blackwood had insisted that they do so. On long missions like this, she reasoned, it was important to let the crew get out and stretch their legs now and again. It was not only good for morale, but for their physical and mental health. After more than a thousand hours underway, in tight quarters, tempers tended to shorten, and people got a little claustrophobic. They needed a break, and a couple days off the ship would let them relieve some pent-up tension.

With a smile, Nickson decided that a little female companionship wouldn't kill *him*, either. He did worry about whether someone would try to kill Zander Krycek again, though. There'd been no sign of the *Bonaventura* since leaving New Austin. Until sensors came back online, there was no telling if it was in this system, or docked at Hannibal's Reach. They wouldn't find out until they got closer.

Log Entry 137
Mission 815-707-SSOC
Reconnaissance Ship 505

The target ship Andromeda *has entered the system, and is en route to Shen Long–28/Hannibal's Reach. We are tracking them on passive sensors, and the drive signature matches. While in transit, we varied our configuration, drive output, and transponder data. We are presently docked at Shen Long–28/Hannibal's Reach, and are waiting for the* Andromeda *to arrive. There are no assets stationed at Hannibal's Reach; AI/CORE recommends that we deploy our on-board asset, SACRED WRAITH. Doing so requires the concurrence of AI/CORE, the ship's commander, and the ship's political officer. Concurrence was reached. The asset will be retrieved from cold sleep and sent into the asteroid.*

CHAPTER 21

The Privateer Ship *Andromeda*
***Hannibal's Reach* Space Habitat**
Shen Long–28 Binary System

With approval from Captain Blackwood, Nickson had worked out a liberty rotation for the crew while the *Andromeda* was docked with Hannibal's Reach. The ship didn't technically need to be manned at all while docked, but given the threats against Zander Krycek's life, someone would have to stay behind and stand watch. Nickson had volunteered to stay behind first, with Kimball and Indira Nair.

The ship was docked with a massive superstructure protruding from one of the oblong asteroid's poles. This construct did not rotate with the asteroid, and had docking points for dozens of ships. The *Andromeda* had secured a berth about halfway up the structure. The ship was locked in, with the manipulator arm deployed and holding on. Interior trams zipped up and down the structure, ferrying passengers from the docking ports to the interior of the habitat.

Presently, most of the crew was assembled in the

cargo bay, and Nickson was giving them a safety briefing before they went on liberty. "Remember, you need to read and understand the rules of this station before you disembark. You all should have been sent a summary. Big thing is, no ranged weapons. No guns, no lasers, no plasma projectors, none of it."

The crew groaned.

"I know, I know, it's dumb, but don't get caught in violation. You'll be arrested, and we'll have to bail you out. Looking your way, Kimball."

Cargomaster Kimball grinned and waved, to the laugher of the crew. Nickson had read the logs about his ordeal on Opal, and he absolutely didn't want a repeat of that.

"Does anyone have any questions about the rules? Okay, good. Now, I know we've been cooped up in here for a long time, and everyone is excited to get out and have some fun. That's fine, but take a buddy with you. Don't go anywhere alone if you can help it. Watch out for each other. Everyone needs to keep a communicator on them at all times, and at the first sign of trouble I want you to hit the panic button.

"Be smart, and try to stay to the common areas of the station. Stay out of the tunnels and habitats beneath the interior surface level. Nobody come back pregnant, or with any diseases. Don't bring back any live animals, produce, or people. No one who is not a member of the crew is allowed on the ship. Do not tell anyone which ship you're from. Don't tell anyone where you're going. Remember, people are looking for our client, and they're dangerous. We'll be docked for fifty-four hours, and I want everyone back and accounted for two hours before we depart. Make the most of the time we've got. Any questions?"

There were none.

"Good," Nickson said, grasping a handhold for stability. "Make your way up to the docking umbilical in an orderly fashion. A tram car should be waiting for you. Stay safe and have fun."

A few scattered "Yes, sir!" answers, and the crew headed for the hatch. The ship was docked with the umbilical at its nose, so they'd have to go up a few decks to get there.

"Nix," Captain Blackwood said, pushing herself toward him. She was very graceful in freefall. She had just come on duty, and had been sleeping in her cabin. "Any sign of the *Bonaventura*?"

"No, ma'am. As we approached, we did an optical and electromagnetic scan of the other ships docked at the station. There are presently twenty-one other ships in berth, with several more in nearby parking orbits. Two of the ships we scanned were *Galaxis* class, but neither was an exact match for the *Bonaventura*. Their transponders list them as the *Homestar Runner*, from the Homestar system, and the *Bandou Maru*, registered out of Nippon."

"Hmm. The *Galaxis* class isn't uncommon. They were in production for something like four hundred years. Still, let's be careful. I'd like to get to Ithaca without anyone becoming involved in another gun battle."

"We can keep the crew on the ship, Skipper."

She shook her head. "No. We've a long way to go yet. I want the crew to get off the ship. They need a break."

"What about Zander Krycek?"

"He's our client, not a prisoner. He's free to come and go as he pleases. He's got security. That's up to him. We've largely been paid up front so, as callous as it sounds, if he gets killed because he isn't cautious enough, we turn around and go home."

"I'll find out what his plans are, Skipper. Hopefully he isn't meeting with any more dubious contacts."

"Actually, Nix, *I'll* talk to him. I want you to go. You deserve a break yourself. You've been working very hard since we started. You were almost killed your second day on the job, you were willing to depart on short notice, and you've done an excellent job since. I want you to take the full fifty-four hours off. I'll work out a watch rotation that doesn't include you."

It was incredibly satisfying to Nickson to hear that. "Thank you, Skipper."

"Be safe. Get going, now. I'll see you when you get back."

With a nod, Nickson pushed himself off the bulkhead and made for the ladder.

Grasping a tablet in one hand and gripping a handhold in the other, Marcus Winchester briefed his team of mercenaries on the details of the Hannibal's Reach space habitat. "They're pretty serious about their no-guns policy," he continued, skimming the text of their regulations. "Residents are permitted to own weapons. Transients are not. The penalties for violating the rules aren't too bad, though, just fines. Big fines. You're only looking at more severe punishment if you commit a crime with a weapon." The team was gathered on the personnel deck while the ship's crew had their briefing down on the cargo deck.

"Bah," Halifax spat. "Sounds like a revenue generating scheme to me, Marcus. They know most spacers won't feel safe going into a place like that unarmed, so they come up with a way to shake them down for money."

"Oh, I agree. What this means for us is, if the client wants to go off the ship, we're going to have to be contentious about concealment. Don't get caught and there won't be any problems. I recommend regular guns only, no lasers or anything with a power supply. They have detectors set up to scan for high-density power cells."

"What are the old man's plans, Marcus?" Devree asked.

"He's not going anywhere right now. Seems he's not feeling too well. He's been back and forth between his bunk and the head for hours. The flight medic gave him a sedative and something to settle his stomach. He's asleep now, and will probably be out for a while. So, a couple of us can get off the ship for a few hours." Marcus looked up, and noticed Annie and Liam were hovering nearby. "Oh, hi, honey."

"Hi, Dad."

"Hello, sir," Liam said, politely.

"Where are you two off to?"

"Most of the crew is on liberty. Me and Liam are going to take the tram to the habitat."

"Huh. Devree, how would you feel about taking Annie shopping?"

"What?"

"Dad! I don't need a babysitter!"

"I'm not worried about *you*, honey. No offense, Liam." That wasn't exactly true, but Annie had grown into a lovely young woman, and there were plenty of skags in spaceports that would love to get their filthy hands on her. "Devree, Wade, you two go with the kids, have a good time. Me and Halifax will stay aboard with the client."

"Well, if you insist," Devree said, with a smile. "Annie, honey, wait up for me for a minute? I'm going to change." Marcus and his team weren't given the sage-green flight suits the crew wore as a duty uniform. Instead, they got black coveralls. Nothing said you were a fresh-off-the-ship spacer, ripe for pickpocketing, more than visiting a port city in your coverall. They had all been advised to wear street clothes. In any case, it was hard to conceal a firearm in a one-piece outfit.

"I think that about does it," Marcus said. "Check in every two hours, and be back here in ten. Stick together out there, and be safe."

Annie piped up then. "Captain on deck!" She and Liam both paused as Captain Blackwood came sailing up the ladder from the cargo deck.

"As you were," the captain said, smiling. Grabbing a handhold above the ladder, she aimed herself and kicked off the bulkhead, effortlessly gliding toward Marcus and his team. She stopped herself on another handhold and righted herself, so that she was right side up from their perspective. It didn't really matter in freefall, but it still felt weird talking to people when they were upside down. "Marcus, how's our client doing?"

"He's resting, ma'am. I guess he's got the squirts

and is sick to the stomach. He took a sedative and is asleep."

"Oh, is he?" the captain said, almost-but-not-quite smiling. "What unfortunate timing, to become so afflicted just as we were pulling into port. Oh, well. Perhaps it's for the best. Please let me know if he comes to."

"Uh, yes, ma'am, will do. I'm sending two of my people out for some leave time, and two of us are staying here. When they come back we'll switch."

"Very good. I'm glad everyone is taking advantage of the time we have. I'll be up on the command deck if I'm needed. Carry on." With that, she pushed herself off the deck, angled off the ceiling, and headed for the ladder.

When the captain had left, Marcus turned his attention back to his team. "Holy shit, I think the old lady drugged Krycek."

Devree's eyes went wide. "You think so?"

Halifax laughed. "Lady Blackwood is a clever one, that's for sure. I wouldn't be surprised if she did."

Marcus couldn't help but chuckle himself. "Well, let's not tell him about this. Devree, Wade, you two get going. Enjoy your free time. See you in ten hours."

CHAPTER 22

Ithaca
Ionia-5589 System
Southern Hemisphere

The attack had gone spectacularly well.

Most Colonial Guard personnel hailed from the terraformed zone up north. There, the climate was more temperate, and the flora and fauna were adapted Earth species. There were few among them who had any experience operating in the dense alien jungles of the southern reaches of the continent. The towering, twisting pseudo-trees made aerial and satellite observation of the ground extremely difficult. There were places where the undergrowth was so thick that it was impossible to pass without hacking your way through. Their natural electromagnetic fields interfered with radio waves and compasses alike, and hindered both communication and navigation.

If you weren't careful, you'd stumble into a nest of razor vines and they'd hack you right back. The nocturnal predators that came out during the long nights were fast, vicious, and could see in the infrared spectrum. There were fungal spore-pods, larger than a man's head, that would burst if disturbed or stepped on. The unfortunate victim would be showered in spores and would soon succumb to a debilitating fungal infection. Without hospitalization and treatment, the victim would die.

The Ithacan jungles were no place for the unaware. Had it not been for the guidance of Roc and his Rangers, and that of Follower of the Storm and his people, Adisa undoubtedly would have died long ago.

The Colonial Guard was also inexperienced in combat, and their training had been lackluster as the economic crisis worsened, sapping defense funds. The cease-fire had been in place since Adisa was a baby, and there were few left in the Guard who had ever seen combat. The leadership of the SAZ Civil Defense Force was made up largely of veterans of the colonial civil war, men and women who had fought under her father. It didn't make up for being outnumbered three to one, but it helped.

Adisa wasn't a soldier, and this was her first experience in combat. The walled compound, cut out of the jungle, was no more than a kilometer in circumference and served as a forward operating base for the Colonial Guard. There were no roads out here; it had to be resupplied entirely from the air, as evidenced by the burning wreckage of a VTOL aircraft on the landing pad. The base had been equipped with an aerial defense system, including a sensor-guided, high-powered laser battery, to protect it from aircraft, missiles, and artillery. The Guard had been in the process of emplacing powerful railgun artillery and missile batteries, which would have threatened SAZ-CDF operations for hundreds of kilometers.

Now, as the sun rose, it was all in ruins. Fires still burned. The site was littered with the bodies of dead Colonial Guardsmen, their brown uniforms stained with blood. Adisa walked through the carnage, almost in shock. Roc was still with her; he'd been assigned as her permanent protector. Follower of the Storm was there, too. Just as Adisa was an emissary to his people, he was an emissary to the humans.

"Well done, mate," Roc said, complimenting Follower of the Storm's warriors. A single platoon of SAZ-CDF Rangers and a native war band two dozen strong had breached the wall in the dead of night. The weapons the SAZ defense engineers had devised for them worked splendidly: powerful 9mm semiautomatic rifles, with basic sights tailored to the eyes of the aliens. The ammunition was armor piercing and explosive, and the warriors had used it to grisly effect. They had also been supplied with hand grenades, simple, unguided rocket launchers, and even a flame thrower. "Poor blighters never knew what hit them."

The cover of the jungle had allowed the attackers to get right up to the perimeter wall. The defenders hadn't been prudent about keeping the foliage clear, and they hadn't placed mines. Rangers in thermoptic camouflage had spent hours slowly crawling forward, avoiding detection by automated gun turrets, and placed a huge explosive charge on the wall. The wall exploded, catching the Guardsmen by complete surprise, and then Stormy's war band stormed in. It was carnage.

"What happens now?" Adisa asked. CDF Rangers frog-marched about a dozen surviving Guardsmen, now prisoners, out of a barracks building. They were lashed together with a flex-cable, and their hands were bound.

"We're gathering everything we can for intel purposes. I'm trying to get aircraft out here to pick up those railguns we captured. They're Combine manufacture, I'm sure, and we can use them."

"This was a good battle," Stormy said, his rumbling voice sounding pleased. "We fought well." He bobbed his head toward a line of dead Guardsmen, whose bodies were covered in ponchos. "They died well." Three of the native warriors had been killed in the battle, and one CDF Ranger. The enemy dead was estimated to be well over a hundred. Lizard-like flying creatures circled above, soaring on leathery, meter-long wings, waiting for a chance to swoop in and scavenge the dead.

"We just started the war," Adisa said, wistfully. It was true; while the Colonial Government had been pushing closer and closer to the Southern Autonomous Zone, setting up supply lines and bases, there hadn't been an actual engagement until now.

"We made a statement," Roc said. "The war was inevitable. We couldn't have sat by and let them gain the advantage over us. You knew this was coming."

"I guess you really don't understand it until you see it."

"My father fought in the civil war," Roc said. "Took a break from farming for a while to go fight. He told me some stories as I was coming up. It was bloody awful. I hope it doesn't get that bad, but I'm not optimistic. They've got off-world support now. If we don't win, quickly and decisively, we will lose. Once that treaty is formalized, there's nothing to stop a Combine fleet nuking us from orbit."

The Colonial Government had nuclear weapons, of course, but so did the Southern Autonomous Zone. Both sides also had sophisticated aerospace defense systems. Neither side could simply destroy the other in a nuclear onslaught. It would be a long, drawn out process, trying to wear down the enemy's defenses so that your own warheads could get through.

Perhaps it was the death all around her, but Adisa took no joy from the victory they'd won. "Is there any hope at all, Roc?"

The Ranger simply shrugged. "Above my pay grade, love. Nobody asked me what I think. Supposedly our leadership has a strategy. If your father comes back, we might have a chance. You haven't, by chance, heard anything, have you?"

"Not yet. All we can do is hope."

CHAPTER 23

Hannibal's Reach **Space Habitat**
Shen Long–28 Binary System

"You are amazing," Nickson said, breathing heavily. The woman on top of him leaned forward, smiling seductively, her dark hair framing her face. Her skin was pale but smooth. Her eyes seemed to shine in the dimly-lit hotel room, the dark eyeliner around them giving them a striking appearance. Her pert, perfect breasts, nipples still erect, brushed across his chest as she leaned in.

"You're not so bad yourself," she purred, kissing him with her lush, full lips. "You have good stamina." He'd needed it. The woman seemed insatiable. They'd had sex three times now.

"I've never been with an aug before," Nickson said, as she slid off of him. In some places, referring to a person with cybernetic prosthetic enhancement as "augs" was considered rude, but it was politer than "cyborg." In any case, her augmentations looked natural. You could barely see the lines where her natural upper body ended, and her synthetic lower body began.

"You should try it," she said, softly. Lying next to him, she gently slid a finger down his chest. "I can eat as much as I want, and I'll never get fat. I don't get stomach problems. I don't get sick, aside from maybe an occasional sinus infection. I'll never get diseases of the lungs or heart. I could live for several hundred years."

"Does it, you know, feel the same? When you have sex?" That came out more awkward than Nickson had hoped. But really, was there a non-awkward way to ask a cyborg woman about her artificial vagina?

A playful smile crossed her face. "It's . . . different, but good. So good. When you touch me, it sends neural impulses to the pleasure center of my brain. You'll never experience an orgasm so mind-blowing."

"Was it painful? How did they do it?"

"So many questions," she cooed. "If you won't tell me where you're from, I'm not going to divulge my secrets, either. It's only fair."

"I at least told you my name."

She rested her chin on her hand, propping her body up with her elbow. "You're so sweet, Nix. Very well, my name is Talia."

"Talia. I like it. It's pretty. I've never met a Talia before. That's from Ancient Earth, right?"

"It is. It means *dew from God*. Don't you go falling in love with me now, you sweet man. You know how these encounters always end. We're two wayward ships, passing in the eternal night."

Nickson checked his chrono. "I still have plenty of time before I have to get back, though," he said with a smile.

"Oh my," Talia said, sliding her hand down Nickson's

body. "Are you hoping for another go? I think you are," she purred, taking him in her hand. "Still hard, too."

Nickson grinned. "What can I say? I was cooped up for a long time."

"Oh, I imagine so. It's a long flight from New Austin, isn't it?"

Nickson felt his heart drop into his stomach. "What?" He went to sit up, but she grabbed him by the throat and slammed him back down onto the bed. She was incredibly strong.

"Shh," she said, leaning in, with a finger held up to her lips. Her right hand was gripped around Nickson's neck like a vise. He could barely breath. "Just relax. No harm will come to you if you cooperate."

Nickson felt a fingertip brush against his neck, then a sharp prick, like a needle. "What did you do to me?" he croaked. "What . . ." His head began to swim. His eyesight blurred up.

"Hush now, Nix," Talia said, still holding him down. "It's nothing personal. I like you. But you know, a girl's got to do what a girl's got to do."

Nickson couldn't say anything. Whatever she had injected him with, it was overwhelming him. His muscles relaxed. His body felt warm. Everything faded to black.

"Hey, he's awake!" Marcus said, as Zander Krycek popped the hatch to his berth. "How are you feeling, sir?"

He pulled himself out of the small compartment and into the open air of the personnel deck. "Like I have the worst hangover of my life," Mr. Krycek grumbled, squinting in the light. "How long was I out?"

Marcus checked his chrono. "Almost twelve hours."

"My stomach feels better, though." Grasping the railing of the catwalk, he pulled himself along it, down the steps, to the floor of the commons area. The old man wasn't an experienced spacer and wasn't particularly graceful in zero gravity. "Would one of you mind getting me some coffee?"

"I'll get it," Wade said, pushing off the floor toward the mess area. "How do you take it?"

"Strong and black, if you please." He turned his attention back to Marcus. "Any news?"

"No, sir, not really. We're still docked at Hannibal's Reach. Most of the crew is off the ship on liberty right now. Halifax and I stayed behind to look after you. I can recall Wade and Devree if you feel like going out. I want all four of us with you if you're going to go onto the station."

He rubbed his temple with his thumb. "Later, perhaps. Right now, I need coffee, a shower, and something to eat."

"Now's a good time for it. The ship is almost empty, and we're connected to the station's water system. Plenty of hot water."

"Here's your coffee," Wade said, gliding back into the commons area. A half-liter bulb was in his hands. He brought himself to a stop and handed it to Mr. Krycek. "Careful, that's really hot."

"Mm, yes." The old man sipped the coffee through the straw on the bulb. "Perfect. Thank you."

A tone sounded throughout the ship, over the PA system. "Marcus, this is the captain. I need you up on the command deck right now. Bring our client with you. Quickly, if you please."

Marcus and Wade looked at each other.

"What's going on?" Mr. Krycek asked.

"Don't know, sir. Let's get upstairs and find out."

Up on the command deck, Captain Blackwood was strapped into her chair, and her face was grim. There was no one on deck with her, as the only other officers aboard were the engineer, the cargomaster, and of course, the purser. (Marcus was beginning to wonder if Mordechai Chang *ever* left his tiny cabin.) "Thank you for coming so quickly," she said, as Marcus, Wade, and Mr. Krycek entered the compartment. "We have a situation here."

"What's going on, ma'am?" Marcus asked.

"I received this message a few moments ago. It's coming from somewhere on the station, and I can't trace the location." She tapped her screen, bringing up a recorded video transmission on the main display.

Nickson Armitage appeared on screen. He was bound, gagged, and tied to a chair with cables. His head hung down; he appeared unconscious. "They call me Wraith," a woman said, matter-of-factly. She didn't appear on camera. "You know what I want, Captain Blackwood. I'm sending you a set of coordinates and a time. Bring Zander Krycek to me, and you'll get your first officer back. If you ignore me, I promise you that Mr. Armitage will suffer immensely before I let him die. If you involve the authorities, or attempt any sort of a rescue, he dies." A gloved hand appeared from off screen, grabbed the XO's hair, and pulled his head back. There was a wide black collar around his neck. "This is an explosive charge, Captain. It has multiple fail-safe features, and only I can disarm it. If you try anything during the exchange, he dies in a spectacular fashion."

She let him go, and his head flopped forward. He was breathing, but seemed to be unconscious. "I know this is difficult to accept. No one likes the feeling of powerlessness, but make no mistake, you *are* powerless. Do as I ask, and you'll have your crewman back unharmed. Do anything else, and his life is forfeit. Where do your loyalties lie, Captain? With your own first officer, or with a deluded old war criminal who thinks he can return to power and atone for himself? You're a capitalist, are you not? You've already been paid at least part of your fees. I'm sure the rest isn't worth the life of your crewman. You have three hours to decide. If you're not where I tell you to be, precisely on schedule, then I will rip this man apart, piece by piece, and I'll send you the video. You, personally, need to be there for the exchange, so I know it isn't a trick. Oh, and you should feel grateful. You and your ship are still both wanted by my superiors, but you're not my mission. Consider my letting you live a gift." The screen went dark as the message ended.

"Jesus Christ," Wade said. He looked at Marcus. "What do we do? I mean, she's a Combine operative, right?"

"Seems that way," Marcus said. Zander Krycek looked a little nervous, as if he were concerned the captain would hand him over. "You think you could disarm that bomb, Wade?"

"Maybe. It depends."

"A man's life is at stake, Mr. Bishop," Captain Blackwood said, sharply. "*Maybe* isn't good enough!"

"I understand that, ma'am, but it doesn't change my answer. That bomb collar could be configured a hundred different ways. I'll have to look at it, and even then, I can't make any guarantees. If I can get to him, I'll try my best. It's all I can do."

"Damn it!" the captain snarled, pounding her fist onto the armrest of her chair.

"This could be a trap, ma'am. The Combine wants you dead same as Mr. Krycek here. Let me get the rest of my team back here, and we'll come up with a plan."

"Captain Blackwood," Mr. Krycek said, "may I speak to you for a moment?"

She exhaled heavily. "Mr. Krycek, I assure you, I'm not going to hand you over to the Combine. Even if I were considering it, I wouldn't trust those bastards to uphold their end of any bargain."

"No, I was going to suggest that you use me as bait. Include me in the plan. It's much more likely to succeed if they see me there."

"Are you sure?"

"Captain, our relationship is a business transaction, and I understand that. Even so, I'm asking you to fight for me in a war that isn't your own. If I'm not willing to fight for you, why should you be willing to do so for me? I will help any way I can."

The captain nodded. "Thank you." She looked up at Marcus. "Please hurry. We don't have a lot of time."

When Nickson Armitage came to, it took a few moments for his eyes to focus. He had a dull, throbbing headache, as if he'd been binge drinking. He rubbed his face with his hands . . . or, at least, tried to. His hands were behind his back, and they wouldn't move. He was bound, arms and legs both, in a flexible cable, and was lying on a cold stone floor. A sealing patch was over his mouth, forcing it shut. He vaguely remembered the woman . . . *what was her name? Talia.* Talia had done something to him, injected him with something. *At least she put my clothes back on.* His flight suit, anyway. He had no idea where his boots were.

Where am I? Nothing looked familiar. He was at the intersection of two large tunnels, maybe four meters high by five meters wide. Amber service lights provided the only illumination; the tunnels were long and straight, but the floor curved upward in the distance. The floor was hewn from rock and ground smooth. He was still on Hannibal's Reach, he figured. *Service tunnels, maybe?* It made sense.

What the hell is that? There was something around his neck, maybe five centimeters wide. It was thick, and heavy, but he couldn't tell what it was. He struggled a bit, trying to see if his bindings would come loose. They didn't budge. Rolling over on his other side, Nickson still couldn't see anyone. He tried to scream though the sealant patch. His muted voice was drowned out by the constant dull roar of the air circulation system. No one would hear him down here.

"Don't hurt yourself struggling," a sultry voice said. Nickson flipped back over and found himself looking up into the eyes of Talia. Her face was visible, but the rest of her body was hidden beneath a thermoptic camouflage cloak. In the dim light of the tunnel, it was difficult to make out the telltale light distortion that happened when the cloak moved, folded, or bent. "Your shipmates are coming to get you. Just lie still, and this will be over soon." Her eyes darted upward. "In fact, I think they're here now." Her face was wiped away as she pulled the cloak's hood back over her head.

"MMMMM! MMMMMM-MMMM!" Nickson tried to scream, tried to warn his shipmates, but it was no good. They were walking right into a trap, and he was going to watch them all die. He could hear footsteps coming from one of the tunnels, getting closer and closer. He rolled over again, struggling to see who it was in the dim light. A man could be seen, silhouetted against the amber lights of the tunnel behind him. Another figure was with him, tall and feminine. *Captain? No!* He watched helplessly as Captain Blackwood and Zander Krycek both stepped into the tunnel intersection, looking around wearily.

"MMMMMM!" Nickson tried to shout, and flailed his body around. They saw him! They picked up their pace a little, moving to where Nickson was lying on the floor.

The captain knelt next to him. "Are you all right?"

He jerkily nodded his head.

"Good. Is she here? Your kidnapper?"

He vigorously shook his head up and down. "MMM-MMM!" *Get out of here before she kills you both!*

Captain Blackwood slowly stood up, looking around the tunnel intersection. "I'm here! I brought Zander Krycek! Show yourself!" Nickson strained his ears, listening for her footsteps, but she was quiet, and the air circulators were loud.

"Such a trusting fool, Captain," Talia said. Her voice was being projected electronically. It echoed throughout the intersection and couldn't be pinpointed. "I thought you'd be smarter than to come here yourself."

"You said that I needed to be here. Here I am. Here's the man you want. Now take that bomb off my officer!"

Bomb? This is a bomb?

"I will, but there are some things I need to discuss with you, first."

"Fine," the captain said, standing up. Reaching under her jacket, she retrieved a pair of bulky-looking goggles, quickly put them on, and powered them up. The lenses glowed a dull blue. Drawing her laser pistol, she pressed it out in front of her in both hands and pointed it at . . . nothing that Nickson could see.

"I can see you," she said, with a smile.

"We all can," someone else said. It was Marcus Winchester! He and his team appeared from a tunnel entrance, pistols drawn, wearing the same kind of goggles. "Make any sudden moves, lady, and you'll be dead before you hit the floor. Now disable your camo and put your hands in the air."

Yes! Yes! Take that, you lying Combine skag!

Talia laughed. "Very well. I seem to have underestimated you." She powered down the cloak and appeared before Nickson's eyes, only a few meters away. She slowly raised her hands in the air.

Wade Bishop spoke up, pointing his big revolver at her. "You almost get killed by one asshole in active camo, you take precautions." Thermoptic camouflage didn't make you invisible. When powered on, it would make you appear transparent, making you difficult to see, especially when standing still. Heat sinks allowed it to mask your thermal signature, at least for a time. There were countermeasures, though, goggles that saw in different spectra, which could reveal a camouflaged individual, especially at close range.

Her face was a calm mask. "That collar is on a timer," she said, coolly. "If I don't remove it within a certain time frame, it will detonate. I wonder, do you think the blast will kill him instantly, or do you suppose he'll be able to look around for a few seconds, maybe even see his headless body before he dies?"

"Fortunately, I have a bomb technician with me," the captain said, jerking her head toward Wade. She didn't lower her laser. "In any case, I promise you that if Nix dies, so do you. You need to understand, you're outnumbered. There are six of us, all with weapons on you. No trickery, nothing you can say, will result in you walking out of here alive unless you do exactly what I tell you to do."

"You must be confident in your bomb technician. I promise you it has anti-tamper features. However, I have a way of resolving this impasse in which we both get what we want, and nobody dies here."

"You can't have my client," the captain said, firmly.

"I don't want your client, Captain. I wish to defect."

What?

Captain Blackwood hesitated for a moment. "I'm sorry, did I hear you correctly?"

"You did," Talia confirmed. "I wish to defect."

"You can't possibly expect me to fall for this."

"I assure you, there's nothing to fall for."

"You don't need to defect to me. Take the bomb off my crewman, and be on your way. I'm certainly not going to report you to your masters."

"They can't monitor me down here. The signal won't get through fifteen hundred meters of rock. Everything I say and do is recorded."

"Your electronic comrade?"

"Yes. As soon as it reestablishes connection with my ship, it'll update them. The transmitter is relentless. This is a big station, but not so big that I can disappear in it, and the ship won't leave if they think I'm still here. I'm too valuable. I need to get away from them. I need my ECCOM surgically removed. This is where we can help each other."

"Why us? Why not just get on another ship?"

"Because, Captain, they won't just let me go. I can silence my ECCOM for brief periods of time, when radio silence is needed, but not indefinitely, and not long enough to get out of range. The transmitter is powerful, and it will use a ship's communications systems as a carrier signal if it has to. I only have a limited amount of control over it. Once they realize I'm on another ship, they'll come after me, and if they can't recover me they can remotely kill me. Any other ship will just hand me over. No one will risk their lives for the sake of a Combine operative."

"And you assume that I will?"

"No, but they're looking for you, too. Despite what I told you earlier, they won't ever grant you amnesty or let you go. Any offer promising that is a lie. You colluded with the Vox Populi and destroyed a cruiser. They will never stop hunting you, either. As long as I'm on your ship, I'm as safe as I can be, for now."

"Holy shit, lady," Wade said, exasperated. "All you had to do was say that from the start!"

"No. The captain is understandably suspicious. She won't let me on her ship unless she has to. And, I promise you, she has to. No disrespect to you, Mr. Bomb Technician, but you won't get that device off without killing Nickson here. So, what do you say, Captain? Get me off this station and out of the system, and I'll take the bomb off your officer. Mr. Krycek, in exchange for asylum on Ithaca, I can give you valuable intelligence regarding operations plans for your world. Do we have a deal?"

Captain Blackwood lowered her laser pistol, clenching her jaw. She looked down at Nickson and made eye contact with him, as if to ask what he thought.

Nickson nodded his head. They could deal with her if she caused problems. At the moment, his main concern was cutting the chitchat and getting the bomb off his neck while he still *had* a neck.

Zander Krycek spoke up next, holstering the pistol he was carrying. "Captain, if what she says is true, it's too good of an opportunity to pass up. I need every advantage I can get."

"Very well," Captain Blackwood said, coldly. She looked back up at Talia. "But I promise you this: If you try anything on my ship, or don't cooperate in every way, I won't hesitate to space you. Don't try me. Now, if you won't take the bomb off him, at least remove the binds so he can walk. Otherwise, you're carrying him."

Talia's facial expression changed, subtly. She seemed... relieved? Satisfied? It was hard to tell. "Thank you, Captain. We should go. If I'm offline too long, they'll send people to look for me."

The skipper put her laser back in its holster, underneath her jacket. "Okay, people, let's get moving. Marcus, if she tries anything even remotely suspicious, kill her." She knelt next to Nickson and helped him free himself from the cables binding his arms and legs. "This part might hurt," she said apologetically. Before Nickson could protest, she ripped the seal off his mouth in one quick motion.

"AUGH!" Nickson cried. He rubbed his face with

his hand. "Damn." The seal had pulled out half his beard stubble and had taken some skin with it. "Skipper, I am so sorry."

"Don't worry about it, Nix. Right now, let's just get you home."

Getting from deep in the bowels of Hannibal's Reach back to the *Andromeda* was a time-consuming process, and it included a stop at a clothing shop to get Nickson a new pair of boots. Talia, or whatever her name was, had left his boots in the hotel room. They were undoubtedly gone by now.

The Combine operative was safe while inside the asteroid, but she warned that her electronic comrade would attempt to establish an uplink to her ship while they traversed the docking superstructure on the way back to the *Andromeda*'s berth. She claimed that she'd be able to go radio silent for enough time to allow them to get back to the ship, but she suggested the captain engage the ship's electronic warfare suite to jam the signal.

Captain Blackwood refused to do that. Turning on the ECM before leaving port would interfere with every ship in the area, and the spaceport control authorities might refuse to let them leave until they shut it down. The captain had a better idea: once on board the *Andromeda*, the Combine operative would be sequestered in a smuggling compartment. It wouldn't be comfortable, as there was no acceleration couch in there, but the compartment was so heavily shielded as to act as a Faraday cage. In fact, it was shielded enough that it could work as a shelter from cosmic radiation in a pinch.

Mazer Broadbent and Kimball were waiting for them in the airlock at the ship's nose. Both men were grasping handholds in one hand and laser weapons in the other as the group arrived. Indira Nair was there, too, as the acting commander of the ship.

"All right," the captain said, turning toward Talia. "You're on my ship. Take the bomb off of him and disarm it."

"What, here? So you can just shove me back out the airlock?"

"Talia," Nickson said, speaking to her for the first time, "you have to trust us. We made a deal and we'll stand by it. Antagonizing the captain isn't going to help."

The cyborg sighed. "Fine. Come here." Turning Nickson around, she fiddled with the device around his neck for a moment. It beeped and unclasped itself, popping off his neck and drifting away before a crew member secured it.

Nickson felt relief wash over him. He felt another surge of relief now that he was finally able to scratch his neck. The collar had been itchy and irritating. The skipper turned toward him.

"Nix, I want you to get down to medical and have Harlan check you out. Indira, is everyone accounted for yet?"

"Not yet, Captain. The last few stragglers are on their way as we speak. I will let you know as soon as they arrive." Nickson could only imagine how unhappy the crew was, having its liberty cut short.

"Good. As soon as everyone is aboard, prep for departure. Have Kel plan a minimum time burn to the transit point. I want out of this system as soon as possible."

"Yes, Captain," the engineer said, and she disappeared through the hatch.

Captain Blackwood turned her attention to Talia. The operative's face was a mask, but Nickson thought he could see a hint of fear there. "Mazer, clap this woman in irons. You and Marcus escort her down to the smuggler's hold, and secure her there. Kimball, I want you to conduct an EMR scan of the compartment once it's sealed, and keep monitoring it. She has a transmitter that will try to talk to the Combine ship. If that signal somehow gets through, I want to know right way."

"Understood, Skipper," the cargomaster said.

"Please put your hands behind your back," Mazer Broadbent commanded. Talia complied, her face blank, her eyes locked on Nickson's, as the heavy-duty restraints were locked around her wrists. They connected to another set of restraints which was placed around her ankles, and to a wide collar which went around her neck. The irons, as they were colloquially known, would administer a powerful electric shock if the wearer struggled too much.

Nickson watched in silence as Talia was pushed through the hatch like a cargo pallet, her hair floating wildly around her head. He turned to the captain. "Thank you for coming after me." It would have been easier and less risky to the ship and mission if she had just left him to his fate.

She put a hand on his arm. "I never leave a man behind. Now, go see Harlan."

Log Entry 138
Mission 815-707-SSOC
Reconnaissance Ship 505

We have lost contact with asset SACRED WRAITH. Target ship Andromeda *rapidly departed and left the system. A thorough investigation conducted on Shen Long–28/Hannibal's Reach has revealed no sign of the asset, dead or alive. AI/CORE is CONFIDENT/HIGH/HIGH that the asset went rogue and is no longer on Shen Long–28/Hannibal's Reach. Commander and political officer concur. Furthermore, AI/CORE is CONFIDENT/MODER-ATE/LOW that SACRED WRAITH is on board the* Andromeda. *It is not understood how this came to pass, if it is the case. The* Andromeda *was scanned as it departed, and there was no locator signal. No locator signal was detected at all, from the time the asset went dark until the present.*

RS-505 cannot catch up to the Andromeda *now, unless the target ship stops for an unexpectedly long period of time. We will continue pursuit, travel to Ionia-5589/Ithaca, coordinate with friendly forces, and attempt to complete the mission there. Failure will result in severe disciplinary action.*

CHAPTER 24

The Privateer Ship *Andromeda*
Deep Space
EC-8590-A System

The medical bay was as clean and quiet as ever.
Harlan Emerson, the ship's flight surgeon, was very
particular about keeping his workspace just so. The
Andromeda was cruising at a steady 0.85 gravity as
Nickson Armitage entered medical. The compartment
was divided into three parts: the main area was the
largest part, had two acceleration-capable beds, and
could serve as either an exam room or an operating
room. Dr. Emerson was assisted here by the flight
medic, Felicity Lowlander, and an autodoc everyone
called Dr. Claw (on account of its gripping pincers).
There was a small laboratory off to the side, and an
even smaller subcompartment which the flight surgeon
used as an office.

"Hello, sir," Felicity said. Her frizzy red hair was
done up in a tight bun. Nickson couldn't help but
note her stunning green eyes every time he saw her;
according to the rest of the crew, they were real, and

not cosmetically enhanced. He fair skin was freckled around her nose. "Have you come to see our patient?"

Nickson nodded. "How's she doing?"

Felicity looked over her shoulder. The farthest of the two beds was obscured by an opaque screen, to give Talia some privacy as she rested. "Surgery went well, even though ... Mr. Armitage, I've never seen anyone that heavily augmented before. Even her internal organs have been replaced. She has a completely artificial digestive system, an artificial heart, artificial lungs, and ... well ... there isn't much left of the original woman in there. There's more machine than meat. She even has a high-density power cell in her lower back to power her systems. She's a hundred seventy-seven centimeters tall, and she's thin, but she weighs almost a hundred kilograms. She's got a lot of metal in her."

Nickson shook his head. "Dear God."

"Yeah. Like I said, I've never seen anything like it. The good news is, the doctor was able to remove her electronic comrade, the transmitter and receiver, a tiny nuclear battery, and the explosive charge which served as her kill switch."

"Explosive charge?"

"Yes. It was behind her right eye. We had Mr. Bishop come look at it. It was only a gram of explosives, but it would be enough to cause a fatal hemorrhage in the brain. She wasn't lying, it would have killed her instantly. Anyway, the antenna for her tracking systems is embedded in her spine. We couldn't remove that. But, she's not broadcasting or receiving anymore. The procedure was a success."

Nickson smiled. "Good. Very good. Can I see her?"

"You can. She's awake. Just . . . she acts like she's not, but she might be a little self-conscious about the way she looks. Don't overreact, okay?"

"Um, got it. Say, where is the doc?"

"He's down in his bunk. The surgery took hours. It was grueling."

"Okay. Thank you." Making his way across the compartment, Nickson first pulled back the privacy screen slightly. "May I come in?" he asked, without looking.

"Yes."

Ducking down, Nickson stepped through the doorway on the screen and slid it shut. Talia was on the bed, which had been raised so she could sit up. She was sipping water through a bulb, her hair hanging down so that he couldn't really see her face. When he approached, she looked up. Her right eye was gone. A rigid gray cover had been fastened over the socket.

"Hi," he said, awkwardly, trying not to stare. A metal folding chair, which magnetically attached to the deck, had been placed next to Talia's bed. Nickson sat down in it, which left the two of them face to face. "How are you doing?"

"He had to take out my eye," she said, flatly. "It was part of my ECCOM. On most people, it's external, bolted to the side of the head." She tapped her right temple. "But that won't work for an intelligence operative. Mine was internal."

"It was your right eye."

"Yes. But it's gone, all of it. I'm free." She sounded dispassionate. Nickson wondered if she even knew what *free* meant.

"Yeah, well, I'm glad. I'm glad it worked out."

"I'm sorry," she said, after a long moment. "For what

I did to you. I've been doing this for a long time, you know. You're the first one I've apologized to. The rest are dead anyway. Thank you for what you've done for me."

"It's okay," Nickson said, managing a smile for her. "Can I ask you something?"

"What, this?" she said, holding up the squeeze bottle. "Yes, I still need to drink water. I do have living tissue. My systems supply it to the tissue in the same way yours do."

Nickson actually had been curious about that, but it wasn't what he was going to ask. "No. I wanted to ask you, what made you decide to run? Er, defect, whatever you want to call it. Why did you do it? You took an enormous risk."

She lowered her bottle and broke eye contact. Her remaining eye had a look in it of someone who had been through hell. "You can't imagine what it's like," she said, quietly. "I was a weapon. An asset. They took everything from me, including my name."

"It's not Talia?"

"It was, once. My full name was Seven-Seven-One Talia, Five-Two-One, Oh-Three-Three, Gamma-Nine-Nine."

"That's not a name. It's a number."

"It's how they do it on Orlov. Seven-Seven-One is the year I was born, by the reckoning of the system calendar. Talia is my given name. The rest is my number and identifier suffix. I know it seems strange to you, but you can tell where someone is from and how old they are by their name and number. It's how it's always been done. But they took that away from me, too. They called me Wraith."

"Wraith?"

"It's my asset code name, SACRED WRAITH. They're randomly selected. Mine was just more fitting than most, I guess. Has there been any sign of my ship?"

The Combine special operations ship, the *Galaxis* class they had known as the *Bonaventura*, had changed its configuration before docking at Hannibal's Reach. Nickson was surprised to learn that such ships are capable of altering their external appearance, electromagnetic, and drive signatures. That, combined with a change in transponder identity, can spoof everything but a close-up inspection. Her former ship, Reconnaissance Ship 505, had been in disguise as the *Homestar Runner* at the asteroid station.

"No. We've been watching for them. The skipper fed the information you gave us into the tactical systems. No matter which configuration it's in, we'll be able to identify it." There was a signal hidden within the ship's electromagnetic radiation signature, one that let such ships identify one another, even at great distances. Nickson was sure that the Concordiat OSI would love to know about that. "Standing orders are to evade if we can until we get to Ithaca. If we can't evade, we're going to destroy it."

"Good," Talia said, bitterly. "They kept me in cold sleep most of the time, when we were out on these long-duration missions. The asset has to be preserved, you know. I miss years that way. As near as I can tell, I've been SACRED WRAITH for almost fifty standard years."

"Fifty years! You don't look old enough."

"As I said, I was in cold sleep most of the time. I'd only get to be alive when we were back home."

"That's . . . hell, I don't even have words for how inhuman that is. Is that why you wanted to leave?"

"Part of it. Some of it was impulse. When we first met, I was fully intending to go through with my mission. I was going to use you to get to your ship, and kill Captain Blackwood and Zander Krycek both."

"What changed?"

"I don't know. We go rogue sometimes. We all know about it. No one talks about it. We just pretend it doesn't happen until it does. That's why there are so many methods of control. That's why we're kept in cold sleep."

"You make it sound like you're a robot. You're not a robot. You're a human being."

She looked at her hands for a moment, then back up at him. A dark circle hung under her eye. "Are you sure about that?"

"I am. Robots don't feel sorry for putting bombs on people's necks. They don't enjoy sex. When they go rogue, it's because of a malfunction or a software error. You didn't have a malfunction, you made a *choice*. What they did to you, *that* was the malfunction. It's not natural. It's not *right*."

"I think it was the first choice I've ever made," she said, more quietly than before. "The first real choice. I wasn't deciding how I was going to carry out my orders, or how I was going to navigate the predetermined path in front of me. I didn't think it would work. I thought they would kill me, or your crew would."

"You did it anyway."

"I did. Death on my own terms is better than living like this. It's not even living. It's just . . . existing.

Functioning. Doing as you're told without thinking much about it. No more." She shook her head slowly. "I can't do it anymore."

"If that was your first choice, you made a good one," Nickson managed, trying to sound encouraging.

"Thank you," she said again. "I need to rest now. I feel tired."

"Okay. I just wanted to check on you. Rest up, and I'll be back later."

CHAPTER 25

Ithaca
Ionia-5589 System
Southern Hemisphere

Adisa Masozi wrote in her journal, quietly tapping away on her tablet. Patrol Base Echo was a luxury resort compared to living out in the field, and she had enjoyed being able to shower every day. SAZ-CDF Ranger patrols would go out every so often, only to return days or weeks later, often missing men. The Colonial Government had formally declared the Southern Autonomous Zone in open rebellion, and the SAZ had responded by formally declaring independence. All the formality made the whole thing sound like little more than a gentlemen's disagreement, but the reality was much bloodier than that.

Air attacks on the cities, bases, and critical infrastructure of the Southern Autonomous Zone had become common. Air raid warning sirens blared every few days, forcing citizens to retreat to hastily built underground shelters. The SAZ had spent the last twenty years heavily investing in air defenses, though. Every aerial attack cost the governmental forces dozens or hundreds of their drones. Even intercontinental ranged ballistic missiles were successfully shot down by lasers and railguns. Still, many of the bombers and missile attacks got through, and it was taking a toll on the South. Adisa had been informed that her home in the town of Brandywine had been destroyed.

More and more young men were joining the Civil Defense Force, which was rapidly being reformed into a real military. Up north, the Colonial Guard had been redesignated the Colonial Army, and they were conscripting new soldiers by the thousands. Both sides had vast resources and modern, distributed manufacturing bases at their disposal. Given the right raw materials, a basic commercial electromechanical assembler in someone's garage could build several rifles a day. An industrial grade one could do dozens, or hundreds, and such technology was widespread on nearly every colony world. Neither side had an immediate strategic advantage, and neither side was capable of delivering a knockout blow to the other. It would be a war of attrition and will. The Southern forces' only real hope was to bleed the Colonial Government so badly that they gave up on their pact with the Combine before the delegation arrived to formally sign the treaty.

Adisa was no strategic expert, but she didn't think that was going to work. She expected that, at some point, the Southern government would attempt to destroy the Northern one by nuclear bombardment. *I wonder,* she wrote, *if anyone will be left to declare themselves the winner. Will the colony survive such a blow to our critical infrastructure? Will the Combine come in anyway, and annex the planet while there is no one to defend it?*

Even still, I fear that living in squalor, having survived a nuclear war, is infinitely preferable to living under Combine rule. In that scenario, there is still hope for the future. If the Combine lands, there is no future. I don't care what their propaganda says. I've read too many reports, from credible sources, about them. Once they get a foothold on this world they will never let it go.

Life is fleeting. My own piece of this war is small, and yet I've seen so much death. She looked up, thoughtfully, contemplating her next choice. Having decided, she sent a quick message to Roc, then brought her journal back up. *I've learned that you have to find what happiness you can, while you can.*

Some ten minutes later, there was a knock at the door of her tent. Barefoot, dressed in camouflage fatigue pants and a halter top, Adisa made her way to the door, and opened it.

Roc was waiting for her. "I'm sorry it took me so long to get over here, love," he said. "I was having a shower. What do you need?" He smelled nice, was wearing a fresh set of fatigues, and was clean-shaven. When he wasn't crawling around the jungle, covered in mud and grime, the Ranger was a very handsome man.

"Come in," she answered, stepping back so he could get by. "Close the door."

"Is everything all right?" Roc asked, closing the door like he was asked. "What—" He fell silent as she raised a finger to his lips. Before he could say anything else, Adisa stood up on her tiptoes, threw her arms around his neck, and kissed him, deeply. After a long moment, Roc pulled back, his eyes wide.

Adisa was suddenly very self-conscious, even embarrassed. Had she been too presumptuous? Too forward?

"I'm sorry," she said, meekly. She shouldn't have done that. Technically, she was his superior. It wasn't ethical. It could get him in trouble. "I didn't mean to—mm!" Taking her in his arms, Roc kissed her passionately. Adisa backed toward her cot, pulling Roc with her, never breaking the embrace. He surprised her by scooping her up in his arms, carrying her over, and gently laying her on her rack.

"Adisa, are you sure about this?" he asked, unbuttoning his uniform shirt.

Adisa responded by pulling her top off over her head. "Take your clothes off," she said. She looked up into his eyes, and smiled. "That's an order."

"Yes, ma'am," the Ranger replied, tossing his shirt onto the floor. He kicked off his boots, doffed his trousers, and climbed onto her cot. "What is your next order?" he asked, smiling.

She put her arms around his neck, and wrapped her legs around his waist. "Make love to me," she whispered into his ear. "I need to feel you."

In the Ranger's arms, Adisa was able to forget the world for a while. In that tent, there was only the two of them. No Combine, no war, no death. It had been a long time since she'd had sex, and Roc was *very* skilled. He touched her in ways no man ever had, and made her feel like the only woman in the world.

Tired, happy, and satisfied, Adisa curled up with Roc on her cot and listened to his heart beat. It was so peaceful she never wanted the moment to end. "Thank you," she said, almost a whisper.

Roc ran his fingers through her hair. "I didn't know you felt this way."

"I didn't, either. I'm sleepy now."

He sighed. "I hate to hit and run, as they say, but I've got a patrol-planning meeting to get to. The major will flip his wig if I'm late."

"Which major?" Adisa asked. "Major Angstrom? The one with the awful mustache?"

Roc laughed. "That's the one. The lads just call him *The Mustache,* or *Major 'Stache.* I don't know where they dug him up, but he's real prickly about being on time for his meetings. Reminds me of my primary school teacher."

"Ugh, he's the *worst,*" Adisa said. She hadn't dealt with him much, but he was a dour, perpetually unhappy man, utterly devoid of a sense of humor. "You'd better go, then. He has a temper, that one."

"I'll come back and see you when it's over," Roc said, sitting up.

"Promise?"

The handsome Ranger leaned in and kissed her one last time. "Promise, love. Get some sleep, yeah?"

"I think I will," she said, and felt herself drifting off as her lover left her tent.

Adisa sat up, suddenly, as the air-attack alarm started to sound. *Indirect fire! We're under attack!* The firebase was equipped with laser defenses, but sometimes rounds still got through. She swung her legs off her cot and hurriedly got her clothes on. She needed to get to the shelter. *BOOM!* She gasped as an explosion rocked the base. It was close enough that her ears popped from the concussion.

"Adisa!" It was Roc. He threw open the door to her tent and ran inside. He wasn't in combat gear, but he'd grabbed his rifle. "Come on, love, we've gotta go, now!"

"I'm coming!" she said, jumping to her feet. "Let's get to the shelter!"

"No, not the shelter, it's not—" *BOOM!* Their base was shaken by another explosion before he could finish the sentence. "It's not just artillery, it's an assault. There's too many of them. You need to get out of here, so come on!"

As they left her tent and ran down the gravel road, Adisa barely had time to take in the horror around her. Fires burned. Men and aliens both screamed for help. The artillery barrage had apparently ceased, but a high-pitched whine, like dozens of giant, angry hornets, was filling the night air.

"What is that?" Adisa asked, gasping, running on the road behind Roc.

"Banshees!" he said. "Combat drones! They're—shit, get down!" He shoved her down to the gravel and opened fire. A combat drone screamed into view then, its meter diameter, contra-rotating lift fans keeping it aloft a few meters above the ground. Roc tore it apart with a long burst from his assault rifle. It spun off, out of control, and crashed into the dirt. "Come on, we've got to keep moving!" he said, pulling her to her feet.

"Where are we going to go?"

"The motor pool! I'm going to get you away from here before the base is overrun!"

They were running again as chaos reigned all around them. Native warriors and Southern Rangers fought and died as dozens of Banshee drones swarmed the patrol base. Each was equipped with a visible-spectrum pulse laser, and blue streaks and electric snaps filled the dusty, smoky air as they fired relentlessly, and with grisly accuracy.

"Roc, look!" Adisa pointed as a pair of ducted-fan VTOL aircraft came to a halt over the patrol base. There was nowhere for them to land, as the landing pad had the burning wreckage of an aircraft blocking it, but they didn't need to. Doors opened on their rears, ropes dropped to the ground, and men began sliding down, one after another. Heavy plasma guns on nose turrets sprayed the already-burning base with streaks of blue-white death.

"Shit!" the Ranger snarled, grabbing her by the hand and pulling her in a different direction. The way to the motor pool was blocked by enemy infantry. "This way!" Another VTOL, this one much larger than the others, lumbered past overhead, but Adisa lost sight of it in the smoke and darkness.

Rounding a bend in the road, they were in sight of the seldom-used west gate of the patrol base. The jungle, dark and foreboding, loomed beyond. The pseudo-trees were lit red from the fires, and smoke blocked some of the light from Ithaca's two moons. They took off at a run toward it, as the sounds of gunfire and the screams of men became less frequent. As Roc ran to the controls to try to get it open, Adisa turned and looked at the conflagration behind them. It had been a massacre.

"There!" Roc said, triumphantly. Slowly, the gate, four meters tall and made of high-tensile mesh, began to retract itself, creaking and groaning from lack of use. "As soon as it opens, go. I'll be right behind you. I'll—Adisa, *go!*" Roc dropped to the prone and opened fire. A cluster of enemy soldiers had appeared behind them. Bullets snapped through the air. "I'll hold them off!" he shouted, popping off a round from his weapon's underslung grenade launcher. "*Go!*"

There was nothing else to do. Adisa was armed only with a small pistol. The gate was still slowly opening, but the gap was over a meter wide now. She ran through the gap and was outside of the compound. She didn't have time to stop and think or plan a direction. She just ran. Her heart pounding, her breathing ragged, she ran, down the road, away from the overrun base.

From the darkness, down the road, a bright spotlight turned on. Adisa slid to a halt as she was caught in the light. She couldn't see what it was coming from, exactly, but it was big, and it was getting closer. On the verge of panic, she turned right and ran off the road, jumping the drainage ditch and into the cover of the pseudo-trees.

Barely any moonlight penetrated the canopy of the jungle. The floor here was relatively clear, with bioluminescent fungal-analogues covering the bottoms of the trees and the forest floor. It gave her just enough light to navigate by, and she was grateful for it. Adisa slowed to a walk, trying to catch her breath. Her heart was pounding so hard she could feel it in her ears. She paused, bent over, hands on her knees, wishing she had some water with her. Patrol Base Echo was deep enough in SAZ territory that she didn't think the government forces would try to hold it. Her best bet was to hide in the jungle until Roc found her. She just had to avoid getting eaten by any of the native wildlife before then.

Her heart dropped into her stomach as another spotlight flashed on. She looked up, slowly, at the source of the light, waiting for death to come at any moment. In between the twisting-vine trunks of the towering pseudo-trees, stood a hulking combat mech, maybe four and a half meters tall. Its wide, armored feet thumped and sunk into the soft, fungus-covered ground as it approached. Its main body was boxy and armored, with a cluster of lenses on an articulated "face." Arms on either side housed weapons, and it appeared to have a missile launcher on its back. She had never seen anything like it, even when she lived up north. It was of Combine origin. It *had* to be.

The mech lumbered to a halt in front of her, keeping her in its spotlight. She thought about going for her pistol, but what was the point? A little 5.7mm compact wasn't going to do anything to that armored monster. She could run, but her legs wouldn't move. She didn't know if it was fear or exhaustion or both.

With a sound like a coiling metal cable, an articulated tentacle shot out of the machine's side and wrapped itself around Adisa's waist. Before she could even process what was happening, it wrapped farther around her arms and shoulders, squeezing her so tightly she could barely breath. She tried to scream, but couldn't, as the war machine carried her off into the darkness.

Adisa didn't know where she was, nor how long she'd been there. The cell she was kept in was lit constantly. Every so often, a tube of nutrient paste and a bottle of water would be given to her, but it seemed to be at irregular intervals, and she couldn't use the feed schedule to judge the passage of time.

One end of her cell had a padded mat on the floor. The other had a toilet. There was nothing else, save the camera that was always watching her. It was a turret, centered in the ceiling, too high up to reach.

It tracked her around the cell, constantly, no matter where she went. No one had spoken to her. Occasional footsteps outside her cell door were the only indication she had that there was anyone else around, wherever it was she was being held.

She wasn't sure of that, either. The mech that had captured her brought her to government troops. She'd been promptly disarmed, bound, and a bag was put over her head. She was kept that way for many hours, as she was loaded onto an aircraft and brought somewhere. Her best guess was that she was still in the south somewhere. She didn't recall blacking out for any length of time, and she hadn't been in the aircraft long enough to get back up to the terraformed zone. It was probably one of the Colonial Army's forward operating bases in the southern hemisphere. Even if that hadn't been just a guess, the information did her no good. No one was coming to rescue Adisa. Sooner or later, they would start in on her, and God only knew what she would divulge when they finally broke her.

She should have killed herself before she let herself get captured. She never should have let them take her. She'd been too afraid, though, unable to act when she needed to. Roc was likely dead, and worse, he'd died for nothing. She didn't have the means to do so now. She was given only a coverall and a pair of soft shoes with no laces. There was nothing to hang herself from, nothing to cut herself with, and she was constantly watched.

Adisa despised the coverall. It was bright yellow and had no pockets. It only opened in the front, so she had to strip down to use the toilet, and she wasn't given any undergarments. Whomever was monitoring her got to watch her sit there, all but naked, as she peed. It was humiliating, dehumanizing, and she was utterly powerless to do anything about it.

One day, she sat up as she heard the approach of heavy feet in the hall. The whining of servos and the rhythmic plodding of the steps told her it wasn't a person. When the cell door slid open, her suspicion was confirmed. Standing in the doorway was a bipedal, upright, vaguely humanoid robot. Its right arm ended in what looked like a machine gun. Its left arm was capped with a three-clawed pincer. Its head was a lump-armored can with an ocular cluster and several antennae protruding from it. It had been painted brown, with the symbol of the Ithacan Colonial Government on its chest, but Adisa was sure that it, too, was of Combine origin.

"Step out into the hall," the robot ordered, in a synthesized baritone voice. It stepped back so it wasn't blocking the doorway. Hesitantly, Adisa came to her feet and left her cell. The robot's arm-gun tracked her every move. "Walk that way," it commanded, its pincer arm pointing down the hall.

Adisa looked down the hall, wondering where she was being taken. The hall was more dimly lit than her cell had been, and was quiet save the constant drone of an air circulation system. Nothing moved except camera turrets.

"Move," the robot ordered, jamming her in the back with its pincer. "Comply or you will be shot." Stumbling forward, Adisa regained her footing and walked down the hall, the robot methodically plodding along behind her. Either side of the hall was lined with cell doors, just like hers. The hall terminated in a small foyer. A door on one side led to another room. On the right, there was what looked like a lift. "Turn left," the robot said, and so she complied.

"What do I do now?" she asked, once she had come to the door. It was plain, and made of metal.

"Open the door."

"How?"

"Touch the pad."

Doing as she was told, Adisa touched the small sensor pad on the wall next to the door. The door then hissed open, revealing a dark room.

"Go in. Move."

A sense of fear building inside her, Adisa slowly stepped through the door, into the cool darkness. After a second or two, the lights flickered on and began to buzz, steadily. The walls were lined with equipment and screens, the purpose of which she could only guess at. In the middle of the room, bolted to the hard, ceramicrete floor, was an adjustable, padded chair.

The robot marched into the room behind Adisa, forcing her out of the way. "Sit in the chair," it commanded.

"What is this?" she asked. "What are you doing to me?"

"Sit in the chair," the robot repeated, prodding her with the pincer once again. Struggling to keep her composure, Adisa did as she was ordered.

"Place your arms on the arm rests." As soon as she did so, restraints popped out and fastened her hands and feet in place. Another one slid out from the head rest, wrapped around her forehead, and pulled her head back until it was immobilized. Without saying another word, the robot pivoted around and left the room, the door sliding shut behind it.

For a while, nothing happened. Adisa was alone in the cold room, listening to the incessant buzzing of the lights and the droning of the air system. Something above her clunked. She couldn't move her head to look up, but she could see it as it snaked down from the ceiling. A metallic tentacle quietly slid straight down, then turned ninety degrees so that it was pointing right at her face. On the end was another lens cluster. It stopped a few centimeters from her face.

"Calibrating," another synthesized voice declared. Lights flashed as it scanned. "Calibration complete." It then began to retract itself back into the ceiling.

Adisa had had enough. "What do you want?" she screamed, her voice not even echoing in the insulated room. There was no answer, from man or machine, at least at first. After a few long moments, the door slid open again. A tall, thin man walked in, dressed in a dark gray uniform with a high collar. His face was pallid. He was completely bald, lacking even eyebrows. Without saying anything, he tapped on the controls of some of the equipment.

"Who are you?" Adisa asked, quietly.

The man turned, as if noticing her for the first time. He leaned in, too close, and it made her skin crawl. His eyes were hazel but bloodshot. His lips were cracked and dry, and he kept licking them. On the right side of his head, fastened to his temple, was a small gray box, with a tiny camera and a light on it. His right shoulder was emblazoned, in red, with the rocket, gear, and olive branches logo of the Orlov Combine.

"My name is Gregory," he said, dispassionately, with an accent she couldn't place. His Commerce English sounded a little off. He would sometimes put the accent on the wrong word. "Gregory Nine-Three-Six, Seven-Seven-One. But, please, just Gregory. No need for formalities. I am here to get to know you."

"What do you want from me?"

"As I said, I am here to get to know you."

"What is all this?"

"This is my workspace. This is my equipment. It helps me get to know you, Adisa Masozi. When we are finished, I will know you as if I were your brother. Do you have a brother, Adisa?"

She didn't say anything.

"I know that you do not. But, you will feel as if you do, when we are finished. You will trust me, and you will tell me the truth in all things. I will trust you, and I will believe what you say, because I will know that you are telling the truth."

"I'm a civilian," Adisa said, trying not to sound like she was pleading. "I don't know anything!"

"Adisa, how can I trust you if you lie to me? I know you know things. You know how to speak. You know how to walk. You know how to tell lies. You know that your father is Zander Krycek, and that you sent a message to him, asking him to return. He is on his way, your father. The information I have is old, but he is on his way. He may arrive soon. Are you excited to see your father again?"

Once again, Adisa didn't answer.

"You should be excited. I never knew my father, Adisa. I was raised in a crèche. I learned at a very young age that people tell lies, and that lies make me angry. Lies make me so angry that I dedicated my life to stamping them out. Everyone is honest with me, now, in the end. You will be honest with me, too."

"Are you going to kill me?"

"What?" The interrogator turned back toward Adisa, and once again leaned in, entirely too close. His breath had a disinfectant smell, like a freshly scrubbed hospital floor. "No, no, no, Adisa, I am not going to kill you. You can believe what I say because I only tell the truth. As I said, I hate lies. I am not going to kill you. You and I are going to have a conversation, and that is all. The difference is, if you tell me a lie, I will know, and you will be punished for it. The more you lie, the worse your punishment will be. You will not die, but it will hurt, Adisa. It will hurt in ways you cannot imagine." Adisa was afraid, and closed her eyes. He kept talking. "You see, the only way to weed out man's lies is to change his nature, and the only way to change his nature is through pain. It is through pain that man learns, that man changes, and through pain I will teach you not to lie. But, when you tell me the truth, you will be rewarded. Instead of pain you will experience pleasure, euphoria, a wonderful ecstatic feeling that will make you happy. I want you to enjoy telling the truth. Do you understand?"

A tear rolled down Adisa's cheek. "Go to hell."

The interrogator smiled, licking his lips again. "Let us begin."

CHAPTER 26

The Privateer Ship *Andromeda*
Ionia-5589 System

Captain Blackwood liked to say that space travel was not an endeavor for the impatient. The way Nickson Armitage saw things, she had the right of it. It had taken the *Andromeda* over two thousand hours of flight time, not including stops, to reach the Ionia-5589 system. Now, after so much tedium, the ship could be in real danger as it made its final approach to Ithaca.

Nickson and the captain were both on the command deck for this. The ship's senior officers were on duty and at their stations, strapped into their acceleration chairs. The junior crewmembers, like Liam and the Winchester girl, were secured in their berths, as were all their passengers. Landing was dangerous enough when half the planet wasn't inclined to try and shoot you down. Even under the best circumstances, someone walking around during the final portion of a flight could be seriously injured.

The exception was Zander Krycek. He had insisted on being up on the command deck as they made their final approach. He was strapped into the folding jump seat to the left of the captain's command chair. It wasn't a proper acceleration seat; if the ship had to maneuver, he would likely black out. But it was enough to keep him from flying around the cabin should things get dicey.

As the *Andromeda* approached Ithaca, the captain had ordered the transponder be left off. This wouldn't hide the approach of the ship, of course. There was very little that could hide the signature of fusion rocket, even across great distances. Even still, there was no point in announcing their presence if they didn't have to. Nickson's screens showed a few ships moving in and around Ithaca, and two of them were Combine bulk freighters.

"Captain, we have an incoming message from another ship," Nuchy said, looking at her display. "Her transponder identifies her as the *Lillehammer*, a free trader out of Eden-3. They're on an approach vector, closing speed, sixty kilometers per second. Their trajectory has them getting no closer than fifty thousand kilometers. Looks like they're headed to the transit point."

"Respond to the message. Put it up on the big screen," Captain Blackwood commanded. A moment later, a man's face appeared on their screen. He was an older fellow, with graying blonde hair and a beard. He wore a blue flight suit with four gold captain's bars embroidered on the shoulders.

"Greetings!" he said, his voice pleasant but serious. "I am *Kaptein* Alex Kempton of the *Lillehammer*. Your transponder doesn't seem to be working. To whom am I speaking?"

"Catherine Blackwood," the captain answered, elbows

resting on the arm rests of her command chair. "Captain of the *Andromeda*. What can I do for you?"

"I wanted to warn you, friend, that things are not so good on Ithaca. If you're a free trader, you might want to seek your fortune elsewhere. War has broken out on this colony."

"War?"

"Yes. The northerners and the southerners have started shooting at each other. I don't know over what, exactly. Probably someone is unhappy about these damned Combine ships in the system. But, whether you try to land in the north or the south, the other side may try to shoot you down. I wanted to warn you. All free traders have been fleeing the system."

"I see. Thank you, Captain, for the warning. It is very much appreciated."

"Godspeed, Captain, and safe travels." With that, the skipper of the *Lillehammer* was gone.

Nickson spun his chair around to look at the captain. The color had drained from Zander Krycek's face.

"My God," the exiled president said. "We may be too late."

"Mr. Krycek," the captain said, "it's time for you to contact your people."

"Yes. Of course. You're right. Mr. Armitage, do you have the frequency and codes I gave you?"

"They're in the system." Kya had given him codes that would allow him to securely talk directly with the Strategic Command Authority of the Southern Autonomous Zone. "We can broadcast whenever you're ready. There'll still be lag at this distance, so when you speak, give them a couple seconds to respond." He wondered what kind of reception Mr. Krycek would receive. Kya had promised him that he would be recognized as the rightful leader of the colony, and that his authority would be deferred to, but would that really be the case? What if they really wanted him as a figurehead? What if they didn't care who he was, or what office he used to hold?

"Nickson, attempt to establish communications with the Southern Autonomous Zone authorities, if you please."

"Yes, ma'am," Nickson said, spinning back around in his chair. Tapping his controls, he programmed the broadcast to match the frequency-hopping pattern they were given. He then sent a test signal, a request to establish a live connection, and some basic information about the *Andromeda*. After thirty seconds, the light turned green, and his display flashed CONNECTION ESTABLISHED. "We're live, Skipper."

The *Andromeda* was decelerating, tail first, toward Ithaca at a steady one gravity. Zander Krycek unfastened his restraints, stood up, and walked to the center of the command deck as the feed went live. On the big screen was the face of an Ithacan soldier, wearing a blue dress uniform. Stars on his shoulder indicated that he was a general officer. His white hair contrasted with his ebony complexion. "Mohammed?" Zander said, recognizing the man. "Mohammed Farai! I'll be damned."

"Mr. President," the general said, smiling. "It's been too long. We're glad to have you back."

"It's good to see you, my friend. You've come a long way from being my S3."

"When tensions started to heat up, the government of the Southern Autonomous Zone began recruiting veterans of the civil war. Many of us were given promotions, as we were the only ones with real military experience. I went from a retired major to an active major-general."

As Nickson watched, Zander's facial expression hardened. "It seems you went and started the war without me, Mohammed."

"It was necessary, Mr. President. The Northerners have been pushing deeper and deeper into our territory, setting up railgun artillery, missile batteries, and drone bases. We had to act before we were at a strategic disadvantage. The few moderate voices in the Colonial Government have been purged. We had few allies."

"And now you have none!" He took a breath. "Listen, I have something to tell you. Colonel Starborn is dead."

"What? How?"

"There was an attempt on my life on Heinlein. Your man Sebastian pulled the trigger. He shot Erasmus in the head, then turned his gun on me. My steward bot is the only reason I'm here talking to you."

"Sebastian? Impossible. He was no assassin! He was a political activist!"

"I suspect they got to him, somehow. Perhaps they threatened his family. We've also had a Combine special-operations ship haunting our footsteps the entire way. We'll send you the relevant data, so you know what to look for."

The general seemed stunned. "Merciful Allah. Erasmus was a good man. He was one of the highest-placed moles we had in the Colonial Guard." He hesitated for a moment. "Forgive me, Mr. President, there's something else you should know. They have your daughter. Adisa was captured."

"No . . . no, that can't be right. How? Where was she? Why weren't you keeping her safe?"

"She was the liaison between our Ranger regiment and the native forces. She was in the field with them, and was captured when one of our forward patrol bases fell."

"Native forces? They agreed to help her?"

"That's right. They are fighting with us."

"My God, she actually pulled it off. How many?"

"All of them, I think. They held a conclave and it was decided. I'll send you all of Adisa's reports."

"We have to get her back. Mohammed, we can't leave them in their hands. You know what they'll do to her!"

"I'm sorry, Mr. President. I don't know that there is anything we can do. We have offered hundreds of prisoners in exchange for her release, and they didn't answer. I don't think the Colonial Army has her. I think their Combine *advisors* do."

Nickson turned back to look at Zander. His face was white. He kept his composure, but you could see the heartbreak on his face.

"I . . . understand," Zander said, after a long moment.

"I'm having instructions sent to your ship. You will be given a priority berth at our spaceport. It's under the cover of our air defenses, but you still need to be cautious on your approach. Once they see that you're going to land here, the Colonial forces will try to shoot you down. I'll have my people send everything we have on their surface-to-space weapons systems, so you're not caught unawares. I would not recommend attempting aerobraking."

"Thank you, Mohammed. Please keep me updated."

"Yes, sir. And, for what it's worth, welcome home." The connection was broken, and the big screen changed back to its normal display.

"I'm sorry, Mr. Krycek," Captain Blackwood said. "I don't have children, but I know what it's like to have someone you love taken from you."

"Captain, would it be possible to speak to you and Mr. Armitage in private?"

"Um, certainly. Let me get Mr. Azevedo up here, and we can all meet in the astrogation deck."

"I think that Mr. Winchester should be there as well."

"Very well." She looked at Nickson. "Nix, call them up here."

A short while later, Nickson, the captain, Marcus Winchester, and the astrogator, Kel Morrow, were standing together in the astrogation deck with Zander Krycek. Mordechai Chang appeared on a nearby screen.

"Thank you all for meeting me here," Captain Blackwood said. "Mr. Krycek, go ahead."

"Thank you, Captain. I have a proposal for you all. If you're not aware, those Combine bastards have my daughter. God only knows what they're doing to her. I haven't had time to go into the reports in depth, but she was the one who facilitated the alliance between the Southern Autonomous Zone and the native Ithacan species. That alliance is critical. The war may not be winnable without it. There are fears that without her, the alliance may not last. That notwithstanding, there is also the issue of the immense propaganda victory her capture could be for the Combine. They will break her, and they will use her to demoralize their enemies. This cannot go unanswered."

Marcus Winchester spoke up first. "I understand your reasoning, sir, but I'm not seeing what we can do about it. Even if we knew where she was, my four-man team can't conduct a rescue like that. It's impossible."

"You're correct. I'm not proposing a rescue. I think we should gain some leverage on our enemies and sue for her release."

The captain raised an eyebrow. "How do you propose we do that?"

"There are Combine ships in this system, are there not?"

"There are," Kel confirmed. "There is a *Tyrant-Romeo*-class bulk cargo ship on final approach, the same as we are," he said, highlighting the ship in the holotank. "Its trajectory will put it in a high orbit over the planet. The other is . . . hmm. The computer is only sixty percent confident, but it looks like a *Troubadour* class of some sort. That's the biggest known freighter in the Combine fleet. That one is on approach from out-system. It's at least a hundred and eighty hours out."

Nickson studied the image of the *Tyrant*-class freighter that the astrogator had put on one of the screens. It had a small, spherical primary hull at the top, which housed the crew habitat and command deck. Below that was a cluster of four cylindrical reaction mass tanks. The ship's main body stretched out below that, a narrow spine almost three hundred meters long. At the bottom was the propulsion unit, a cluster of engines and radiators. The spine is where it carried the modular cargo containers. Each was trapezoid shaped, and they mounted to the ship's spine at the twelve, three, six, and nine o'clock positions. The overall length of the ship was four hundred meters. It even carried a small parasite craft, a transatmospheric shuttle capable of carrying six passengers.

"Probably another weapons shipment," Zander said. "They've been supplying Colonial forces with weapons and ordnance under the guise of humanitarian aid."

"Would it be possible to intercept either of them?"

"Wait, intercept them? What are you getting at?" Nickson asked.

Kel didn't wait for an answer. "The one on final approach we could catch fairly easily. It would still be far enough away from the planet that we would be out of range of any surface-to-space weapons they have. Intercepting the other would require substantial consumption of reaction mass, and they would see us coming from a long way out. Our maneuver options would be limited by the time we returned to Ithaca. They could turn around, and possibly beat us back to the transit point." A huge freighter like the *Troubadour* class had significantly more reaction mass than the *Andromeda*.

"Please answer the question, Mr. Krycek," Captain Blackwood said. "What *are* you getting at?"

"I told you we might need the *Andromeda* for fire support. It's time we made a statement."

"I don't see how destroying a Combine merchantman will get them to release your daughter, sir," Nickson said. "I mean no offense."

"I don't mean to destroy it, Mr. Armitage. I mean to *capture* it. Mr. Winchester, do you feel up for a boarding action?"

"Are you serious?"

"Deadly serious. Mr. Morrow, what is the crew complement of the *Tyrant* class?"

"Uh . . ." Kel looked down at a screen. "Eight, normally, sometimes more, sometimes less. They're not warships, so they don't have much need for damage-control functions or crew redundancy."

"Are they armed?"

"Officially, no. Going armed would get them barred from a lot of systems. Unofficially? I wouldn't be surprised if they had lasers or other modest defenses." Armed privateers and free traders were common. Combine ships, however, being an official government fleet, had special rules they needed to abide by.

Marcus rubbed his chin. "Wade and I have EVA training. Devree doesn't have much, just what she's done while on the *Andromeda*. Halifax, I'm not sure. We probably could take the freighter by force, assuming they didn't just surrender. What do you plan to do with it after we capture it? You think it has supplies you can hold for ransom?"

"No, though, if it has any supplies, we may find them useful. I'm suggesting we capture the ship and announce to the Colonial Government that if they do not release my daughter, we will deorbit it and drop it on one of their cities."

Even without the cargo modules, it had sufficient mass that it would likely survive reentry intact. Depending on the velocity, its impact could obliterate an entire city. The collapse of its fusion bottle could cause an additional uncontrolled reaction, adding to the destruction. Nickson looked up at Zander Krycek. "Are you *insane*? Your first day here, and you want to conduct an orbital drop? That's a war crime. Any support you have will evaporate if you do it!" He looked at Captain Blackwood. "Skipper, we can't be a party to this. We can't—"

She held up a hand, and Nickson fell silent. "Mr. Armitage is right," she said, coldly. "Mr. Krycek, I sympathize with your situation. I took my ship and crossed hundreds of light-years to save my little brother. But this, this is different. You're talking about using my ship to conduct unrestricted warfare on your enemies. There are limits on what I'm willing to do, for *any* amount of money."

"The cap'n is wise to be hesitant," Mordechai said, on the screen he appeared on. "Engaging a ship from a merchant fleet, even the Combine one, is questionable enough to begin with. Bombarding a civilian population is something we are not obligated to do."

"It's something we *won't* do," Captain Blackwood said, firmly.

"You all misunderstand me. I do not expect you to actually drop that ship on the colony. Mr. Armitage is correct, it would only serve to coalesce the entire population against me. I'm going to bluff."

"I don't see how bluffing is any better than actually doing it," Nickson said. "The people will still think you're capable of doing it. Wouldn't that still hurt your cause?"

"We won't tell the people anything. Perhaps our former-Combine friend belowdecks can help us communicate directly with the Combine forces on Ithaca. We will make the threat directly to them, and their Colonial liaisons."

"What makes you think they'll believe you?" Nickson asked.

"Why wouldn't they? I'm the Butcher of Sargusport, aren't I? I'm sure the story has gotten ever more gruesome in the retelling. I'll make them believe it."

"That still doesn't help your PR problem," Marcus said. "The moment you make that threat, they'll broadcast it across the entire system, and everyone still turns against you."

"I don't think so. I think they'll keep it secret, especially if they release Adisa. They don't want to be seen as weak. If I promise to keep it a secret, they may agree to the terms. Even if they do release it, I'll deny it. Footage like that can be easily forged, and they've been propagandizing me for so long that I'm sure many are numb to it. Why, I've watched footage of me, personally, executing prisoners, and I assure you that never happened. We can use their own propensity to lie against them."

"And what if they call your bluff? What if the Combine refuses to release your daughter?"

"Then we still have a freighter full of goods that our allies can use, and their forces will be deprived of equipment. We need to try, though. It's critically important that we get her back, and not just because she's my daughter."

The captain raised an eyebrow. "Oh?"

"Adisa's grandmother was Queen Mirembe, husband of King Khari the Fifth. When her mother was killed, Adisa became the only surviving member of the royal family."

"Wait a minute," Nickson said. "You overthrew the king, didn't you? You're telling me that you were married to a princess and she was okay with that? What are you not telling us?"

He sighed. "It's . . . complicated, Mr. Armitage. The queen died when my wife was just a baby. She took her own life, and her loss was, I think, the thing that started the king on his spiral into madness. The king met with the native Elders, and something went wrong. I never did find out what happened, exactly, but the natives at the meeting were all killed. The king blamed them for her death. That's when the troubles with the natives began."

"How did you come to know such sensitive information?"

"As a young officer, I was given the honor of transferring to the Royal Guard. That is how I met Neema, the princess. My wife. It also allowed me knowledge of many royal secrets over the years."

"That's how you got close enough to the king for your coup," Nickson suggested.

"Yes. You must understand, this was not a decision we made lightly. The king's crackdowns on the natives were getting out of hand. People he suspected of disloyalty were not treated any better. The people grew afraid of their government, and came to resent the king. We feared that if nothing was done, there would be a revolt, even a civil war. None of us wanted to see the colony torn apart like that. None of us wanted to be publicly hung, either. So, we began making plans in secret."

"Was your wife involved?"

The old man smiled. "You could say that . . . the coup was her idea. She was . . . passionate, in her politics, and cared very deeply for the people. She would have done anything to protect them, even usurp her own father. She also desperately wanted peace with the natives. My original idea was to put her on the throne as queen. In retrospect, I wish we would have. It might have stopped the civil war from happening. Neema might...she might still be alive."

"Why didn't you?"

"My wife refused. She sincerely believed that replacing one absolute monarch with another wasn't a solution. With her father gone, she publicly abdicated the throne, and announced that she was going into exile off-world. The nobles and their royalist supporters pushed back, squabbling over who was next in line for the throne, and a political crisis turned into a civil war. I was chosen, by the Revolutionary Council, to be the first president of the colony. I was reluctant, but Neema insisted."

"What happened to your wife, Mr. Krycek?" the captain asked, gently. "Forgive me for asking."

"Royalist traitors in my own ranks attempted to assassinate me with a bomb. The plot failed, but the bomb did not. My wife was killed. I was so angry. I made...poor choices, in the aftermath. You must understand, I was fighting two wars at once, against the Royalists and aliens both. The natives rejected our attempts to sue for peace, so there was no choice but to take them on as well." He took a deep breath. "We had such plans, you know. When the war was won, we planned to call together leaders from all over the colony and hold a constitutional convention. We had drawn up a declaration of rights that would ensure our people would be protected from the excesses of royal power. Some on the Revolutionary Council had... other ideas. The Sargusport incident was the excuse they needed to be rid of me, and set themselves up as the permanent ruling committee." He smiled, humorlessly. "Fortunately for them, I beat the natives in battle and got them to agree to the peace treaty, before I was ousted. The damned fools had no plan on how to handle that mess, save attempting xenocide."

"You said your daughter was important to your plans," Kel said.

"Adisa doesn't know her true heritage. Her mother and I were married in secret; the king never would have allowed it. The official record shows that Princess Neema, unmarried and with no children, abdicated the throne after the coup and left the planet. That was all a story, something we manufactured to protect our unborn child. Neema took the commoner name Masozi. As far as those same records are concerned, we were never married, but I acknowledged being the father of her child. We intended to tell our daughter who she really was, when she was old enough, and after things had stabilized. We . . . I . . . never got the chance."

"Are you planning on installing your daughter as queen? Is that what this is about? Who else knows about this?"

"That is my hope," Zander admitted. "The Khari Dynasty founded this colony. Khari the Fifth was a tyrant, but before him, we enjoyed centuries of relative peace and prosperity. I believe . . . at least, I want to believe . . . that restoring the crown will unite the various factions. A simple DNA test will prove that Adisa is of the Khari bloodline. But, I don't intend to merely bring back the monarchy. We will have a constitution, with the declaration of rights my wife wrote. There will be a division of powers between the crown and an elected parliament. As for who else knows ... I believe Colonel Starborn was the last person who knew. There were always rumors that a surviving scion of the royal family was out there, but we covered our tracks well."

"So, if she's going to be queen, what is your role? Will you still be president?"

"No. The Southern Autonomous Zone is mostly loyal to me, but I'm ... controversial. I have many enemies. There are too many who lost family in Sargusport, and family is everything in Ithacan culture. If we win this fight, and if we're successful in creating a new government, I intend to retire from public life altogether."

"I have a question," Nickson said. "If we're going to capture the freighter, and threaten to destroy a city, why not demand the immediate surrender of the Council? Tell them to stand down or you'll drop the freighter on them. You have a trump card. Couldn't it be used to end the war?"

The old man shook his head. "If I thought that would work, I'd try it. They'll be willing to release a prisoner, I'll bet, but they won't be willing to capitulate. It slides the risk scale too far. The more demands I make, the more likely it is they will call my bluff. If I try to get too much, I'll get nothing."

"You really think they're so desperate to hold onto power that they'd risk you destroying an entire city?"

"They're desperate enough to climb into bed with the Combine, Mr. Armitage. I would put nothing past them at this point."

"You must realize, this will only work once," the captain said. "If we attack the Combine merchant fleet, they *will* send armed escorts next time. Interstellar law allows for that."

"Warships are coming anyway, Captain, if we don't win this war. If we lose, it won't make a difference."

"Even if you win, it could still be used as a justification for a punitive expedition to Ithaca."

"Possibly, but we need to focus on the immediate future. Right now, God only knows what those monsters are doing to my daughter. Please, Captain. We're her only hope."

"Please excuse us, Mr. Krycek. I need to discuss this with my officers. I'll come talk to you when we've reached a decision."

"Very well. Thank you, Captain." Without another word, Zander Krycek left the astrogation deck.

She wasted no time getting down to business. "Okay people, you heard the pitch. What do you think?"

"I say no, Skipper," Nickson said, earnestly. "All we have to do is get him to the surface of the planet, and we've completed the terms of the contract. I think the best course of action is to get paid, resupply, and get out of here before this colony blows itself to hell. Mr. Krycek has good intentions, but the odds are not in his favor, and he's probably going to lose this war. If we stay and get involved, we could all end up in a Combine prison, or worse."

"Thank you. Marcus?"

"Honestly, ma'am, taking that freighter is doable. I have a daughter myself, so I know what he's feeling. I can't speak to whether or not his plan will work."

"But are you willing to try and carry it out?"

"I'll have to talk it over with the team, but I think they'll be on board with our part of it. Provided the payment offered is adequate, of course."

"Mordechai?"

"Cap'n, we're in a tough situation here. The money we make will be enough to keep us in business for a couple more years, but it doesn't compare to a free port of harbor and a cargo hold full of treasure. Of course, that assumes that Mr. Krycek is successful, which is emphatically *not* a safe assumption. There are also legal ramifications to consider."

"Such as?"

"Capturing that freighter will be an act of piracy unless we formally declare ourselves as military combatants. Once we do that, we are a valid military target to not only the Ithacan Colonial Government, but to the Combine as well. The Combine won't have to hunt us in secret anymore. They can lawfully engage us in any system they encounter us in. This holds for Mr. Winchester and his team as well."

"I see. Kel?"

The astrogator was quiet for a moment. "Captain, I don't know that our client's personal vendetta is worth risking the ship for. But I want you all to think about this: Is the fate of an entire *planet* worth risking the ship for? Sure, we can take our money and wash our hands of the entire situation, but is that the moral thing to do? We're in a position to actually *do something*. That's rare in life. Are we going to squander it, and let the damned Combine take this system? Or do we take a stand and fight?"

Nickson had to think about that for a moment. Privateering, by its nature, often meant getting involved in someone else's war. He and the entire crew of the *Madeline Drake* had nearly died defending New Babylon from a lost fleet. He sincerely regretted Captain Ogleman's decision to pursue that cruiser, but he had no such qualms with the mission itself. Protecting an otherwise defenseless system from raiders was noble, even if you made a credit or two in the process. Somebody had to do it. "Captain," he said, looking back up at her, "you know we'll support you, whatever you decide. I'm going to admit that Kel made me think about this in a way I hadn't before. Maybe there is something at stake more important than our paychecks... or even our own safety."

"It's worth pointing out that they're already after you," Marcus said. "On account of that cruiser you blew up last time. I don't see how them hating you a little more will make a difference. There are worse fates than to be the enemy of the worst people in the galaxy."

Captain Blackwood looked thoughtful for a moment. "Thank you, all. I believe I've decided. Mordechai, draw us up a contract addendum. We will provide the fire support Mr. Krycek is asking for, including capturing that freighter. Just give us an out. I'll not be contractually obligated to die fighting in someone else's war."

"I'm on it, Cap'n."

"Nix, Kel, start plotting an intercept trajectory. Wait until the last moment possible to change course. I don't want that *Tyrant* to have time to turn and run."

"You know, Captain, if we capture that ship, it seems wasteful to not use it," Marcus said. "We take everything it's got, sure. Maybe we can rig it to drop the cargo containers in friendly territory. But using the ship itself as a weapon is a sound strategy. Not on a population center, of course, but maybe there is a Combine base down there? A valid and lawful military target, I'm saying. Whether or not they release the old man's daughter, knocking out an enemy base is worth the risk."

"You raise a good point, Marcus, but I don't think so. I'm assuming the freighter will be damaged when we capture it. We won't be able to just program an impact trajectory. We may have to push it, nudge it out of orbit ourselves. This is not very accurate. Being off by a few degrees can translate to hundreds of kilometers on the surface. Hitting anything smaller than a large city would be difficult, and would carry the risk of unintentional civilian deaths. Work with Nix and Kel, and get to planning your assault. I'll go talk to our client. All right everyone, we've got work to do. Get to it."

CHAPTER 27

The Privateer Ship *Andromeda*
High Ithaca Orbit
Ionia-5589 System

"Captain, we have a missile launch, coming from the *Tyrant!*" Nuchy said, excitedly.

Captain Blackwood chuckled, under the strain of acceleration. "So much for their unarmed freighters."

"Targeting!" Nickson said. "It's just one, it won't get through. We've got an incoming transmission from the target ship."

"If they're announcing their surrender, they've got a hell of a way of showing it. Nuchy, put it up on the big screen."

"Yes, ma'am!"

Nickson glanced up at the main screen as the connection was established. Reclined in his acceleration chair, he could keep an eye on it without having to look away from his own screens. A pale, panicked-looking Combine officer appeared on screen. His gray uniform was damp with sweat.

"Pirate ship *Andromeda*," he began, "this is Freighter Two-One-One of the People's Combined Collective

Merchant Fleet. We are a civilian cargo vessel. This attack will be considered piracy if you do not break off at once!"

Even mashed in her acceleration chair at three gravities, Captain Blackwood sounded uncompromising and resolute. "Freighter Two-One-One, this is the *Andromeda* of the Free Ithacan Space Force. We believe you are transporting weapons and military munitions intended for the enemy. You are armed, in violation of interstellar treaty and custom. Power down your engines, disarm your weapons systems, and stand by to be boarded. If you comply, you will not be harmed. If you wish to defect, we can accommodate you. My flight surgeon is getting quite skilled at removing your electronic comrades."

The screen went blank. "They cut the link, Skipper," Nickson said.

"How's that missile doing?"

"I've got a firing solution on it ... firing! Missile splashed." Nickson was startled by a loud, metallic bang. "We just came into laser range!"

"Colin, evade!" the captain ordered. The skilled young pilot didn't waste time responding. He vectored the thrust of the ship's four main engines and fired the maneuvering thrusters. Powerful g-forces started to drain the blood from Nickson's head as the ship slewed, still under acceleration. Laser weapons took time to penetrate armor, especially ablative armor like the *Andromeda*'s honeycomb energy-absorber layer. Maneuvering the ship reduced the ability of laser weapons to penetrate any one spot in the hull. "Nix, target their propulsion system, two missiles, low yield. Fire!"

One missile spat out of each of the *Andromeda*'s

rotary launchers, angling forward at incredible g-forces as they maneuvered toward their target. They were capable of omnidirectional targeting. It helped, because the ship didn't have to be pointing in the direction it wanted the missiles to go. "Missiles away!" Nickson announced. "Tracking, tracking . . . shit, they splashed one!"

"Steady, Nix. How's the other one doing?"

"Good hit!" Nickson announced, more excitedly than he'd intended. "They've lost an engine and a radiator." There was another bang on the hull as the Combine laser hit the *Andromeda* again.

"Colin, angle us for a railgun shot!" the captain ordered. "Nix, target that damned laser turret."

"It's on the propulsion unit, Skipper." Blood rushed to Nickson's head as the ship maneuvered again without cutting its acceleration. "I've got firing solution. Firing!" The ship's acceleration was reduced, slightly but perceptibly, by the incredible recoil of the railgun firing. "Good hit!"

"It knocked out another engine, Captain!" Nuchy announced. "They lost another radiator, too. Their acceleration is dropping. They cut their engines."

It made sense to Nickson. Dumping propellant into a damaged fusion rocket, with missing radiators, could result in an engine meltdown or an explosion. "We've got another incoming transmission, Skipper!"

"Seems they've changed their minds, hey? Put it up."

"We surrender!" the Combine officer said. Warning klaxons blared in the background. Sweat globules drifted off his brow.

Another crewman could be heard speaking from off screen. Nickson didn't understand their language, but the computer automatically translated, and flashed subtitles on the screen. *AI/CORE says we cannot be captured. It says we must self-destruct.*

The officer turned to his off-screen comrade, angrily yelling in his native language. *I don't give a damn what the computer says. I'm not dying for this trash heap!* He turned back to the screen. "*Andromeda*, are you receiving us? We surrender!"

Nickson exhaled heavily. *Thank God.*

"Colin, turn us over and begin deceleration. Match trajectories with the *Tyrant*." The captain addressed the Combine crew next. "To whom am I speaking? Are you the ship's commander?"

"Yes."

"Am I to understand that your *computer* is ordering you to destroy your own ship?"

"Yes. The AI/CORE. All ships have one."

"I assure you, there's no need to die at the behest of a machine, Commander. You will be taken prisoner, but you will not be harmed. Have your crew stand down. If you do not comply, my next railgun shot will be right through your hab module. Am I making myself clear?"

"Yes! We have no personal weapons. We are standing by for boarding."

"Excellent. You made a wise choice." She muted the communication with the Combine officer. "Marcus, is your team ready?"

"Standing by, Captain."

"Excellent. Nix, as soon as we cut acceleration, head up to the airlock and suit up. You're on."

Up in the nose of the ship, Marcus and his team were standing by, in space suits, armed with laser weapons. Kimball and Mazer Broadbent were there too, suited up, and armed. Their suits were locked into safety docks all around the compartment, immobilizing them while the ship was accelerating. He'd nearly blacked out, being held upright at three gravities, but things had calmed down now. The ship's XO had just arrived, and was clumsily trying to hurry into a space suit. "Wade, help him, will you?"

"On it." Wade disconnected himself from the wall, and pushed his way over to the XO. "Here, here, I got it. Okay, put your legs in now." Once he was suited up and sealed, Wade ran him through the checklist. "O2 looks good. Heating and cooling is good. You've got a positive seal. How are your comms?"

"I can hear you," the XO said. "Loud and clear. My boards are green."

"All right." Wade turned to Marcus and shot him a thumbs-up. "We're good to go, boss."

"Skipper, this is Nix," the XO said, "we're standing by. Commence docking operation."

"Everyone, lock yourselves in," Marcus ordered. He didn't want anyone to go flying when they made contact.

The Combine *Tyrant*-class transport was still coasting, tailfirst, toward Ithaca. The *Andromeda* had had to swing around, match velocities, and meet the other ship nose-to-nose. As Marcus understood it, the *Andromeda* was going to lock onto the bigger ship and nudge it into a stable orbit. An occasional dropping or turning sensation indicated when the ship was using its maneuvering or retro thrusters. With a rough bump, the two ships were connected.

"Marcus," the captain said, from the command deck, "we're locked in. Manipulator arm is latched on. We're not extending the docking umbilical. We're nose to nose. As soon as the inner hatch opens, be ready."

"Copy that, ma'am." He turned to his team. "You heard the lady! Unlock, weapons hot, and be ready for anything." The crew had claimed they wanted to surrender, but you could never be too careful. Many of the Combine's citizens were fanatically loyal, a product of centuries of cultural and political indoctrination. There was no telling what they might try. That was one of the primary reasons they were all wearing space suits. Some eager fool, ready to die honorably, might attempt to depressurize the ship while the boarding team was aboard. The space suits also had maneuvering jets, which would allow the team better mobility in a microgravity environment.

An alarm sounded, and an amber light flashed as the docking port above the boarding team slowly opened. Air rushed, briefly, as pressure equalized. The team took up positions, orienting themselves toward the hatch, weapons at the ready, as the door opened all the way. The light went from amber to green, and they were connected.

"We're docked, Skipper," the XO said.

"Excellent," the captain replied. "Marcus, proceed with caution."

"Copy that," Marcus said. "All right, boys and girls, let's go. Mr. Armitage, you hang back with Kimball and Broadbent until we've secured the ship." Their job would be securing the prisoners. The fact that they were all wearing space suits meant that, in the event the prisoners got froggy and tried to overpower them, the *Andromeda* could simply depressurize its docking bay, solving the problem.

Weapons ready, Marcus and his team jetted forward, traveling up through the hatch. The Combine ship's docking port was lit red, and an atrociously loud alarm kept blaring. There was no one in the other ship's docking port waiting for them. Once through, the boarding team rotated ninety degrees and planted their feet on the floor of the docking bay, engaging magnetic boots as they did so. The hatch leading to the interior of the enemy ship was still closed. A pair of bewildered-looking faces watched them through a porthole on it.

"Open up!" Marcus ordered, pointing his laser pistol through the porthole. The Combine officers' eyes went wide, and they did as they were told. The hatch hissed and clicked as they undogged it. Marcus stepped back, his mag boots thumping on the metal deck, to give the hatch room to swing inward. "Hands up!" he ordered, his voice broadcasting over his suit's loudspeaker. "Which one of you is the commander?"

Neither of them answered. "I don't think they understand you," Devree said. "Hold on." A moment later, the loudspeaker on her suit said something in a language Marcus didn't understand. The native tongue in the Combine was some far-removed descendent of ancient Ukrainian, mixed with Commerce English and Esperanto. Devree had her suit automatically translate her commands for her. The two crewmen seemed to understand. They slowly raised their free hands, though each was still grasping a handhold. They pointed toward another hatch and said something back.

"They say the commander is down on the command deck, Marcus."

"Good. Tell them to go through the hatch, to the

Andromeda. Kimball, this is Marcus, we've got two prisoners headed your way."

"Understood, Mercenary Winchester! We are standing by."

Marcus grabbed one of the Combine spacers by his flight suit coverall and dragged him forward, into the docking bay. The other one got the hint and followed. "Okay people, let's keep moving." Around a dogleg was an open hatch, with a ladder, which led down into the ship.

Wade pulled up next to Marcus and clamped to the floor, looking at a wrist-top display on his suit. "I think that's the command deck down there."

"Okay. I'll go first. Wade, you come down right after. Devree, Halifax, you two hold up here until we call you." Everyone acknowledged their orders. Marcus disengaged his mag boots and pushed himself off the deck. Directly above the hatch, he pushed away from the ceiling, sending him straight down the ladder feetfirst. "Everybody, hands where I can see 'em!" he ordered, brandishing his laser. Four Combine officers were present on the command deck, three men and a woman. Wade was down next, weapon up and ready. "Who's the commander?"

"I am," one of the men said, gripping a handhold on the bulkhead. The light on his electronic comrade was blinking red. "I'm the commander. Comrade-Merchant-Commander Dak Two-Two-Zero-One-Four. Please, don't shoot. We surrender."

"Nobody will get shot so long as everyone cooperates. Two of my men are waiting up the ladder," he said, pointing upward with his free hand. "Have your men proceed, one at a time, up the ladder, through the docking port, and into the *Andromeda*. If anyone is injured and needs medical attention, send them first. We have a doctor ready to receive patients. How many personnel do you have?"

"Seven," the commander answered.

"Okay, make sure they're all accounted for before you leave. We don't want anyone left behind on the ship, for their own safety. If you or any of your men wants your electronic comrade removed, ask the doctor about it. He can do it."

"What?" the commander said, touching the device grafted to his temple. "They can . . . remove it? That's impossible."

"It's not impossible," Marcus assured him. "I've seen it done. None of your crew has to go back if they don't want to."

One of the other crewmen, a short, heavyset, sickly looking man, grew angry. He was still strapped into his acceleration chair, unlike the others. He shouted something at the commander in the Orlov dialect. Marcus's suit computer translated it: *Traitor!* The angry officer looked around the cabin, shouting at the others. *You're all traitors! Traitors and cowards!*

"Commander, you need to calm that man down, right now!" Marcus ordered, pointing his laser at the upset officer. "Tell him if he doesn't relax, I'm going to shoot him."

"He is a political officer," the commander said, almost apologetically. He turned back toward the man and started shouting back. Marcus's translator couldn't keep up with who was saying what. After a few more seconds of bickering, the agitated political officer hit some controls on his console.

"What is he doing?" Marcus demanded. "Tell him to stop. Tell him!" More shouting. Now, the three other Combine officers were shouting at the man, who seemed like he was threatening to do something. He mashed a button on his console, and Marcus fired. The electric snap of the laser stunned everyone into silence. The beam was briefly visible in the dimly lit compartment, a quick, pulsing flash of bright blue. The political officer's face was ripped open, with globules of blood drifting out of the smoking hole in his skull. *God damn,* Marcus thought. The heavy laser pistol he was using had done a number on the guy. Devree was on the radio, asking if everything was alright, but he didn't have time to answer.

"He reactivated the AI/CORE!" the commander said.

"What? What does that mean?" Before he got his answer, a serpentine tentacle appeared from a port in the ceiling. It was capped by a metal housing with a cluster of lenses, one of which was glowing red.

It said something in the Combine dialect. Subtitles appeared on Marcus's display. *Scanning. Threat assessment: maximum. Engaging.*

"Engaging? What is it—?" The robotic snake turned toward the closest Combine officer, and shot him with a laser weapon. The man shrieked, tumbling in the cabin, as the machine turned toward the next one. "Wade *shoot it!*" Both men opened fire on the robotic monstrosity as the two surviving crewmembers tried to take cover. Multiple laser shots burned and blasted the machine, severing the front of its ocular cluster and leaving it a smoking ruin.

"What the fuck was that?" Wade asked, breathing heavily in his suit.

"That was the AI/CORE," the ship's commander said, sounding tired. "We shut it down before you boarded. I'm afraid the political officer has the authority to reactivate it." He turned to his shipmate, and said something to her in his native tongue. *How is Vasyli?*

He is dead, Comrade-Commander, the woman said, checking her shipmate. *I am apologizing.*

"Are there any other surprises we need to know about, Commander?" Marcus asked, keeping his weapon at the ready.

"The AI/CORE has another such observer unit in engineering. I suggest you keep your men out of there."

"Can you shut it down again?"

"I will try."

"Good. Do that, and have the rest of your crew head over to the *Andromeda*."

"I appreciate your restraint," the commander said, sounding tired. He turned to his crew and started giving them orders in his own language.

"Mr. Armitage," Marcus said, into his radio. "You're up."

"Roger that," Nickson said. "I'm on my way." Using the maneuvering jets on his suit, he moved past the pair of restrained Combine prisoners, through the airlock, and into the other ship.

"This way," someone said. It was the mercenary, Halifax, stuck to the floor with mag boots. "The command deck is through this hatch." Following his instructions, Nickson pushed past Halifax and Devree Starlighter, who were guarding the hatch and watching the entrance to the airlock, and moved down onto the command deck.

"He's here," Wade Bishop said, getting Marcus Winchester's attention.

Nickson's feet hit the floor and stuck as he activated his mag boots. Looking up, he froze as he took in the grisly scene on the command deck. One man was strapped into an acceleration chair, dead. Two Combine officers were wrapping another body in a burial shroud. Globules of blood floated all about the cabin, and were sticking to bulkheads and screens. "What the hell happened in here?"

"Their political officer reactivated their AI system. I shot him. Then, that tentacle thing there came down from the ceiling and shot that other poor bastard before Wade and I were able to knock it out."

"Yeah, it's a mess," Wade agreed. "You okay?"

"Yeah, fine, great," Nickson said. The mangled bodies, the smoke, the blood drifting in freefall, it all brought him back to that day on the *Madeline Drake*. He had to fight to keep his hands from shaking. The Combine officers started pulling themselves up the ladder, one after another. *Get it together,* he thought, harshly. His mag boots clomping on the deck, Nickson moved to an empty console and got to work.

The captain spoke in his ear. "Nix, what's the status of that freighter?"

"The controls aren't locked out, so that's good," he said, squinting at the displays. The writing was mostly in Cyrillic, but his suit display was set to translate for him. "They sustained heavy damage to the propulsion unit. I don't know if it's safe for this ship to move under its own power. The engines might explode, or melt down."

"Understood. What else?"

"Apparently their ship AI tried to murder the crew."

"We saw that on the feed. Can you figure out how to program and release the cargo modules?"

"It'll take me a little while, Skipper, but I think so."

"Good. I want you to keep working on it. We're going to begin moving this tub soon. You may experience some negative acceleration. Mr. Krycek is preparing his statement for broadcast."

"Understood. Don't toss me around too much."

"I'll be gentle, Nix, I promise," the captain said, with a chuckle.

CHAPTER 28

Ithaca
Ionia-5589 System
Southern Hemisphere

Adisa laid on her mat, trying to forget the world around her. She had no idea how long she'd been in this place. She didn't know what information she'd given up to her Combine interrogator; her memory grew increasingly hazy. Sometimes, it seemed like days, even weeks, would go by before the robot would march her down the hall, into Gregory's interrogation room. He would hook her up to his vile machines, show her seemingly random images, inject her with chemicals, and ask her questions. Every time she lied or tried to evade the question, he would hurt her. She had no bruises or scars. The machine merely stimulated the pain receptors in her brain, and it was the most agonizing pain ever. The first time he did it, she emptied her bladder, right there in his chair.

She hadn't heard from Gregory in a long while now. Occasionally, a scream would echo down the hall; another soul at his mercy, no doubt. Adisa had stopped eating the nutrient paste they were feeding her. She was losing weight. Her stomach growled. She was weak. She didn't care.

Adisa's eyes went wide as she heard the clunking of the security robot's feet approaching. The noise grew louder as the machine drew near, and she closed her eyes, tightly. Tears streamed down her face as she prayed. *Please, God, not me, not me, not me.* She felt ashamed. Every time the robot stopped at another cell, that meant some other poor bastard was going to Gregory's chair. At that moment, all alone, she didn't care. She just didn't want to go through it again.

She found herself wondering if she could get the robot to kill her. Maybe if she attacked it, or ran, it would shoot her like it always threatened to. They couldn't extract any more information from her if she was dead. Death seemed to be the only honorable way out. It was only a matter of time before they broke her completely, before she betrayed her comrades and friends.

Adisa held her breath as the robot's footsteps drew near to her cell door. She heard another set of footsteps with it. That was different. She didn't want to look up, didn't want to breathe. Maybe if she held still enough, they would forget she was there.

The robot stopped outside her door.

In that moment, Adisa made her choice. She would make the robot kill her. They would get nothing further from Adisa Masozi. The world would never know how she died, but she'd know, and that was all that mattered. She sat up, wiping the tears from her eyes, as the cell door slid open. Taking a breath, she turned around, and was horrified to see Gregory standing there, smiling at her.

"Hello, Adisa," he said, with that unsettling, ever-present grin. He entered the cell, and the security robot marched in after. "I hear you haven't been eating. Is the food not to your taste? You can have better, you know, if you will simply be more cooperative."

"What do you want?" she asked, coldly.

"I have a surprise for you, Adisa! Do you like surprises?" She didn't answer. "I see. Well, perhaps you will like this one." He turned to his robot. "Play the video, please."

"Playing video," the robot announced. Adisa stepped aside as it projected against the back wall of her cell. The wall was blank, at first, but then a man's face appeared. She didn't immediately recognize him, but he seemed familiar somehow. Fair skin, dark hair going gray, intense eyes...

"My name is Zander Krycek," the man said. Adisa's heart dropped into her stomach. "I am the rightful president of this colony. People of Ithaca, I have returned."

Father? She turned back to the interrogator. It had to be a trick. This was another one of his games. Gregory said nothing. He just kept smiling at her.

"I went into exile, so many years ago, believing it was in the best interests of the colony. In the aftermath of the Sargusport incident, I was little more than a distraction, a polarizing figure causing disunity and strife. I would not be here, today, had I not been asked to return. I left, in peace, wishing nothing but the best for my homeworld. I return to find your leaders, pathetic, power-craving cowards that they are, about to sign a military pact with the Orlov Combine.

"Make no mistake, my fellow Ithacans. Whatever

the text of this pact says, the results will be the same: Ithaca, your home and mine, will be nothing more than a vassal of the most oppressive regime in all of inhabited space. A client state, little more than a port of harbor for their ships, and another world they can extract resources from. This is not acceptable. This cannot be allowed. *I* will not allow it.

"I know you've been desperate. I know that a hungry man seldom cares who provides him with a meal. Your leaders, this so-called Revolutionary Council, and their never-ending Interim Government, have led you to poverty and ruin. How is it, in the modern era, with all our technological marvels, that people can be going hungry? How is this possible? I will tell you how: incompetent, self-serving governance from the fools on the Council. They have taken this colony and driven it into the ground. Rather than doing the right thing and abdicating power, as I did, they desperately cling to it, going so far as to look for off-world benefactors to prop them up.

"Is this what you want for your children? Do you want them to live under the boot of the Combine? Will you stand idly by and watch as your fellow citizens are implanted with their so-called *electronic comrades*, as our world is raped for its resources, and as they exterminate the natives we once forged a peace with? Will you believe Combine propaganda over what you know to be true? Will you do nothing, or will you say, *no more*?

"The colony is on the verge of tearing itself apart. North versus South, Autonomous Zone versus the Colonial Government. I offer you a different way. Join me! Take back your world. Unite as Ithacans, as free men and women of an independent world, and drive back those who lay supine before the Combine! To the Colonial Guard I once led, I ask you, is this what you signed up for? Is this what your oath entails? Would you fight a war, killing your fellow citizens, just so your leaders can hand the planet over to the Combine? The choice is yours."

The message ended. A few seconds later, another one began, and her father's face reappeared. He seemed to be looking right at her. "This message is for the so-called Revolutionary Council. It has come to my attention that Combine forces are holding my daughter, Adisa Masozi, as a prisoner. She will be released, alive and unharmed, immediately. If this does not happen, the consequences will be dire."

Her father's face disappeared, replaced by a projection of the blackness of space. From the bottom of the screen, stretching off into the distance, was the vast gray bulk of one of the Combine transport ships.

"I have captured this freighter. Its mass is four hundred thousand tonnes. If my daughter is not released, in the condition I specified, I will drop it on the Combine embassy in Mombasa. At eight kilometers per second, your chances of stopping it are low, even if you use fusion weapons. It will destroy the entire city, including the spaceport and your military command facilities. You people have called me the Butcher of Sargusport in your propaganda, so you know what I'm capable of. You've tried to kill me multiple times, and all your assassins have failed. I suggest you do not test my patience any further. I await your reply." The image disappeared as the message ended. Adisa stared at the blank wall for a few moments, in disbelief. Slowly, she turned to look at her interrogator, who was still calmly smiling at her.

"Are you excited, Adisa?" he asked. "I would not have let you go. I do not believe in negotiating with terrorists, but your world's leaders, they are weak. They are afraid. They intend to give in to his demands."

"What? This is a trick."

"No! No, no, no, Adisa, I assure you, no trick! I have told you so many times, I only tell the truth, and the truth is, you are going to be released. Are you excited?"

What Adisa was, was in shock. She had all but given up, and now this? Now her father was threatening to destroy a city of five million people just to save her? She didn't know if she should be excited or horrified.

"So, you're just...letting me go?"

Gregory moved in close. Adisa stepped back, the hair on her arms standing up. "Not...just yet, Adisa," he said, licking his cracked lips. "In due time. There is...one more thing we need to do, first."

"What are you going to do?"

Gregory didn't answer. He only smiled.

CHAPTER 29

**The Privateer Ship *Andromeda*
High Ithaca Orbit
Ionia-5589 System**

Annabelle Winchester went about her appointed tasks on the cargo deck. The ship was quiet, now, after so much excitement and commotion. The *Andromeda* was still docked with the Combine cargo ship, so her present acceleration was very low, only 0.25 gravity. It was enough to keep you planted on the floor, but you had to be careful when you walked. She found that she could quickly get around the ship by hopping in the low gravity.

In the center of the cargo deck was a large mesh dome, fastened to the deck and the ceiling. In it, five Combine prisoners were being held. They had sleeping bags, secured to the deck, to rest in, and were routinely given food and water. The portable head they used for a bathroom didn't leave much to the imagination, though, so Annie made it a point to keep them out of sight. In any case, she had been ordered not to talk to them. They were watched constantly by Jerkins, the robot that Zander Krycek had bought with him. It had a laser weapon on its back, was plugged into the ship's electrical system for a steady power supply, and was magnetically clamped to the floor by the cage. It had been programmed to shoot anyone who got out.

The prisoners weren't causing any trouble, though. They talked quietly amongst themselves in whatever language it was they spoke, and barely made eye contact with anyone. Her dad had told her that two of them were killed when they captured the ship, so maybe they were in mourning.

"Liam!" Annie said, happily, when her friend slowly fell down the ladder. He landed dramatically, going down on one knee, with an arm up in the air, like a netcast superhero. "You goober. What are you doing down here?"

Liam smiled as he bounded over to her. He looked good; he'd lost some weight, and seemed more confident than before. "Visiting you. How are you doing?"

"It's been quiet."

"Is it weird, being in here with the prisoners?"

"Nah. They don't bother me. I reckon they know that if they try to get out, that robot'll fry 'em. Besides, where they gonna go? We took their ship."

"That's not all we did."

"What do you mean?"

"Zander Krycek threatened to drop the ship on the colony!"

Annie's eyes went wide. "What?"

"It's true! The Combine has his daughter. He made the threat to drop the ship to get her released. That's why we captured it."

"Holy shit. I can't believe Captain Blackwood would go along with that."

"That's the thing. It was a *bluff*. They fell for it. She wasn't actually going to go through with it."

Relieved, Annie felt silly for ever doubting the captain. "What's going on now? Nobody tells me anything." Liam spent a lot of time in astrogation, so he always knew where the ship was headed.

"We're pushing the ship on an orbital trajectory that will take us over the Southern Autonomous Zone. They're going to drop all of its cargo containers to friendly forces in the south!"

"Holy hell. That was a good plan. What's in the containers?"

"Weapons. Heavy weapons. Railgun artillery, missiles, things like that. After that, we're going to push it on a to a high solar orbit, far enough away from the planet that they can't reach it with any shuttles they have. The captain wants to keep it for salvage. After all that's done we're going to land."

"Finally. I want to walk in real gravity again."

"It's going to be scary, Annie. They're going to try to shoot us down as we get close to the planet, and again as we land. The captain is going to put everybody in general quarters until we're on the ground. It looks like we're going to be providing fire support for the Southern forces, striking at surface targets from space."

"Wow. It's a real war down there, huh?"

"It is. Are you scared?"

"A little."

"I am too."

"Liam, listen. Everything is ..." Annie fell silent as someone else came down the ladder. It was the Combine cyborg, the one they called the Wraith. She landed gracefully on the deck, barely wrinkling the tight black flight suit she wore. Her black hair now had purple streaks in it. Liam was agog at her as she approached.

"Hello, Annabelle," the former assassin said. "And... I'm afraid I don't know your name, young man."

"L-Liam, ma'am."

She smiled. "Liam. I like that." Her stupidly perfect face was only sullied by the metallic plate over her right eye socket.

Liam stared at her, almost slack-jawed. Of course, her flight suit was unzipped just enough to show off her cleavage. Annie rolled her eyes. "What can we do for you?"

"Is it all right if I talk with the prisoners some more?"

"Sure. Kimball said you had permission."

The Wraith smiled again. "Thank you." She turned and effortlessly bounded across the cargo deck before sitting on the floor, by the edge of the mesh cage.

Annie looked over at her Liam. "Oh, my *gawd*, you're like a love-sick puppy."

Liam's face turned beet red. "I am not!"

"You were practically drooling, staring at her tits! Hard to miss 'em when she's got 'em hangin' out like that."

"She's beautiful."

"You know she slept with the XO? Banged him and then kidnapped him."

"She defected. But, aren't they worried she's trying to plan something with the prisoners?"

"Nah. Jerkins is watching, and everything they say is being recorded. I think she's talking to them about getting those little camera boxes taken off their heads."

"Can you imagine living like that, Annie? Having everything you say and do monitored for your entire life? Having some computer listening, making sure you didn't think or say the wrong thing?"

"I suppose it's normal for them."

"I suppose it is. But, listen, there's another reason I came down here. Your dad wants to talk to you."

"Huh? About what?"

"I don't know. He wasn't mad or anything. He's up on the personnel deck. When I told him I was coming to see you, he asked me to see if you could go up and talk to him for a minute."

"Oh . . . well, okay, I guess. Can you finish these system checks for me?"

"What?"

Annie shoved her tablet into Liam's hands. "The checklist is on the screen. I was almost done. Thank you!" Before he had a chance to say anything else, she had already bounded up the ladder.

Up on the personnel deck, she found her father and his team lounging around in the commons area. "Hey, sweetie!" her father said. "I need to talk to you a minute."

Bounding over to where he was, Annie managed to land in an empty chair next to him. She was getting quite adept at navigating in the low gravity. "What's wrong, Dad?"

"Listen, I'm going to be leaving the ship when we pass over Ithaca."

"What? How?"

"Mr. Krycek needs to get down to the surface. We're doing a low pass over the Southern Autonomous Zone to drop that Combine ship's cargo pods. Well, that ship also has a small shuttle attached to it. During the pass, the old man's going to take the shuttle down, and we're going with him."

"That's crazy! They'll be trying to shoot you down!"

"They will, but we've got a plan for that, too. We'll be fine. The captain will be announcing the plan soon, but I wanted to talk to you first. I wanted to make sure you'll be okay without me for a little while."

Annie had been on the ship without her father before, but that was when they were planeted on Zanzibar. The idea of being out in space without him was a little scary. "Yeah, I'll be okay," she said, putting on a brave face. "You have a job to do, too. Just . . . you better be okay."

Her father put a hand on her shoulder. "I'll be fine, baby girl. I'm like a cockroach: hard to kill and good at getting away from danger. You just mind yourself while I'm gone, okay? And look after Liam."

"I will. You look after Uncle Wade."

Wade looked up from his handheld. "What? Why do I need looking after?"

"Well," Annie said, a grin forming on her face, "I figure Zander Krycek is taking his robot with him. I don't want you to get frisky with it and get your face melted off."

"She's right, Wade. I'm pretty sure Jerkins don't swing that way."

Wade folded his arms across his chest. "You know . . ."

Nickson found Talia down on the cargo deck. She was at the bottom of the ladder, talking to Liam, the young junior crewmember.

"Sir!" Liam said, standing up straight, when Nickson drifted down the ladder.

"As you were, crewman," Nickson said, smiling. "Say, what are you doing down here?"

"Crewman Winchester asked me to cover for her

for a little bit. She took her break to go talk with her father before he leaves."

Nickson nodded. "That's fine. But I want you to head to supply. Quartermaster Chang needs help with a project."

"Yes, sir!" he said, earnestly. He turned to Talia, his eyes darting down to her cleavage before he caught himself. "Please excuse me, ma'am." Without another word, he was up the ladder and gone.

Nickson grinned at the former Combine assassin. "You're going to give that poor little virgin a heart attack, dressed like that."

Talia actually smiled, and it wasn't the cold, calculating smile from before. There was a bit of warmth there, something Nickson hadn't seen before. "He's sweet. He needs to find himself a nice girl."

"Do they, you know, do that, like normal, on Orlov?"

"Do what? Meet girls?"

"Yeah. Sex, romance, courtship. What's it like?"

Talia looked down at the deck for a moment. "I was just a girl when they took me for the program. I never got to have a, how would you say, boyfriend."

"You didn't seem inexperienced to me." As a matter of fact, Nickson couldn't remember the last time he'd bedded a woman as carnally skilled as Talia.

"I'm not. As soon as we were old enough, they started teaching us sexual techniques, how to seduce men. We were required to have intercourse with some of the instructors as a test."

Nickson's mouth fell open. She'd said it so matter-of-factly that it took him a moment to process what he'd heard. "My God, that's . . . that's monstrous. I'm sorry. I didn't mean to bring something like that up."

"It is okay, Nickson. It feels, I don't know, good to talk about this. Everything about the program is a state secret. We entered the program as girls and left as women." She looked down at her hands. The pseudo-skin covering them looked real enough. "Not women. As machines. Killing machines."

"Talia, you're *not* a machine."

"I'm not a woman, either. Women can have children. They can create life. I am a . . . a human head on a mechanical puppet body."

Nickson's mind raced. He just wanted to see how she was doing, and in opening his big, stupid mouth, he'd really upset her. He desperately tried to think of something to say that would make her feel better, but what *could* he say? What had been done to her was a vile injustice. It was inhuman. There were no words that could help with something like that.

"I could have incapacitated you at any time," she continued, looking into his eye. "I didn't have to have sex with you. I just . . . I wanted to feel *alive*. To feel *human*. I wanted to do something because *I chose to*. I . . ." She fell silent for a moment. "I am sorry. I did not mean to get so personal. This is difficult for me."

"Talia, it's okay. Look, I'm not going to pretend to understand what you've been through, and . . . hell, I don't even know what to say. I can't pat you on the head and say, *there, there*, and make it all better. But if talking helps, then you can talk to me."

"Thank you, Nickson. There are not many on the ship who will talk to me."

"Is that why you're leaving? I heard you were going down to the surface with the old man."

"I am of no use here. I can, perhaps, be useful

to Zander Krycek. He said that I can stay on Ithaca if I like."

"Well...look, don't disappear when you get down there, okay? I'd like to see you again."

Talia smiled again, and oh, what a smile it was. "You're sweet, too, Nickson." Without warning, she leaned forward and kissed him on the mouth. "Thank you for your kindness."

"Wow...hey, anytime." He shot her his own best smile, the one that the ladies all loved. There were few, in Nickson's experience, who could resist *the smolder*.

Talia, still smiling, shook her head. "I must go get ready. I will see you again when you land." She started to head up the ladder.

"Promise?"

"I promise," she said, and then she was gone.

CHAPTER 30

Combine Merchant Ship 211
Low Ithaca Orbit
Ionia-5589 System

The Combine *Spiral*-class shuttle was cramped and uncomfortable, especially when the passengers were all wearing space suits. The tiny cabin had three seats on either side, and not so much as a window to look out of. *Probably for the best,* Marcus thought, his stomach already churning. *It's better if you can't see.* The *Andromeda* was pushing the captured combine freighter on a very low orbital trajectory over Ithaca. The turbulence was jarring as the ships skimmed the upper reaches of the atmosphere, their hulls heating from the friction.

Everyone on board was connected to the same network, so they could talk to each other through their helmet's radio. Marcus, Wade, Devree, and Halifax were all on board, as was Zander Krycek. Kya was supposed to have gone, but she had flatly refused the shuttle ride. Space travel was hard on her, but the prospect of riding down in the shuttle seemed to terrify the poor woman. The old man told her to stay on the *Andromeda* until it landed.

The Wraith, she was a surprise last-minute addition, taking Kya's seat. Captain Blackwood had been fine with her leaving. In fact, she seemed happy to have the cyborg off her ship. Just about everyone did. Marcus didn't blame the crew for not trusting her, but he couldn't help but feel a little bad about the cold shoulder she'd been getting from almost everyone.

Colin Abernathy, the junior flight officer, was at the controls of the shuttle. He had spent some time familiarizing himself with the controls, and even ran a couple of simulations to help himself get a feel for it. Even still, Marcus wasn't thrilled that the kid's first time actually flying this Combine piece of junk was a high-speed atmospheric reentry under fire.

"This is like the combat drops we did in the Espatiers!" Marcus said. "It's been a long time!" *Not long enough.* Despite the protestations of his stomach, he was the team leader and he had to show confidence, even as the shuttle threatened to rattle itself apart around them.

"Thirty seconds!" the pilot announced. "Listen, I'm going to have to do this manually. I wouldn't trust whatever piece of shit autopilot this thing has, even if it *was* programmed to do what we need to do. Fortunately for y'all, I'm *really good* at this. Ten seconds! Stand by!"

It really did feel like a combat drop for Marcus. Memories, not all of them good, came flooding back. While he'd trained for it dozens of times, he'd only conducted one real combat drop during his time in the Espatier Corps. A lot of Espatiers had died on that drop. He closed his eyes and tried to push it all from his mind. "Hang on!" he warned. "This next part isn't fun!"

"Release!" With a loud, metallic *THUNK*, the *Spiral* was free of the Combine freighter, which was still being pushed, tailfirst, by the *Andromeda*. Relative to the planet, the shuttle was flying backward. Marcus' stomach lurched as the small, lifting-body craft dropped away from its mothership. It hit the upper atmosphere like a runaway train, shaking and rattling like they were all about to die. The Abernathy kid knew what he was doing, though. A burst from the maneuvering thrusters had the shuttle flipped around. More maneuvers got it out from underneath its mothership, but following closely enough to mask its thermal and radar signature. The shuttle rumbled as the main engines fired. They needed to keep up with the *Andromeda* and the freighter. "The freighter is about to release the cargo containers!"

Bringing his arm up, Marcus tapped his wrist-top display. He was treated to a view from the nose of the *Andromeda*, looking down the length of the freighter she was pushing. The trapezoidal cargo modules began to release, one after another, in a spiral pattern: *top, left, bottom, right,* around and around, down the length of the ship's spaceframe. Each used automatic maneuvering jets to right itself, so that the heat-shielded side was down, and to get on the right trajectory. Meanwhile, the *Andromeda* and Merchant Ship 211 were both blasting their electronic countermeasures. The *Andromeda* was releasing decoys as well, and had its lasers ready to shoot down incoming missiles.

"We're beginning our descent," Colin said. "I don't

want to freak anyone out, but...well, I've got some good news and some bad news. The good news is, we're low enough and far enough south that enemy laser and railgun batteries don't have a shot at us."

"What's the bad news?"

"Nobody freak out, but I'm tracking several dozen inbound missiles."

"What are they targeting?" Marcus grunted.

"Everything! The *Andromeda*, the Combine ship, and the cargo modules. Mostly the ships. Nothing is pinging on us, yet. I think we're lost in the fray. Everybody hold onto your butts, it's gonna get real choppy!"

"This isn't already choppy?" Wade asked. "Jesus Christ!"

Eyes clenched shut, Marcus gritted his teeth as the shuttle plummeted into Ithaca's atmosphere. It stayed close to the ejecting cargo containers and tried to mimic their trajectory. Agonizing minutes ticked by, punctuated by the occasional sudden maneuver or burst of the thrusters. The pilot wasn't saying much now, only tersely reporting his status to the *Andromeda*. They were already at the upper limit of the shuttle's reentry velocity rating; much faster and they'd start to burn up.

"How's everybody doing?" Marcus asked. He still needed to look after his team. "Wade?"

"Fantastic! I am fantastic!"

"Woo-hoo!" Devree exclaimed. The former police sniper always did strike Marcus as an adrenaline junkie.

"Halifax? You alright?"

"He's asleep," Devree said.

"What?"

"He's asleep! No shit!"

Unbelievable, Marcus thought. "Mr. Krycek, you hanging in there?"

"Fine," the old man grunted, tersely. He was breathing rapidly.

"Wraith, what about you?"

"Hm? Oh, I'm fine," the assassin said, conversationally. "Thank you for asking." She sounded downright serene. Marcus wondered if she had a wire that rerouted fear or something. He snapped back to reality when the shuttle started shaking, harder than it had before. Instead of a constant vibration, the bumps were jarring, frequent, and irregular. An alarm sounded.

"Colin, what the hell's going on?"

"We're fine! Everything is fine! Just going in too fast. The cargo modules are, ah, rated for a higher reentry velocity than we are, so—shit!"

"Shit? Shit what? What's going on?"

"A missile just hit one of the cargo modules, that's all. We're fine. Couple missiles got through to the freighter, too, but it's still intact."

"What about the *Andromeda*?"

"No hits on her. She's pushing the freighter back into space now. They're fine, too. Just relax. This is still a controlled descent. You know, mostly. I need you to let me concentrate, okay?" Marcus didn't answer. The kid was right, he needed to concentrate, and backseat flying was never helpful. He closed his eyes again, made a few promises to God, and hoped for the best.

When he opened his eyes next, things were going much more smoothly. There was no more of the bone-jarring turbulence. At the front of the cabin, past the pilot's seat, Marcus could see out the canopy, and instead of the blackness of space there was a vividly blue sky. The shuttle's air-breathing engines rumbled to life. The alarms had all ceased.

"I think we're in the clear," Colin said, sounding relieved himself. "Altitude is thirty thousand meters and descending. Wing dihedral set for atmospheric flight. Control surfaces are responding. Boards are green."

Oh, thank you, Jesus, Marcus thought to himself. "Are we still being targeted?"

"No. They concentrated most of their fire on the freighter and the *Andromeda*. I think four or five of the cargo modules were hit, but the rest have deployed their parachutes. We're in the air defense envelope of the Southern Autonomous Zone now, so we've got cover. We've got a squadron of air defense drones on an intercept course, ground control says they're our escorts. I'm locked in on the nav beacon at the spaceport. We should be on the ground in, uh, maybe thirty minutes. Everyone alive back there?"

Marcus looked around, making sure everyone was okay. "Yeah, we're fine. That was some damned good flying, kid." He looked at his teammates again. "Somebody wake up Halifax."

After landing, Marcus immediately put his team to work. Doffing their space suits, they offloaded their gear (and Jerkins) from the cargo bay of the Combine shuttle (which had been claimed by the Southern Autonomous Zone forces and was already being repainted in their standard green/blue/brown camouflage scheme). The team and their equipment, loaded onto a caravan of armored trucks, were rushed away from the spaceport. The convoy moved quickly, through a small city, and then onto a military base on the outskirts of it. They were driven into a tunnel in the side of a mountain. Black Mountain, as it was called, sat above the Southern Autonomous Zone's military headquarters. The tunnel, long and straight, terminated at a massive cargo elevator. The elevator slowly descended, carrying all three trucks down at once, finally stopping a kilometer underground. Climbing out of the truck, Marcus and his team found a military honor guard and a group of generals waiting to meet his client.

There was also someone there Marcus didn't expect: a two-meter-tall saurian alien!

"Holy shit," Devree whispered. "Is that one of the native Ithacans?"

"It is," Wade answered. "Wow." The being was wearing blue garb that resembled the Ithacan generals' uniforms. It spoke with Mr. Krycek in halting Commerce English, its voice deep and rumbling.

"Ain't that a sight?" Marcus mused. He'd seen a few alien species in his travels, but rarely did one find a race that so closely interacted with humans. He looked back at his team. "Let's have a huddle real quick, guys, while the mucky-mucks exchange their greetings and salutations and whatever. Listen, it's going to be hectic while the old man gets settled in. I'll see about securing us all beds and chow. I don't know how long we're going to be down here. Once we figure out what the situation is, our client doesn't go anywhere alone. Someone will be on him at all times, unless he specifically orders otherwise. If he's in a meeting with some general, eating his dinner, screwing his secretary, or taking a shit, one of us will be with him. Clear?" Everyone acknowledged. "Good." Marcus waved at the Wraith, signaling for her to join the group.

"Yes?" she asked, sounding a little hesitant.

"Wraith, I wouldn't tell these people about where you come from."

Her eye narrowed. "*Talia*, Mr. Winchester."

"Huh?"

"My *name* is *Talia*."

Marcus nodded. "Please accept my apologies, ma'am. I meant no offense."

"I apologize as well. I do not mean to be so, ah, touchy. I am still adjusting to all this. I have already discussed this with Mr. Krycek. As far as anyone here is concerned, I am his assistant and lover. I was in a terrible accident that resulted in my augmentation."

She certainly had the looks for it, Marcus thought, despite the metal plate over her right eye socket. "That should work. A guy like that would be expected to have a mistress, I suppose."

"You should know, I will likely have restrictions placed on where I can go while we're down here. I will be debriefed by intelligence personnel when he feels the time is right. He is not so trusting of these people yet. I will assist you as I can, but I may be of limited help."

"Understood. Thank you for that." Marcus didn't think limiting her access to the Southern Autonomous Zone's command bunker was a bad idea. There was always the possibility that her real mission was to kill not only Zander Krycek, but the entire SAZ leadership. A decapitation strike like that could cripple their ability to conduct the war. He didn't think that scenario was very likely; she had asked to have her electronic comrade removed, after all, even though it meant the loss of her eye. If it was a setup, it was ridiculously elaborate. Even still, nothing could be ruled out, and he wasn't ready to trust her a hundred percent.

Mr. Krycek looked over at the group. "Marcus? May we speak with you for a moment?" Walking over, Marcus was introduced to the general officers by his client. "This is Marcus Winchester," he said, "the commander of my protective detail. I would not be alive, if not for him."

"Just doing the job you hired us to do, sir."

"Such modesty. This man and his team put down a cybernetic Combine assassin on New Austin, armed only with handguns. They're quite good. Marcus, I would like to introduce you to Follower of the Storm. He's the native liaison who was working with my daughter."

"Greetings, Mar-cusss," the alien said, dipping its head. It stuck its hand out.

Marcus took the alien's offered hand. Its two thumbs wrapped completely around his wrist as they shook. "It's good to meet you," Marcus said, in awe.

"There is also news of my daughter."

Marcus turned back toward Mr. Krycek. "Really? Good news, I hope."

"Indeed," one of the SAZ generals said. He was a white-haired man in a blue dress uniform. He offered Marcus his hand, and the two men exchanged an Earth-style handshake. "General Mohammed Farai, SAZ—er, Free Ithacan Defense Force. Forgive me, our name change was quite recent. In any case, yes, we do have good news. The Colonials were dragging their feet in response to President Krycek's demand that his daughter be set free. That low orbital pass your ship conducted scared them, it seems. They thought you were going to send that Combine ship straight at them. Shortly after you landed, they contacted us and agreed to release her immediately, so long as the freighter is removed from Ithacan orbit."

"I believe Captain Blackwood intends to push it into a solar orbit," Marcus answered.

"Excellent," the general answered. "We're sending an aircraft to pick Adisa Masozi up. She's being held at one of their forward operating bases in the southern hemisphere."

"Marcus," Mr. Krycek said, "I want you and your team to go. You've already demonstrated that you can handle yourselves. There is no one I would rather have on the job, should they try anything."

"I appreciate that, sir, but I really think we should stay here, with you."

"I assure you, I'll be fine. These men," he said, indicating the general officers, "served under me in the civil war. I trust them. In any case, we're fourteen hundred meters underground. I'm as safe here as I am anywhere on Ithaca. And, I'll have Jerkins with me."

The robot, quietly idling off to the side, beeped approvingly.

"Please, Marcus, go get Adisa. Bring my daughter home."

"I'll begin preparations. Don't worry, sir, we'll bring her back."

"This one will go also," the alien rumbled. "A-disss-a is my . . . friend. We learned much from each other. We faced battle together. She taught me many human

words. This one...I...was there when she was...
taken...by alien machines. There was too much
fighting. I could not..." The alien paused, trying to
find his words. "Save. I could not save her. I failed.
I must go."

Marcus nodded. "No one gets left behind."

The alien seemed pleased with that.

CHAPTER 31

Ithaca
Ionia-5589 System
Southern Hemisphere

When the doors opened, the light was so bright that it hurt Adisa's eyes. She wanted to take a moment, to let her eyes adjust, but the guards didn't let her. They ordered her to move, and roughly pushed her forward. They were Colonial Army soldiers, clad in brown uniforms. As her eyes cleared, Adisa realized she was on the roof of a building. Looking back, she saw Gregory, standing in the doorway with his hands folded behind his back. Small, round sunglasses concealed his eyes, but he was smiling as always.

Adisa was startled by a loud, shrill roar, and looked up. A large VTOL aircraft was slowing to a hover above the landing pad. It was a boxy machine with a squared-off nose, and rotating engine nacelles at the end of its short, straight wings. It rotated to the side as it descended. FIDF was painted on its tail boom, in white letters that contrasted with the blue, brown, and green camouflage scheme. It touched down, curtseying as its landing gear suspension compressed under its weight. The engines roared, then quieted down to an idle.

The guards escorting Adisa stopped at the foot of the steps that led up to the landing pad. "Go," one of them said, brusquely. She hesitated for a moment, and the guard pushed her. "Go!" he repeated. She climbed the stairs, slowly, squinting in the sun as she looked around. A squad of Colonial Army soldiers was on the roof, weapons pointed at the VTOL. Up on the landing pad, more soldiers were waiting for her, but they were wearing different uniforms. With each step, her stomach and sides hurt, and she didn't know why. At the top of the steps, one of the soldiers extended his hand to her.

"My name is Marcus," the man said, his voice raised so that he could be heard over the sound of the aircraft's jets. He wore a combat helmet and tinted smart goggles. His uniform was a mottled camouflage scheme similar to the paint job on the aircraft. "Your father sent me. I'm bringing you home."

Adisa nodded, and the man named Marcus hurried her toward the VTOL. Follower of the Storm was there, inside, waiting for her. "Stormy!" she said, almost sobbing. If he was there, it meant it wasn't a trick. This was really happening! As the other soldiers on the landing withdrew back to the aircraft, she threw her arms around Stormy's neck and hugged him.

"I thought you died," she sobbed.

Stormy awkwardly but gently placed his hands on Adisa's back, trying to mimic what she was doing. Hugging wasn't a concept his people had, but in that moment, she didn't care. She was so happy to see him.

"I am . . . full of regret, A-disss-a," he said, as the doors closed. "I tried to find you. I failed."

"It's not your fault," she answered, stepping back. She hesitated for a long moment. "Did . . . what happened to Roc?"

The alien was silent for a few seconds, his dark eyes unreadable. "Roc died a good death, like a warrior should. His . . . absence . . . is felt. I am full of regret, again."

"No," Adisa said, weakly, tears streaming down her face. "Oh, God, no." She leaned into Stormy again and started to cry.

The soldier named Marcus appeared next to them, speaking softly. "I'm sorry, folks, but you need to strap in. We're taking off." One of his soldiers, a woman, carefully helped Adisa into a seat and buckled her restraints. Stormy's tail stump made it so he couldn't use a chair built for humans, so he sat on the floor next to her. Her stomach lurched a little as the aircraft took off and quickly dove to treetop level, speeding southward.

"I don't feel good," Adisa said, still in tears. Her insides hurt, like she was having the worst cramps ever. Her heart hurt as well. Roc had died saving her. It wasn't right. It wasn't fair. He didn't deserve that.

The female soldier put a hand on her shoulder. "Hang in there, honey, we'll get you looked at as soon as we can. Try and get some rest. Here's some water if you're thirsty."

Adisa was exhausted. The tightness in her chest just wouldn't go away, and she couldn't hold back the tears. She found solace in sleep.

❖ ❖ ❖

Marcus Winchester hurried down a corridor, trying to remember which way to go. The subterranean complex was sprawling, and labyrinthine, and which corridor led where was not always readily apparent. Turning a corner, he found himself at a transparent door, leading to the executive office suite that Mr. Krycek had been set up in. He waved a hand in front of a panel with a red light on it. Recognizing his biometrics, the light turned green and the door opened.

Inside, Talia was sitting at a desk, looking bored. Halifax was seated against the wall, fiddling with his handheld.

"Marcus?" the red-haired mercenary asked. "What's wrong?"

"I need to see the old man," Marcus said. "I tried to message him, but there was no response."

"He's in a private meeting right now," Talia said. "Is everything alright?"

"Is he in there?"

"He is, but he said he absolutely wasn't to be disturbed. He has guests. Natives."

"He'll want to be disturbed for this," Marcus said. "It's about his daughter. Let me in."

"If you insist." She tapped her console.

"Thank you," Marcus said, and pushed the door to the inner office open. "Mr. Krycek, I—" He found himself at a loss for words when he realized that there were four Ithacan aliens in the office with his client. One of them was Follower of the Storm, the warrior who had gone with him to recover Adisa. The other three were smaller and slenderer in build. *Females?* They were draped in identical robes, crimson in color. Their faces were veiled, revealing only their eyes.

"Mar-cusss," Follower of the Storm said. "You were not . . . invited."

"My, uh, apologies for charging in like that. It's important."

"Something troubles you, warrior," the three females said, in unison. Their singsongy voices had an ethereal quality. They sounded almost like they were in your mind instead of your ears.

"Mr. Krycek, it's your daughter."

"Oh my God," the old man said, standing up. "What's wrong?"

"The doctor did a full imaging scan of her. They found something inside her."

"What do you mean?"

"I mean, something was planted inside of her body. You should really come with me, sir. The doctor can give you the details."

The color had drained from Mr. Krycek's face. "Of course." He turned his attention to the three veiled aliens. "Forgive me. I must tend to my daughter."

The aliens said nothing. The old man hurried out of the office, and Marcus followed. "Halifax, go with him," he ordered.

"On it!" He hurried out of the office, after the client.

"What is going on?" Talia asked.

"It looks like those bastards planted something inside Adisa."

"What? What do you mean?"

"Doc says they cut her open and stuck something inside her body. It's a sphere about yay big," Marcus explained, holding his hands a few centimeters apart. "They don't know what it is."

Talia said something in her native language that,

judging from the way she spat the word out, must have been an epithet. "I'm coming with you. That object is a bomb."

"What?"

"I'll explain on the way. We don't have much time."

"Understood." Marcus tapped his earpiece. "Wade, where you at?"

"In the break room, boss. What's going on?"

"I need you in medical right away. It's Adisa. The Combine put a bomb inside her."

"What? How do you know?"

"I'll talk to you in medical. Double-time, Wade. Out."

The medical clinic was getting crowded by the time Marcus and Talia got up there. Mr. Krycek was surprisingly calm as he spoke with the doctor about the situation. Tapping a console, the physician brought up a 3D representation of the object on a holotank.

"This is the foreign object we found inside your daughter's abdomen, Mr. President," the doctor said. "It is a nonmetallic sphere, six centimeters in diameter. As you can see, our x-ray imaging was able to penetrate the object. It appears to have circuitry inside. A tracking device, perhaps?"

"It serves as that," Talia said, "but that is not its primary function. It is a bomb."

The doctor's eyes went wide. "Are you sure?"

"Quite sure," Talia said. "I am . . . familiar . . . with such contrivances of Internal Security. I've seen this before."

"What do you think, Wade?" Marcus asked. His partner had been a Nuclear/Explosive Ordnance Disposal technician in the Concordiat Defense Force. If anyone in the room had any idea what to do, it would be him.

"I don't have any reason to doubt Talia," he said,

looking at the hologram. "That dark blob there, that's likely the explosive charge. That looks like a power source. Talia, how is it initiated?"

"It can vary," she said. "It will have a timer. If we do nothing, it will detonate."

"It might have antiremoval features," Wade said. "Mr. Krycek, I'm sorry, but if we try to pull it out of her, it could explode."

The old man shook his head. "Why would they let her go, only to do this? What is the point of this?"

"They know she's valuable to you," Talia answered. "This is what they do. The Combine may be trying to goad you into overreacting, which could hinder your efforts to counter them."

"I should've dropped that damned freighter on those bastards," he said, coldly. "What can we do?"

"If I can get to the device, I may be able to access its functions."

The old man looked at the former assassin, his eyes almost pleading. "Will you try? Adisa is important. Not just to me, she's important to the future of this world."

"If I am unsuccessful, I could cause the device to detonate."

"I know what I'm asking, Talia. Will you try?"

"Hang on a second," Wade said. "Don't you people have N/EOD techs of your own? Surely they have a manipulator bot. Have the autodoc cut her open, then have the robot remove the device. It minimizes the number of people put in jeopardy."

"There isn't such a team on site," Mr. Krycek said. "Black Mountain doesn't store ordnance, so they didn't station a team like that here. You must understand, our forces don't have very many such assets."

"I don't think that will work in any case, Mr. Bishop," Talia said. She held up her left hand, pointing her index finger at the ceiling. A needlelike metallic key poked out of the tip of the finger. "I can only access it through my interface. The Combine very rarely employs wireless interfaces for such things, it makes them too easy to hack. I have to connect with it directly, and I may not be able to access its programmed functions."

"Shit. Well, okay." He looked up at the doctor. "Doc, prep your autodoc for surgery. Talia and I will take care of the device."

"Wade, are you sure?" Marcus asked.

"Hell no, I ain't sure, but if Talia is going to be in there, finger-fucking this thing, then so am I."

"That's not necessary," Talia insisted.

Marcus shook his head. "Devree is gonna be pissed at you, Wade."

"Yeah, well, get her some chocolates for me, okay? She likes dark chocolate. Mr. Krycek, tell your people to get their own bomb technicians up here anyway. We're going to get to work. I don't think we have much time."

"The device may be connected to her biological functions," Talia suggested. "Keep her sedated. Waking up, or an elevated heartrate, or physiological stress may activate it."

"She is under anesthetic now," the doctor said. "But, Mr. President, there is one more thing you should know about. We did bloodwork on her as soon as she came in. We just got the results back." She seemed hesitant, looking at everyone in the room. "It's rather personal."

"Doctor, there's no time. I assure you, my body-guards and staff are discreet professionals."

"Adisa is pregnant, sir. It's still very early in her term, but I'm certain about it. Congratulations."

The old man blinked a few times, seemingly in shock. "My God, I'm going to be a grandfather."

"You are, sir," Wade said. "Talia and me will get that thing out of her."

"Please, young man, try your best. And Talia? Whatever happens, thank you for trying."

"Don't get yourself killed, Wade," Marcus said. "Devree will never forgive me."

"No promises. Come on, Talia, let's get to work."

Marcus felt bad for his client. He'd seen a lot of terrible things in his career, but he couldn't imagine what it would be like to sit there, watching helplessly, while your daughter's life hangs in the balance. He wondered, if it were Annie on that table instead of Adisa, would he have the same composure the old man did? He doubted it.

Zander Krycek sat quietly, chin resting on inter-laced fingers, watching the operation on the video feed. The clinic and the entire level it was on had been evacuated, leaving Wade and Talia alone to do what needed to be done. Follower of the Storm stood behind him, in silence, his alien face unreadable to Marcus. The doctor was also watching, and was in direct communication with the two of them, should there be any unexpected medical complications that the autodoc couldn't handle.

Devree and Halifax were there, too. The sniper was standing against the wall, arms folded, watching the displays in silence. She was scared. She didn't get scared often. Halifax, he didn't seem too stressed.

He just watched intently, occasionally telling Devree not to worry.

"If he doesn't blow himself up I'm going to kill him," she said. "That idiot always has to volunteer for stuff like this."

"Aye," Halifax agreed, "he's an idiot, but he's a brave idiot. Sometimes there isn't much difference 'tween the two."

The autodoc methodically made an incision in Adisa's abdomen, vacuuming up the blood as it did so. Marcus had seen his share of blood and guts, but nonetheless cringed as retractors were used to pull open the incision and keep it open.

"I see it," Talia said. Both she and Wade were dressed in surgical scrubs and protective clothing. "There." A different camera zoomed in, and there it was: a gray ball, covered in blood, lodged deep in the young woman's abdomen. "I need suction. Doctor, have the robot apply suction. I need the device cleaned off, so I can find the interface."

"Very well," the doctor said. "Stand by." She tapped her tablet a few times, and the autodoc responded. A clear tube slid into the incision and turned red as it sucked out the blood.

"Can you see it?" Wade asked.

"Rotate it," Talia said. "Slowly. See those receptors? That's where it's connected to her body. Be careful not to break the connection."

"Christ," Wade blasphemed. "Hey, what is that?" On the camera feed, Marcus could see a small circle engraved on the device, with a dot in the middle. Another line went around the circumference, probably where the two halves were sealed together.

"Yes," Talia said. "Steady." Removing her surgical glove, she extended the tiny interface pin from her left index finger and, very slowly, inserted it into the device. She closed her eye.

"What's going on?" said Mr. Krycek.

"Quiet," Wade said. "Let her work."

"There," Talia said. The bomb hissed as the seal was broken, and it opened, slightly, along the seam.

"What's it doing?" Wade asked. "That scared the shit out of me."

"I have opened it. I cannot turn it off."

"Okay, okay, hang on . . . Doc! I need more suction! It's filling up with blood!"

"Yes, of course, sorry!" the doctor said, hurriedly tapping her tablet. "Is that better?"

"Yeah. Stand by." Mr. Krycek stood up as Wade leaned in close, using a head lamp to peer into the device. "I see it." He looked up. "Talia, you get out of here now."

"No," she said, flatly. "Continue working."

Wade nodded and looked back into the incision on Adisa's abdomen. "I need, like, some teeny little pliers. Needle nose." A wide array of tools, both surgical and electronic, had been set out for them on the surgical cart. Talia handed him a very small set of pliers. "Okay. I see the power source. As near as I can tell, it's the only one. Looks like a . . . holy shit, this is a nuclear battery." He looked back up at Talia. "Why would they put a long-duration nuclear battery in something like this?"

"These devices can be used to gain compliance from an individual for a very long time," she said.

"Damn. What kind of asshole thought something like that up?"

"Internal Security," she answered, flatly. "This and worse. Things you wouldn't believe."

"Yeah, well, I don't wanna find out. Okay, guys, this is it. I'm going to take out the power source. If it doesn't, you know, explode and kill us all, it should be disarmed."

"Mr. Bishop," Krycek said, "I have received word that a bomb disposal team has arrived at the mountain. They have all their equipment with them. The commander asked if there's anything he can do to assist you."

"Yeah, have them bring down an explosive containment vessel. I need somewhere to put this thing."

"I will relay. Whatever happens, Mr. Bishop . . . thank you."

"No problem." He looked up at the camera. "Devree, I love you." Looking back down, he gently tugged on the battery, popping it loose from where it sat. Nothing happened. He exhaled heavily. "Okay, so far so good. Doc, I need you to tell the autodoc to detach these receptors from the tissue, without jarring the device. I'm afraid I'll cut something important."

"On it," the doctor said, working the controls on her tablet. "Please stand back." The autodoc's three-fingered hand reached into the incision, and paused. Another, smaller arm deployed out of the hand and opened three fingers of its own. This happened a third time, and three tiny fingers began delicately detaching the bomb's receptors from Adisa's tissue.

"Wow," Wade said, looking on. "A fractal-arm robot."

"The receptors are disconnected," the doctor confirmed. "Is it safe to remove the device?"

"I'm as sure as I can be," Wade said. "Go ahead

and lift it out." Very slowly, the robotic arm lifted the device out of the incision in Adisa's abdomen. It had to close the two halves of opened bomb, to fit it through without tearing more tissue. Once clear of her body, the robot took the device, dripping blood, and gently set it on a wheeled cart. "Okay, it's clear. I'm going to push this thing down the hall, get it away from medical."

"Those bomb techs should be waiting for you down the corridor," Marcus said.

"Perfect. Doctor, we're done here."

"Very good, Mr. Bishop," she said. "I'm going to inspect the wound, repair any damage I find, and then close. Patient's vital signs are stable."

President Krycek sat down in his chair, exhaling heavily. "Mr. Bishop, thank you. You have the gratitude of my homeworld, and of a relieved father. Talia, you as well. We couldn't have done this without you."

"You couldn't have," she agreed, bluntly. "I am... happy... to have helped." Marcus chuckled at how awkward it sounded.

Zander Krycek turned to the doctor. "I'm going to go to my office, tell the Elders what happened, and have a stiff drink. Please alert me when Adisa is awake."

When Adisa opened her eyes, she wasn't sure where she was, but she knew she didn't feel good. She was lying in bed, in a bright, white room, but she couldn't make out any details. It took what seemed like a long time for her eyes to adjust. She sat up a little and rubbed her eyes. It was then she realized there were tubes and wires connected to her. *Am I in a hospital?* Confused, she struggled to remember how she got wherever she was. Her last, hazy memory was of being strapped into a seat on an aircraft, and being told that Roc was dead.

"Oh God," she whispered, quietly. Tears formed in her eyes as she struggled not to break down and sob. "Roc..."

"Hello, Adisa," someone said. She startled at the sudden realization that she wasn't alone. "You don't need to be scared. You're safe. We got you away from the Combine."

The voice was familiar, yet not someone she knew. "Where am I?" she asked, blinking away the tears and rubbing her eyes some more.

"You're in the medical facility of the Southern Autonomous Zone military command complex. Do you know who I am?"

Adisa forced her eyes to focus on the man sitting next to her bed. "Father?" she said, after a moment. "Is that really you?"

"It is, my darling," he said. "I'm sorry it took me so long to come home."

"You came," she said, weakly. She remembered the message from him that her interrogator had shown her. "You...you threatened to destroy an entire city to save me! How could you?" She tried to sit up, her heart racing. "How could you? You risked everything we've been fighting for for one person!"

"Adisa, please, stay calm."

"Don't tell me to stay calm! Do we have *any* allies left, now?"

"Adisa, *please*," her father said, sharply. "You've just had surgery. You need to be still."

"Surgery? What did I have..." she trailed off, barely

remembering the abdominal pains that she felt upon her release. "Oh, God, what did they do to me?"

"They planted a bomb inside you, Adisa."

"A bomb?" she repeated, on the edge of panic.

"Yes, a bomb. You're safe now. We had it removed. And, listen to me, please. I did threaten the colony for your safe return. It was a bluff. I never would have done such a thing."

"I want to believe you, Father."

Your father speaks the truth, young one, a voice sang into Adisa's ear. Or was it into her mind? The voice was familiar, comforting, yet . . . alien.

"Are the Elders here?" she asked. "They're here, aren't they?"

"Three of them are, yes," her father said. "How . . . how did you know?"

"One of them spoke to me."

"Ah. They spoke directly into your mind, didn't they?"

"You . . . know about this?"

"Yes, my dear. Do you think I was able to engineer a peace treaty between our two races without undergoing such contact? I submitted to their psionic link many years ago. That is how I earned their trust after so many years of hostilities."

"You never told anyone of this?"

"I didn't. They asked me to keep it secret, and so I did. But, Adisa, there's something else I need to tell you. You're pregnant."

Her eyes went wide. "What?"

"You're pregnant," her father repeated. "Doctors confirmed it in your blood tests. And, before you ask, no, the surgery didn't harm your pregnancy. You're healthy."

Adisa's head was spinning, her heart started to race. "Oh, God."

Her father raised an eyebrow. "Please, forgive me for prying, but...who is the father?" Tears formed in her eyes again. She placed her hands on her belly, and this time, couldn't stop herself from sobbing. "Adisa, what's wrong?"

"He's dead," she said with a sniffle.

"I see. Damn it all. I'm so sorry. Who was he?"

"A soldier. An SAZ Ranger. He was my escort. He... he died trying to protect me, the night the Combine took me. He's dead because of me." Tears streamed down her cheeks. Her father stood up, then sat on the bed next to her. Hesitating for just a moment, he took Adisa into his arms, and held her as she cried and cried.

"My God, I'm so sorry, my darling," he said softly. "I know this pain. I know it well. I loved your mother deeply, you know. She was the light of my life. When I lost her, I wasn't whole anymore. Part of me died with her, and I have never been the same."

"How do you live with this?" she sobbed. "Does it ever stop hurting?"

"No. No, child, it doesn't. In time, you...you learn to live with it. But listen to me. He's dead, but not gone. He lives on inside you, in your child. You need to focus on that, on the future. That was the only thing that kept me going after your mother died. The only reason I didn't lay down and die was...well, you. Out of death and tragedy, comes life, a new beginning."

"Thank you for coming here, father," she said, wiping tears from her eyes. "I'm sure it wasn't easy."

"You don't know how right you are. But, I'm here now, and one way or another, I'm here to stay."

"How is the war going?" Adisa didn't know how long she'd been in captivity. She'd had no way of telling time. "Is it bad?"

"It's mostly an air war now, and that's been something of a stalemate. We've burned through much of our war materiel, and so have they. We prevented a planned ground offensive deeper into our territory, but are unable to launch an offensive north. We're not losing, and they're not winning. Unfortunately, they don't *have* to win. All they need do is hold out until the Combine delegation return with military escorts, and then we will lose. We cannot hold out with them having space superiority and unlimited reinforcements from off-world."

"Is it hopeless?"

"There is hope, Adisa. My hope, *our* hope, lies within you."

"Me? What can I do?" Adisa was confused. She wasn't a soldier. She wasn't a great military leader. Her primary area of education was xenoanthropology.

"My dear, there is something else I need to tell you. It's time you learned who you really are."

Log Entry 139
Mission 815-707-SSOC
Reconnaissance Ship 505

We have entered the Ionia-5589 system. Long-range sensor scans show one Polaris-*class patrol ship approaching the planet. AI/CORE is CONFIDENT/HIGH/HIGH that this is the* Andromeda. *It is not known why they haven't landed yet, or if they have and have taken back off again.*

There is a Type-38 freighter in a high solar orbit that is not responding to normal laser pulse hails. It appears to be damaged and abandoned. We attempted to remotely access its logs, but they have been wiped.

AI/CORE has conferred with friendly forces on Ionia-5589/Ithaca via the extremely long-range encrypted communications array. Messages received via the ELRECA confirm that Zander Krycek has arrived on the planet. We have failed.

There is another friendly ship in the system, a Type-54 covert battleship disguised as a Type-19 heavy freighter. It is on a trajectory from out-system and will be entering the Ionia-5589/Ithaca orbital sphere soon.

AI/CORE will confer with friendly forces on Ionia-5589/Ithaca and stand by for instructions.

With the aid of an excellent doctor, Adisa was healing quickly. It had been several days since her father had revealed her true heritage, and she was still having a hard time wrapping her brain around it. When she was a child, growing up, her father would make up stories about her. He would entertain her with thrilling tales of Princess Adisa, and her magical adventures across the universe. She realized now that when he called her *princess*, it wasn't just a cute nickname, it was her *actual title*.

It meant that her unborn child was destined to rule, someday, if her father's plan of restoring the crown worked. The child would never know her father. She struggled to hold back tears just thinking about it. It wouldn't do for royalty to be seen crying. How amazing was it, though, that this child, the product of one night of reckless passion, of love previously unexpressed, might grow up to be king or queen?

It amazed her how readily everyone accepted her newfound status. The south had been wary of the crown for generations, and among them were the most fervent supporters of abolishing the monarchy and moving to a republican form of government. And yet, the leadership of the Southern Autonomous Zone had declared their support for the crown restoration. That her father was also the *father of the revolution* probably helped. She'd also made it known who the father of her child-to-be was. The south had never been well-represented in the previous regimes. It was an open secret that they had been despised by the nobles, especially King Khari V's court. Having the future king or queen be of southern blood seemed to have softened their opinions on the monarchy.

Her father was hoping that the north would be as willing to recognize her legitimacy as the south, with or without the council. He intended to reveal her to the world, declaring her to be the rightful queen of Ithaca, and ask for a cease-fire. He was optimistic, but Adisa wasn't. He hadn't lived on Ithaca in years, whereas she'd grown up there. She knew how deeply the divisions ran. Even if the people would accept her, the Revolutionary Council surely would not just give up.

Despite her doubts, she agreed to go through with it. What other choice was there? The war had ground into a stalemate, and they were running out of time. Her father assured her that he still had back-channel contacts to the north, and was busy laying the groundwork for her. She desperately hoped that this wasn't all for nothing. If the Combine arrived and began orbital bombardment, the war was lost no matter what. Adisa would be queen of the ashes.

Arriving at her quarters, she turned to her escort. He was a short, burly man with a scruffy beard and a blade of red hair sticking up out of his head. Halifax, his name was. He was one of the mercenaries her father had brought from New Austin. "I'm going to go in and rest."

"Aye, Princess," Halifax said, giving her a polite nod. He wore the fatigues of the Southern Autonomous Zone Defense Force, though they lacked insignia. "I'll be outside if you need me."

Adisa didn't think she needed to be guarded all day, every day, but her father was insistent. She thanked the mercenary, waved her hand over the access panel, and entered her room as the door slid open. As the door closed behind her, she felt strange. Not sick, or dizzy, or anything like that. She felt like she wasn't alone, but the presence wasn't alarming. It was familiar, almost comforting. "Hello?" she called out. There was no answer.

Crossing the foyer of her suite, she went to her bedroom. Inside, the lights were off. The room was illuminated only by the scented candles she'd lit before leaving. Adisa startled when she realized that there were three figures there, concealed in the shadows, watching her silently.

"Do not be afraid, young one," three voices sang, in unison. The figures, veiled from head to toe, barely moved. "We have met before."

It was the Elders! "I apologize. You startled me. I wasn't expecting you."

"We move in secret when we need to. We mean you no harm. We have more to show you."

"Will I need to drink that elixir again?"

"No. Your mind is receptive to psionics, more developed than most of your kind. Once we learned of your true bloodline, we understood."

"I'm glad you understand, because I'm confused."

"Sit, young one. Let us show you where you come from." Adisa kicked off her shoes and did as she was asked. Her bed was adjusted so that she could lounge on it without lying flat. "Clear your mind," the Elders sang. That was a little bit harder. She had a *lot* on her mind.

Nothing happened. "I don't know if this—" Adisa fell silent as images came flooding into her mind. She witnessed the arrival of the first colonists on Ithaca, centuries ago.

"Your kind was already known to us when these settlers arrived," the Elders said. "There had been expeditions before, but the aliens who landed were few, their habitats temporary. We stayed hidden, and observed without being detected. This landing, the one which brought your ancestors, was different. There were thousands of you, and it was clear that you intended to stay.

"Many of us were afraid. There were calls, amongst the Elders, to utilize the technology and the weapons that we had buried so long ago. They demanded your extermination. This is *our* world, they lamented, and had we not already lost everything? Would we let you take our home from us? Worse, it was feared that with you here, *they* would find us again."

You were afraid we'd lead the Maggots to you. But you had the means to destroy us? Adisa thought.

"Yes, young one. Most of our people are unaware, but we did not land on this world unprepared. We brought weapons with us, ancient and terrible, and some Elders called for their use."

Images flashed in Adisa's mind of beam weaponry obliterating the newly landed human ships and nascent colony. She was being shown not what happened, but what might have been. *Why didn't you?*

"Some of us are old enough to remember the last war. We may be all that is left of our race. We are few in number and lack the means to travel the stars. We believed, rightly, that you were part of a vast empire. If we wiped out the few invaders, it would certainly not be the last we saw of your people. A habitable world is far too precious to simply abandon. More would come, and if we started a war, we would not win. We chose instead to do something that our race had not done in an age."

Adisa watched as a delegation of the Elders' people approached the human settlement, appearing out of the jungle. Their first communication was made only with hand gestures. None of the humans or Ithacans involved had ever participated in such a first-contact scenario before. A human contingent appeared, led by King Khari I himself!

"We determined that this one was your leader. We did not understand your words, but it was obvious that he was in authority. We sensed psionic ability in him, although it was weak and undeveloped. We saw promise in this, a potential for communication. He, and a few of his advisors, were led to a meeting place, where we three awaited them."

Through the eyes of the Elders, Adisa saw the king

and his entourage come to a clearing in the jungle. The Elders were there, in the shade of an ancient stone obelisk. It was a monument they had constructed upon first landing on Ithaca.

"We offered your king the elixir, and though his subordinates argued against it, he drank. His mind opened to us easily and without pain. That is how we were able to talk with your ancestors, young one. That is how we ensured peace between our two races. We told them which territories we claimed as our own, and they told us where they wished to build. We agreed to peaceful trade and noninterference. There were few among you who knew the truth, but the peace held." Native Ithacans helped the early human settlers build the colony. They instructed the humans on the dangerous beasts which lived in the jungle and seas. The northern plains were safer than the savage jungles of the south, but there was nowhere on Ithaca that was not perilous for humankind.

This is not what I learned in school, Adisa thought. *We were told that your people had warred with ours from the start, that you sought to kill us all and eat our flesh. I realized later that it was propaganda from the king's education ministry, but there were many of us who believed it.*

"Yes, young one. The fifth of your kings, he lacked the psionic abilities of his forbears. He tried to commune with us, and brought his mate. We warned against it, but they insisted. In the name of continued peace and cooperation, we attempted the communion. It . . . went poorly."

Adisa watched as the king and queen both drank the elixir, and attempted to open their minds to the

Elders. Within moments they were in agony, writhing on the ground, screaming, clawing at their heads. The Royal Guardsmen panicked and opened fire, killing the three Elders and their entire entourage. Only then did the agony stop. The king had blood trickling from his nose. The queen fared even worse.

"To those without psionic ability, however latent, the communion can be like having the mind ripped open. It can be agonizing. We tried to warn your king, but he would not listen. Yet, he was strong of mind and will. For him, the process was painful, but not dangerous. Your queen's mind was troubled. A dark cloud hung over it, a sickness, deep-rooted and hidden from view. The communion nearly killed her, and left her mind scarred and traumatized."

She killed herself when my mother was just a baby, Adisa thought. *My father told me that the king blamed you, and this is what started the conflict between our peoples.*

The Elders' song was mournful now. "It's true. With the murder of our sisters, there were calls for war. Anger is not something we are prone to, but such a killing was seen as an act of unwarranted aggression, a threat to our existence. Some of us argued against violence even then, but your people began to strike at ours, and we would not allow ourselves to be exterminated."

But you didn't use your hidden weapons.

"No. Those of us calling for restraint were able to convince our sisters to not reveal our true ability. We feared such a thing would bring more of your kind from off-world, and that we would inevitably lose. Instead, we played the part of the primitives, and sacrificed many of our own people as a result. Our intention was not to defeat you, but to get you to leave us in peace once again. Some tribes took matters into their own claws, however, and much blood was spilled."

Adisa saw, in her mind's eye, flashes of bloody battles between native warriors and human settlers. The natives took and learned to use human weapons, like guns, and learned to make primitive bombs. Small settlements were wiped out, and those massacres were answered by human reprisals.

"Something changed unexpectedly. Your people began to fight amongst themselves. Your king...met a bitter end."

An image of King Khari V appeared in Adisa's mind. He was bound to a chair. A man approached, pistol in hand. It was her father! He was younger, clean-shaven, with a short military haircut. He raised the pistol and shot the king through the heart.

"We did not understand what was happening. This new human leader, the one called Krycek, he fought harder than your king had. His soldiers respected him. We suffered defeat after defeat, and we feared he would press the attack, find our hidden cities, and wipe us out. Yet, he did not."

Now Adisa saw her father, alone and unarmed, approaching the three Elders. "He asked to meet with us," they sang. "He said he wanted to end the war. We agreed, but we needed to know if he was sincere. We asked him to drink of the elixir. He had no psionic ability that we could detect. We warned him of what had befallen your king. He persisted, drank, and opened his mind to communion." She saw her father writhing in agony, clawing at his head, as the Elders probed his mind. They looked on coldly as he screamed. "He was telling the truth. He wanted peace. We agreed to his terms, and the war ceased immediately. It was a momentous occasion for our people. The last time we had such an agreement with an alien race was so long ago that it was all but forgotten. This meeting changed the course of our history, and yours. Your father risked his life, his mind, to make peace with us. We have not forgotten that."

Why do you show me this now?

"We asked you to help us return to the stars in exchange for our aid. You agreed, without hesitation, and in return our people are fighting, and dying, alongside yours. We believe the tide is turning. Your people are rallying to you, and to your father, against this... Combine. But they will not let go of this world willingly. They will not be driven from our world so easily. We must prepare to defend our home, to whatever end, should they attack from space. Even now, our people are delving into rock and stone, retrieving the weapons that have been dormant for so long. We will reveal ourselves for who we truly are, and show your people what we are truly capable of. But, the price of this will be high, and we must ask for something in return."

Anything. Name it.

"You must protect us, Adisa, from your own people. We know how your species craves lost technology, how it values the remnants of the ancients. They will come for us. They will try to steal our technology, to exploit our people. You must protect us, Adisa, until we can return to the stars and begin our great journey."

You have my word. I will not let anyone exploit your people. But, you must understand, we are still a small and weak colony. Even if we drive the Combine away now, they may return with a full invasion fleet, especially once they realize that there is lost paleo-technology here. I may have to seek alliances with other foreign powers. I swear to you, though, I will not break my promise to your people.

"We know you will not, Adisa. Even still, the risk is great. Great, but necessary."

If we fail, the Combine will find you eventually.

"It is known. Even if they do not, our race has long been stagnant. With each generation we lose more of our heritage and our history. The Elders alone cannot maintain our culture. If we stay here in seclusion, we will devolve into savagery. We will be little more than beasts, fashioning crude stone tools, and looking up at the stars in ignorance. This cannot be allowed to pass."

Thank you, Elders. You may have saved our world.

"Rest now, young one. Without the elixir, even your mind will need time to recover. We must begin preparations. You will know when we are ready. You must understand that the war is not yet won. Suffering and death still awaits us. You must find your strength. Farewell."

When Adisa opened her eyes, her room was dark. The candles had burned down and gone out. Her head spun as she sat up; it was all she could do to turn the lights on. Looking at the chrono, she realized that she'd been asleep for twelve hours.

Just then, her communicator beeped. "Yes?" she asked, groggily, rubbing her temple.

It was her father. "Adisa, you should come down to the war room. There's something you need to see."

CHAPTER 32

The Privateer Ship *Andromeda*
Ithaca Orbit
Ionia-5589 System

Nickson Armitage awoke suddenly. A priority-communication alarm was beeping in his berth. He fumbled for the lights and to answer the call, almost bumping his head on the padded ceiling in the process. "This is Armitage," he said, groggily, eyes half open.

It was Captain Blackwood. "Nix, I'm sorry to interrupt your rack time. I wanted you to know that our stalker, that *Galaxis* class, has entered the system. We detected the translation thirty minutes ago, and the drive signature just now. Computer says it's a seventy-five percent match."

"Sounds good enough for me, Skipper. We going to battle stations?"

"Not yet. There's no need. They can't catch us before we land, and I don't want to use up the remass going after them."

Nickson rubbed his eyes, and took a sip from his

water bulb. "Is it going to be *safe* to land?" The
Southern Autonomous Zone had good air defenses, but
railgun shots from a fast-moving ship were damned
hard to intercept. A planeted ship was vulnerable.

"I've been assured that they can move the ship to
an underground silo after we land. Apparently, some
of their landing pads are on elevators."

"Why do they have all this stuff if they don't have
any functional ships?"

"That's the thing, they're trying. Both sides have
been trying to refurbish old ships from before the war.
The Combine has refused to sell the Colonial Government any spacecraft, aside from shuttles, fortunately."

"Hey, what's the status on that other freighter, the
Troubadour class?"

"It's in a deceleration burn right now. Its current
trajectory will put it in a geostationary orbit over the
Northern Hemisphere."

"Odd that they're still headed in-system after we
captured the other one. You want to go after it? We
could make it two for two."

The captain smiled. "Feeling a little more aggressive, Nix?"

Nickson shrugged. "If we're going to fight this war,
I think we should win it. That's all."

"I agree, but we're going to hold off for now. The
situation on the surface is dynamic. Here, you need
to see this."

"See what?" Before Nickson could even finish his
question, the image of the skipper was gone. In its
place was the face of Colin Abernathy, down on the
surface of Ithaca.

"Captain," the young pilot said, "I just wanted to

give you an update. All is well here. They successfully removed the explosive device from Mr. Krycek's
daughter, and she's recovering. They're changing tactics,
I think. Just watch."

The image once again cut away. Now, instead of
the *Andromeda's* flight officer, Nickson found himself
looking at Zander Krycek. Standing at his side was
Adisa Masozi, his daughter. With her was a huge
reptilian alien, one of the native Ithacans, wearing a
blue outfit that resembled a military uniform. Behind
them all was Talia, standing quietly with her hands
behind her back. *What is she doing?*

"People of Ithaca, this is Zander Krycek, broadcasting from a secure location in the Southern Autonomous
Zone. Before, I asked you all to join me, to protect our
world from the machinations of the Orlov Combine. I
know you've been blasted with pro-Combine propaganda, before then and since. I know they say some
terrible things about me. Some of them are even true!
But this, this isn't about me. It isn't about me returning
to power. I have made up my mind on the matter: I
will do no such thing. If we survive the coming days, I
will assume no role in the new government. There is,
however, someone I would like you to meet."

His daughter stepped forward then. She was also
dressed in a blue uniform, but one more elaborate
than the ones the SAZ generals wore. It had more
piping, more finery, and in place of the rank on her
shoulders there was only an emblem of a golden crown.

"This is Princess Adisa Cosette Masozi," she said,
solemnly. "I am the last scion of the Khari Dynasty and
the rightful heir to the throne of Ithaca. Included in
this transmission is DNA encoding that will verify my

claim to the throne. I am Zander Krycek's daughter. My mother was Princess Neema, daughter of King Khari the Fifth and Queen Mirembe. She did not leave the planet in exile, as you've been told. She stayed. She was married to my father. She loved him, and the bomb that was meant for my father claimed her life instead.

"I know this is a lot to take in. Only recently did I learn of my true heritage. I have lived among you my entire life, as a commoner, fighting for the future of my world. I didn't ask for this. Never in my life have I sought power or prestige. For most of the past year, I've been living in the jungle with the Rangers of the Southern Autonomous Zone, trying to reestablish peaceful relations with the Ithacan people, with whom we share this world. My father made peace with them once, and they have agreed to fight for me. You've read the reports of them in battle, of their ferocity and fearlessness. I assure you, if anything, those reports have been understated. I also have a warship in my service, and I needn't remind you what kind of advantage that gives me in battle.

"I do not come before you today to make threats, however. There is a long history of animosity between the north and the south, between republican and royalist, and between the Interim Government and the Southern Autonomous Zone. These divisions need not define us. We are, all of us, Ithacans. We have all suffered and bled. We have all lost ones we love. Northerner, southern, human, or alien, we shared this world peacefully once, and I believe that we can do so again. I grew up in the north. I was born and raised in Mombasa. I've also lived in the south. There are differences, yes, in culture and custom, but those differences are not worth killing each other over!"

Adisa lowered her eyes briefly, as if this was difficult for her to say. "A man named Roc taught me that. He was a Ranger, brave and loyal. I... I loved him. He died trying to protect me from Combine forces." She looked back up at the camera. "Make no mistake about it, they're here. Their soldiers, weapons, advisors, and spies are already on our world, despite their insistence to the contrary. I know this for a fact. I was captured, and they tortured me. That wasn't enough for them, either! When my father successfully bargained for my release, they put... they put a bomb inside my body!" While she said this, the screen was filled with footage from her surgery. Talia and Wade Bishop were shown working delicately to remove the bomb. "This device was designed to kill me and everyone around me. That is who they are." Adisa returned to the screen. "That is what they are bringing to our world if we do not stop them. Talia?"

Talia stepped forward then. She introduced herself as a former assassin from Combine Internal Security. She relayed the story she had told Nickson, but in more gruesome detail. She laid out the horrors that she had seen and that she had participated in. "I know they are promising you autonomy," she said, her eyes like ice. "I know they say it is a partnership. Those are lies. For a while, perhaps even a generation, things will appear to stay the same. Slowly they will work their way into every part of your lives. They will control what you see, read, hear, and think. Any dissent will be silenced without mercy. Every form of media you see will be embedded with their propaganda. They will take boys and girls, as innocent as I once was, and turn them into killing machines, like me. By the time you realize how far gone you are, it will be too late. Your colony will hold a vote to join the People's Combined Collective in totality, and the measure will win with an overwhelming majority. Then, everything you are, your history, your culture, your language, this will all be erased. To them, people are nothing but livestock to be managed, assets to be cultivated and expended. Do not believe their lies."

Adisa returned to the screen. "I ask you all to join me, your queen, and let us end this madness before more lives are spent needlessly. I am calling for an immediate cessation of hostilities. I will oversee the peace talks myself. We will bring all factions to the table: Revolutionists, Republicans, Royalists, and our Native neighbors, and we will forge a new and lasting peace for our world. There will be amnesty for all past transgressions and offenses. There will be no show trials or executions. We will start anew, and craft for ourselves a government that is accountable to the people and limited in its power. I will personally submit the declaration of rights, that my mother wrote, to be considered for inclusion in a new constitution for our colony. The people should not fear their government. No president, king, council, or legislature should have absolute, unchecked power.

"We can achieve this goal, but we can only achieve it if we end this war and come to the table. We cannot do it with foreign forces operating on our soil. I demand an immediate withdrawal of all military personnel, advisors, attachés, and servants of the Orlov Combine. As your queen, I am exercising my ancient right to refuse any treaty that I believe is not in the best interest of the colony. This is nonnegotiable. If you accept the cease-fire, the Combine must leave. If they do not, then I will consider it an act of war.

"To the Revolutionary Council, I say this: allow the cease-fire and peace talks to go forward. If you do so, you will all be granted amnesty, and your voices will be heard in the creation of our new government. If you refuse, each one of you will be considered to be in open rebellion, and I will not rest until I see each of you hung. To the Colonial Army, I would like to remind you that your oaths are to the colony, not the Council. You are not obligated to obey any illegal orders. Please, do the right thing, and stop the fighting. I'm not asking you to retreat or surrender, only to accept a cease-fire so the peace talks can begin. If you won't do it for your queen, do it for your families, and your world. There has been too much bloodshed already."

The image changed again. Nickson found himself looking at something he couldn't immediately identify. It looked vaguely like one of the native Ithacans, but it was *huge*. It had to be 30 meters tall! Its body was covered, from head to toe, in dull armor plating. On its back was a boxy attachment, looking almost like a backpack, with cooling fins sticking out of it. Some sort of weapon was mounted on its shoulder. It raised its head to the sky and roared.

"Captain, what . . . what in the hell is that?"

"Paleotechnology," she answered. "I received a private encoded message from Mr. Krycek. The Ithacans, they're not native to this world at all. They were once a spacefaring race, and they landed here and hid to escape the Maggots."

"My God," Nickson said, staring at the screen. The footage was recorded from an aircraft. It zoomed out, and showed dozens of the creatures, lumbering out of caves and tunnels. "How...I have so many questions."

"I don't have answers for you. We'll get them when we land, I suspect. Keep watching."

Adisa returned to the screen. "I have terrible weapons at my disposal, ancient, alien technology capable of unbelievable destruction. I do not wish to use it. Our world has seen enough war. I implore you not to test my resolve, however. I await a reply. I will not wait forever." The message ended, suddenly, and the captain's face reappeared on Nickson's screen.

"Holy shit," was all he could say. He blinked a few times. "Do you think this will work?"

"It is already. This broadcast went out six hours ago. Both sides have accepted the cease-fire, more or less. Kya is in contact with her people dirtside, and she says that the Council refused the offer, but most of their army disobeyed their orders. The fighting has stopped, for now."

Nickson could hardly believe it. Having come up in a culture where royalty was unheard of, he had a hard time understanding such dogged loyalty to a relative of someone who used to be important, but he was thankful for it. He guessed that when you factor in ancient alien technology, that changes things. Maybe they really *would* get through this without firing another shot. "So, Skipper, are we cleared to land, then?"

"We have been ordered to stand down, yes. Friendly air defenses are still active, so we'll have top cover, but they're worried having us in flight could jeopardize the peace talks. We're set to hit the atmosphere in about six hours."

"You need me up there?"

Captain Blackwood shot Nickson her famous lopsided grin. "You know, I'll be fine. I'm going to head up to the flight deck and pilot her in myself. Colin will have to forgive me."

Log Entry 140
Mission 815-707-SSOC
Reconnaissance Ship 505

The situation on Ionia-5589/Ithaca is rapidly spiraling out of control. Zander Krycek's meddling has resulted in a breakdown in relations with the host government. This government is no longer in control of its armed forces, eighty percent of which have stood down.

We have confirmed reports of sophisticated alien paleotechnology on the planet. Local command reports that previously unknown weapons have appeared alongside opposition forces. Information and analysis is included in this log entry.

Ionia-5589/Ithaca has summarily been upgraded from STRATCAT VALUABLE to STRATCAT CRITICAL PLUS. The capture and analysis of alien technology of the utmost importance. We will coordinate with the Type-54 covert battleship and plan orbital strike missions on key colony infrastructure. AI/CORE is CONFIDENT/MODERATE/MODERATE that an overwhelming strike, now, can break colonial resistance sufficiently for the planet to be held until reinforcements arrive.

The planetside AI/CORE/PRIME has authorized unrestricted warfare on military and civilian infrastructure.

RS-505 will not be able to assist. Our instructions are to observe, collect data, and return to home station.

CHAPTER 33

The War Room
Black Mountain Command Complex
Southern Autonomous Zone

Everyone rose as Adisa strode into the war room. "As you were," she said, before she could be formally announced. There was no time for royal frivolity. At the center of the room was a huge holotank, the biggest she had ever seen. Projecting an image of Ithaca, it was surrounded by her generals and advisors, along with her father.

"Apologies for disturbing your rest, Your Majesty," General Mohammed Farai said. "I know that you are still recovering."

That was true, and Adisa's insides hurt, but now was not the time for such weakness. "No, you were right to notify me. Please update me on the situation."

Her father spoke up first. "When I arrived in system, we were tracking two Combine ships. One, the *Tyrant*-class freighter, we captured. That ship is disabled and is now in a high solar orbit." The image on the holotank zoomed out. A blue, curved line represented the orbit of the captured transport ship. "The other, a much larger *Troubadour* class, was on approach from out-system." Ionia-5589's third transit point, the one which led to Orlov's Star and the frontier beyond, was far from Ithaca at present. Orbital mechanics put Ionia-5589 between the planet and that transit point. "This ship is, only now, approaching our orbital sphere."

"We didn't expect it to arrive so soon," General Farai said. "A fully laden *Troubadour* class can't even manage one gravity of acceleration under normal circumstances. This ship sped up to two gravities, and held that acceleration for over an hour. We're also detecting some unusual electromagnetic interference from the ship that our technicians believe to be electronic warfare systems. Your Majesty, we believe that this *Troubadour* is, in fact, a large warship in disguise."

"That is a known tactic of Combine forces," Zander said. "The ship that stalked us all the way from Heinlein was a special-operations craft disguised as a common tramp freighter. It demonstrated the capability to alter both its physical configuration and its drive signature to mask its identity."

"What are our options?"

"We don't have many, Your Majesty," General Farai said. "With sufficient velocity, such a warship can launch missiles from a great distance away. A ship that large could be carrying heavy planetary-assault weaponry as well."

"What kind of weaponry?"

"Mass drivers for orbital bombardment. Also, the Combine is known to have in its inventory several types of large fusion-drive missiles. These can accelerate for days, obtaining very high velocities, and carry a dozen nuclear warheads. If even one such device gets through our air defenses, it could all but wipe out the colony."

"Are we not capable of shooting them down?"

"It's not so easy," her father said. "These weapons have antimissile lasers and electronic warfare suites of their own. They're strategic weapons, almost never used, but we can't rule them out now. Worse, once that ship gets close enough, it could start pounding us with a capital ship–sized mass driver. The projectiles will be small, very dense, and accelerated to extremely high velocities. This makes them very difficult to intercept, and they will target our aerospace defense network first. Our defenses are not state of the art. Far from it."

"What about the northerners? Do they have better weapons?"

Her father shook his head. "The Combine wouldn't sell them weapons that could threaten their own ships. I have to assume that, all along, they planned to take the planet by force if diplomatic maneuvering failed. The reveal of the technology of our native allies likely solidified their resolve."

"You're sure of this, Father?"

"Not sure, but we can't afford to assume anything but the worst. Their trajectory puts them on a high-speed pass of our planet, a standard hit-and-run tactic for orbital bombardment."

"I will talk with the Elders and see if they can help us. What other options do we have?"

General Farai took control of the holotank display. "The best strategy would be to engage them at a distance. They would have to launch their weapons from much farther away, giving us more time to intercept them, and if sufficiently damaged they may turn back."

A pit was forming in Adisa's stomach. "Do we have any ships?"

"Only the *Andromeda* is fully operational, Your Majesty," the general said. "It is low on reaction mass and is on approach to land. They will need to resupply if they're to engage. There is one other, but she has not been certified as flightworthy yet."

"Tell me more."

"We call her the *Independence*," her father said. He tapped his controls and brought up a representation of the ship in the holotank. It was a midsized, three-engine design. "We once had four of these in the Orbital Guard, but they were mothballed before you were born. The *Independence* is the only survivor. They've been working on her for years, trying to get her operational."

"Can she fly?" Adisa asked.

"She can," General Farai said. "A combat test flight is not ideal, but we are out of options right now. I don't know that the *Andromeda* can take on that warship alone and prevail. I don't know that both of them, together, can take on that battleship and prevail. A capital ship–sized mass driver is not optimized for space-to-space engagement, but is more than capable of destroying a patrol ship in a single hit. There's also the matter of crewing the ships. We've had crews training on the simulator, but none have actually flown a ship like that before. The few experienced pilots we have all fly shuttles."

"Get me a direct feed to the *Andromeda*," Adisa ordered. She was becoming more comfortable with her newfound authority. "We need to ask them for help."

"On it!" a technician said, getting to work.

Her father turned to Marcus, his bodyguard, and asked him about the pilot that had flown him down to the surface.

"Who, Colin?" Marcus asked. "Yeah, he's a good pilot. You thinking you want him to fly your ship? You're going to have to ask Captain Blackwood about that, but I'll get him down here."

A few moments later, the technician looked back at Adisa. "We're connected, Your Majesty. It'll be on the right screen."

"Thank you. Put her on."

A woman's face appeared on the screen. She was tall, of fair complexion, and had her hair done up in a tight bun. "Your Majesty," she said, cordially, "it's a pleasure to finally meet you. I'm Catherine Blackwood, captain of the *Andromeda*. How may we be of assistance?"

"Captain, first I would like to thank you for all you have done. I understand that you undertook my father's mission as a business venture, but all the same you risked your life, and the lives of your crew, to get him here. Your capture of that Combine freighter allowed my release, and if not for Mr. Bishop and Ms. Talia, I likely would have died. I owe you my life. I have no right to, but I must ask more of you."

"I'm listening, Your Majesty."

"As we speak, that second Combine ship is headed toward us. Have you been tracking its trajectory?"

"We have. It's suspicious."

"We have reason to believe it is, in fact, a covert warship preparing to conduct a high-speed pass for orbital bombardment of the colony. We have one ship of our own, but it's untested and the crew has never been in space. With your permission, I would like to ask your pilot if he would fly it for us."

"You can ask," the captain said. "I will not order him to do so. It's up to him."

"That is fair. There is one more thing I must ask. Will you engage this ship for us? I understand the gravity of what I'm asking, Captain. I would not ask if it were for my own sake, but millions of lives will be lost if nothing is done. Our surface defenses will not be enough."

Captain Blackwood was quiet for a moment. "I'll need to discuss this with my crew. I'm also very low on reaction mass." She looked away from the screen for a moment. "Without topping off, I will be unable to intercept."

Adisa's father stepped forward. "Captain, we can launch resupply tanks to you. It is how we planned to resupply our own ship, in orbit, without having permanent orbital supply points that would have been vulnerable to attack from the ground."

"I see. And you're certain we won't take ground fire from the north?"

"As certain as I can be, Captain."

"I will consult with my crew and get back to you. *Andromeda* out." With that, the screen went dark.

"Do you think she will help us?" Adisa asked.

"I hope so," her father said.

CHAPTER 34

The Privateer Ship *Andromeda*
Ithaca Orbit
Ionia-5589 System

Floating in freefall, Nickson held onto a handhold as the ship's crew assembled on the cargo deck. He knew what the meeting was about, but many of them were still in the dark about it. Everyone was present, save young Luis Azevedo, who was monitoring the command deck, and Mordechai Chang. The reclusive purser had not, as far as Nickson knew, left his personal compartment even once since they'd been underway. He was monitoring over the video feed, however.

"Thank you all for coming," the captain said, grasping a handhold at the front of the group. "We haven't much time, so I won't mince words. There is, at this time, a capital-class Combine warship headed toward Ithaca. It's a battleship that had been disguised as a *Troubadour*-class bulk freighter. Our analysis indicates it intends to conduct a high relative velocity flyby of the planet, which is an attack pattern consistent with orbital bombardment strategy. With the loss of their political allies on the ground, and the reveal of alien technology, friendly intelligence believes they intend to take the planet at all costs.

"Our clients have at their disposal one ship that they've never flown. It's untested and they have no experienced spacers to fly it. They're going to ask Mr. Abernathy to fly it, as a matter of fact, but there's no guarantee it'll even get off the ground. For the time being, we are all that stands between millions of colonists and the Combine.

"You all must understand; this warship outclasses us completely. The *Polaris* class, in any configuration, was never intended to take on a capital ship alone. Our odds of success are not good. We will likely only get one pass, and we'll have to hope we can hit them hard enough to prevent them from launching any strategic weapons they may have on board."

There were murmurs from the crew, but no one spoke up.

"If we go through with this, we will not have time to land," the captain continued. "They will resupply us in orbit, and we will proceed on an intercept trajectory. That is why I'm bringing this to you. You have worked hard, and risked much, over the years. We have lost friends. This action is outside the scope of our contract, and it may cost us our lives. We are privateers, not soldiers. We are not duty bound to lay down our lives for someone else's world. I will not make this decision without hearing from you. If you have something to say, please, let your voice be heard."

Kel Morrow spoke up first. "I have not changed my mind from before, Captain." He turned to his shipmates. "You are all my family. I understand the consequences of taking on that battleship. I don't suggest we do so lightly. But, please, think of this: if not us, then who? Do we stand by and do nothing while the Combine enslaves this world? While they do God knows what to the native species? Do we simply fly away and let millions die?"

"I'm afraid I must disagree with you, Kel," Indira Nair said. "Captain, this is not our fight. The Combine is here because these people invited them here. This is all their own doing."

"I'm with Chief Engineer Nair," Dr. Emerson added. "What good will it do those people if we all die in an unsuccessful attempt at stopping a huge capital ship? The end result won't change. The only difference is, we all die too."

"I say we fight!" It was Mazer Broadbent this time. "No, this isn't our world, and these aren't our people, but they're still human beings. There are innocent people down there who don't deserve to be vaporized from space. We wouldn't be fighting to save one government from another, we'd be fighting to save children from being slaughtered. If that's not worth risking death for, then what is? If you get home safely knowing you allowed such an atrocity to happen, will you be able to live with yourself?"

There was more murmuring now. That moved them. Annabelle Winchester raised her hand, like a polite school pupil.

The captain smiled. "Go ahead, Annie."

"I know I'm new," she said, raising her voice so that she could be heard. "And I don't want to die. But my dad is down there. My family. What are we going to do, just leave him down there? And Colin? So we can turn tail and run?"

"No one was suggesting that, Annie," the captain said.

"Then how are we going to get home? If we refuse, and they're all as good as dead, why should they give us any reaction mass? They might try to steal the ship to go fight themselves, and I wouldn't blame them."

"What are you suggesting, Crewman Winchester?" Kimball asked.

"I'm suggesting we go kill that Combine piece of junk, even...even if it means we die. I'm scared, okay? I'll admit it. But the people down on the planet are scared, too, and we're their only hope."

"Thank you, Annie," the captain said. "Nix?"

Nickson thought for a moment. He had to choose his words carefully. "Like Crewman Winchester, I'm new. Hell, I'm newer than her. She's been with you all in combat before. I was against taking on the Combine. My last ship was crippled trying to engage a cruiser that wasn't nearly as big as this Combine battleship. My captain died, and we were only barely able to limp home. I promised Captain Blackwood that I wouldn't be afraid to speak out if I thought she was making a bad decision that would get us all killed. This, this is a little trickier. This is a decision that might get us all killed...but isn't necessarily a bad one."

He thought about the stories that Talia had told him, of what was done to her. "The Combine is *evil*. There's no other word for it. If we do nothing, millions of people are going to die, and the rest will be enslaved. It won't simply be a matter of replacing one government with a worse government. You've all seen what they do. They implant people with machines and manage them like animals. Human lives are just... just a resource to be expended as necessary. I wouldn't wish that on anyone, even if their leaders were dumb enough to invite the Combine in. Skipper, I say we stand and fight. We might die, but we'll all die together, and we'll die trying to do the right thing. There are a hell of a lot worse ways to die. And if Colin agrees to fly their ship? He's still part of the crew. He'll need help. It's not hopeless. With two ships, we might be able to beat that monster. A lot of its weaponry will be geared toward surface bombardment. It's armored, but it's not invulnerable. One good hit and we can kill it."

The crew seemed to largely agree. Captain Blackwood was quiet for a few moments before addressing the crew again. "I could not ask for a better crew. It has been my honor to fly with you all. I'm going to contact Mr. Krycek and tell him he can count on us. We've already declared ourselves as combatants in this war. It wouldn't do to abandon our allies now. Thank you, everyone, for giving me your honest opinions. It will be some time before we depart, but we need to begin preparations now. I want top-to-bottom systems checks. I want the ship cleaned. Make sure the damage control and emergency medical stations are stocked. Every single crewmember needs to have a space suit checked out and ready to use."

"Yes, Captain!" the crew shouted.

"Excellent. Move out, everyone."

CHAPTER 35

The War Room
Black Mountain Command Complex
Southern Autonomous Zone

Adisa was in the war room, tracking the movements of the ships in the system. The second suspected Combine ship, a *Galaxis* class, was too far out to be a factor in the battle ahead. The huge battleship had cut its engines and was coasting, but made no effort to decelerate. Its trajectory would allow it to target both the terraformed zone up north, and the Southern Autonomous Zone, without slowing down. The bastards weren't even broadcasting a demand that Ithaca surrender. They were just going to destroy the colony. Not for the first time, she silently cursed the Revolutionary Council, and considered revoking her offer of amnesty to them.

She looked up as an aide got her attention. "Begging your pardon, Your Majesty, but we're receiving a transmission from the *Andromeda*."

"Thank you," she said, managing a smile for the man. "Please put it up on the screen." A moment later, she was once again face to face with Captain Blackwood.

Before either woman could say anything, Colin Abernathy, the brave young pilot of the *Andromeda*, stepped forward to address his captain. "Ma'am, I gave it a lot of thought, and I'm going to fly their ship for them."

"I see. Are you sure?"

"I am. It's not right to just do nothing and let the Combine bomb this planet. They need at least one spacer who's actually been in space in the last thirty years. The ship's skipper was retired and hasn't flown since before I was born."

"Well, we've got good news for you, Colin. You won't be out there alone." Captain Blackwood looked up at Adisa. "Your Majesty, the *Andromeda* is at your service. I'm sending down a list of supplies we need, including reaction mass. Please send them up as soon as you are able."

"Launch preparations are already underway, Captain," her father said. "I can't thank you enough for doing this."

"Everyone on Ithaca thanks you, Captain," Adisa said. "No matter what happens, you have our unending gratitude. As of this moment, you and your entire crew are hereby granted Ithacan citizenship, and you will forever be welcome on our world."

"That's kind of you, Your Majesty, but we still have to get through this battle."

Her father spoke up once again. "There's more good news, Captain. Our native allies have a weapon they dug up. With the help of their Adepts, we're working to get it mounted to the *Independence*."

"What is it?"

"Some kind of beam weapon. It's been buried for a thousand years, but they assure us it's still operational. It's going to change the flight characteristics of the ship, however. We'll be slower."

"Understood," the spacer said. "Wait, *we*?"

"Yes, Captain. I will be aboard the *Independence* as well."

Adisa turned to her father. "What? I did not authorize this!"

"I didn't ask, my dear." He looked back up at the screen. "We'll send you launch information on your supplies, Captain."

"Thank you."

Before Adisa could say anything else, her father's bodyguard stepped forward and looked up at the screen. "Captain?"

"Hello, Marcus."

"My daughter is on your ship."

"I know," she said softly. "She'll be secured in her berth, as safe as any of us can be."

"I don't want to distract her right now. You've got work to do. But, when you get a moment, will you tell her something for me?"

"Of course."

"Tell her no matter what happens, I love her, I'm so proud of her, and I'm sorry I can't be there with her."

"I will, Marcus. I will do everything in my power to bring her home to you."

"I know you will, Captain. Thank you."

With that, Captain Blackwood was gone, and Adisa turned back to her father. "There is no reason for you to go. Captain Murphy is an experienced spacer. You are not."

"Adisa, I have to go. It has to be me."

"But why?"

"Because that man over there," he said, pointing at his bodyguard, "his teenage daughter is risking her life for our planet. Because too many times, death claimed someone else when it should have been me. Like Colonel Starborn, or your mother. And because I'm responsible for all of this. I began the revolution, I killed the king, I destroyed Sargusport, and I left the Revolutionary Council in power. All this death and suffering is *my fault*, don't you see? I have to make it right."

The queen wasn't supposed to cry in front of her people. Adisa fought back the tears. She had a terrible feeling that she would never see her father again. "I could order you to stay," she said, quietly.

"You could, my queen, and I promise you that after I return, I will submit myself to the Queen's Justice. In the meantime, though, unless you lock me up, I'm getting on that ship before it lifts off." He put his hands on her shoulders, and looked down into her eyes. "I see so much of your mother in you. I always knew you were destined for greatness. No matter what happens, be strong, Adisa. Be a better leader than I was. Protect our people." He let go, and stepped away.

"Your queen orders you to return home alive," she said, still fighting back tears.

"Yes, Your Majesty," he said, dutifully, with a bow. "I love you." Without another word, he turned and left the war room. Marcus Winchester went to follow, but Adisa motioned for him to stay. There was nothing his bodyguard could do to protect him now.

CHAPTER 36

**The Privateer Ship *Andromeda*
Ithaca Orbit
Ionia-5589 System**

Nickson Armitage sat behind the controls of the *Andromeda*, alone on the flight deck, as preparations began. His acceleration chair was reclined, so that he could look out the ship's only windows without having to crane his neck. The view before him was breathtaking. Ithaca, beautiful in blue, green, and white, hung below him peacefully. One could almost forget that there was a battle yet to be fought.

On his screens, he was able to track the resupply launches as they came up, one after another, from several bases in the Southern Autonomous Zone. The reaction mass they were to take on wouldn't come close to filling their tanks, but it would hopefully be enough to carry them through the battle. They also received a shipment of nuclear warheads that they could fit onto their existing supply of missiles. Under ordinary circumstances, a privateer like the *Andromeda* wouldn't carry such weapons, and wouldn't be permitted to operate in many systems if she did. Besides that, they were often of limited utility in space combat. In the vacuum of space, they didn't produce the incredible blast and shockwave effects that they were known for. Their effective ranges were greatly reduced, especially if the target ship had heavy X-ray shielding. Even still, these were not ordinary circumstances, and any advantage they could get was welcome.

The resupply was not a short process. It had taken several orbital changes to intercept the various supply shipments, and in order to save reaction mass the maneuvers were done with minimal delta-v expenditure. A shuttle came up to collect the Combine prisoners they had been holding on the cargo deck. The shuttle was tiny, a local design intended to be as light as possible. It only had four seats, but they managed to stuff all five prisoners into it, plus poor Kya, the SAZ political attaché, and get them off the ship. They'd been barely able to get the hatch closed, and Nickson didn't imagine that it was a comfortable ride.

All this served to kill time while they were waiting for the *Independence* to launch, however. They'd spent days, planetside, hurriedly trying to get the old rust-bucket ready to launch. Nickson hoped to hell that Colin's skill was enough to fly that thing, especially with some mystery alien weapon bolted to the side. All the while, the Combine warship drew ever nearer. The *Galaxis* class had put itself on a long, slow trajectory that would take it out-system, presumably back to Orlov's Star.

It was during the seemingly endless wait for the launch of the *Independence* that Nickson received a private message from Ithaca. Nuchy, down on the command deck, had very politely routed it up to him so that he could view it. He tapped his console, and Talia appeared on screen.

"Hello, Nickson," she said. She seemed a little uncomfortable, almost as if she were nervous. "I... look, this is not easy for me to say. Please come back safely. I look forward to seeing you again. You are... you were good to me. Kind. You didn't have to be. I haven't forgotten. Please be safe." That was it; the message ended.

He smiled, and realized that he missed the former Combine assassin. It wasn't just because she was beautiful, or just because it was the best sex he'd ever had. She was sweet, in her own way, once you got to know her. She'd been denied so much of life, of what it means to be human, that this was all difficult for her. Even so, she was trying her best, and Nickson respected that.

A beeping console alerted him to an approaching ship. "Holy shit," he said aloud. "They actually got it off the ground." He watched his sensor feed as the *Independence* appeared over the planetary horizon, on a trajectory to match orbits with the *Andromeda*. She was an old tub, a *Reliant* class that was probably almost a hundred years old. Two centuries before, *Reliants* were all over inhabited space, but they were rare in the modern era. Her spaceframe had been modified, and from the drive signature, Nickson could tell that she'd been re-engined at some point. The *Reliant* had a blunt nose, a straight, cylindrical hull, and a bulbous engine cluster at her stern, surrounded by airfoils and radiators. Old spacers derogatorily referred to them as *dildos*, given their unfortunate resemblance to sex toys.

Zooming in the optical tracking camera, he was able to get a good look at her. Along the hull was a long, organic-looking . . . *appendage*. It ran the length of the ship and protruded past the nose. Fins and protrusions jutted from it, and at its base was an oval-shaped structure. A power plant, perhaps? Maybe a coolant tank? An energy weapon that big would need its own reactor, most likely. It boggled Nickson's mind that such a thing could have been preserved for a thousand years, but still be made to work. Most of the Ithacans knew very little of their own ancient technology, but they had Adepts, engineers and scientists, who passed this arcane knowledge down from one generation to the next. Apparently, their collective knowledge had been enough to not only resurrect their terrifying, monstrous super-soldiers, but to graft this beam weapon onto an old human ship. It was unbelievable.

A transmission came in from the rising Ithacan ship. A heavyset old man, with a gray beard and bald head, appeared on the screen. "This is Captain Lucian Murphy, commander of Her Majesty's Royal Space Force Ship *Independence*." He was breathing heavily, straining under the acceleration. "Glad to finally catch up, *Andromeda*. It's good to be back in space. It's been a long time."

"We're happy to have you with us," Captain Blackwood said. "Is your new weapon operational?"

"It is. The Adepts told us it'll only be good for one or two shots before it burns out, though. Range is limited to a few thousand kilometers. We'll have to get close. But, if it works like it should, it should punch through all but the thickest armor, and give the crew a nice dose of radiation while it's at it."

"*If* it works?"

Captain Murphy smiled, apologetically. "It's a thousand years old, Captain."

"Fair enough. We're ready to get underway, *Independence*. Have you received the flight plan?"

"Received and loaded into the nav computer. President Krycek is going to broadcast a speech to the planet as we depart. And, Captain? Thank you. I'm a fat old man now, but I've got grandchildren down there. No matter what happens, it's an honor to be here with you."

"You're too kind, Captain. May I speak with my flight officer?"

"Colin? Sure! He's a fine pilot, better than I ever was. I'll put him on."

A moment later, Colin Abernathy's face replaced the captain's. He was smiling. "Hey, Skipper!"

"Are you doing okay over there?" Captain Blackwood asked.

"Oh yeah. This ship is super old, don't get me wrong, but she's flying. We'll be right by you all the way to the end."

"Very good," the captain said. "Mr. Nickson, take us out."

"Yes, ma'am," he replied. He tapped the control for the ship's PA system. "Attention all personnel, stand by for acceleration, I say again, stand by for acceleration. One point five gravities, T-minus two minutes."

CHAPTER 37

**Black Mountain Command Complex
Southern Autonomous Zone**

Looking up at the night sky, Marcus had never felt so small and helpless. Somewhere up there, his daughter, his seventeen-year-old baby girl, was flying off into a battle that she probably wouldn't win. Instead of keeping her safe, or at least being there with her, Marcus was stuck down on the ground.

He'd found a quiet spot to sit and look at the night sky, away from much of the light pollution of the sprawling Black Mountain complex. It was quiet, mostly, save the occasional aircraft, ground vehicle, or . . . *whatever the hell those are.* The alien monster lumbered past, its huge head scanning for threats. Thirty meters tall and covered in armored plate, the ancient Ithacan weapons were a sight to see. The creature paused, turned its head, and looked down at Marcus. He couldn't see its real eyes, if it even had any; they were concealed underneath the helmet that covered its head. It contemplated him, quietly, for a few moments, before looking away and continuing on.

They were nuclear powered, he'd been told. The things that looked like backpacks on them were armored casings for compact fission reactors. They were cyborgs, a combination of living being and armored war machine. Marcus hadn't been able to figure out why they'd made them so big. Sure, they were terrifying, but they had to be impossible to hide and difficult to move. *Who knows? It must have made sense to them at some point.* They hadn't been tested in battle on Ithaca. The Colonial Army had agreed to the cease-fire as soon as they were revealed. He didn't know if that was mostly loyalty to the royal family, fear of these giant alien monsters, or a genuine desire to not be conquered by the Combine, but it didn't really matter. All that mattered to him was whether or not his little girl came back alive.

"Those things freak me out," Wade said, startling Marcus.

"Holy hell, Wade, how'd you sneak up on me like that?"

"Hard to hear me coming when that thing is stomping past. I wasn't sneaking. You okay, boss?"

"Yeah. No."

"I know you're worried about Annie. I am too."

"This was a mistake, Wade. This whole thing was a mistake."

"Maybe so, but it wasn't all your decision. She's the same age we were when we joined the Defense Force. She's just doing what young people do."

"Most young people don't get into lopsided battles with Combine warships."

"No, but you know better than I do how many kids get ground up in countless little wars all over inhabited space. I saw some shit myself, and I was

Fleet. We'd hear all kinds of horror stories about what Espatiers went through."

Marcus looked back up at the sky. "I guess I never thought I'd be the one stuck behind, waiting and worrying. I can't believe Ellie stuck with me all these years."

"She's a good woman, Marcus. But after this one, maybe you should be done, you know?"

"Yeah. I've got a son to raise. I don't want him to grow up without me around like Annie did, when she was little."

"She'll be okay. Captain Blackwood knows what she's doing. And, they got that big alien death ray bolted onto that other ship, so maybe they've got a fighting chance."

"God almighty, Wade, I hope you're right."

Log Entry 141
Mission 815-707-SSOC
Reconnaissance Ship 505

Hostile forces on Ionia-5589/Ithaca seem to have realized that the Type-19 Freighter is actually a covert battleship. Two patrol ships, a Polaris *class and a* Reliant *class, are moving to intercept. AI/ CORE is CONFIDENT/HIGH/MODERATE that the battleship will destroy the inbound attackers and complete its mission. The Type 54's AI/CORE has informed us that as soon as the immediate threat of the two intercepting ships is dealt with, it will continue on with its primary objective. It carries thirty-six fusion-drive strategic missiles, each equipped with twelve variable-yield, independently targeting nuclear warheads. We have been relayed a strategic targeting plan that would destroy every population center on Ionia-5589/ Ithaca. The missiles will not be launched while there is a danger of enemy ships intercepting them.*

AI/CORE states that victory is assured. The political officer is in concurrence. I am not. Too much has gone wrong on this mission to make such assumptions. RS-505 will remain in-system long enough to record the battle and ascertain the results of the orbital strike.

CHAPTER 38

The Privateer Ship *Andromeda*
Ionia-5589 System

Wearing a space suit and strapped into the acceleration chair on the flight deck, Nickson's primary job would be to target and fire the railgun. Given its limited range of adjustment, the ship itself would have to be maneuvered to fire it. As a last resort, he could use the ship's exhaust plume to vaporize incoming missiles, but with a closing speed of over a hundred kilometers per second, there likely wouldn't be enough time for that to work. The good news was, once the ships got past the merge with the missiles, there was no way they would have enough delta-v to flip around and pursue from the rear.

Though still tens of thousands of kilometers away, the Combine warship loomed large on Nickson's displays. The *Andromeda* and the *Independence* were flying relatively close together; not close enough to see each other, but close enough to cover each other with lasers. The *Independence* didn't have a working electronic warfare suite, and would be a damned missile magnet because of it. If it was going to live long enough to use its alien beam weapon, the *Andromeda* would have to cover it.

At the closing speeds involved, on a normal ship, a simple railgun hit would be catastrophic. Talia uploaded information about the battleship in question, though, and it seemed that it was covered in ablative, energy-absorbing armor. It could take a hell of a lot more of a pounding than either of its opponents could, and they were only going to get one pass. Captain Blackwood had decided that a direct intercept was the most survivable course of action. The Combine ship had God only knew how many missiles aboard, and neither intercepting ship was likely to survive a long-range missile-throwing contest with it. They had to get close enough to use the beam weapon and the nukes, and for that they needed speed.

The enemy wasn't making it easy. It started by vomiting out salvo after salvo of interceptor missiles, and employing a powerful ECM suite. On top of that, the son of a bitch was *maneuvering*. Not much, just little course corrections here and there, at random, enough to make long-range railgun targeting even more difficult.

"Tracking Salvo-Delta, eight missiles, closing fast!" Nuchy said. "Salvo-Echo, eight missiles! I'm trying— damn it, salvo fox, eight missiles!"

"Holy shit," Azevedo said.

"Calmly, people," the captain warned. "Focus."

"Salvo-Golf, eight missiles!"

"Leave the lasers on autotarget. Let the computer select which missiles to intercept, and in which order. Nuchy, you focus on ECM, see if you can fry a few of the incoming. Deploy decoys at your discretion, just remember we only have so many of them. Luis, get me a firing solution on our bandit. Nix, you awake up there?"

"Awake? Hell, Skipper, they'll never find the seat cushion when this is over!"

"Ha! Listen, don't waste railgun shots trying to intercept missiles." She was right; at the speeds they were operating at, and the way the missiles were maneuvering, the railgun would be useless. "Get me a hit on the enemy ship."

"On it, Skipper. I'll try and get us a lucky shot!"

Sweat beaded down Nickson's face, pulled toward the back of his helmet by multiple gravities of acceleration, as he maneuvered the ship from one firing solution to the next. The sensitivity of his controls was turned way down, to the point where the course changes didn't even use the ship's maneuvering thrusters. Very slight vectoring of the primary exhaust, combined with the internal gyro, was enough. Salvo after salvo of missiles were launched at them, the Combine ship having a seemingly endless supply.

"Firing!" Nickson announced, squeezing the trigger on his manual control stick. Felt acceleration dropped as he fired once, twice, then three times, launching three slugs toward the enemy ship. The first two missed, but the third one? "Impact!" he announced, excitedly. "Good hit."

"Excellent, Nix, now do it again. I want you to expend the entire railgun magazine by the time we merge, you understand?"

"On it, Skipper!"

"Missiles away!" Azevedo announced. "Missiles away!" He fired two pairs of missiles at the same time the *Independence* did, the eight warheads shrieking toward their target at unbelievable velocities. "Damn it!" he snarled. None of them made it through.

"Don't worry about that one, Luis, just get me another firing solution."

Nickson made up for the lull in missile firing by salvoing more railgun shots. He was startled by a loud bang and a terrible metallic groan, coming from somewhere in the ship. It knocked him off course, and he had to adjust. "What the hell was that?"

"We're hit!" Nuchy said. "We lost the number two airfoil."

"Holy Christ," Azevedo said, "Good thing it wasn't a nuke! I've got target lock again, firing! Two missiles away!"

Colin Abernathy's voice came over Nickson's headset. "*Andromeda*, this is *Independence*, you okay?"

"We're okay," Nickson said, trying to sound reassuring. "They took off a wing, but it's not a problem right now."

"None of our missiles are getting through!"

"I know, ours either. Keep trying. I pegged 'em with my railgun once."

"I saw that, good shooting."

"What's the ETA on that beam weapon?"

"They're calibrating it now. Time to fire, two minutes."

"I'll keep you covered, you just keep your maneuvers coordinated with mine."

"Roger that, sir!"

"Boom! Yes!" Azevedo cried, triumphantly.

"Did we get a hit?" Nickson asked.

"Close-in intercept, but it was one of the nukes. They got cooked a little."

"Outstanding," Nickson said, grinning in his helmet.

"It's not over yet, people," Captain Blackwood reminded them. "I need another hit like that, Luis!"

"We're running low on missiles, Captain!"

Nickson fired more rounds from the railgun, as fast as his need to maneuver and the weapon's cycle time would allow. *BANG!* The noise was so loud, and so close, that he had reflexively tried to duck. A warning klaxon sounded, and over the noise cancellation of his helmet he could hear a loud hiss.

"Nix, are you alright?" the captain asked.

"Yeah, I'm fine, Skipper. We got a hull breach up here. Small one, piece of fragmentation maybe. Scared the shit out of me." More loud pings and bangs resonated through the hull, and more warning lights lit up.

"Multiple damage reports coming in."

"Skipper, I think they're using fragmentation warheads on us now." Even a tiny piece of metal, at these speeds, could do significant damage.

"Concur. Nix, I need you to—" She fell silent as one of Nickson's screens lit up. The *Independence* fired its alien weapon, and it was unlike anything he'd ever seen. A visible, coherent white streak flashed from the *Independence* to the Combine warship, lasting for half a second.

"Holy shit," Nickson said. "Did they hit? They hit!"

Azevedo spoke up. "Captain, sensors are showing damage on the bandit. That was a good hit. It's not dead, though." It *was* damaged, though. Around where the beam had hit, the ablative armor had been blasted away. Secondary explosions blew bits and pieces off the battleship, but it kept coming.

"Colin, that was some damn fine shooting!" Nickson said. "Can you do that one more time!"

"We can, we just gotta wait for it to cycle. Give it...what? Yeah, give it two minutes. Can you—" He was cut off. A red warning light flashed on Nickson's display, and he zoomed in on the *Independence*.

Oh, no. "Skipper, the *Independence* is hit!"

"What? How bad?"

"It's bad. Near miss from a nuke. They got fried. Their acceleration is dropping. I'm trying to raise Colin. Keep firing. *Independence*, this is *Andromeda*, come in, do you read?"

"I'm still here, sir," Colin said, after a long moment. His voice was strained, and the transmission was filled with static. As Azevedo fired the last of the *Andromeda*'s missiles, Nickson tried to do a damage assessment on the *Independence*.

"You took a pretty good hit there. You gonna make it?"

"We're losing thrust. Laser targeting is fried. We're leaking propellant and atmosphere. I...my suit says I just took a lethal dose of X-rays. I think we all did."

Oh, God, no. Colin was a dead man, one way or another.

Despite the acceleration, Captain Blackwood's voice was calm and clear. "Colin."

"It's okay, Captain," he said, weakly. "Listen, the weapon was damaged. We're almost at the merge. We're out of time."

Another loud bang, and more red lights. The *Andromeda* lurched as a missile sliced through the honeycomb energy absorber layer, blowing a chunk of it off and breaching the hull. Acceleration was dropping. The railgun was having a difficult time charging its capacitor. One more good hit and they were done for.

"It's been an honor flying with you," the young pilot said. As the two intercepting ships merged with the oncoming battleship, Colin tapped his controls and altered course just enough to ensure collision. As the *Andromeda* flashed past, both the *Independence* and the Combine warship disappeared in a flash of light. The *Andromeda*, heavily damaged, lurched as the number one engine exploded. The crushing g-forces of the sudden slew sent all the blood to Nickson's feet, and he blacked out.

Log Entry 142
Mission 815-707-SSOC
Reconnaissance Ship 505

The Type-54 battleship has been destroyed. The two intercepting ships utilized an unknown weapon, possibly of alien origin, which damaged it. One of the ships, the Reliant *class, then rammed it. Given the extremely high relative velocity, both ships were lost. The* Andromeda *appears crippled on long-range telemetry, and is coasting out-system, but that is all we know.*

We will be returning to home station. All of this must be reported to command.

CHAPTER 39

The Privateer Ship *Andromeda*
Ionia-5589 System

"Liam, can you hear me?" Annie was scared. In a space suit, secured in her berth, she didn't know what was going on with the battle. The feed from the command deck had stopped. The engines cut out, and they were now in freefall. Through the little window on the hatch of her bunk, the red hull breach lights were flashing. The *Andromeda* was hurt, and she was hurt badly.

"I'm here," Liam said. "Is it over?"

"I think so. We should go see if anybody needs help."

"We were told to stay here until they called for damage control."

"Liam, I haven't heard *anything* on the ship net for a while now. I think it's down."

"Then how are we talking?"

"The suit's short-range internal radio. We're close enough." Annabelle and Liam were the only ones in their berths on the crew deck. Everyone else was in the acceleration couches at their battle stations. Junior crewmembers didn't have battle stations, so they had basically been told to go to bed until it was over. "Look, something's wrong, okay? We need to go help."

"Okay, okay. I'll meet you outside."

"Your suit is sealed, right? There's a hull breach." The individual berths could hold atmosphere of their own, but they would depressurize when the door was opened.

"I'm good. I'm coming out."

Annie did the same. Moving in the berth, which was little more than an oversized coffin, was difficult under normal circumstances. Having the suit and helmet on didn't help. She managed to hit the door release latch with her heel and use her toe to actuate a lever, undogging the hatch. The air sucked out of her berth as she kicked the door open and pushed herself out.

"Holy shit," she said, looking around the personnel deck. It had completely depressurized, but there wasn't any apparent damage.

Liam finally managed to get himself out of his berth, barely managing to catch the railing before he went spinning across the compartment. Righting himself, he clicked on his mag boots and clamped to the floor. "What happened? My suit says the atmospheric pressure in here is almost zero, but I don't see a hull breach."

That *was* strange. Any hole big enough to drain the air that quickly should be easy enough to spot. "I don't know. Let's go down to the cargo deck and check on Kimball. Follow me." Keeping the channel with Liam open, she activated her own mag boots and locked onto the catwalk. Moving through the compartment was oddly soundless. Annie could hear herself breathe, and Liam could talk to her. Each magnetized step in the boots made a dull *thump* that resonated through her suit, but there was no sound coming from the world around them. It was like watching a video with the sound muted.

The hatch leading up to the above deck was sealed, indicated with a red light. That was supposed to happen in the event of depressurization. The hatch leading down to the cargo deck, however, was stuck about halfway open. The light flashed red and yellow, indicating a problem.

"Oh, no," Liam said. "I bet the cargo bay depressurized, too."

"We gotta get down there and check on Kimball! Go to the damage-control station and get the rescue jaws. Move slow, don't get your heart rate up. Conserve your air." Doing as he was asked, Liam clunkily walked over to the damage-control locker and came back with a large orange case. Inside was a set of powered jaws, which they placed on the stuck hatch. Activating it, the device turned its main screw, pushing and pushing with many tonnes of force, pushing the jammed hatch open.

Annie removed the jaws from the hatch. "I'm going to go down first. You follow me." She grabbed the ladder with her hands, deactivated her boots, and pulled herself through the hatch headfirst.

Her stomach lurched when she got down to the cargo bay and righted herself. The lights were flickering. The compartment was a hard vacuum. Where the sealed cargo doors should have been, Annie could see a million stars and the blackness of space. The damage was extensive. Part of the deck was missing as well. She wondered how the ship even held together.

Liam pulled himself down the ladder a moment later, and swore aloud when he righted himself and saw the damage. "Holy shit, Annie. What happened?"

"I don't know. We must have got hit pretty bad. We're not spinning anymore, so that's good. Come on, let's go to Kimball's station." The cargomaster's acceleration couch was in the tiny office, along the edge of the cargo bay, but it was empty. Kimball wasn't anywhere to be found, and they still hadn't heard anyone else on the radio.

"What do we do now?"

Annie honestly wasn't sure what to do. She didn't know if she and Liam were the only survivors, or if the ship was about to explode. Her mind and her heart both raced as she struggled to keep it together. "Let's . . . let's keep going down. We can't go up, the hatch is sealed. Look at the damage to the deck. Engineering might be depressurized, too. We should go see if they're okay."

"I don't know, Annie, maybe we should stay here."

"We *can't* stay here!" she snapped. "Look at that, Liam, the ship got *fucked up*! If you just stand here with your dick in your hand, people are gonna die!"

"Okay!" he answered, meekly. "I'm sorry. Lead the way."

Annie hadn't meant to bite his head off. She was scared. What if she and Liam really were the only ones left? Would they die out here? Was the Combine ship on its way to bomb the planet?

When they got to the hatch leading down to engineering, Annie and Liam found it open. Someone had tripped the emergency release, manually opening the hatch. That was a good sign! Someone had to be alive to do that! "I bet Kimball is down there," she said, pulling herself through. "Hello?" she asked, boosting the power to her suit radio. "Can you read me?"

"Crewman Winchester?" Kimball asked. "Is that you?"

"Yes, sir! Oh my God, I'm so happy to hear your voice. Where are you?"

"Around the dogleg. You're supposed to be in your berth!"

"We were, but we thought you might need help."

"I do. Hurry, please."

When Nickson opened his eyes, everything had stopped spinning. That was a good sign. Someone had gotten control and stabilized the ship. They were in freefall, and his suit said that the compartment's atmospheric pressure was dangerously low. "Skipper, what's our status?"

"Nix! Oh, thank God. Are you all right?"

"I think so. Still got a slow leak up here. Looks like...yeah, the hatch sealed behind me. Do you have pressure down there?"

"We do, but we have a major hull breach belowdecks. The personnel deck, the cargo bay, and engineering have all been depressurized. Comms are down, sensors are down, navigation is down. We can only talk through suit radios, and the shielding in the damned hull means I can't hear anybody."

"How bad are we hit?"

"We're dead in space, Nix. I don't know if Indira is alive or dead. We're locked out of engine control."

That was a standard, automatic safety mechanism that engaged when the engines were damaged in such a way that operating them risked a catastrophic failure. "I'm going to head down and start getting crew accountability."

"I can help."

"No, you stay where you are and see if you can patch that leak. I don't know how long we're going to be out here, we need to conserve our air supply."

"Roger that, Skipper," Nickson said, unfastening his harness. He retrieved the emergency patch kit, opened it, and got to work. There was a small, colored-smoke dispenser to help him find the leak, and a variety of patches in different sizes. The smoke dispenser had a magnetic clamp on it. He set it down and activated it. A thin, wispy strand of purple smoke drifted from the dispenser and toward an upper corner of the compartment. *There!* Fortunately, the hole wasn't very big, only about a centimeter across. It was located between two pieces of paneling, and there was no good way to attach the seal. He'd have to use the foam sealant.

"Test, test, can anyone hear me?"

The ship's network was back online! "Copy that, this is the XO, up on the flight deck. I read you, loud and clear. Who's this?"

"Mordechai. I had to reroute comms through some undamaged relays, but we can talk, for now. How bad is it?"

"Bad. Can you get the cameras back up?"

"I'll get to work on it."

"We need help down here!" It was the Winchester girl.

"Crewman Winchester? Is there a problem in your berth?"

"I'm not in my berth. I'm down in engineering. Kimball and Liam are with me. The damage is bad down here. Big hull breach where the engine blew. The chief engineer is pinned into her acceleration couch and we're scared to move her."

"It looks like her suit was punctured," Kimball said. "If we remove the debris, it may lead to blood loss and suit depressurization. I need Doctor Emerson and Med Tech Lowlander down here at once."

"Captain, you copy all that?" Nickson asked.

"Copy all. We need to find a way down there. We've lost pressure on the lower three decks. We may have to do an EVA out the docking bay and come in through the cargo deck. Kel was able to pull up a camera feed and the cargo deck is open to space. I don't want to risk further depressurizing the ship. Kimball, hold on down there. I'll get medical assistance to you as soon as I can."

"Kimball," Nickson added, "where's Enzo? Is he okay?"

"Unconscious, but alive. His station separated from the floor in the explosion. Only the power conduits saved him from being lost through the hull breach."

"Thank God," the captain said. "I've already lost one man today, I don't intend to lose another."

CHAPTER 40

The War Room
Black Mountain Command Complex
Southern Autonomous Zone

Adisa stared at the images displayed in the holotank, and barely registered what the general was telling her. There was a battle, but they'd *done* it. The *Independence* and the *Andromeda* had done it. The Combine battleship had been destroyed, but the cost? He said something about the other Combine ship fleeing the system, and something else about more translation signatures, but she cut him off. "Tell me about the battle. What happened?"

"We monitored the entire engagement with telescopes, radar, and infrared, Your Majesty. It appears that the *Independence*, heavily damaged, rammed the enemy ship, destroying them both. I'm . . . I'm sorry. They are heroes, now."

Adisa had lost the father of her child, and then her own father, in a matter of weeks. She'd not had enough time to get to know either man. She had never in her life felt so alone. "What is the status of the *Andromeda*?"

"She's still out there. We've been trying to contact them but have not received a reply. It's likely the ship was heavily damaged in the engagement and lost communications."

"We need to go help them," she said. "At once. We need to get someone out there and bring them back!"

General Farai looked at his queen, apologetically. "We can't, Your Majesty. She's too far away, and moving farther away very quickly. None of the shuttles we have could hope to catch her."

"No, no, this is unacceptable. Unacceptable, you hear me? I am not going to go and tell Mr. Winchester that his daughter is still alive, but because we're such a primitive backwater world, we lack the means to go pick her up and bring her home, that she's going to die anyway. Find a way!" she shouted, slamming her fist on the holotank.

The assembled officers looked at each other, uncomfortably. They were right, and Adisa knew it. It was all just so wrong. It was unfair. Those brave spacers had saved her world, and now they were doomed to die out there. She tried to think of what to tell Marcus Winchester, and couldn't find the words.

A young technician came running up to the holotank. "We're receiving a transmission!" he said, excitedly.

"From the *Andromeda*?" Adisa asked, hopefully.

"No, ma'am—I mean, Your Majesty. That translation signature we picked up a while ago? Well, just watch. Here." He tapped his handheld a few times, and routed the message to the big screen.

A man in a sage-green flight suit appeared, with graying hair and a trimmed mustache. "This is Colonel Dietrich Cutter of the Concordiat Defense Force, commanding officer of the *Trafalgar*. We are here as neutral observers, and we request permission to approach Ithaca."

"I don't understand," Adisa said, still trying to process what she was seeing. "Why is the Concordiat here?"

"Your Majesty, it seems that before he left New Austin, your father contacted the Office of Strategic Intelligence, telling them that the Combine was planning on annexing our world. He requested Concordiat observers. Last we discussed it, he didn't think they would actually send someone, but it seems that they have. The *Trafalgar* is a heavy battlecruiser. Today, of all days, they arrive, after the battle is over, no less."

"That doesn't matter right now. General, I want you to contact them and ask them to intercept and rescue the crew of the *Andromeda*. Tell them that if they do that, they may not only approach, but we'll fully brief them on the entire situation."

"Yes, Your Majesty." He turned to the technician. "Prepare a laser pulse transmission for that ship, with authentication codes."

Thank God, Adisa thought, hoping against hope that the Concordiat cruiser wouldn't be too late. She wondered if anyone on the *Andromeda* was even still alive.

CHAPTER 41

Black Mountain Command Complex
Southern Autonomous Zone
Eight Local Days Later...

On a warm morning, in the shade of Black Mountain, Nickson Armitage stood next to his captain, both wearing fresh flight suits and peaked caps. Behind them, the crew of the *Andromeda* was assembled, standing in a formation. Indira Nair was in a powered mobility chassis, which allowed her to walk without placing any pressure on her healing legs. They'd even managed to drag Mordechai Chang out for this, though Nickson had never seen a man so uncomfortable with being outside.

Thousands of people had assembled for the ceremony. There was an honor guard from the Southern Autonomous Zone Defense Force, and hundreds of soldiers in formation. Marcus Winchester and his team stood quietly behind the queen, ever vigilant. A huge delegation of natives had arrived, hundreds of them, to pay their respects to Zander Krycek. Behind them loomed a squad of their nuclear-powered super soldiers, silent and imposing.

A military band had been assembled off to the side, though they were silent now. A couple thousand civilians from the nearby city had shown up as well. They all knew what had happened, now: the *Andromeda* and the *Independence*, with a weapon from the natives, had destroyed the Combine battleship and saved Ithaca. The queen read each of the names of the lost crew, and told the crowd a little about them.

It was a very thoughtful gesture, Nickson thought, and yet bittersweet. There was one person missing from his formation. He'd managed to get everyone on his ship back alive, but they'd still lost a man.

"Next," Queen Adisa said, "let us all remember a young spacer named Colin Abernathy. Born on Earth, he spent his life amongst the stars, and had been with the *Andromeda* for several years. He arrived on Ithaca, separated from his shipmates, only by chance. He flew the shuttle that delivered my father safely to the surface, braving an active, hostile air defense network that desperately tried to shoot them down. When we approached him to fly the *Independence*, we did so with great hesitation. It wasn't his ship. This isn't his world. This wasn't his war. The odds of success were not great. I wouldn't have held it against anyone had they refused.

"Yet, Colin didn't refuse. He told me that he would help because it was the right thing to do. He asked for nothing in return. He was a privateer, a spacer who makes a living pursuing contracts like this, and he offered to fly my ship without so much as requesting a bonus. The *Independence* was heavily damaged in the battle. The powerful beam weapon our allies gave us was no longer operational. The Combine ship was still closing on Ithaca, and was still firing at both ships. Colin chose to make the ultimate sacrifice. Instead of letting his ship be destroyed, or risking the enemy getting past him, he rammed the enemy warship. He died, out there, so that millions of us down here may live."

The queen turned, looking over at the assembled crew of the *Andromeda*. "Captain Blackwood, I know flowery words and gratitude don't bring a lost comrade back. I know the pain of losing a part of your family, and it's plain to see that your crew *is* your family. But please know that you, your crew, and Colin have the eternal gratitude of the Ithacan people. Without you, the war would have continued, and we would be doomed to annexation by the Combine. I promise you that his sacrifice will not be in vain, nor will it be forgotten."

The queen began to clap, and the crowd followed suit. The next thing Nickson knew, thousands of people were clapping and cheering for his crew. It was overwhelming. He looked over at the captain, but her face was a mask. She was the sort to internalize loss. He would have to talk to her later. Perhaps she, like him, was having a hard time focusing on much of the pomp and circumstance, since there was still so very much to do.

The *Andromeda* hadn't been destroyed, but she'd been crippled. The Concordiat battlecruiser *Trafalgar* had towed her back to Ithaca orbit. The ship couldn't land, and the Ithacans lacked the means to repair her in orbit. Given the extent of the damage, Nickson wasn't at all sure that the ship *could* be restored. It seemed likely that it would be a total loss after all. Losing a crewmember is one thing; losing a crewmember and your ship is worse. Nickson knew, he'd been there, and he sympathized with his captain. He'd definitely have to talk to her later.

There was also the matter of how they were going to get home. Aside from the *Trafalgar*, there were no transit-capable ships in the Ionia-5589 system. The Concordiat ship, having been briefed on the situation and having seen the alien technology, wouldn't be leaving until it was duly relieved. The queen had formally requested protection from the Combine, and given that there was incredible alien paleotechnology on Ithaca, they seemed happy to oblige. Nickson didn't know what the future held for Ithaca. The Concordiat might try to pressure the colony into joining just to have control over the alien technology. He wasn't sure that that would be a bad thing, either. Ithaca had a lot of promise, but what it needed was stability and peace.

"Thank you," Captain Blackwood said, her voice hushed so only they could hear.

"For what, Skipper?"

"For being a damned good exec. I would happily keep you on, but without a ship, I'm not really a captain anymore."

"I don't think this is the end of our adventures," he said, managing a smile. "You can't keep a good spacer in the dirt, and frankly, you're the best spacer I've ever met. The *Andromeda* is a fine ship, but there are other ships. We'll bounce back, Skipper."

"Thank you, Nix. I rather needed to hear that."

As the ceremony dragged on, Nickson contemplated just how damned lucky he was to be alive. Between his first mission aboard the *Andromeda* and his last mission on the *Madeline Drake*, he should have been dead several times over. Yet, here he was, alive, and kicking, when so many others were not. It made him, perhaps, a little more appreciative of life. He looked over at Talia, who was quietly observing the ceremony, and decided that there was something he needed to do.

As the ceremony concluded, Nickson begged his captain's leave and walked over to Talia. He hadn't seen her much since his rescue, given that most of the past eight days had been spent in transit and recovery.

"I'm sorry for your loss," she said, quietly. She'd done her hair up nice, though she left it hanging over her right eye to conceal the metallic plate that covered it. "I didn't talk to Colin much, but he seemed like a sweet boy. He was too young to die. I am happy that you made it back. I was . . . I was worried about you."

"I thought about you while we were trapped out there," Nickson said. "When I found out that we were going to be rescued, my first thought was that I was so happy because I'd get to see you again."

Talia's pale face turned a little red. "No one has ever said such things to me before."

"What's next for you, Talia?"

"The queen has promised me an implant for my eye, so I will at least look whole again. After that, I don't know. I may stay here."

Nickson took a breath. "I don't think you should stay here."

"I don't understand. This seems like a good place."

"No, it's not that, it's . . . stay with us. With me."

"What?"

"We will get a new ship, and we will be back in business. When that happens, I'd like you with us."

"I'm not a spacer."

"There are plenty of spacers, Talia. There's only one you."

She blushed again. Before she could say anything else, Nickson leaned forward and kissed her. It took her by surprise. She almost pulled away. But, after a moment, she put her arms around his neck. He pulled her close and kissed her, deeply.

"I think I understand now," she said, looking into his eye. She was smiling, too, and what a smile it was. "But, *you* must understand, I have . . . I have a long road ahead of me. I need to learn who I am, what kind of person I am. This, so much of this is new for me."

"I'll help you however I can, Talia. If you need me to back off, I'll back off. If you want more, you can have more. That's why you should come with us. You'll travel, you'll be surrounded by friends, and you'll have all the time you need."

"Okay," she said.

"Wait, really?"

"Yes. I will go with you, if the captain will allow it."

"You won't regret this."

She smiled again. "If I do, it was still my choice. That is important. I decide where I go, now. It will take some getting used to."

Marcus Winchester sat with his daughter, watching Ionia-5589 slide below the horizon. The clouds were lit up in every shade of pink, red, and gold, and it was beautiful.

"I hope Mom and David are okay," Annie said. "I miss them."

"I'm sure they're fine, honey. You come from tough stock."

"I know. I just wish I could send them a message, let them know we're all right."

"It's the nature of the beast when it comes to interstellar travel. It was hard on your mom when I was in the Espatiers."

"When we get back, I might stay home for a while."

"Really? I'm sure Captain Blackwood will offer you a crew position when she gets a new ship."

"Maybe, but I don't know when that will be, or where she'll fly out of. I don't think I want to leave you guys and never see you. I want to be there for my little brother. It's important that he not grow up without his sister."

"What brought on the change of heart?" Marcus was certain he knew, but he didn't want to put words in her mouth.

"I almost died out there, Daddy. I was scared."

"I know, baby. The captain told me what you did, braving the damaged ship, rescuing the engineer. I want you to know that I'm damned proud of you. I was scared, too."

"You were?"

"Of course I was! My little girl was out in a space battle, and I was stuck down here with no way to help. That's a hell of a thing for a father."

She looked up at him. "Also, I don't think you should leave again, either. I think both of us being gone is really hard on Mom."

"I know it is. After this one, I'm done, I think. I just want to stay home and be with my family."

"What's going to happen to this place?"

"Ithaca? It's hard to say. You know, we changed the course of history for this world."

"We did that on Zanzibar too, kinda."

"You're right, we did. Doing that twice in a few years is pretty good, huh? I bet none of your friends can claim that." He laughed. "But no, I don't know what's going to happen. The queen told me that the Ithacans want to start going back into space. They want to see if they can find more of their own people."

"Do you really think they're out there?"

"Anything is possible. It's a big universe. I guess they'll have to go find out for themselves."

Annie rested her head on Marcus' shoulder. "I just want to go home."

"Don't worry, kiddo. We'll get there."

Sitting in a big, plush chair in her chambers, Adisa wrote in her journal, and tried to reflect on everything that had happened. The battle was over, but there was still so much to be done. Soon, the reunification talks would begin. It would not be easy. The Southern Autonomous Zone leadership had thrown in with her in the hopes of winning the war, but animosities ran deep between the two halves of the colony. There would be many who refused to recognize her authority as queen. The road to a lasting peace and prosperity would be hard, and there was no guarantee of success.

They had a chance, however, and sometimes that was all one could hope for. *I barely knew my father,* she wrote, *and yet I miss him, dearly. Whatever happens, I won't let his sacrifice be in vain. His counsel and political experience will be missed in the days ahead.* She put a hand on her belly. *I miss Roc most of all. My father was right, though, part of him lives on inside me, and our child will go on to do great things. I owe him that much.*

More Concordiat ships have arrived, and I should be able to arrange transport home for the crew of the Andromeda. I offered to let them all stay, of course, but I don't think any of them will. The promises my father made to them will be honored, though, and I will ensure that they are taken care of.

Already, I am being pressured to apply for membership in the Interstellar Concordiat. It seems their fleet captains double as salesmen, and I've been getting the pitch almost nonstop. It is something we need to discuss at the reunification talks. We won a victory here, but we are still vulnerable. If the Combine shows up tomorrow with an invasion fleet, there is nothing we could do to stop them. Now that they are aware of the technology the natives possess, I wouldn't put such a thing past them. Membership in the Concordiat may be our best hope of remaining free. It would virtually guarantee off-world investment and trade, and those are things my people desperately need. It bears consideration.

The natives are no longer living in the shadows. The Elders tell me that they are educating their own people on their real history, and are trying to relearn that which has been all but forgotten. They may yet have more secrets buried here, and everyone in inhabited space will soon be flocking to Ithaca. Upholding my promise to them, protecting them from exploitation, may be the most difficult challenge that lies ahead.

It's wonderful, though: two species sharing a world, working together to rebuild it. Intermingling, learning *about one another, someday going into space together. I don't think such a thing has happened in the history of either of our races. This could be the start of a new chapter for both our peoples. This could change everything, and I am proud that it happened on my homeworld. Somehow, the universe feels a little less lonely.*

Adisa looked up from her tablet, and put a hand on her belly again. "Roc," she said aloud. "After your father, if you're a boy. If you're a girl . . . how about Catherine?"

IF YOU LIKE...
YOU SHOULD TRY...

DAVID DRAKE
David Weber
Tony Daniel
John Lambshead

DAVID WEBER
John Ringo
Timothy Zahn
Linda Evans
Jane Lindskold
Sarah A. Hoyt

JOHN RINGO
Michael Z. Williamson
Tom Kratman
Larry Correia
Mike Kupari

ANNE MCCAFFREY
Mercedes Lackey
Lois McMaster Bujold
Liaden Universe® by Sharon Lee & Steve Miller
Sarah A. Hoyt
Mike Kupari

MERCEDES LACKEY
Wen Spencer
Andre Norton
James H. Schmitz

LARRY NIVEN
Tony Daniel
James P. Hogan
Travis S. Taylor
Brad Torgersen

ROBERT A. HEINLEIN
Jerry Pournelle
Lois McMaster Bujold
Michael Z. Williamson

HEINLEIN'S "JUVENILES"
Rats, Bats & Vats series by Eric Flint & Dave Freer
Brendan DuBois' *Dark Victory*
David Weber & Jane Lindskold's Star Kingdom
Series
David Drake & Jim Kjelgaard's *The Hunter Returns*

HORATIO HORNBLOWER OR PATRICK O'BRIAN
David Weber's Honor Harrington series
David Drake's RCN series
Alex Stewart's *Shooting the Rift*

HARRY POTTER
Mercedes Lackey's Urban Fantasy series

JIM BUTCHER
Larry Correia's The Grimnoir Chronicles
John Lambshead's *Wolf in Shadow*

TECHNOTHRILLERS
Larry Correia & Mike Kupari's Dead Six Series
Robert Conroy's *Stormfront*
Eric Stone's *Unforgettable*
Tom Kratman's Countdown Series

THE LORD OF THE RINGS
Elizabeth Moon's *The Deed of Paksenarrion*
P.C. Hodgell
Ryk E. Spoor's Phoenix Rising series

A GAME OF THRONES
Larry Correia's *Son of the Black Sword*
David Weber's fantasy novels
Sonia Orin Lyris' *The Seer*

H.P. LOVECRAFT
Larry Correia's Monster Hunter series
P.C. Hodgell's Kencyrath series
John Ringo's Special Circumstances Series

ZOMBIES
John Ringo's Black Tide Rising Series
Wm. Mark Simmons

GEORGETTE HEYER
Lois McMaster Bujold
Catherine Asaro
Liaden Universe® by Sharon Lee & Steve Miller
Dave Freer